Matchmaker

Weddings

Two Contemporary Romances Under One Cover

Matchmaker
Weddings

ANNALISA DAUGHETY
& KIM O'BRIEN

BARBOUR
PUBLISHING

A Wedding
BLUNDER
IN THE BLACK HILLS

KIM
O'BRIEN

Nothing is so common as the wish to be remarkable.
WILLIAM SHAKESPEARE

Chapter 1

"He's your *dentist*, Mom. I'm *not* going on a blind date with your dentist."

Millie Hogan stabbed her knife into the tub of mustard then swiped it across a piece of pumpernickel. She'd only broken up with Karl Kauffman a couple of weeks ago, and already her mother was trying to set her up.

Peering over the top of the glass deli counter, Howard Glugan, the chief of police and one of the café's regulars, strained to watch. "Take it easy, Millie," he said. "I'd hate to charge you for assault and battery to a slice of bread."

Millie managed to laugh. She arranged slices of ham and swiss cheese on the bread, stuck a colorful toothpick through the center, and added a handful of chips. "Pie, Chief?"

"What kind?"

"Blueberry, pecan, or rhubarb."

"I could manage a piece of rhubarb."

Millie cut him an ample slice and rang him up on the register.

"Of course you're going out with Dr. Denvers," her mother stated. "It's all arranged."

"Then unarrange it. Shouldn't you be working the grill?" Millie turned to the town's librarian. "The usual, Mrs. Ellison?"

"Yes, please. I hate to say it, dear, but Eva's right. Dr. Denvers is a real catch."

Her mother laughed as Millie ladled out a bowl of chicken noodle. She knew Mrs. Ellison liked a buttered roll and a cup of herb tea with her soup. She'd practically grown up here in Dosie Dough's, and the same people had been ordering the same thing for years. She knew most of the people seated at the booths and tables. Unfortunately, this meant that everyone was so familiar with one another that they ended up discussing everything in front of everybody, like now.

"Why are you so stubborn?" her mother said. "Just because you broke up with that policeman doesn't mean you give up on all men."

"And bless his soul is that boy cranky," Aunt Lillian remarked from her wheelchair. She was sitting with the other aunts at her usual spot at the table in front of the bay window where they could see the town square and comment if they saw something interesting. "He's practically shaking the parking meters in hopes of giving some poor soul a ticket," Lillian continued. "Can't you talk to Karl, Chief?"

The chief wiped his mouth with a napkin. "I don't discuss police business."

Millie scooped out a generous portion of tuna salad. She really didn't want to talk about Karl Kauffman anyway. He kept leaving parking tickets on her car with notes that said, *Call me*.

"I hear we've got more snow coming." Millie glanced over at Aunt Keeker for help. Of all the three women who made up Eva's best friends and Millie's "aunts," Keeker could always be counted on for a lively discussion about the weather. She particularly enjoyed being the bearer of bad news when it came to storms, and today she was wearing her sheepskin bomber hat, a sure sign that Deer Park was due for a major snowfall.

"As a matter of fact—" Keeker started.

"Dating is like riding a horse," her mother interrupted. "If you fall off, you should get right back on again."

Millie lifted the lid off the steaming pot of tomato soup. She was pretty sure the nearest her mother had ever been to a horse was watching a rerun of *Bonanza* on television.

"Mom, I'm done with blind dates. I'm not going out with the electrician, the UPS guy, or anyone else." She ladled the soup into the bowl and in her best and most dramatic stage voice, declared, "I'm off men. Forever."

"Let's not get melodramatic," her mother said dryly. "You know you like going out on dates."

"That was before," Millie said. "I've decided to concentrate on my acting career now."

"Dr. Denvers is perfect for you," her mother insisted. "Smart, good looking, and nice. He has that doctor thing going, too. You'd have excellent medical benefits."

Millie gave her a look. "We have medical coverage, Mom."

"But he's a *dentist*," Aunt Mimi called out from the aunts' table. She was a tiny woman with a cloud of permed apricot-colored hair that matched the coat of the toy poodle that snored in her lap. "Do you know how hard it is to get good dental benefits?"

"If she's going to date him," Jeff Gulden, a thin, wiry-haired mechanic with huge ears and a chronically sad face, said, "could she at least wait until next week? I have a root canal scheduled for Friday, and it'll probably go better if the doc doesn't have a broken heart."

"Remember it took Erv Michels two weeks before he stopped throwing the UPS packages into the bushes after Millie dumped him?" Aunt Mimi agreed. "Not that I blame you, Millie honey, for passing on that boy. I saw him kick his dog when he thought no one was watching." She stroked her poodle lovingly.

"All of you," Millie said, waving a serving spoon, "need to stop talking about my social life. If you want to help me, think of things for me to write about in my application for *Chef's Challenge*. The deadline's coming up." She pointed to the back kitchen. "Mom, don't you think you ought to go flip those burgers?"

"Lottie's got the grill." Her mother's brow creased. "I don't know why you keep trying to get yourself on those mindless reality shows. What if some crazy person saw you on TV and started to stalk you?"

Millie blinked innocently. "Well, I guess if he was single, you'd probably try and set me up on a date with him."

Her mother pursed her lips firmly together. "I'm just trying to help you, honey. I don't want you ending up like me, with no one to keep me warm at night."

"I'll keep you warm," somebody called out. Millie thought it was Will Gavinski, who worked on the sunflower farm ten miles north of town.

Millie didn't think that thirty-one was exactly ancient, however, she let her mother's comment pass. "What can I get for you today, Mr. Lawrence?" Millie asked the next customer in line.

"He'll have liverwurst," Millie's mother announced before the manager of the town's movie theater could reply, "and I'll get it. You need to go home and get ready for your date."

Millie swiped a generous amount of mayo on the bread. Hadn't her mother heard a word she'd said? So what if David Denvers was a good dentist. It didn't mean he'd be a good date. In high school, he'd been a year ahead of her. She remembered a nerdy kid on the short side with big glasses and ears that bent out slightly at the sides.

"If you like him so much, Mom," she joked, "why don't you go skiing with him?"

Her mother set her hands on her ample hips and locked eyes with Millie. "If you won't, I will. I'm not standing the boy up."

The restaurant became so quiet that Millie could hear the hum of the refrigerator in the back room. Was her mother serious? This from a woman who got in her car to drive twenty yards to the mailbox?

At age sixty-four, overweight, and a diabetic, the last thing her mother needed to be doing was putting on a pair of skis. As if reading Millie's thoughts, her mother said, "I'm sure my old skis could still get the job done."

Her mother had to be bluffing. Millie folded her arms and ordered herself not to give in.

"Don't wait up for me," her mom continued. "Unlike some people"—she paused to give Millie a significant look—"I have not forgotten how to have fun."

"Mom, you can't go skiing. You could hurt yourself."

"Before you were born, I used to be quite the ski bunny, and I still have the trophies to prove it."

She might have been a ski bunny once, but Millie tactfully restrained from pointing out that most bunnies didn't top the scale at over two hundred pounds. "Mom. . ."

"Your father has been gone for twenty years. It's high time I put myself back on the market. You gotta live, Millie."

I would, Millie thought, *but you won't let me.* Immediately she felt a stab of guilt. This was her mother, who loved her more than anyone else in the world. If her mother sometimes tried to run her life, it was only because she wanted Millie to be happy.

"You're acting crazy, Mom. Skiing is risky."

Her mom rolled her eyes. "I'm not a novice. And if I do get hurt, at least I'll be with a doctor."

"Dentist," Millie corrected.

"They both go to medical school," Millie's mother announced. "Don't worry about me."

Clumping across the wooden floor in her trademark UGG boots, her mom added, "I'll tell him you were having female problems, Millie, but you want to reschedule."

Why? Millie scrunched her eyes shut. *Why me?* She didn't know whether to laugh or cry. Her mom loved her dearly yet couldn't see she was killing her. Watching her mom's broad frame navigate around the crowded room, Millie knew she should stop her, and yet part of her wanted to let her go. If she kept caving in to her mother's demands, she'd never get her mother to leave her alone.

Why couldn't she have a mother who didn't guilt her daughter into blind dates or wield her health as a weapon?

Her mother had reached the coatrack. Hardheaded, stubborn, and proud of every drop of German blood—that was her mother. Millie clenched her jaw. Her mother wasn't going to win. Not this time. "You'd better check your blood sugar before you go."

"No time," her mother replied. Her hand was on the doorknob. "See you later, honey."

The door was open now. A cold draft snaked its way across the floor, and she could see the light bouncing off the gleaming heaps of snow half burying the parking meters on the sidewalk.

"Hold it," Millie ordered. "If I do this for you, you have to promise me—no exceptions—that this is the last time you set me up on a blind date."

Her mother turned. "Of course, dear."

"No meddling of any kind in my social life."

"Scout's honor," her mother replied and held up two fingers for Millie to see.

"No more talk about me getting older or settling down or having kids."

"I promise."

Millie studied her mother's face a moment longer. She probably couldn't trust her, yet she didn't want her going off and trying to ski just to make a point. "Okay," Millie said, "I'll do it. I'll go skiing with Dr. Denvers."

Her mother's face relaxed into a broad smile. "David will be waiting by the ice sculpture of the dolphin—and sweetie, don't forget to floss before you go."

Chapter 2

It'd been years since Millie had skied. In the ladies' room at the ski lodge, she squeezed into her one-piece ski outfit. The zipper was a bit tighter than she remembered, and the sleeves seemed to have shrunk. Then again, she'd been sixteen when she'd bought this outfit.

Sixteen. She'd had such big dreams then—of going to Hollywood and being discovered or living in Manhattan and starring in a Broadway show. She and Oprah would nod to each other casually at cocktail parties, and Millie would appear periodically on shows like *Larry King Live* and *Good Morning America*.

Millie tugged her zipper. She'd never seen herself as a permanent fixture at Dosie Dough's, and at the rate she was going, the best she could hope for was a spot on *Dr. Phil* for a special on dysfunctional relationships. All too easily she could picture her aunts, mother, and former dates squeezed onto one couch while Millie sat across from them trying to explain that she didn't have commitment issues— just a desire to find out if there was more to life than what Deer Park had to offer.

Surveying herself in the mirror, Millie couldn't decide if she looked more like a fat Judy Jetson or the Michelin Man. In either case, the way the material strained at the zipper suggested that the first time she hit a mogul she was going to burst out of this ski suit like a parboiled tomato.

She tucked her mass of dark, curly hair into a bright yellow Turtle Fur hat and settled her goggles on top. Who cared what she looked like?

Blinking, Millie stepped outside into the blinding light of snow reflected off the mountain. She scanned the group of skiers who clustered in groups around the ski racks or slid past on their way to the lift line.

She didn't see a short man with glasses who had ears that kind of stuck out at the sides waiting next to the ice dolphin. Then again, it'd been years since she'd seen him. After high school, he'd gone to dental school in California and gotten married. According to chatter at the café, he'd returned to Deer Park six months ago to take over his father's dental practice.

Pushing up her tight sleeves, she checked her watch. It was a little after four o'clock. Maybe he wasn't coming. She felt something hopeful stir inside, and then a deep voice said, "Millie? Millie Hogan?"

A medium-sized man wearing black ski pants and carrying a pair of Rossignols over his shoulder walked up to her. "David Denvers." He extended his free hand for Millie to shake.

"I know," Millie said. "I mean, I remember you from high school."

"Me, too," David said cheerfully. "Only you looked a lot taller then."

Back then she'd been a giant compared to him. Not anymore. He wasn't a very tall man, but he still had several inches over her. His face was lean now, and he carried the skis easily. The glasses were gone, too. She couldn't tell if his ears still stuck out though. His wool ski cap hid them.

"Nice to see you again," Millie murmured, reduced to falling back on good manners and hoping that he wouldn't bring up the time when she was in ninth grade and he had asked her out in the middle of the cafeteria line. She'd said no, and the cafeteria lady had looked as if she wanted to throw the spaghetti and meat sauce at her.

"Hope you haven't been waiting long," David continued, glancing over his shoulder. "I was getting us lift tickets." He handed her a sticker and a thin metal hanger.

"Thanks," Millie said, threading the thin wire through her coat zipper. "Let me pay you back."

"It's my treat," David said.

"I insist." The more she let a guy pay for her, the bigger the guy's expectations at the end of the date. Millie never intended to feel obligated to anyone.

David shrugged. "We can settle this after we finish skiing. We don't want to lose the light."

Millie bent to put on her skis. She hadn't used them in years and was more than a little relieved when the bindings snapped neatly shut. "David," she said and straightened. "I should warn you, I haven't skied in quite a while. Would you mind starting out on a blue trail?"

David didn't answer. She looked over her shoulder and saw a slender blond standing nearby. The woman was wearing tight black ski pants that outlined her long, thin legs and a black ski jacket that ended at her trim hips. The woman's big blue eyes were fixed on David.

"David," Millie prompted sharply enough to get his attention.

"What?" His voice sounded strained, and the way he now looked at Millie reminded her of someone who was trying to put a good face on something unpleasant, like spending the afternoon with an IRS auditor.

Great. She could win a Michelin Man look-alike contest, and her date wished that he were with someone else. Her toes pinched in the boots that, like the snowsuit, had mysteriously shrunk in the closet. When she got home, she and her mother were going to have a very long conversation.

When David saw that Cynthia had followed him to the ski area, he almost groaned. During the past few weeks, he'd tried talking to her, ignoring her, and once hiding from her in the office supply room. Cynthia, however, had proved to be both unshakable and relentless.

He supposed that he could get a restraining order, but he suspected that Chief Glugan would laugh at him if he tried. Cynthia wasn't threatening or dangerous. She was just a lonely young woman, recently divorced, who like him had returned to Deer Park after being away for years. Besides, his parents and Cynthia's parents were good friends. He suspected the reason she was so good at finding him was that his mother was helping.

Digging his ski poles into the snow, David pushed forward, heading for the lift line. He had a vague plan about getting to the top of the mountain ahead of her then disappearing with Millie down one of the lesser-known trails.

The lift line moved agonizingly slow. He had to fight himself not to glance over his shoulder again to make sure she wasn't standing right behind him. He wished with all his heart that two weeks ago Cynthia had walked into a different dental office. He probably shouldn't have complimented her so much on her dental hygiene or accepted that offer of coffee and donuts. She'd mistaken friendship on his part for something more.

It didn't help either that his mother was firmly on Cynthia's side. *"You can't mourn Lisa forever,"* his mother had said when all of this started. *"Bart needs a mother, and you need a wife."*

"She's stalking me, Mother. That's not a good start to a relationship."

"Of course she isn't stalking you. Her family and ours have been friends for years. Besides, David, it's been five years. How much longer are you going to wait?"

Giving in to the urge, David glanced back over his shoulder. Cynthia beamed at him. David groaned involuntarily.

"Are you okay?" Millie asked.

"Oh, yeah."

"You sounded in pain."

"I'm fine."

"It's this date, isn't it? I'm going to kill my mother," Millie announced. "How'd she blackmail you into this?"

David looked more closely at Millie, whose face was all but hidden under a fluffy yellow hat and goggles. It had not occurred to him that he was not the only one who had been talked into this date. "She didn't blackmail me."

"Then what?"

"Nothing. I haven't been skiing in a long time. And she said you hadn't either."

Millie studied his face. "Look, we don't have to do this. We can end this date right now. No hard feelings."

David glanced back at Cynthia. If he backed out of the date now, it'd only encourage Cynthia to pursue him harder. Of course, he couldn't explain this to Millie. "We're here," he said. "It's a beautiful afternoon. We should enjoy it."

A moment later, the chairlift lightly bumped the back of his legs, and he settled back as the cable pulled the chair into the air.

"If it wasn't blackmail, then it was a bribe," Millie mused. She was wearing a one-piece down outfit with a lot of insulation. Their shoulders touched, although he was aware that she was sitting with as much space between them as possible. "What'd she promise you? Apple caramel pie? Black Forest cake? Strudel?"

David cast a nervous glance over his shoulder. There were only two lift chairs between Cynthia and himself. "She didn't bribe me. I wanted to come." The false note in his voice hung in the air as obvious as the small puffs of his breath. "Hey, how about this weather? Feels like snow, doesn't it?"

Talking about the weather. How lame was that? He wiggled his fingers inside his thick gloves to warm them and tried not to think how long it'd been since he'd been on a date.

"Snow?" Millie picked at the thread of conversation. "We're already ten inches above average for the year."

He looked at her to see if she was being serious or poking fun at his awkward attempt at conversation. "At least the trails will be in good condition."

The chair bounced slightly as it rolled over the top of a support tower. They glided past ponderosa pines, their branches glistening with two inches of fresh snow. Far below them, skiers traversed the slope gracefully. David envied their freedom.

The wind picked up as they neared the top of the mountain. Seeing the safety netting below, David raised the safety bar and inched to the edge of the chair. The lift leveled, and David pushed off. Millie skied off beside him, mirroring his movements as they slid away from the lift area.

David wanted to waste no time putting distance between

himself and Cynthia. If they hurried, they might be able to choose a trail without Cynthia seeing them. "Let's try Sidewinder," he suggested. "It's on the far side of the mountain, but it's usually not very crowded."

"What color trail is it?"

David kept moving. "It's a blue trail. An intermediate."

"Okay," Millie agreed.

It was windy and much colder at the top of the mountain. Most of the surface was flat, and they had to use their arms and move their skis in an awkward ice-skating motion. Both of them were panting by the time they reached the top of Sidewinder.

Normally David would have paused to admire the view. Today he just wanted to get out of range of Cynthia. "You first," he said.

Millie pushed off. He felt something inside him relax as she put a nice edge into the first turn. The snow sparkled in the late afternoon sun, and the air that filled his lungs tasted pure and chilly. His face burned pleasantly from the cold, and the world opened up to him in a way that he had almost forgotten.

Casting one more look over his shoulder, he used both his arms to swing off the lip and launch himself down the slope. The powder felt as good as it looked. He took the fall line at the edge of the trail where fewer skiers had skied and the snow was deeper.

He picked up speed quickly but controlled it with quick, short turns that sent the snow spraying behind him. Just in front of him, he watched Millie making her way down the trail. She traversed the mountain easily although cautiously, avoiding the few moguls that had formed out of the turns of other skiers.

Millie paused where the trail flattened. Digging his edges into the snow, David checked his skis to a hard stop next to her. In the distance, the ski lodge looked tiny, a dollhouse version of the sprawling wood-and-glass building.

"This is great," Millie said, slightly breathless. "I'd forgotten how much I like to ski."

"Me, too," David said.

She lifted her goggles onto the top of her fluffy yellow hat. "Hope I'm not holding you back."

"No. Not at all. You're a terrific skier."

"Thanks. You're pretty good, too."

For a moment their gazes met. Millie's eyes were the same, a clear shade of gray as they'd been in high school. She had a nice smile, too. He liked the slight crookedness of her incisors. It was an honest smile, the imperfections telling him it was the smile God had given her.

Looking at her heart-shaped face and stonewashed eyes, it was impossible to think so many years had passed. She looked exactly the way he remembered from high school. She'd been the girl of his dreams, and he'd prayed that she'd go out with him. It hadn't worked out that way, but he had no regrets or complaints. He'd had seven amazing years with Lisa. God had blessed them with a son, and he thought it was more than one man could ask for or want.

It surprised him though to look at her and feel the slightest stirring of interest. He remembered she'd been a girl with big dreams—voted most likely to be a movie star. Instead, she'd stayed in Deer Park.

"I'm really glad you could come today, Millie," he said, but couldn't help glancing up the hill to make sure they hadn't been followed.

"Me, too," she said, sounding unconvinced.

"We should probably get going."

She peered down the trail then back at him. "It's getting steep.

Maybe you'd better not watch me—this might not be pretty."

He laughed. He'd forgotten that she had a great sense of humor. It amazed him to realize that if it hadn't been for Cynthia, he'd be genuinely enjoying himself. "I'll be right behind you," he promised.

She tugged her goggles into place, took a deep breath, then pushed off.

He watched her bend and rise out of the turn and felt that little spark of interest again. Not that he was going to do anything about it. He already had one too many women to deal with. A quick glance confirmed Cynthia was schussing down the slope with determination toward him.

He considered waiting and telling her to back off, but the trail was steep, and he'd promised Millie that he would stay close to her. Pushing off the lip, he let his skis run down the hill and wondered what it was going to take to get rid of Cynthia Shively.

Chapter 3

"Hi, Mom," Millie called as she dumped her boots and ski suit in the laundry room. "I'm home."

Following the sound of the television, Millie hurried into the family room where her mother sat in the leather recliner watching the Food Network.

Her mother punched the MUTE button and stared up at Millie. "You had a great time, didn't you? I told you he was perfect."

"Well, not exactly." Millie eyed the bag of caramels in her mother's lap. "How many of those have you had?"

Her mother giggled. "I don't know, and I don't care. Tell me about David. Did he kiss you?"

Millie reached for the bag of candy, but her mother lifted it out of her grasp.

"Paws off, Millie. I'm serious. You get your own." Her fingers tightened as Millie managed to get a hand on it. "Look," her mom said in an obvious attempt to distract her, "*Dinner: Impossible* is coming on. Robert Irvine is practically exploding out of his T-shirt."

Millie snatched the candy from her mother's grasp and studied the brightness of her mother's eyes. She didn't trust the excitement she saw in them. "Have you checked your blood sugar?"

"Maybe later." She glanced at her mother, but as usual Eva

avoided her gaze. "Millie, relax. Every once in a while it's okay for me to eat a little candy. Besides"—she wagged a finger at Millie—"I'm eating those caramels for your own good."

Millie crossed into the kitchen. Pushing aside the familiar clutter on the counter, she searched for her mother's blood sugar monitor. She found it beneath a Pottery Barn catalog and her mother's red wool hat. Taking a clean lancet and a test strip, she returned to the family room.

"It's not okay for you to eat this stuff," she informed her mother. "And you know it. If your blood sugar gets too high, you could go into shock or pass out."

"Stop being a wet blanket." Her mom rose from her chair and stepped behind it. She looked prepared to make a run for it if Millie came one step closer. "Besides, I'm not finished yet." She pointed to her teeth. "My filling is still in place, but don't worry, honey, I'm going to loosen it if it takes all night."

Millie blinked. Who on earth would *want* to go back to the dentist? Then it hit her. A matchmaking mother would welcome an excuse to go back to the dentist if she was interested in setting her daughter up on another date. "Mom," she said sharply. "He has a girlfriend. She was following us all afternoon on the ski slope."

Her mother waved her hand indifferently. "If the girlfriend was serious, David would never have agreed to go on a date with you. He's not that kind of man. So, Millie, the appointment is at nine. You'll take me of course."

"Mom, you're scaring me."

"If it's a girl, you can name her after me. And if it's a boy, you can call him Everett. Rhett for short. Isn't that cute?"

"There isn't going to be a first child," Millie interrupted, advancing a step. "And I'm not taking you to the dentist tomorrow.

Now come here and let me test your blood."

"Vampire." Eva made a cross with two fingers. "Stay back."

Millie struggled to keep her temper. *It's the diabetes talking,* she reminded herself. Her mother's moods often were directly related to the levels of her blood sugar. If it was high, her mother's spirits soared. She went about the house singing, almost giddy. Low blood sugar, on the other hand, made her defiant and irritable.

"Come on," Millie coaxed. "If you let me test your blood, I'll tell you a little more about my date."

Her mother's face brightened instantly. "You're going to break the Hogan curse; I just know it. You're going to be the first Hogan woman in three generations to get the happily-ever-after."

Millie took another step toward her mother and wondered how she was going to put a positive spin on a date that had consisted of David covertly peering around for glimpses of another woman while she pretended not to notice.

"He's grown," she said. "I don't tower over him like a giant anymore. Now give me your hand if you want to hear anything else."

"Oh all right." Her mother extended her right hand. "Did you notice his eyes? They're the color of the Caribbean Sea."

Millie placed the pencil-shaped instrument on the pad of her mother's index finger and pushed a button. The device released the needle in a loud *click.* A small dot of blood formed on her mom's finger, and Millie dipped it onto the test strip.

Her mother was capable of using the device herself, and it never failed to puzzle Millie how her mom could take such a casual approach to a potentially life-threatening disease.

She stuck the test strip into the monitor and waited. A few seconds later, the number flashed on the screen. "380," Millie announced. Worry made her voice sharp. "Did you take any medication today at all?"

"I'm not senile. Of course I did."

Millie studied her mother's face. Eva's brown eyes sparkled, and a becoming blush the color of pink geraniums bloomed in her cheeks. She didn't look like a woman on the verge of a diabetic coma, but that was the problem. With diabetes, you couldn't tell what was happening on the inside.

"I'm going to call your doctor," Millie announced, wondering if she should simply take her mother to the emergency room. "You keep watching *Dinner: Impossible*."

"I want to hear about your date," her mother insisted. "Wait until you're in the dental chair and he leans over you. I haven't had such a hot flash since I went through menopause."

Millie knew Dr. Wong's number by heart. She left a message with the answering service and hung up. Although she pretty much knew the drill by now—*"Keep a close eye on your mother and check her blood sugar in an hour or so"*—she still needed to hear the orders come from a physician. She didn't want the one time she should have called to be the one time she didn't.

Sinking into one of the ladder-backed kitchen chairs, she tucked a piece of hair behind her ear, but it wasn't long enough to stay, and it fell forward, tickling her cheek. She pushed it again anyway. A cup of coffee, half empty from the morning, sat on the table. Millie sipped the cold beverage and waited for the doctor to call.

She stared at the yellow walls. For as long as she could remember, she and her mom had been saying they'd change the color, but whenever they got to the paint store, they ended up coming home with the same shade of egg-yolk yellow. The fading print of a rooster hung over the Formica table, and the speckled linoleum floor was thirty years old.

A gallery of photographs on magnets covered three sides of the refrigerator. Her gaze lingered on the sight of herself elbow deep in bread dough and her mother standing beside her laughing.

Millie couldn't remember what had been so funny, but it didn't matter. The photo captured the essence of her mother, who thought the only good life was one with joy and laughter. Of course her mother didn't have to worry—she had Millie to worry for her.

"Millie? What's taking so long?"

Millie hesitated. She needed a few seconds before she faced Eva again. She reminded herself she and her mom were the M&M's—Mom and Millie. She, Millie, was the plain kind; Eva, the flamboyant, nutty one.

She picked up the bag of caramels and bit into one unhappily. *She's my mother, and she loves me. She's just trying to do what she thinks is best.*

Millie popped another caramel into her mouth and then another. She chewed unhappily and wished the doctor would hurry up and call. Suddenly her teeth clamped down on something hard as a rock. She moved it around her mouth, but with growing certainty realized this couldn't be a caramel. Her tongue found an unfamiliar gap in the back of her mouth.

She didn't need to see the silver evidence to know that she'd just dislodged a filling, and from the size of the hole, maybe even part of her tooth.

Chapter 4

Aris waited for him as he stepped into the kitchen. Seated at the wooden table, his housekeeper was wearing an ankle-length down jacket. Her long silver braid extended from a fur hat with a raccoon tail. She gave him a sour face and tapped the face of her watch.

"Sorry," David said, remembering belatedly that his housekeeper met with the Garden Club at the library on Tuesday nights.

"Oh well, it's no problem," Aris replied in a tone that said the exact opposite. "Tuna casserole's in the oven, salad in the refrigerator." She swung an industrial-sized purse over her shoulder. "Your mother called. She wants to know if you can take her to the Saint Francis cemetery this weekend."

To photograph ancestral graves. His mother's latest obsession. David nodded. "How's Bart?"

Aris shrugged and picked up a key ring that jingled with at least a dozen keys. "He's upstairs on the computer. Says he's working on homework, but. . ."—her eyes narrowed—"when I brought him milk and cookies, he almost dove into the computer screen trying to cover up what was on it." She put her hand on the doorknob. "We should check his IMs."

David shook his head. A month after Aris had moved with

them from California, she had joined the Deer Park Garden Club. It hadn't taken her long to become moderator of the club's online "loop," a position that allowed her to review all the notes posted on the web page. With the new responsibility she had acquired some new computer skills and an insatiable urge to become a cyber detective.

"Instant messages," Aris said very deliberately, as if he hadn't understood the acronym. "I can show you how to pull up his history. We can trace where he's been. Make sure he hasn't been visiting the wrong websites." She paused dramatically. "The web is full of nudie pictures."

David shook his head and tried not to think about how Aris knew about these places. Still, she made a good point, and he made a mental note to ask Bart what sites he'd been visiting online. "No thanks, Aris."

The elderly housekeeper shrugged. "Okay then. I'd better get going, or I'll be late for my meeting."

With a blast of frigid air and the firm click of the door, Aris left him alone in the kitchen. David hung his parka on a hook. He gave Tank, their English bulldog, a pat on the head then crossed into the living room.

Pulling aside a hand's width of the cranberry-colored drapes, he pressed himself tightly against the wall and peered out the window. *This is ridiculous,* he told himself. *I'm acting like a fugitive in my own house.* Still, he couldn't resist gazing up and down the street.

There—in her cherry red Miata—was Cynthia Shively. She had a pair of binoculars trained on the house. He let the curtains fall and stifled a groan. Turning, he saw his son, Bart, standing behind him.

"Hi, Dad," Bart said cheerfully. "She's late tonight."

David stiffened. He didn't like the idea of Bart being any part of this whole unpleasant business with Cynthia. "She stopped at KFC on the way home from the ski hill." He'd felt a brief moment of hope when he realized she wasn't going to follow him the entire way home. But then he'd seen her pull into the drive-through and knew she wasn't giving up—she was simply gathering ammunition in the form of one of Bart's favorite fast-food options.

"KFC?" Bart's eyes lit up. He was eleven years old, not quite five feet, and had the appetite of a starving Russian soldier. "I love KFC."

David was pretty sure his mother had made sure Cynthia knew this and that it was very likely she'd be knocking at the door in a few minutes to offer them some. He ruffled Bart's short black hair. "We've got tuna casserole in the oven." He tried to make this sound like a good option and watched his son's face fall.

"Every night it's either tuna casserole, chicken noodle soup, or macaroni and cheese."

"Not every night." Although privately David agreed that they had eaten enough of these foods to last a lifetime, he also knew that without Aris their lives would be completely chaotic, not to mention more than a little bit empty. She might have started off as their housekeeper, but somewhere along the line, Aris had become family. When he'd talked about moving back to South Dakota, she hadn't blinked. She'd just nodded and said she was tired of Los Angeles and that she hoped he planned on buying a house big enough for them all.

He glanced down into the always serious face of his son, a face slowly edging its way toward manhood, but still round and soft. He made a split-second decision. "Come on, buddy, we'll go to Pizza Palace tonight for dinner."

"No!" Bart said so loudly that David blinked in surprise. "I mean," he added more quietly, "we should stay home. It's a school night, and I have a lot of homework to do."

Something pinged David's parental radar. "Aris said you finished your homework."

Bart folded his arms, and an expression of guilt washed across his boyish features. "Well, I just remembered that I have more, uh, math homework."

"It's only six o'clock," David pointed out. "We'll be home by seven if we leave now."

"I'm really kind of tired tonight."

David's suspicions raised another notch. Usually Bart jumped at the opportunity to go to Pizza Palace. Not only did he wolf down enormous slices of pepperoni pizza, but also the two of them enjoyed playing the arcade games afterward. "What's the matter?"

Bart's gaze slid past his face. "I just want to stay home tonight, that's all. Maybe I'm getting sick or something."

David placed his hand on Bart's forehead. No temperature. He sighed. All he wanted to do was turn on CNN and collapse on the couch with the newspaper. The last thing he wanted was another problem. And yet one look into his son's eyes and David found himself prepared to do whatever it took to erase the look of unhappiness from Bart's face. "Okay, buddy," he said. "We'll stay home."

Not even a hint of a smile formed on Bart's round face. "Thanks, Dad."

David hesitated, unsure of the words that needed to be said to draw his son out. If he pushed, the boy would clam up. And yet if he didn't, how would he find out what was bothering Bart and help him?

The phone rang.

David guessed it was his mom calling about the Saint Francis cemetery. Well, he wouldn't answer. The phone rang twice more, and then the answering machine picked up. David's voice, sounding low and deep and not quite the way it sounded to himself, asked the caller to leave a message.

"Hey, Barty," a voice called in a high, squeaky voice that was obviously a boy trying to sound like a girl. "This is Lauren. I *love* you. I want to get *married* to you. I want to have your babies!" There was a sound of air kisses, a chorus of not-so-nice male laughter, and then the caller hung up.

David looked at his son's tomato-red face. "Bart?"

Wordlessly, the boy turned and charged up the stairs. His door slammed shut in reply. A moment later music blasted through the house.

Tank shuffled into the room and glanced up at David. Heartfelt sympathy seemed to flow from the bulldog's liquid brown eyes. The thump of the bass drew David's gaze to the ceiling. He pictured Bart facedown on his bed, blasting his music as if he could drown out his own thoughts. David knew a lot about unwelcome thoughts. They slid through your mind like ghosts, and the more you tried to bat them away, the more they multiplied.

What he didn't know was how to reach his son who was growing up faster every day, becoming more distant, more plugged into his computer, his friends, and his MP3 player than he was to David. At the same time, like now, he knew the tough exterior was nothing more than a thin shell that Bart hid behind. Inside, he was still a little kid—smart as all get out—but not particularly tough.

David glanced down at the bulldog, who wagged her stubby tail hopefully. "What do I do, Tank?"

The round bulldog flipped onto her back and stuck four short paws into the air. "Play dead?" David asked. "That's the best you can do?"

The dog wiggled happily on the floor, almost but not quite in time with the beat of the music. David rubbed the back of his neck and glanced up once more in the direction of his son's room.

He put his foot on the first step of the staircase. Bart probably wouldn't talk to him. Quite possibly he'd make things worse by pushing the boy. David was a man, but not so old that he'd forgotten how much he'd wanted his father's approval, not sympathy. Maybe the best thing to do was ignore the whole telephone thing.

From the upstairs, the music continued to pound. David looked up the stairs and sighed. He knew he would have to talk to Bart about girls—something he had not expected to do for a long time. He'd give Bart a few days to get past the embarrassing phone call, and then he'd talk to him.

Chapter 5

The sound of easy-listening music filled Millie's ears as she stepped inside the second-floor office. Glancing around the small, windowless room, she walked past the burgundy-colored leather couches to the receptionist, an older woman with ash-blond hair, a narrow face, and a friendly smile looked up at her. "Can I help you?"

"I'm Millie Hogan. My mother, Eva, is scheduled to see Dr. Denvers at nine, but I'd like to take her appointment if that's okay."

"Millie Hogan?" The polite smile remained on the receptionist's face, but something flickered in her eyes. Setting her reading glasses on her nose, she studied the appointment book with the concentration of someone who'd been told they had two minutes to study before a pop quiz. "I'm sorry," she said. "We can't just substitute patients like this."

"Why not?"

The woman's gaze stayed in the appointment book. "Because"—she paused—"your name is not in the book."

"Can't you add it?"

"There's another name there already."

"But my mother isn't coming," Millie repeated.

"I could probably fit you in a week from next Thursday," the receptionist said.

"I don't think I can wait that long," Millie said. "Look, I'm sure if we ask David, he'll be glad to let me use my mom's appointment."

"Dr. Denvers," the woman corrected sternly, "cannot be bothered with scheduling conflicts."

Millie ran her hand through her hair. Why was the receptionist being so difficult?

The hall door opened, and a woman stepped inside. Millie immediately recognized the woman from the ski hill. She looked even more stunning in slim-fitting winter white pants and a camel-colored wool turtleneck. Her gold necklace and earrings were flawless.

The blond stepped across the room on thin heels that gleamed as if they'd never set foot in a snowy, salt-strewn South Dakota street.

"Veronica," the blond exclaimed. "I made muffins." She handed the receptionist a basket covered with a checkered cloth. "Banana chocolate chip. And they're still warm."

"Oh, they're David's favorite," the receptionist exclaimed. "I'll go get him right away."

She must have pressed a secret bell or something because almost immediately the door to the patient area opened and David appeared in the doorway. He was wearing a white, thermal shirt beneath a pair of light-blue scrubs. His face brightened when he saw her. "Millie?" he asked. "This is a nice surprise."

Before she could reply, the blond said, "Have a muffin, David."

"They're your favorite—banana chocolate chip," the receptionist confirmed. "Wasn't that thoughtful of Cynthia to bring them?"

A tiny muscle jerked in the corner of David's mouth. His gaze swung to the tall blond who beamed back at him. "Try one," Cynthia said. "They have a secret ingredient that I think you'll like."

"Uh, no thank you," David said, backing up a step. "But maybe later."

"Now's a good time," the receptionist said. "Your nine o'clock patient just canceled."

"Actually," Millie said, "I'd love to take my mother's appointment. I lost a filling and was hoping that you'd be able to take a look at it."

Relief washed over David's face. "Come on back, and let's have a look."

"David, you can't do that. I don't have her insurance information."

Millie took her insurance card out of her wallet, handed it to the receptionist, and followed David into the examination room.

"Thanks, David." Millie set her purse on the windowsill. "Your receptionist sure is protective."

"That's my mother."

Millie's head swung around. "Seriously?"

David smiled apologetically. "When I took over my dad's practice, I sort of inherited her, too. She's actually very good at the job."

"Oh. Say no more." Thousands of hours of running the café with her mother flashed through her head. Sometimes her mother nearly drove her crazy, and other times her mom's sense of humor had her laughing so hard she could hardly stay upright. She settled into the reclining dental chair and tried to relax as David snapped on a pair of latex gloves.

"So what happened?" David asked, adjusting the arm of a high-tech light. He pressed a button, and the seat reclined. The world tilted, and she found herself staring up at the tiled ceiling blocks. He aimed a strong light on her face, and she was suddenly conscious of every imperfection of her face.

"I was eating caramels," Millie confessed. "Suddenly I felt this little hard rock in my mouth and a space where my filling used to be."

"Caramels?" David repeated, frowning. He rolled his stool closer to her. "I was just telling your mother yesterday that eating caramels was almost guaranteed to pull out a filling."

"I know," Millie said. "I confiscated the candy from her."

"That's odd. She thanked me yesterday for telling her." He frowned thoughtfully. "Well, let's take a look." He picked up one of the slim, stainless steel tools lying on an adjustable tray and gently probed the hole in Millie's mouth. "Does that hurt?"

"Sort of," Millie said. With David's hands in her mouth, it came out, "Thort off."

"That's a pretty big hole back there," David mused, bending so close she smelled the faint odor of soap. "I'm going to clean it up a bit and then patch it."

"Great," Millie said. She just wanted the whole thing over. She flinched though at the sight of a scary-looking needle in David's hands.

"Just some Novocain," he said cheerfully. He dabbed her gums with something that tasted like banana then injected her. Millie focused on his eyes and decided her mother was right. They were the exact shade of the Caribbean. Not that either her mother or herself had ever actually seen the Caribbean. Nope. For them it was Lake Bluckman, which they'd dubbed Lake Blue Lips, because even in the summer the water temperature rarely rose to sixty degrees.

"We'll just give you a few minutes to let that numb up." David gave her a confident smile. He had nice teeth, even and white.

"I had fun skiing yesterday," he said casually, perching on the stool and watching her with that look doctors use when they're making a clinical assessment while trying to appear as if they aren't.

Millie nodded. "Me, too." She was trying not to touch the cavity with her tongue, and her gum felt increasingly foreign and tingly. "I was really sore this morning. I'm not used to so much exercise."

"We got in a lot of runs," David agreed. "How's that gum feeling?"

"What gum?"

David laughed. "Open, please."

"Uh, David," Millie said, eyeing the scary-looking tool in his hand. "I want to apologize for yesterday. My mother never would have made you go on a blind date if she knew you already had a girlfriend. I'm really sorry if we caused you problems."

"Girlfriend?" David repeated.

"Cynthia—the muffin woman. I saw her yesterday at the ski hill watching us."

"She's not my girlfriend," David said, his face tightening slightly.

Millie's eyebrows drew together. She'd seen the way the woman looked at David. "She isn't?"

"No," David said firmly and advanced with the drill.

"Oh." Millie involuntarily shrank back. "She was following us all day. She couldn't take her eyes off you. And here she is today in your office."

"I know," David said calmly.

"So, she's what? A bill collector?"

He laughed. "No."

She was prying but couldn't seem to help herself. Dental offices always made her a little nervous, and the sight of the adjustable arm of the drill struck dread in her heart. It was getting harder to feel part of her mouth, and she concentrated on getting the words out clearly. "A stalker then?"

David's cheeks turned pink. "Don't you remember Cynthia Shively?"

The name was familiar, but Millie couldn't quite place it.

"Dr. Shively? The optometrist?" David prompted.

"She's his daughter? You're kidding me." But it clicked. The Shivelys had several children, and all of them had attended private boarding schools, mostly in Europe. "That's Cynthia Shively? I thought she was in France married to some bigwig plastic surgeon."

"She's divorced," David explained. "Came back to town a couple of weeks ago. We had coffee because she seemed kind of down, and ever since then I haven't been able to get her to stop following me."

Millie was fascinated. "She's stalking you?"

"Aggressively pursuing," David explained. "Our mothers are friends. They sort of made some kind of marriage pact while we were in elementary school."

Millie would have laughed, but David looked so unhappy over the whole situation that she felt a bit sorry for him. "How long has she been stalking—I mean, aggressively pursuing you?"

"A couple of weeks," David admitted. "I hoped if she saw me with you, she'd realize that I'm not interested in her. It didn't work."

So he'd only gone out with her to try and shake Cynthia. Millie should have felt insulted. Instead, she was relieved. David hadn't wanted to be on that blind date with her yesterday any more than she had. No wonder the date had felt so awkward.

"It's not that you're not an attractive woman, Millie, but I'm not looking for a relationship right now."

"Neither am I," Millie agreed. "But my mother, well, she'd probably throw herself in front of a bus if the driver was male, single, and she thought it'd get me a date."

"Don't say that in front of Cynthia," David said dryly. "It might give her ideas."

She met David's gaze and felt the understanding pass between them. "My mother was only eating caramels because she wanted to dislodge her filling. She planned to have me come with her so she

41

could get us together again. She already has names for our children."

"You know. . . ," David began then shook his head. "Bad idea. Very bad idea. Probably wouldn't work."

Millie sat up as straight as the sloped chair would allow. "What? What probably wouldn't work?"

David reached for a surgical mask. "I was just thinking. . .that maybe. . .no." He shook his head. "It's a bad idea. Let's get back to your tooth. That's something I can fix."

"You can't do that," Millie protested. "You can't tell me that you have an idea and then not say what it is."

He'd put on the surgical mask, which was cheating, since it hid his expression while he could see her entire face very well. He tried to move the arm of the drill into position, but she pushed it away. "Tell me."

He hesitated a second longer then said, "Okay. I was thinking that if we pretended to keep dating, then maybe Cynthia would stop stalking me. Plus, your mother would stop setting you up on blind dates." He paused. "We'd both get a little breathing room."

Millie blinked. Pretend to date David? Wouldn't that just fuel her mother's dreams of grandchildren? Then again, if she didn't go out again with David, she suspected Cliff Johnson, the pharmacist from CVS, was next on the list.

"You know, that's a fantastic idea," she said. "It might be hard to pull off though. I mean, to be believable, we'd have to do a good job of pretending that we were really into each other."

"But only when we were around other people," David pointed out. "And only for a short time."

"And then, when we break up, we could tell everyone that we have a broken heart and need time to recover. I would probably have to take a vacation," Millie mused. "You know, get out of town for a little while." She brightened at the prospect.

"And by then Cynthia would have found someone else."

"We could call it off sooner if either of us wanted," Millie qualified quickly. "With no hard feelings. You know. If it wasn't working."

"No hard feelings," David echoed. "So what do you think?"

"I don't know. What do you think?"

"It might be worth trying."

"As long as we both understand that it's only pretend." Millie looked at him carefully. "When we go on dates, we bring a book or something. No personal questions."

He seemed to consider the plan a bit longer then extended his hand. "I'm fine with that," he said.

The latex hand felt a little weird. To be honest, the whole plan felt a little weird, but Millie figured this was the only way to get her mother off her back.

Chapter 6

Both Cynthia and Mrs. Denvers were wearing polite smiles when Millie returned to the reception area. Given what David had just told her, Millie could almost see their brains whirling, trying to calculate just how big a threat she was to them.

"Did everything go well, dear?" Mrs. Denvers asked.

Cynthia covered the muffins and looked prepared to defend them physically if Millie so much as stepped in their direction.

"Yeth," Millie said, the Novocain making the right side of her mouth feel roughly the size of a bowling ball. Remembering her role, she added, "David ith a wonderful dentith."

As if on cue, said dentist popped out behind her. "It was so wonderful to see you again, Millie," he said into the back of her head and with way too much emphasis on the word *wonderful* to be completely believable.

Millie shifted so they could actually look at each other. "You, too," she said, smiling—well, at least she hoped she was smiling. For all she knew, she could be drooling like a Newfoundland. "And I'm really looking forwarth to tomorrow evening."

"Yes, tomorrow evening," David repeated so loudly that someone standing by the building's elevators could have heard. "I'll pick you up at seven, right?"

Millie winced. David might be a good dentist, but so far he was proving to be a lousy actor. "Right," she agreed, trying to signal with her eyes for him to tone it down a bit.

He didn't seem to get the message, because the next thing she knew, he was patting her shoulder much too enthusiastically. To make it worse, his gaze stayed pinned over her shoulder, probably watching his mother's and Cynthia's reactions.

This won't do, not at all, Millie thought. *Better help the man out.* She raised herself on the tips of her toes and gently kissed his cheek. The side of her mouth that had feeling registered the warmth and smoothness of his skin. She let her lips linger for a moment then added, "Thanks for fixing my toof, David."

"Anything else you need fixing, you just call me," David said, still sounding like a really bad actor reading a script.

"I will." Millie gave him a final, sultry look. "Thee you tomorrow night." She strutted past Cynthia and David's mother. "Have a nith day," she said grandly, putting a little hip action into the final few steps to the door.

As she stepped into the hallway, she heard Mrs. Denvers say, "David, don't you know who that girl is?"

She paused, held her breath, then heard David say, "Not entirely, Mother, but I intend to." The words sounded believable—as if he really meant them. As Millie stepped toward the elevators, she thought that maybe this plan might just work after all.

It started to sleet on her way back to the café. The gigantic éclair on top of the café's roof glistened in its case of ice. The wind had picked up, too. When she stepped out of her car, icy wind grabbed the door and slung darts of frozen rain against her cheeks. She hunched over and hurried into the café.

At least half a dozen customers looked up, called a cheerful,

"Hey, Millie," and waved as she moved inside the warm restaurant. A log crackled in the corner fireplace, and the smell of freshly baked bread sweetened the air. Millie hung up her coat, and as Tim McGraw sang softly in the background, she braced herself for the onslaught of questions.

"You get your tooth fixed?" Jeff Gulden asked. His perpetually sad face looked even more worried than usual. He'd finished his plate of scrambled eggs and hash browns. Millie automatically scooped it up and checked the level of his coffee cup.

"Yes, thanks," Millie replied. Half her lip felt numb, but her tongue no longer felt huge in her mouth.

She picked up a few more empty plates on her way back to the kitchen. Dumping them in a tub near the sink, she grabbed two orders from under the warming lights and ran back to the front of the restaurant before her mother could start asking a million questions. Millie didn't want Eva getting suspicious if she gave up the information too easily.

She set the plates down in front of the older couple at table five then picked up the coffeepot from the hot plate and began walking around the room refilling cups.

"How's it going, Mrs. Benson?" Millie asked. "Cold enough for you today?"

Like most of the regulars, Mrs. Benson was retired and spent weekday mornings at Dosie Dough's sipping coffee and reading the morning paper. She looked up at Millie and smiled. "It says in the paper that it's going to get even colder." She held her cup up for a refill. "Obviously global warming has not come to South Dakota."

Millie laughed and moved to the next table. A husband and wife were seated with their two young kids. Tourists, she thought and topped off their cups, all the while engaging in small-town talk.

"Millie," Aunt Mimi's voice boomed across the room. "We cannot wait a second longer. Come over here and tell us how your visit with Dr. Denvers went."

The coffeepot jiggled in Millie's hands. It wasn't as if she could pretend that she hadn't heard what Aunt Mimi had said. Although Mimi was so tiny her head could barely be seen when she drove a car, she more than made up for it with her voice. Naturally loud, it boomed across any distance. When she'd worked as a crossing guard, her voice had kept both traffic and children well in line.

"Talk loudly," Aunt Lillian called from her wheelchair at the bay window. "I want to hear everything." As usual, her white hair was tucked into a neat chignon. Today she was wearing her favorite pair of faux diamond chandelier earrings—the same ones she'd worn the night she'd been named Miss South Dakota in 1965.

"Not much to tell," Millie said but smiled as if there were a lot to tell. "Where's Aunt Keeker?"

"Right here, honey," Keeker said, walking out of the kitchen area with Millie's mother. "I was just talking to your mother for a moment." She fingered the brim of her Chicago Cubs baseball hat. "How'd your appointment with Dr. Denvers go?"

"It went fine," she said.

Keeker exchanged a look of satisfaction with Eva. "And that's the power of a good hat."

Millie gave what she hoped was a believable sigh and shook her head. "Aunt Keeker," she said, "getting my tooth fixed had nothing to do with your hat."

"We're not talking about your tooth." Keeker's large brown eyes blinked innocently.

Keeker firmly believed in wearing lucky hats. When a friend got sick, Keeker would trot out the herbal hat; when someone had sleep problems, she wore her dream-catcher hat; and whenever Millie started to date someone, she wore her lucky baseball cap. The cap, she claimed, had helped the Cubs break a fifteen-game losing streak back in the seventies.

"Tell us about the doc," Eva pressed.

Busying herself with the coffeepot, Millie shrugged in response to her mother's question. "I don't know what to say."

"Say you're going to see him again."

The room became dead quiet. Millie could feel all gazes turned toward her, waiting for her response. Even Thomas and Melvin Dittmore, the twin brothers who sat in front of the fireplace playing a game of chess that involved about three moves a week, had stopped studying the board and were looking at her instead.

"Well." Jeff cleared his throat. "I don't mean to pry, Miss Millie, but my root canal is scheduled for Friday, and if you think it'd be better for me to give the doc a couple of days to himself, I'd sure appreciate your saying so."

Could she really pull this off? She wasn't sure, but the sight of Cliff Johnson, the CVS pharmacist, casually eating a cinnamon roll at table three helped make up her mind. Picking up a hot pot of coffee, she walked over to Jeff and filled his cup. "Keep your appointment, Mr. Gulden, and don't worry about a thing."

"That means she's got another date," Aunt Mimi boomed out, startling her little poodle so badly it jumped up on the table and started mindlessly barking. "Hallelujah!"

Millie chuckled. "Is there nothing better to discuss than my social life? How about that malfunctioning traffic light on Bender Road?"

"She's got a date," her mother confirmed, beaming.

"If you ask me, she doesn't look too happy about it," Jeff

ventured, the wrinkles in his weathered face deepening. "Maybe I should reschedule."

Millie touched the right side of her mouth to make sure the expression she'd formed was indeed a smile. "I am happy," she said. "It's just the Novocain. I feel like I have a fat lip."

Aunt Keeker placed her hand, blue-veined and gnarled with arthritis, on Millie's arm. "I have a feeling," she said, "that he could be the one. I'll wear my red beret on your next date. I wore it when Roland kissed me for the first time. It fell off when I swooned, and he caught me."

"You don't need to do that," Millie said, but she smiled and squeezed Keeker's hand back. No matter how many times Keeker told this story, her eyes still filled. Millie wondered if she'd ever feel that way about anyone.

"What Millie needs," Aunt Mimi said, her small, wrinkled face breaking into a smile, "is a new dress. Something that shows off her figure." She stroked her dog. As long as Millie could remember, there had been a small apricot poodle in Mimi's lap, and all of them had been named Earl Gray. This one was probably Earl Gray the sixth or seventh, and it was the nastiest one so far. It had snapped at everyone in the café. "Wouldn't Millie look pretty in something the same orange color as your coat, sweet baby dog?"

Millie's tongue rolled over the place where David had fixed the cavity. Aunt Mimi had a good idea. She'd make that trip to Swaggers and buy herself something pretty to wear on her next pretend date with David. She wouldn't buy a marked-down dress either. A full-priced dress said she was serious.

Picking up a rag from behind the deli counter, she began wiping down an empty table. She wanted to rewrite her essay about why she'd make a good candidate on *Chef's Challenge*—a new reality show on the Food Network. Of all the dozens of casting calls she'd responded to, this one was the most suited to her. The show was a combination of *Survivor*, *Amazing Race*, and *Top Chef*, and Millie felt sure she had all the right skills necessary.

Somebody honked, and Millie automatically glanced out the front window. It was a big black Expedition, impatient with the car in front of it, which was waiting for a parking spot. Probably a tourist coming to town for the skiing. She looked past the gray, slushy street and sharp-tipped grains of sleet. The mountains were lost in the haze, but she really wasn't looking for them.

Someday her cell would ring, and it would be a casting director calling for her. She imagined herself in a chair in front of a mirror almost as big as the café's front window. Her hairdresser and makeup artist would be fussing over her, preparing for taping the next episode of *Chef's Challenge*. If she tried hard enough, she could almost hear the whispers of their voices. Closing her eyes, Millie smiled and dreamed of being somebody.

Chapter 7

"Hah!" Bart exclaimed as his Porsche 4000 sideswiped David's Audi. David's remote control vibrated in his hands. His car spun around and ended up, once again, on the TV screen facing backward.

It was worth it to see the look of excitement on Bart's face. "Come on, Dad. Catch up to me. I'll wait for you."

"So you can crash into me again," David observed, valiantly manipulating the controls so that his racer once more faced the correct direction.

Video games weren't his thing. He much preferred playing chess or backgammon, or even a long game like Monopoly. But Bart's generation played video games—increasingly sophisticated ones, too. David had to admit that his son, who pretty much tripped over his own feet in any kind of sport, could play any kind of video game like a professional.

From her place at their feet, Tank snored peacefully, ignoring Bart's shout of satisfaction as David's car once more plunged into the side rail.

"So," David said casually. "How was school today?"

"Fine."

Bart's racer accelerated, achieving a speed of 120 miles per hour, and left David's car in the dust.

"Those kids give you any trouble?"

Bart's gaze stayed glued to the television screen. He appeared not to have heard.

"Anything you want to talk about?" David accelerated his Audi with the determination of a father on a mission. Showing more skill than he had the entire game, he chased down Bart's car then deliberately slammed into it.

Both cars hit the side rail. Bart whooped in joyful surprise. "Good one, Dad!"

"You know," David said. "When I was your age or maybe a little older, I liked this girl. She was gorgeous—tall, wild brown hair, and a smile like an angel. I used to follow her around like a lost puppy."

He glanced at his son, who studied his remote control as if he'd never seen one in his life.

"There was this thing at school called Teen Night. Nothing big, just music and dancing in the gym. Finally, I got my courage up and asked her to go with me." David paused. "We were standing in the cafeteria line." He tried to see some sign that Bart was listening.

"And?" Bart asked, still fiddling with the remote but doing nothing to actually move his car.

"She looked down at me—I was about three inches shorter than her—and said no."

"I'm sorry, Dad."

"The point is that I asked her, and it didn't work out. That's the way it is sometimes."

Bart snorted. "It's not that simple anymore, Dad."

"No, it probably isn't," David agreed, thinking, *Talk to me, Bart.* "Nobody called me up on the telephone and harassed me. In fact, the cafeteria lady felt so sorry for me that I got extras at lunch for about a week."

Bart lifted the television remote. "At our cafeteria," he stated flatly, "you don't want extras."

His son turned up the volume of the television, and with a screech of tires and the roar of an engine, he once more focused his attention on the screen.

David surprised them both by reaching over and removing the remote from his son's hands. "I can't help you if you don't talk to me."

"Talk about what?"

"You know. That phone call."

"It's no big deal, Dad," Bart said without looking at him. "I have two Laurens in my address book on my phone, and I texted the wrong one. She forwarded the message to a bunch of people."

Ouch. David tried not to wince. Although he would have paid money to know what his son's message to the girl had been, he forced himself to assume Bart's casual tone and expression.

"Well," David said. "I'm sure this all will blow over."

Bart shot him a look that said it would when you-know-where froze over. Instantly David knew he'd said the wrong thing.

"Maybe you shouldn't let it blow over," David heard himself suggest. "Instead of taking your licks, you should use what's happened to your advantage."

"Huh?"

"Yeah," David said, searching his brain for a plan. "This girl you like. Why not text her again? Maybe she'll be flattered that you like her so much that you keep trying. Getting her to go out with you would make everyone stop teasing you."

Dead silence. Bart didn't look at him. "You could ask her to go to the movies," David suggested, knowing that he was doing all the talking but seeming unable to stop himself. "There must be something PG you could go to—or ask her to go ice-skating with you."

The image of his own unsuccessful skiing date with Millie flashed before his eyes. He stomped it down as quickly as he could. That was different. Neither of them had gone on the date for the right reason.

Bart punched the POWER button on the game console, and David had the sickening feeling that his son also was shutting down any further discussion about girls or dating. He could have kicked himself for failing. There was so much he wanted to say to Bart about this new stage of his life, but he didn't know how. Even now he wanted to hug his son but knew Bart would only shrink away.

"PG is for little kids," Bart stated without emotion. "And even if our movie theater was showing one, my friends wouldn't want to go. Mostly they like PG-13 or R movies."

Eleven-year-olds watching R-rated movies? What in the world are their parents thinking? David bit back the lecture forming and said, "Why don't we check the newspaper and see what's playing and then go from there?"

"If I see something good," Bart began, "could we have popcorn and sodas and candy?"

"You bet." David pushed down the dentist inside him that told him Bart shouldn't eat popcorn with braces on his teeth. He thought, too, of Lisa and how their first date had been to see *Titanic*. Would it help Bart to hear how awkward that date had been? How he'd dropped his soda and soaked the feet of the people in the row in front of them? Or would it merely serve to remind Bart of the mother he had lost?

"Dad?" Bart was studying his face, his eyes owlish behind the thick lenses of his glasses. "How do you get a girl to like you?"

David swallowed. He wasn't ready for this. Not ready at all. Yet he had no choice. The question had been tossed to him, and he could either fumble the ball or answer it as best he could.

"Well," he began, dismissing his first answer—the "just be yourself" answer that had probably been said about a hundred million times. "There's lots of ways. You compliment her. You give her gifts. You find out about her likes and dislikes." He paused. "You go slowly, Bart. You talk to God about it."

A long pause, and then Bart said, "Oh, okay," and punched back on the game console, filling the silence between them with the noise of a band that seemed to be shouting rather than singing.

David thought, *That's it? That's all he's going to say?*

Apparently it was. David followed Bart's cue and picked up his remote control. On familiar ground, he allowed himself to relax. All too soon he had a feeling that Bart would think playing video games with him wasn't cool.

He shot Bart a sideways look as his car drew even with the Porsche. He wondered if all parents had as much trouble letting go as he did or if it was because he was a single parent that watching Bart become more independent made him want to jerk him back into childhood. He felt as if he hadn't had enough time to fully appreciate it.

Above the ear-jarring music with lyrics that sounded like someone with a sore throat was screaming, "Raba-daba-jam, JAM!" over and over, there was a screech of tires and Bart's car fell back. A second later the finish line flashed in front of David's car. As he crossed it, his heart beat a bit harder, not because he'd won, but because he knew it was Bart's way of saying that maybe he wasn't ready to let go either.

Chapter 8

The doorbell rang at 6:55 p.m. Millie smoothed the folds of her new black silk dress—exquisitely cut but much too lightweight for the January night—and reached for the matching satin handbag.

Her mom, as if fearing that David might change his mind if kept waiting for longer than two seconds, flung open the door. "David!" she cried. "So wonderful to see you!"

Although it wasn't a date, not a real one anyway, Millie gave him credit. His dark gray pinstripe suit fit his lean torso perfectly, his shoes were polished, and in his hands were two red roses.

"For you," he said and extended one of the flowers to Millie. "You look very nice."

Millie's nose wrinkled. *Very nice?* That's what her mother said whenever Millie cut her hair too short. It was not something you said to a woman who'd just spent a hundred and fifty dollars on a dress she had bought specifically for him. She arched one eyebrow. "Thank you," she said. "You look very nice, too."

He gave her a flower and a small kiss on the cheek. The cool fragrance of his aftershave wafted over her. It smelled classy and expensive. And the long-stemmed rose was fresh and neatly bundled with baby's breath. She decided to forgive his lukewarm compliment about her appearance.

"Mrs. Hogan," David said, stepping back. "This rose is for you."

Her mother took the rose, and her face flushed with pleasure. "This is so sweet of you." Her mom turned the flower to admire it from another angle. "Thank you."

"You're welcome." He smiled, and in the space of a few seconds an awkward silence fell among them. This surprised Millie, because her mom was never at a loss for words. She was turning the rose in her hands, and there was a soft look on her face as if she was remembering another time and another rose.

"So, Eva," David began, breaking the silence. "How's that filling working out for you?"

Her mother beamed. "Perfectly." She turned to Millie and winked, making it clear it wasn't just her filling that she was talking about.

Millie touched David's arm. She didn't want him to get side-tracked with talking about dentistry. "Maybe we ought to get going."

"Oh, we have plenty of time," David said. "Our reservation isn't until eight o'clock."

Okay. The flowers had been romantic, but settling in for an extended visit with her mother wasn't. Millie had the awful thought that with any encouragement, he'd be happy to plop down on their couch and talk to her mom. That definitely didn't sound like a romantic first date.

Fortunately, Eva shook her head. "No, no, you kids get going." Her mother waved her arms as if she were shooing chickens. "*Dinner: Impossible* is about to start. That Robert Irvine is a fantastic cook. You ever watch the Food Network, David?"

"No," David replied. "I'm not much of a cook, I'm afraid."

"Everyone can cook," Millie's mother assured him. "It's just a matter of practice. I have some very easy recipes, and I'm sure Millie wouldn't mind showing you how to make them."

Millie almost laughed. Touting her culinary skills was just another way her mother was trying to make Millie seem like wife material. She handed her mother the rose. "Could you put this in some water for me? David and I really should get going."

"It was good to see you, Eva," David said. "Have a nice night."

"Enjoy yourselves," her mother said, fingering a rose petal. "But drive safely."

Millie grabbed her coat out of the closet. Slinging it over her arm, she yanked open the front door without even putting it on. The blast of cold air immediately stung her cheeks, and the slice of wind went straight through the hair she'd spent an hour straightening. She didn't look back as she hurried to David's SUV.

"Well, all in all, I think that went pretty well," Millie said, settling into the cold leather seat in David's black Lexus.

The car jolted slightly as David shifted into REVERSE. "You think so?"

"Absolutely. The flowers were a great touch." Millie checked the back of one of her earrings to make sure it was tight.

"Thank you."

She leaned back and watched the scenery flash before her eyes—houses frosted with a few inches of snow and streetlights throwing buckets of light onto the slick black street. They rode in comfortable silence through Millie's neighborhood then turned right onto the back road that led to town. "You know, I like what we're doing—this not dating," she said. "Normally I'd be trying to come up with stimulating conversation or wondering if you liked my dress or if I had lipstick on my teeth. This is much more relaxing."

David smiled. "I know what you mean. There's no pressure, no awkward silences while you wonder what the other person thinks of you. No expectations."

"Nope," Millie confirmed. "We're just two people helping each other out."

"Um-hum," David murmured and glanced in the rearview mirror.

She followed his gaze. "Is Cynthia following us?"

"I thought I saw her car a little ways back," David admitted. "But I guess I was wrong. I made sure she was within hearing range when I told my mother our plans." He flashed a sideways grin. "I told my mother that I thought you might be the one."

The one? Millie sat up straighter. She hadn't expected him to make such a bold statement so early in their relationship. "You think she believed you?"

"Well," David said, "she got very quiet and asked me if I was taking any new medications."

They both laughed. "You have to go more slowly, David, or you're going to give your poor mother a heart attack."

"I tried subtle," David said. "It didn't work."

Millie smoothed her dress. "I guess you're right. Sometimes it's best to be direct, especially when it comes to relationships. You have to make a clean break. Dragging it out just makes things worse."

She'd learned this firsthand. Men tended to ignore the signs that things weren't working out. Things like avoiding eye contact, not talking very much, and/or claiming to be too busy to go out rarely did the trick. People tended to see what they wanted to see and ignore the rest. "When I need to break up with someone, I tell them it's been nice, and then I shake their hand and say, 'It's over.' "

David slowed as the lights of the town came into sight. "And they just go away?"

"Most go passive-aggressive. Erv—the UPS guy—threw my packages in the bushes for two weeks before he got over it, and Karl Kauffman—he's a policeman—left me a couple of bogus parking tickets. But basically they knew going into it that I wasn't looking for a serious relationship." She noticed a Jonas Brothers CD sitting on top of a recording from the Chicago Symphony Orchestra.

"People should accept that a person doesn't have to be in a relationship to be happy," David said.

"Exactly," Millie agreed. "Marriage isn't for everyone. Some of us want other things."

David shot her a sideways glance. "Like what?"

Millie glanced out the window. Lights were still on in the CVS, but the windows to the adjacent UPS store and dry cleaner's were long dark. Ahead, the parking lot was half empty at the movie theater that had been playing the same two films for a month. "Options," she said, "which is something this town doesn't give you."

He took her to Ben's, which was the expensive restaurant in town. Mostly people went there to celebrate important family milestones, and it was pretty much booked all through the warmer months for wedding receptions. Millie was suddenly glad she'd worn the new black silk as she followed David through the foyer, where an enormous stone swan statue spat a flow of water. The crimson and gold carpet sank luxuriously beneath her feet.

"Hope this place is okay," David said as they waited to be seated. "I just thought, you know, that if we wanted people to think we were dating, I should bring you somewhere nice."

The last time Millie had been here was a few years ago when the aunts had brought her mother here to celebrate her sixtieth birthday.

There'd been a terrible scene when Aunt Mimi had tried to sneak her dog into the restaurant in a large purse and they'd been discovered. Aunt Lillian had jumped to Mimi's defense, but her story about Earl Gray being a service dog didn't keep them from getting escorted to the door. Millie remembered all of them grumbling as they walked back to the car, and then Keeker had triumphantly pulled out the loaf of french bread she'd stolen off the table when Lillian and Mimi had been arguing with the manager.

"It's perfect," Millie replied as a woman in black with oversized silver jewelry led them to their table.

Couples bent over tables talking. A tall guy in a brown suit laughed and clinked glasses with a cute redheaded woman who ducked her head as if she'd just received a very lavish compliment. Across from them a bald man with a silver mustache and his white-haired wife were sharing a large piece of chocolate cake. On the dance floor several couples were moving slowly to the piano player's rendition of Elton John's "Your Song."

Millie picked up her menu and studied the selections. She tried not to worry when she saw the prices.

"See anything you like?" David asked.

"It all looks great." Millie lowered the menu. "Hope you know we're splitting the check."

"I appreciate the offer, but I can't let you do that."

She studied the serious line of his mouth. "David," she said. "Don't you know going dutch is the number one rule in the official book of un-dating?"

"You must be studying an old version," David replied and broke a piece of bread off the end of the loaf. "According to the International Council of Un-dating, or ICU, the number one rule is to make people believe we are actually dating, which means the guy picks up the check."

"The ICU?" Millie laughed.

"Which covers both national and international rules."

"I see. . ."

"U," David finished.

"No. I mean, I see what you're saying, but I'm paying you back when we get in the car."

"Millie," David said. "Thanks for offering, but I've got it. What would you like to drink?"

"Water. If I agree to let you pay this time, will you let me get the check next time?"

"No," David said. "When we're on a date, I pick up the check."

"That's not fair," Millie pointed out. "Why should you always have to pay?"

"To do otherwise would be an insult to you."

He said it matter-of-factly, but Millie's skin tingled pleasantly. She liked being treated as if she mattered to him, even if they were only pretending. She lifted the menu to hide her pleasure and resolved to order the second cheapest thing on the menu.

The pianist struck up a melancholy tune. "Maybe we should suggest a Jonas Brothers' song," Millie suggested.

David's eyebrows pushed together. "The Jonas Brothers?"

"I saw the CD cover in your car. I figured you were a fan."

He laughed. "Oh. My son likes them."

Millie blinked. A son? He had a son? Why had she not heard this before? She vaguely remembered the conversation that had swirled around Dosie Dough's when David had taken over his father's practice, but mostly people had been speculating on whether he'd be as good a dentist as his dad or if they should look for someone older and more experienced.

She realized that she was gripping her water glass way too hard and consciously relaxed her fingers. She was going to kill her mother for failing to mention David's son. She never dated men with children. Never. Her mother knew that.

"He's eleven going on sixteen," David said, and there was an undeniable note of pride in his voice. "Want to see a picture?"

Millie set the water glass on the table with a definite thump. "I don't date men with kids."

He frowned. "Why not?"

"Because kids complicate things."

"Such as?"

"Breaking up. I don't want to have to tell some boy or girl that I won't be seeing them because I've broken up with their father." She shook her head. "I'm sorry, David, but we're going to need to rethink our plan."

"I understand your reservations," David said. He realigned his silverware then looked up at her again. "But I don't think we'll be together long enough for Bart to get attached."

Millie cocked a brow. She wasn't used to men being so clearly uninterested in her. Although it wasn't flattering, it was intriguing. "I agree. If we date, it would have to be short-term."

"Just long enough to be believable," David began.

"And short enough that there's no hard feelings at the end."

David nodded. "Of course, if you don't like being around kids, then you're right—this plan wouldn't work."

"No, it's not that at all. I love kids. I just wouldn't want to hurt anyone." It was her turn to realign the silverware. "What would you tell him about us?"

"I'd tell him that you're a very nice woman and that I'm going to be spending some time with you."

"You don't think he'd see right through us?"

"He's very smart," David agreed. "But we won't be around him that much—and when we are, we'll just be ourselves. You know, friends." He picked up a spoon and turned it over in his fingers with the same dexterity Millie remembered from the way he'd handled the dental tools. "I haven't dated much since my wife's death. This might be a good thing for him."

Millie dropped her gaze to the pretty little pearl ring on the fourth finger of her left hand. Maybe she was being a little too rigid. David had made some good points, and she would be careful to make sure that she kept a safe distance from Bart—for his own good of course. She could look at this as a test of her acting skill—a perfect opportunity to work unscripted, just as she would on a reality television show. She found herself nodding. "Okay, I'll do it."

David smiled in relief. "Good," he said.

They turned back to their menus. A waitress silently materialized at their table before Millie had decided what to order. She ran her finger down the price list. She was pretty sure David would call her on it if she ordered the cheapest thing. "The artichoke and chicken ravioli looks good."

"I'll have the New York strip steak."

As soon as their waitress left, David said, "In the interest of making our plan a success, we should probably get to know each other a little better. I should know what your favorite color is and things like that."

"That's a good idea," Millie agreed. "It's periwinkle. What's yours?"

"Gray. What's your favorite movie?"

Millie frowned. Gravestones and rain clouds were gray. So were trash cans and elephants. "Gray is depressing," she said. "We need to find you a better color to like."

"Hold on," David said, his eyes narrowing and his body stiffening slightly. "I can't believe it." He lowered his voice. "It's her. Cynthia. She's here—and heading right for us."

"Don't worry." Reaching across the table, Millie placed her hand over David's, startling him so badly that he nearly knocked over his water glass. "Remember, we're on a date. Look at me like you mean it."

David leaned forward and locked gazes with her. After several moments, Millie realized that he wasn't blinking. "Not like we're having a staring contest," she whispered, "but like we're really into each other."

Just to show him what she meant, she leaned forward and gazed deeply into his eyes. They really were lovely. Full of color and depth. She'd never seen that particular shade of blue before either. She felt something in her stomach flutter. Her gaze lowered past his sculpted nose to the molded fullness of his lips. She considered kissing him— not because she was attracted to him or anything—but simply in the spirit of being a good team player.

She might have done it, too, if David would stop looking at her as if he were an optometrist sizing her for contact lenses. She kicked him under the table.

"Hello, David," a husky female voice said, and Millie looked up to see Cynthia Shively standing over them wearing a lemon chiffon dress with multilayers that parted in all the right places.

"You remember Millie Hogan," David said gesturing.

"Yes, of course," Cynthia said smiling as if David had just awarded her the Miss America title. "I hope your tooth infection is clearing up."

"It was a filling," Millie corrected. "A very small filling."

"Of course it was." Cynthia laughed as if Millie had said something highly amusing. Even in the soft light, her perfectly aligned teeth gleamed pearly white, clearly demonstrating that she was a no-cavities kind of girl.

"What are you doing here?" David asked.

"Eating dinner," Cynthia replied innocently. "Your mother stopped to talk to the maître d' about a table. I'm sure she'll be along shortly."

Sure enough, Mrs. Denvers, wearing a floor-length blue dress that looked as if it had been plucked straight from a rack of mother-of-the-bride gowns, was making her way steadily toward them.

"Good news," Mrs. Denvers said after murmuring a polite hello to Millie. "Our table is almost ready."

"Why don't you have a drink with us while you wait?" Millie suggested, ignoring the frantic look David was signaling with his eyes.

"We'd love to," Mrs. Denvers said. She motioned to one of the waiters, and almost magically two additional chairs appeared. "We don't mean to intrude on your date"—she paused to give David an inscrutable look—"but we needed to celebrate."

"Celebrate what?" David asked.

"Cynthia's return to Deer Park," Mrs. Denvers said. "We should have a toast to a long, happy life here." She looked around for a waiter. "What are you drinking, Millie?"

"Ice water."

"Oh, that's right. I forgot. With the medication you're taking for that awful gum infection, you shouldn't have anything alcoholic. Hope you don't lose that tooth."

Millie smiled sweetly. "Thank you for your concern, Mrs. Denvers, but David replaced my filling, and I'm just fine now." She shot David an adoring gaze. "Aren't I, pooh bear?"

He blinked twice. "You certainly are—*muffin*." Turning to his mother, he added, "Want me to check and see if your table is ready now, Mother?"

"No," Mrs. Denvers said. "It's all taken care of."

A few minutes later, Mrs. Denvers's table did open. Millie wasn't surprised when it turned out to be one right next to theirs. She didn't fight it when Cynthia suggested they push the two tables together.

"Do you see what I'm up against now?" David asked. They had escaped to the small dance floor and were slowly moving as the pianist played the love theme from *Titanic*.

"It'll be okay," Millie assured him, moving her feet slowly in time to the music. "Once they see how happy we are together, they'll give up."

David's eyes crinkled attractively. "I hope so, *muffin*."

"That reminds me," Millie said, enjoying the firm band of his arm around her. "You have to come up with a different endearment for me. Calling me muffin makes me feel fat."

"You aren't fat," David stated firmly. "But would you prefer *honey*?"

"It's still food-based, but better." She breathed in a little more of his faint but expensive-smelling soap.

"You're awfully choosy," David complained, tightening his arm around her and smiling down at her when she glanced up in surprise. "How about something Italian, like *cara mia*?"

She laughed. It was amazing, really, how easy it was to pretend to be thoroughly enjoying herself. She should have come up with this idea of un-dating years ago. There was no pressure wondering where this date was going or worrying about someone else's feelings. She looked up at him flirtatiously from under her lashes. "Since when do you speak Italian?"

"There's lots of things you don't know about me," David said.

His face loomed closer. "You ready for a dip?"

The next thing she knew, she was bent back over David's knee, her hair all but touching the floor, and David was standing over her, holding her effortlessly. Someone applauded, and from this upside-down position, it almost looked as if Mrs. Denvers was smiling at her.

When she returned to the table, Millie excused herself to the ladies' room to check her hair and makeup. Inside, she plunked down in a purple upholstered chair with gold fringe and regarded her image in the mirror. Her hair was getting curly even though she'd spent an hour straightening it, and the freckles across her nose and cheeks looked more pronounced than ever. She dabbed a little powder on them.

The door opened, and Mrs. Denvers walked into the room. She zeroed in on Millie and seated herself on an upholstered chair next to her. They regarded the other's image in the mirror. Mrs. Denvers took out her lipstick. "I'm so grateful that you're sharing your evening with David with Cynthia and I."

"No problem," Millie replied.

Mrs. Denvers began outlining her lips. "Cynthia's mother and I have been friends for years," Mrs. Denvers said, still regarding Millie in the mirror. "When Katherine was trying to decide what boarding school Cynthia would attend, she consulted me. We studied every school in the country before we sent Cynthia to France. Katherine was determined that her daughter was not only going to get a first-rate education, but also learn how to be a lady. We were both so proud when Cynthia married that plastic surgeon—of course the marriage didn't take—but when Cynthia came back to Deer Park just like David, we saw all along that God had been working behind the scenes. It was much too big of a coincidence for everything to happen the way it did."

Millie's stomach tightened. Something in the other woman's eyes told her that Mrs. Denver had something else to say. Something unpleasant about Millie. She wanted to bolt from the room, but at the same time felt firmly rooted to the seat.

"Look," Mrs. Denvers said pleasantly, blotting her mouth with a tissue and still addressing Millie in the mirror. "I know you see an attractive, educated man like David and think you're holding a winning lottery ticket." She smiled sympathetically, but then her lips tightened. "David has to be protected from his own niceness." She snapped the top back on the tube of lipstick. "I don't want him hurt again."

Millie's chin came up a notch. "I may not speak French," she said, "but at least I'm not a stalker."

Mrs. Denvers put her lipstick back in her purse and snapped it shut. "Give my regards to your mother. Tell her we miss seeing her in church."

Millie stiffened. Neither she nor her mother had set foot in church in two decades. "I won't have people staring at the back of our heads," Eva had said. "Either pitying us or judging us or just plain wondering if we're going to burst into flames."

Judging, just like Mrs. Denvers was doing right now, and the woman couldn't have made it any plainer that Millie wasn't good enough for David. She might not have said it, but the word *tramp* was easy to read in her eyes.

Standing, she stretched herself to her full five foot eight—five foot eleven, actually, in her shoes. She wanted to say that going to church didn't make Mrs. Denvers better than Millie, but she refused to let David's mother know that the comment had hurt her. Instinctively, she knew a better way to get back.

Leaning forward, Millie pouted her lips as she studied herself in the mirror. She gave herself a final smoldering look that said she was every mother's nightmare. And then putting everything she had into the sway of her hips, she strutted out of the room without a backward glance.

Chapter 9

Tank greeted David at the back door with an enthusiastic, if not somewhat asthmatic sounding, series of welcoming snorts. Her rear end swung back and forth so energetically that the plump bulldog nearly lost her balance.

Straightening, David dropped his keys on the counter and slung his coat over the back of a kitchen chair. "Hey, Aris, I'm home."

No response. Crossing into the living room, he found the housekeeper sleeping on the leather couch. He started to pull a thick knitted afghan over her, but her hazel eyes snapped open.

"I wasn't sleeping," she stated. "I was just resting my eyes."

David smiled. "Go back to sleep."

Aris sat up and surreptitiously wiped a small amount of drool from the corner of her mouth. "I'm fine. How'd it go? Your date with Millie?"

"Great," David replied, stiffening slightly. Before he'd left, Aris had made sure he knew about Millie's reputation for dumping a man after a few dates. His mom had basically given him the same lecture a couple of days ago, and it had really bugged him.

"You're going out with her again." Aris shook her head sadly.

"She's a very nice woman." She was funny, smart, kind. He remembered all these things from high school. She'd been beautiful back then, too, with those big gray eyes and generous smile.

"I don't think this is a good idea," Aris protested. "She'll only hurt you."

"Not likely," David said, thinking of his foolproof plan. Although he felt the same attraction for Millie as when he'd been fifteen, he had no intention of getting personally involved. He wasn't a nerdy little kid with a huge crush anymore. He was a grown man—a father—and could clearly see that he and Millie weren't right for each other. If he ever got serious about someone, it would be with someone more grounded. Someone more like his wife.

"I'm just warning you," Aris said. "You've got a faraway look in your eye."

"I most definitely do not," David declared, blinking. "The only things in my eyes are my contacts."

"If you say so," Aris said, clearly not agreeing.

David decided to change the subject. "How's Bart?"

Aris sat up a bit straighter. "Ah yes. We need to talk. You know how I was telling you about all those sites on the Internet? The ones with the nudie people?"

David's stomach tightened. He hoped he wasn't about to hear that his son had been visiting one of those sites. "Yeah?"

"I wanted to make sure that Bart wasn't logging on to any of those places or visiting those chat rooms—those are the places where the child predators lurk," Aris explained. "You might think you're talking to another eleven-year-old boy, but you're really communicating with—"

"Aris, I'm familiar with the dangers of online chat rooms. Bart and I have talked about them. Are you telling me that he disobeyed me?"

"Not exactly," Aris said. "I sort of distracted him with peanut butter cookies, and while he was eating them, I sneaked up to his room and took a peek at his computer."

David felt his features freeze. Aris had been part of their family before Bart had even been born. She'd been their housekeeper then their nanny. While he and Lisa had been building their dental practice, Aris had spent hours playing LEGOS and watching Disney movies with Bart. He'd never forget coming home one evening to watch Aris and three-year-old Bart dancing as Sebastian the crab sang "Under the Sea." But violating Bart's privacy? "You distracted him with cookies and then peeked at his computer?"

"You'll be happy to know that when I checked his history, he hadn't been to any sites with nudies."

David ran his hands through his hair. He didn't like that Aris had invaded his son's privacy. At the same time, he knew that she'd been trying to check up on his son—something that maybe he might not be doing enough.

"That's good," he said but didn't let his guard down completely.

"I decided that as long as I was there, I ought to check his e-mail. You know, make sure that he didn't have any inappropriate communications. You should see the e-mails I get advertising all sorts of enhancements for parts of your body that. . . Well, let's just say there are some pretty sick people out there."

"I know you mean well, but you shouldn't invade Bart's privacy like that. He's a good kid."

"I guess you probably don't want to hear what I found then."

Despite himself, David's interest piqued. "Is it something that I need to know as a father?"

Aris shrugged. "Probably, but seeing that you don't want to invade his privacy, I guess you don't want to know."

David forced himself to relax his jaw. He'd seen enough patients with teeth worn down from grinding to know how much damage that could do. "Obviously you think I should know what you discovered, so just tell me."

"Okay," Aris agreed. "But first, did you know that there's a program, a kind of spyware, you can use to pull up everything that's on somebody's computer, even if they delete it?"

Although David wasn't a computer expert, he knew about parental controls. He nodded.

"You wouldn't believe the things that people share over the network." She shook her head. "Enough to turn my hair gray. Oh right, my hair is already gray." She laughed.

I don't want to hear it, David thought, sensing that with any kind of encouragement Aris would happily spill the beans on her fellow garden club members. He closed his eyes and sighed. *My housekeeper, the cyber spy.* "What did the e-mail on Bart's computer say?"

"It was an IM," Aris corrected, obviously enjoying drawing out the story as long as possible. "And the tricky thing about recalling those IMs is that they're not in the deleted folder where most e-mails go. You have to recall them by—"

"Aris, just tell me!"

"The message read, 'Next time you'll lose more than your hat if you don't leave Lauren alone!' The alias was 'GorillaGuy.' "

David rubbed the skin on his face hard. He felt something primitive and fierce rise up in him. No way would he stand back and let a bully go after his son. He'd call the parent tonight. Go over there if he had to. The phone calls he could dismiss as a prank, but stealing Bart's hat? That was an act designed to humiliate, and he wouldn't have it. The only trouble, he realized slowly, was that he didn't have a name.

"I was thinking that if we log onto Bart's computer, we could draw out GorillaGuy. You know, pretend to be Bart."

David shook his head. "No."

"We could tell GorillaGuy," Aris added, completely ignoring him, "that we'll chop-suey him if he doesn't return Bart's hat."

"No," David replied firmly. "We can't chop-suey anyone."

"Of course we can," Aris assured him. "There are instructions for everything on the Internet. It's simply a matter of using the right search engine. I like Bing."

"It's not that," David said. "It's the wrong thing to do."

"What? You're just going to sit there and let Bart get bullied by this. . .this King Kong person?"

David nearly smiled at the look of outrage on the elderly housekeeper's face. She looked prepared to go one-on-one with GorillaGuy if necessary. As much as he felt the same way inside, he knew it wouldn't help Bart, not in the long run. "I'll handle this."

"How?"

"First, I'll talk to Bart and get him to tell me the name of the bully. Then I'll talk to the principal and the guidance counselor."

Aris laughed. "In what world do you live?"

David just looked at her.

"In a perfect world, your plan would work perfectly. In reality, David, you're not going to get anything accomplished unless you're sneaky. Our best strategy is to covertly draw out this bully and then. . ." She hesitated. "I don't know. Maybe we threaten to chop-suey him if he doesn't stop."

"That's not how I do things," David said. "I'm going to talk with Bart in the morning." He thought a moment. "If you could sleep late tomorrow, I'll make a good breakfast and talk to him one-on-one before school starts."

Aris rolled her eyes. "You cook breakfast?" She snorted. "That's funny."

"Even I can manage eggs and bacon."

She shook her head. "I think you're going to need me there—but if that's the way you want it. . ." The look in her eyes suggested a disaster of epic proportions was imminent.

He nodded. "I think it should come from me."

"Okay, but you're going to have to tell me everything he says."

"We'll see how it goes," David said. As he walked upstairs, he rubbed his face wearily. The pleasant glow from his un-date with Millie was fading, and it pained him to think of some kid picking on Bart. He dreaded the conversation with Bart in the morning. How was he going to explain just how he attained this information?

What David really wanted, he realized, was for Bart to come to him for help. He hadn't—and there had been plenty of time when Bart had been sitting on David's bed as he got ready for his date with Millie to ask.

That Bart had shut him out of a major conflict in his life was another issue—and something else he was going to have to address. Sighing, David walked down the silent hallway. All in all, a root canal was so much easier than parenting, and in the long run it was much less painful for everyone.

Chapter 10

The next morning all the aunts were huddled outside the café when Millie and her mother arrived just before five o'clock. She quickly unlocked the door. "What are you all doing here so early? Is everyone okay?" Millie scanned their red, weathered faces. It couldn't have been more than ten degrees, and she had no idea how long they'd been standing there. "Aunt Lillian," she said. "Can you feel your toes and fingers?"

"All eight of them," Lillian quipped from her wheelchair. "We're here early, Millie, because we want to hear the details about your date with David last night."

Her mother flipped on the lights as they moved inside the café. Aunt Lillian flicked the lever on her electric wheelchair and rolled into the room. Aunt Mimi, clutching her dog, clip-clopped in the three-inch high heels that just brought her over the five-foot mark, heading straight for the kitchen. "Hold on while I get my tea," she called. "Nobody say anything interesting until I get back."

Millie hurried to the stone fireplace and began stuffing newspaper between the layers of logs and kindling. The last time Aunt Lillian had gotten so chilled, she'd developed a bad case of bronchitis. Who would have guessed the one morning she was running late would be the one morning they would decide to show up at 5:00 a.m.?

"What time did he pick you up?" Aunt Keeker asked. Her flyaway gray hair stuck out from beneath a black bowler hat out of which an enormous purple ostrich feather flew.

"He came early," her mother informed everyone smugly. "Brought us both roses. I'm telling you, when he walked in the room, it was like the temperature went up five degrees. He isn't cheap either. He took her to Ben's."

There was an appreciative chorus of *oh*s and an exchange of impressed looks.

"The boy is smitten," Aunt Keeker pronounced. "As you can see, honey, I'm wearing my ostrich plume fedora—typically the male bird flaps his wings and shows his feathers when he's trying to attract a mate, but I have found that it works just as well when the female wears it."

Aunt Mimi's voice boomed from the kitchen. "You all are saying interesting things without me."

"He brought Millie flowers, and Eva had a hot flash," Lillian yelled. Her voice softened. "I want to hear if you had a good time. Did you, sweetie?"

Millie stepped back as the kindling caught fire. She closed the wire gate. "Aunt Lillian, it's warmer over here." Of all her mother's friends and Millie's aunts, Lillian was the most fragile. She'd been a Realtor, and had, in fact, sold Eva the small house on Cherry Lane more than thirty years ago. The two women had quickly discovered they had two things in common—a shared love of freshly baked pastries and parents who lived with them. They started meeting for coffee and muffins and had been friends ever since. While a degenerative neurological condition had progressively weakened Lillian's arms and legs and ended her Realtor's career several years ago, her mind was as sharp as ever. With no kids of her own, Lillian, of all the aunts, was like a second mother to Millie and could read her almost as well as Eva.

Millie ducked her head to avoid Lillian's gaze and minimize her chance of the older woman suspecting anything wrong. "This is way too early to be having this conversation. But yes, I had a good time."

"That's all I got out of her last night," Eva confirmed. "I nearly broke my neck running down the stairs to peek out the living room window, and all I saw was David walking back to his car."

"Millie, we didn't get here at 5:00 a.m. to see which of us has the worst bed head," Aunt Mimi said. She was clutching a red Dosie's mug in one hand and holding the dog with the other. "Did he kiss you?"

Millie started removing chairs from on top of the tables. "You all have to give me some space."

"When are you going to see him again?" Aunt Keeker fingered the ostrich plume in her hat. "And what will you be doing? I have to know what hat to wear."

"I don't know," Millie replied. "Maybe in a week or so. I don't want him to think I'm too available."

"Don't wait too long," her mother advised. "He'll think you aren't interested."

"Men have fragile egos," Aunt Lillian stated. Her blue eyes peered up at Millie very seriously. "You have to praise them a lot and make sure you flatter them. Even if it's over something silly— like the way they fold their socks. It's the secret, honey, to a healthy relationship."

"They're like dogs," Aunt Mimi added. "Most have to be trained. You give them a cookie when they do something right, and you yell at them when they're bad." She kissed her poodle on the top of its small orange head. "When I met Maurice, he was immediately put into puppy training to learn the basics. Gift giving, sensitivity—that sort of thing."

Millie laughed. "David is well past puppy training. He has great manners and even dances divinely." She remembered the way David held her when they danced and smiled. His body was lean and strong, like a runner's. It'd taken mere seconds for him to adjust to her size and shape, and then it'd felt like they'd been dancing together for years. She didn't know how he'd done that.

Finishing with the chairs, Millie realized Aunt Lillian was staring at her. "Can I get you some hot tea?"

"In a minute." The older woman's sharp blue eyes fixed on Millie. "Something is different about you." She drummed her fingers on the arm of the wheelchair. "I can't put my finger on it, but I feel it. A little sparkle or something."

"That tingle you feel is the circulation returning to your fingers," Millie quipped, but she busied herself with lining up the salt and pepper shakers that were already sitting side by side, like an old couple.

"Don't you think something's different about Millie?" Lillian asked Keeker.

"Absolutely," Keeker agreed. "She's a girl with a secret in her eyes. It was like that for me, too, when I met Roland." She smiled at Millie. "I understand, honey. When something special comes along, you have to protect it. So stop looking at her like that, Lillian, and come help me decide if I should spend Easter in Chicago or Denver. Jessica's pregnant and shouldn't travel, and Brianna has all those kids to organize. Not to mention how expensive it would be for her to fly. . ."

Millie recognized her escape and left the two women by the fireplace talking.

"Bart?" David knocked on his son's bedroom door. "Are you up?"

"Yeah. I'll be down in a minute."

He'd been saying this for the past fifteen minutes. David thought about the eggs and bacon sitting on the kitchen table getting cold. He was due at the office at seven thirty to prep for Mrs. Daniels, who was always early and would have an anxiety attack and leave if he wasn't there to coax her into the examination room. And there was still the matter of the instant message Aris had found on Bart's computer. David had hoped to discuss this over breakfast.

Opening the door, he stepped into the room. A boy-sized lump lay in the middle of the bed. "Bart? You're still in bed?"

Bart mumbled something unintelligible.

"It's six thirty," David said. "We're going to be late."

"Why are you waking me up so early?" Bart mumbled sleepily. "The bus doesn't come until eight."

"I made breakfast," David said. "We need to talk." Reaching for the bedside lamp, he clicked it on, and the room exploded with light. Out of her silver frame, Lisa smiled serenely from her spot on the bedside table. He met her gaze for a moment, wondering how she would have handled this. She probably would have known— without asking—who the bully was, called up the bully's mother, retrieved the hat, and set up a playdate, all before Bart left for school.

"Talk about what? Your date?"

Blood rushed unexpectedly to David's face at the thought of Millie in that black silk dress with her dark hair falling around the creamy white skin of her shoulders. "No," he said. He and Bart had a long talk on Wednesday night about David seeing other women and how it didn't mean he loved Bart's mom less. Bart had seemed fine with it, more curious about the logistics than the implications. However, looking down at his son, David wondered if Bart was as fine with him dating as he seemed. "Please get up," he said. "The eggs are getting cold."

Bart stretched but made no move to get up. "Can I have contact lenses?"

David blinked at the unexpected change in topics. "Well, yeah, you can. But you have to take care of your eyes, make sure you clean the lenses every day." The piles of clothing that lay on the floor were mute testimony to Bart's sloppiness.

"I'll do it," Bart said. "And I want karate lessons."

Because of the whole bully thing? *Great*, David thought, *Aris has been talking to him about chop-sueing people.* "Why the sudden interest?"

Bart shrugged. "I just want to stop looking like a nerd."

"There's nothing wrong with the way you look," David pointed out, trying not to think about how late they already were going to be and that they really needed to talk about that IM.

"Dad, I have braces and wear glasses. I'm short, and the only thing I'm good at is computer games. Face it. I'm a nerd."

"That's not true," David said. "You're good at lots of things."

Bart stared at him in silent challenge. *Like what?* his huge blue eyes seemed to say.

"You won the geography and math bee last year, and you're great in science, and. . ." David paused, thinking hard but unable to name a single thing that didn't support Bart's nerdiness. He raked his fingers through his hair. "You can have karate lessons if you want, but don't try and be someone different. I like you just the way you are."

"You're my father," Bart stated. "You have to like me. It's like a law or something."

"Other people like you, as well," David stated firmly.

Bart's mouth took on a tight, pinched look, and his gaze slid away from David's. "Not everyone."

He'd intended to have this discussion downstairs, where Bart would see that David had made Bart's favorite breakfast and understand that David had Bart's best interests at heart. However, it felt like Bart had opened the door to the conversation, and after a brief hesitation, during which David prayed he'd have the right words, he said, "Listen, Bart, I know about your hat. I know you're being bullied at school. We need to talk about it."

Bart's mouth opened and closed. Color flooded his round cheeks. "What are you talking about?"

"Who's GorillaGuy?"

His son's lips shut tightly. "That's none of your business. You've been on my computer, haven't you? That is so low, Dad. I can't believe you would do that." Pushing back the covers, Bart sprang from the bed and marched across the room.

"If you're being bullied, I need to know about it."

Bart grabbed yesterday's blue jeans from the floor and a shirt that hung on the back of his desk chair. "You think *spying* on me is going to help?"

"How I found out is irrelevant," David stated firmly. He wasn't about to throw Aris under the bus. "The point is that some kid at school stole your hat and threatened you. I take that seriously."

Pausing at the connecting door to the bathroom, Bart looked back at him. Defiance flashed from his eyes, and yet he looked vulnerable, too, standing there in checkered flannel pajamas that were just a bit too big for him. "Stay out of this, Dad. And stay out of my computer."

"We need to talk to the principal, Bart, and tell him everything."

"Like *that'll* help." Bart's voice rose. "All it'd do is get me beaten up or labeled a tattler."

"Were there any witnesses? Did this boy do anything else?"

"I can handle this," Bart said. "Why can't you trust me?"

Despite his fears for his son, David felt a small stirring of pride rise up inside himself at his son's determination to handle this problem himself. "I do trust you, but it's my job to make sure you're safe at school."

"I can take care of myself."

"I know, but. . ." David sought valiantly for a response that wouldn't hurt his son's feelings. The truth was, his son was short, kind of round, and apt to trip over his own feet. In other words, the Denvers's genes took a lot of time to mature.

"But you don't think I can do it."

"Of course I don't think that," David said.

"Then stay out of this."

"I'm your father," David said, trying not to get frustrated at the way this conversation was going. "My job is to take care of you the best way I can. Now I'm asking you to tell me the name of this boy."

Bart folded his arms. "No."

"No?" David couldn't ever remember Bart defying him like this. He felt that if he didn't deal with this correctly now, he was setting a new standard for their future arguments. He raised his voice slightly so Bart would know he was serious. "You will tell me the name of this kid, and you'll do it now."

"No," Bart said meeting his gaze levelly. "And you can't make me."

David considered agreeing with his son then grounding him for the rest of his life, but then he realized it probably wouldn't do either of them much good. "Look," he said, forcing himself to stay calm, "we're on the same side here. I'm trying to help you."

"Then stay out of this. Stay out of my computer."

"I'm your father, and I'll do whatever I need to do to keep you safe." David realized that he was grinding his teeth again and forced himself to relax his jaw. He briefly considered bribery—pizza primarily—then steeled himself to finish their argument. "Do you want to lose your computer privileges?"

Before Bart could reply, there was the sound of breaking glass.

As David sprinted to the top of the staircase, he heard more noises, china clinking against china, and a grunting noise. Hurrying into the kitchen, he saw Tank standing on top of the table. She'd knocked over the pitcher of orange juice—that was the crash he'd heard from upstairs—and was currently cleaning off a plate of scrambled eggs floating in an orange pool. The dog grinned happily. *Come on*, her brown eyes invited. *There's plenty for both of us.*

For a moment, David stood there, stupidly surveying the mess and fighting the urge just to leave it. Grunting, he hefted the dog off the table, carried her into his study, and shut the door so she couldn't get cut on the glass before he cleaned it up. Returning to the kitchen, he lifted the corners of the tablecloth and marched the contents of the table to the garbage in the garage and threw it all out. However, when he tried to get back in the house, he discovered he'd locked himself out. On the way to the front door, he spotted Cynthia, who was parked across the street.

She waved at him cheerfully from behind an oversized pair of dark glasses. "You're running a little late this morning, David. Want me to take Bart to school for you?"

David counted to ten then yelled back, "No thanks." As he

turned to go back inside, he thought about fixing another breakfast then decided there wasn't time. They'd talk in the car. He'd stop at Dosie Dough's for some coffee and muffins. It'd be quick and easy and was right on the way to his office and Bart's school. He brightened unexpectedly at the thought.

Chapter 11

Millie almost dropped the double stack of gingerbread pancakes she was balancing on a tray when David and a boy who looked so much like him that it could only be his son walked into the café. What were they doing here? She hadn't expected to see him so soon and especially not with his son. Setting the plates down, she wiped her hands on her apron and hurried up to the front counter.

"David—what a nice surprise." She kissed his cheek lightly then turned to the boy, who crossed his arms and looked as if he'd rather be struck by lightning than be hugged by her. "You've got to be Bart." She flashed her best smile and stuck out her hand. "I'm Millie Hogan."

Bart mumbled something and gave her a jellyfish for a hand. David shot him a warning look.

"We had a breakfast malfunction this morning," David explained. "Tank—that's our bulldog—jumped on the table and ate the eggs and bacon." He glanced sideways at Bart. "I mean bacon and eggs." He laughed uncomfortably.

Bart shifted his weight and completely ignored his father. Millie chuckled politely but didn't quite get the joke. "No worries—we've got plenty of eggs and bacon here." Millie picked up a couple of menus. "Let's get you a table."

"Actually, we don't have time. If you could just get us some coffee and donuts and orange juice for Bart, we'll take it to go."

"Sure." Millie lifted the dome off the glass case with the pastries. "What kind would you like?"

Bart's eyes widened behind his oversized glasses when he spotted the fresh-baked donuts. However, when his father asked him to pick out a few, he shrugged and the sullen look returned to his face.

"We'll have chocolate frosted," David supplied. "And a couple chocolate ones with sprinkles. I usually don't let him have so much sugar for breakfast, but I figure once in a while it's okay."

"Especially on mornings when you have a breakfast malfunction."

David laughed, but Bart didn't. As she placed the pastries in a paper sack, she watched David attempt to meet the boy's gaze. The kid ignored him, pulled out his cell, and started fiddling with the keys. Millie wondered if it was always like this between them or if they'd had an argument. If it was the latter, she hoped it had nothing to do with her. "I'll just get the juice. Back in a minute."

When she returned, Bart was alone at the counter, still punching buttons on his cell. Millie added the bottle of orange juice to a second bag then filled a large Styrofoam cup to the brim with coffee. She threw a couple of creamers and some sugar packets into the bag. "Where's your dad?"

"He had to take a phone call. He said he'd be right back."

Millie took her time arranging the food in the bag, adding napkins, extra creamers, and more wooden stirring sticks than he could possibly use. Eventually she ran out of things to add, and there were only so many ways to fold shut the top. Bart watched her closely. She pretended not to notice and wondered if he was totally freaked out at the idea of his dad dating her.

She wished David would get back. Over the top of Bart's head, she looked through the bay window into the parking lot. She spotted David pacing back and forth with his cell pressed to his ear. He wasn't alone, however. He was being trailed by Cynthia Shively. The blond finally managed to catch him and tap him on the shoulder.

David turned around, saw Cynthia, and jerked visibly. Millie almost laughed as she watched David try to manage a polite smile.

Now that she'd caught his attention, Cynthia went into full manhunting posture. Millie gave the woman full points for her moves: a perfect flip of her long blond hair, a bright smile that showed off excellent orthodontic work, and graceful footwork in the high-heeled boots as she advanced into David's personal space.

David, who was taking one step backward for every one Cynthia took forward, glanced at the café, and even from where she stood it was an obvious cry for help.

Millie looked at Bart, who also was watching the scene in progress. "I guess I should go rescue him."

"He's fine," Bart said. "Can I have a donut?"

Millie watched Cynthia pin David against the side of a red pickup truck. "My goodness she's aggressive. Your poor dad looks like he wishes the earth would swallow him up."

Bart laughed. "Dad always says we should be tolerant of others—even the ones that bug us the most." His blue eyes, so like David's, looked up at her seriously. "We should probably leave them alone to work things out."

Millie looked down at David's son in surprise. He sounded like a mini-adult—a little mini-man.

"We don't have much time before school starts," Bart added. "Maybe I should eat while they're talking."

She gave one last glance out the window. Part of her still wanted to go out there and rescue David, but another part of her thought it would be a good opportunity for David to tell Cynthia that he had a girlfriend now. The message would be better delivered without Millie rushing to his defense.

"Okay," she said and led him to an empty booth then plopped down across from him. "So what grade are you in?"

A long pause, and then he said, "Sixth."

"Oh. Middle school." Millie's nose wrinkled. Those years had been the worst for her. She'd never forget all the rumors and whispers that had followed her around like a bad smell. She pushed aside the thought and focused on Bart's round face. "You like it?"

"It's okay."

"What's your favorite subject?"

There was another long hesitation. "Science."

"Science?" Millie opened the take-out bag and handed him a double chocolate frosted donut. "What kind of science?" She hoped it wasn't biology. She'd nearly failed that one. The terminology had been incomprehensible, and never once had she managed to see the stupid little cell thingies through the microscope.

He took the donut. "Nuclear physics," he said and bit into the donut.

Millie felt her jaw drop. This was even worse than she feared. "Nuclear physics? They didn't teach that when I went to middle school."

Bart snorted. "I studied it at camp last summer in California—at UCLA."

"You went to nuclear physics camp?" She had never heard of any kid going to nuclear physics camp. "Are you a genius?"

Bart swallowed another bite of donut. "I don't know. We called it nerd camp. This is a pretty good donut." It was gone in the blink of an eye, and before she could pull the bag back, he'd grabbed another.

"So what's nuclear physics about?"

"Well," he said, "you study the interactions of atomic nuclei."

Millie swallowed. "That sounds interesting," she said but had no idea what he was talking about. "You want some juice?"

"No thanks," he said and grabbed a third donut.

This is it, Millie thought. *I can't carry on a conversation about nuclear physics, and I doubt he caught last night's episode of* Top Chef. She looked around for help, but no one would make eye contact, although she felt sure everyone had been furiously eavesdropping or staring moments before.

"Who's that?" Bart was pointing to a black-and-white photo on the wall.

"That's my mother."

"She looks like you."

"Yes, she does." In the photo her mother was in her early forties. Her hair was still dark brown and curled to the top of her shoulders in a style similar to Millie's. Eva had yet to gain weight, and her body was slim and athletic looking in a one-piece ski outfit that Millie was pretty sure was still hanging in her closet.

"That's an old photo of her at the Winterfest Snow Carnival box sled races." She pointed to the rectangular cardboard sled just behind her mother. "That's her sled—it's a giant chocolate éclair."

Bart reached for a fourth donut. There were two more in the bag, and at the speed he was eating, she feared he was going to get sick. She didn't think David would appreciate it if his son barfed all over the front seat of his car on the way to school.

"It's an interesting story," Millie said and picked up the Bavarian cream. She really didn't need the calories—if she ever got cast on a reality television show, the cameras would add ten pounds to her weight. However, there was probably only one way to keep Bart from eating it. She stuffed a large bite into her mouth.

"When I was about your age, my mom wanted to start a restaurant. We didn't have much money, and every time she tried to get a business loan, she got turned down. She hadn't had a job in years—and to be honest, we were pretty close to being bankrupt. The owners of Deer Park Mountain were trying to promote the idea of a family fun day at the ski hill and came up with the idea of a box sled race. So my mom basically challenged the owner of the bank to go head-to-head in the race. She wagered him a lifetime of strudel against a loan for her restaurant if he beat her. She pushed him in public, he took the challenge, and well, you can probably guess the rest—my mother won the race and got the loan."

She and Bart split the last donut. Only a few sprinkles were at the bottom of the bag.

"That's so cool," he said. "I've heard about that race at school. A lot of kids are entering it."

"I'm not surprised. It's a very big deal here. Last year we even had people who came down from Canada." She read the interest on his face. "There's lots of categories—most creative and of course the adult and junior race categories."

"When is it?"

"The first Saturday in March."

"When are entries due?"

"Right up until race day." Millie studied his face. "Are you thinking of entering? My mom and I would help if you wanted. Her sled still holds the winning time."

"Maybe," Bart said. "Hey, I see my dad—I'd better get going."

She looked at the entrance, and sure enough David was standing just inside the door. He shook his head when he caught her eye and made a long-suffering face. Millie smiled sweetly at him and waved.

"Hey, Bart," she said, "before you go, let me put in a few more donuts for your dad." She saw some chocolate icing on the corner of his mouth. "Maybe you should tell him you've already had a couple." Maybe she shouldn't have let Bart eat so many. "Then again, maybe you shouldn't."

"Don't worry," Bart said. "He really doesn't care what I eat."

Millie frowned. Bart's face was neutral, as if he'd just reported on the temperature outside, but the remark had a slightly bitter undertone that resonated inside her. Adding a couple of donuts to the bag, she remembered feeling that way as a child when Eva had been so busy starting the café that it seemed like Millie only existed in context to it. She wanted to question Bart more deeply, but he grabbed both bags and headed for the door. She didn't know what she would have said anyway.

David tried to pay, but she told him it was on the house and then changed the subject to what a great time she'd had last night at Ben's. When the last jingle of the bell faded behind them, the café seemed to come to life again. Aunt Lillian proclaimed that "the child was adorable enough to eat," and Aunt Keeker fanned herself with her sombrero and declared David was the best-looking man she'd seen in twenty years. Even Aunt Mimi stroked her dog and declared happily, "And his dog eats off the kitchen table. What could be better?"

Hollywood, Millie thought but was wise enough to keep her mouth shut.

Chapter 12

For their second un-date, David and Millie went cross-country skiing. Millie wasn't too keen on such an athletic date, but she liked the idea of going somewhere private so neither of them would have to pretend they liked each other in front of other people. After some more discussion, they agreed to go on Saturday afternoon while Bart was at the movies with some friends.

At 2:58 the bells on the café's door jingled, and David walked inside. His ski jacket was unzipped to reveal a lean torso, and his black ski pants molded around a pair of muscular thighs. His blue eyes were even a more vivid shade than she remembered. When that gaze came to rest on her, she felt a small tingle but pushed it firmly to the back of her mind.

"Hi." She gave him a kiss on the cheek and breathed in a little of that yummy soap. She let herself linger a minute in his arms. It wasn't that she enjoyed the feel of his arms around her, she assured herself. She was simply getting into character.

Behind her one of the aunts laughed and asked if Millie was planning on introducing him or if she was going to hug him for the rest of the afternoon.

"You can meet him if you promise to behave," Millie warned. Taking his arm, she led him to the table by the picture window.

"These are my aunts—Mrs. Keeker Dupree, Mrs. Lillian Wade, and Mrs. Mimi Decker—that's her dog Earl Gray."

"Technically, we're ABCs—aunts by choice." Aunt Lillian reached out a blue-veined hand and flashed a smile that had earned her the title of Miss South Dakota in 1965. "I'm so glad to meet you."

"The pleasure is mine. Millie has told me so much about you all."

Millie kept her smile firmly in place. She hoped David remembered how carefully he had to act around them. *The aunts have known me since I was born, and all their senses are going to be on high alert when they meet you,"* she'd warned him when they'd planned this date. *"They can smell a skunk a mile off."*

David had been fascinated with the idea of Eva's best friends forming a tight-knit group of aunts and had listened closely as Millie had explained how the circle had started when Lillian had sold Eva her house and then widened as Eva met Keeker in the grocery store and had become fascinated by the plastic fruit in her hat. They'd been interrupted by a small, apricot-colored poodle that had run up to them with Mimi chasing it and the store manager chasing Mimi.

Turning to Aunt Keeker, David extended his hand to hers and gave her a smile that Millie had to admit looked 100 percent believable. "Nice hat," he said.

Aunt Keeker touched the blue-and-white ski cap. "Thank you, David. It's made from the hair of the Tong sheep in China, which graze on herbs that appear to make them exceptionally fertile." Her brown eyes twinkled as she stared at David. "Would you care to smell it? It has a very mild but pleasing scent."

"No," Millie all but shouted. She took a deep breath. "I mean, ha-ha, Aunt Keeker is only joking. Right, Aunt Keeker?"

"I have six children," Keeker replied proudly. "My youngest,

Jessica, just returned the hat a few weeks ago. She lives in Chicago and is having triplets in July. That'll give me fifteen grandchildren." She removed the wool hat and extended it toward them. "Here," she said. "You can keep it as long as you want."

Millie looked at David, who had a wicked grin on his face and looked as if he might actually reach for the hat.

"No," Millie said firmly. "We are not going to smell, touch, or wear that hat." She took David's arm and redirected his attention. "Have you met my aunt Mimi?"

"Nice to meet you," David said. His gaze fell on Earl Gray who was sitting up in Mimi's lap and wagging his tail. "What a cute dog. I love dogs."

Before Millie could warn him that the dog couldn't be trusted, David reached to pat Earl Gray. The poodle gave a death growl and launched itself at David's hand. David jerked his arm away as the dog sank its fangs into the sleeve of his coat. He stepped back, the poodle dangling from his arm.

"Earl, you let go right now!" Mimi tugged ineffectively at the dog, which was still growling through its clenched jaws. "Bad boy!"

The dog held on tightly as Mimi put all of her ninety pounds into pulling him off David's sleeve.

Millie grabbed a glass of water. She dumped half the contents on top of the dog's head. It immediately released David's sleeve, and Mimi snatched it away.

"Are you okay?" Millie asked.

"I'm fine," he said, eyeing the small puncture marks in his jacket.

"I'm so sorry, David," Mimi said. With one hand, she gave him a paper napkin to dry his sleeve, and in the other she clutched her dog to her chest like a football. Her large hazel eyes looked up at him apologetically. "Earl only does this when he likes someone."

"It's true," Eva announced, striding into the room. "He only snaps at the nicest people." She cast the dog a withering glance. "Stupidest animal in creation."

"It's not stupidity," Mimi shot back. "It's a confidence issue. Earl only bites nice people because he knows they won't bite him back. It's actually a very smart strategy." She stroked the dog's curly coat. "Little by little, Earl is learning to believe in himself. Someday his big moment is going to come."

"More likely he's going to hurt somebody and you're going to feel awful," Eva warned.

"Stay back, David," Keeker warned as David moved closer to the table. "The thing jumps like a squirrel."

"You'll see," Mimi said. "Poodles are highly intelligent. When the time comes, Earl Gray will rise to the occasion." She kissed the top of the dog's head. "Won't you, sweet baby?"

"Sweet baby, my foot." Eva turned to David. "I'll sew up your sleeve for you if you give me a minute."

"It's fine," David said. He looked at Millie, who sent him a mental apology. "We really should get going."

"Well," Eva said, "have fun, but be careful. Don't ski into a tree or get lost or eaten by a bear or something." She thrust a pack into Millie's hands. "Don't forget your snacks."

Millie took it from her hands. She'd purposely left her mother alone with it so Eva could inspect the contents. By the smile on Eva's round face, she knew her mother not only had peeked inside, but that she approved the choice of items. "Thanks," she said.

"Millie, it's colder than you think outside. Why don't you borrow Keeker's hat? It would go beautifully with your parka."

The Tong sheep? No way. "No thanks."

"We probably should get going," David said, coming to her

rescue. "Are you ready?"

"Yes," Lillian, Keeker, Mimi, and her mother replied simultaneously.

Thirty minutes later she was half sliding, half jogging behind David. She wasn't very good at cross-country skiing, but she was keeping up. The temperature had risen to a balmy thirty degrees, and the snow was so bright it hurt to look at it. For once the wind had died down, and the great dark mountains covered with the dense ponderosa pines made her feel like an explorer—as if she might be part of a documentary on the Black Hills. She imagined a camera crew from National Geographic following them with cameras perched on their shoulders.

"How are you doing?" David called over his shoulder.

"Great," Millie panted, trying not to sound out of shape, which was impossible because she was out of shape. She tightened her grip on the poles and promised herself to start working out more regularly. She couldn't narrate a documentary if she didn't have the breath to speak.

David slowed as the trail began a slow climb. Millie turned her feet out, tramping upward in a classic V pattern that made her feel like a giant duck waddling up the hill. From the back, it probably was the most unflattering camera angle possible. She decided to stop fantasizing about being filmed.

David waited for her at the top. His eyes were hidden behind mirrored sunglasses, but his smile was wide and open. "I haven't done this in years," he said. "Next time I'm going to bring Bart. He needs to get out more and spend less time playing video games."

Millie leaned heavily on her poles. She was too out of breath to do anything but nod. The man had lungs like Lance Armstrong. He wasn't even sweating. How far had they gone? Five miles? Ten? A hundred?

Just as she was about to call it quits, she spotted a small log cabin a short way off. The rest station. She sighed in relief and steeled herself to ski the remaining distance. When she got to the picnic area, she popped her bindings gratefully and stepped out of the skis. Dusting snow off a bench, she flopped down.

David shrugged off his backpack and stepped out of his skis. Still looking pretty fresh from their skiing, he unzipped his jacket and sat down across from her. "No way is Cynthia going to follow us here."

"Don't be too sure," Millie said, still sucking an embarrassing amount of air into her lungs and trying to pretend her heartbeat wasn't off the charts. She was sweating and unzipped the front of her parka.

"She is pretty persistent," David agreed. He began to unpack the contents of the backpack. Pulling out a checkered wool blanket, he laid it over the top of the table then pulled out a silver thermos and two cups. "She came by the office this morning, and guess what her latest scheme is."

Millie watched him pour the coffee into one of the Styrofoam cups. Small curls of steam released into the air. "What?"

"She's thinking of becoming a dental hygienist and wants to be my assistant so she can observe what dentistry is really like."

"What'd you tell her?"

"That I was afraid you wouldn't be comfortable with the idea of me spending so much time with her. And I offered to make a phone call or two into Sioux City to see if another dentist could use her help."

Millie laughed. "Good answer." She took a sip of the hot liquid. "You don't think she's dangerous, do you?" An image of Glenn Close in *Fatal Attraction* flashed through her mind.

"Oh no. She's just lonely and confused. She'd probably have backed off already if my mother wasn't encouraging her."

Now that her breathing had slowed, Millie went to work helping David unpack their picnic. She opened a container of a fruit and cream cheese chutney and began spreading it on some crackers.

"That looks really good."

"Hope so," Millie said, biting into the cracker. "It's a new recipe. I invented it for our date."

"Really?"

She nodded, pleased that he seemed impressed. "I knew my mother would be interested in the food messages I was sending you."

David helped himself to another cracker. "Well, the food message I'm sending you is that I'm about to make a total pig of myself."

Millie laughed. "In our food language, if you eat everything, then you're saying that you like me as much or more than I like you."

"What?"

"The food, David. It's a conversation. The amount of food and the effort that went into preparing it says I'm very interested in you. The kind of food says that it's a romantic interest."

David studied the cracker with interest. "It says all that?"

"Absolutely," Millie told him. "If I was trying to express doubts about our relationship, I would have made baked brie and cheese."

"That's good, too."

"No it isn't. Not in my dating language. Baked brie is a safe choice to serve. I would never serve that to a guy I really liked." She nibbled a cracker. "The mango and coconut flavors in the chutney are supposed to invoke an image of tropical islands. You're supposed to taste something exotic and slightly seductive." She frowned a little. "But not too seductive. More like something you want to have a little more of."

"Well it's working. I do want more of it," David said, polishing off another cracker. "What else is in the backpack?"

"Oh," Millie said. "Prosciutto and Jarlsberg cheese on baguettes with butter lettuce and tomato. Some sweet potato chips—and dessert."

David brightened. "Dessert?"

"Mini-carrot-cake muffins with cream cheese frosting."

"Carrot cake is one of my favorite desserts."

"I know." Millie beamed. "Your dad told me. I tried calling your office to ask your mom what you liked, but she kept putting me on hold, and then"—she made quotation marks with her fingers—" 'accidentally' hanging up on me."

"Sorry about that," David said and wiped his mouth on a crisp white linen napkin. "She's been in a horrible mood ever since we went on our date last week."

"That's good—it means she's taking our relationship seriously."

"She is." The sandwich was gone in a couple more bites, and he was reaching for another. He wasn't a tall man, or a heavy one, and watching him pack away the food made Millie wonder where he put it all. "She was so desperate to prove that Cynthia is the right woman for me that she went to the Saint Francis cemetery and photographed graves to prove my family and Cynthia's were friends as far back as in the 1800s."

Millie put her sandwich down and frowned. "Well, I hope it doesn't mean I'm about to get visited by the ghosts of your relatives who want you to marry Cynthia Shively."

David laughed. "Don't worry. No family ghost would want me to marry Cynthia. She's nice, but she isn't for me." He shook his head. "I was lucky once. My wife, Lisa, was an amazing woman—I don't think I'll ever feel the same about any other woman."

Something in Millie's gut clenched. What about her? Why didn't he think she'd ever be good enough for him? She almost asked, but then she remembered it wasn't a real date. She flushed, realizing she'd almost overreacted. The point was that David was talking about his dead wife and that had to be painful for him. She touched his arm. "I'm sorry. Really sorry."

"Yeah—me, too," David said in that same matter-of-fact voice. He took another bite of baguette, but the expression on his face suggested he no longer tasted it.

Millie studied her half-eaten sandwich. She wanted to find out more about David's late wife but knew it was none of her business and a clear violation of the spirit of their plan. It didn't stop her, however, from thinking about David's wife. She remembered seeing a photograph in the local paper shortly after David had gotten engaged. Lisa had been lovely—a petite California blond with delicate features and a lovely smile. She'd been a pediatric dentist, and Millie remembered thinking David had done well.

"Oh, by the way," David said. "Tomorrow morning you're going to get a dozen white roses from me. I arranged for them to be delivered to the café."

Millie sipped her hot coffee slowly. "Nice touch," she said. "I'll call on Monday to thank you, but if you don't hear from me, it means your mother is putting me on hold again. By the way, that background music is really, really annoying. All it plays is a string rendition of 'My Heart Will Go On.' "

David chuckled. "I didn't know—it was one of the things I

left the same when I took over my dad's practice. I'll do something about it." His grin widened. "What do you like? When I have the music changed, it'll be one more example of how I'm really falling for you."

"More likely, I'll never get through on the phone." She smiled though. "You should change it to something *you* like."

Millie thought of her mother's stubborn determination to hold on to the past. It was as if change, even a small one, would upset the balance of the universe and end in disaster of epic proportions. Eva stubbornly refused to redecorate either the café or their house. Even small stuff—like Millie suggesting some changes to the menu—was met with resistance. *"Good idea, honey,"* Eva would say. *"I'll think about it."* But nothing would ever happen.

"Try this," she urged, handing him a mini-carrot-cake muffin. "The frosting got a little smushed, but it should be pretty good."

He chewed slowly, swallowed, and looked at her. "You made this?"

Millie nodded. "I thought about making you something chocolate, but thought it was a little too soon. I decided we should work up to it. I'll make you cheesecake next."

"I hope there's a lot of working up to do," David said happily.

Millie nodded but let silence creep into their conversation. They weren't supposed to be engaging in so much small talk. They weren't supposed to be enjoying themselves—they'd come here so they wouldn't have to pretend in front of other people. She was glad David got the hint when a few moments later he pulled their books out of the backpack. He handed her a copy of *Acting in Television Commercials: For Fun and Profit* without comment.

Millie started the first chapter—"The Million-Dollar Minute."

"Did you know," she read, *"that most people make their first impression of another person within the first three seconds of meeting them?"*

That seemed far too short. There was even the five-second rule for food that fell on the floor. She glanced at David, intending to ask his opinion, but stopped when she saw the title of his book: *HELP! My Child Is Being Bullied.*

Millie frowned. Bart bullied? She pictured the boy's pale complexion, thick glasses, and chubby cheeks. *Do not get involved,* she ordered herself. *Do not ask why he's reading that book.* She forced her eyes back to the page.

"How do you make that first impression be a good one and clinch that role? First you have to do your homework. Before you even step into the room, you have to decipher the meaning behind the commercial script."

Millie looked up. David's brow was creased. It seemed a long time before he turned the page. She looked back down at her book.

"How do you decipher the meaning behind the commercial script? How do you. . ."

She glanced up. Bit her lip and looked down at her book again. The words on the page blurred. She reminded herself firmly that whatever was happening in David's personal life was none of her business and venturing into those waters was a very bad idea. And then she heard a voice that sounded very much like hers say, "Is your son being bullied?"

David looked up. "Uh, sort of. I'm meeting with the principal on Monday to talk about it."

"Oh."

Rex Woody was a tall, thin man with a bad comb-over who wore black suits and a perpetually sad expression. He was a nice guy but had trouble making up his mind about things. Whenever he came into the café, he would spend long moments with his gaze fixed to the menu board then end up ordering a plain cheeseburger.

"Oh what?" David prompted.

"Oh, probably nothing," Millie murmured. She turned back to her book. "It's just, well, Rex can be a little wishy-washy."

"I've been thinking the same thing," David admitted. "He had a very hard time deciding if Bart should skip a grade or not when I enrolled him. In the end, he gave me the choice, and I thought Bart would be happier with kids his age. Maybe that was a mistake."

"I'm sure you did the right thing," Millie assured him. "This kid, whoever he is, he isn't hurting Bart physically, is he?"

"No. So far it's just a prank, a note, and a stolen ski hat."

"It's still bullying." Millie curled her hair around her finger. "The chief of police eats lunch at the café. The next time I see him, I could ask him to talk to this kid for you."

David shook his head. "I don't want to involve the police at this point."

"Well, how about calling the kid's parents?"

"Bart won't tell me the name of the kid. All I know is that he goes by the alias GorillaGuy."

"How'd you find that out?" The little voice in her head warning Millie not to get involved made a weak protest, but she drowned it out with a swallow of coffee.

"It's a long story."

"I like long stories." She set her book on the table. "Maybe you should start at the beginning."

The light was beginning to fade by the time David finished his story. "He thinks I spied on him—and he's pretty upset with me right now." David turned his empty coffee cup absently in his hands. "He's pushing me to let him handle this himself, but I'm afraid he's going to get creamed if he gets into a physical fight."

Millie pictured Bart's sweet round face and agreed with David.

"Maybe he could figure out a way to stand up to this kid but not actually fight him."

"I don't think a kid who goes by the alias GorillaGuy is going to accept a challenge to take on Bart in the Math Olympics."

She thought hard but was distracted by a crunching sound in the woods. "Maybe the solution is to find out if this girl Lauren likes Bart back. You could ask him to have one of his friends ask one of her girlfriends. That's the way we used to do it." She remembered just a little too late that David had been the exception to the rule. He'd just walked up to her one day in the cafeteria line and asked her out—and she'd simply said no.

"And if she says no, then Bart would stop trying to get up his nerve to ask her out, and the bully kid might back off." David stroked his chin. "Not a bad idea."

Something snapped in the woods. It sounded like a branch. Millie paused, listening, but the vast woods once more went silent. "Did you hear that?"

David held up his hand, indicating for her to be silent as another cracking noise popped loudly in the woods, followed by smaller but nonetheless unmistakable sounds of something picking its way through the underbrush.

It's Cynthia, Millie thought. Who knew the woman had the nose of a bloodhound? More branches popped, and Millie had the uncharitable thought that Cynthia might have a nice figure and face, but she wasn't very light on her feet. Either that or she'd brought Mrs. Denvers along with her. Even as she thought it, she glimpsed a large shadow moving between the trees. This was much bigger than a human.

"David," she squeaked.

Chapter 13

David began stuffing things into the backpack. "Come on," he said. "We've got to get going."

Millie strained to see the dark shape in the woods. Whatever it was, it had four legs. And it was *big*. She froze on the seat, hoping that whatever it was, it would go away. Instead, she glimpsed massive branches moving toward them then realized a tree wasn't moving—the branches were a huge set of antlers.

"Millie," David said quietly. "We need to get out of here."

Move? She could hardly breathe. Moose, especially bull moose, could be aggressive if they felt threatened—if they thought their territory was being invaded or they were protecting their young. Quite possibly she and David were sitting in the moose's favorite feeding ground. Quite possibly it was deciding between death by impalement or death by trampling. She had the sudden strong urge to pee and felt every ounce of the dark Colombian coffee pressing urgently against her bladder.

"Millie," David whispered more urgently, "let's go."

This might be true, but from the state of her limbs, she wasn't going anywhere. The moose was staring right at her. It could probably smell her fear.

"Move slowly, and don't look it in the eye."

Millie reminded herself that she'd dealt with worse than a moose. She'd had to knee a guy in the crotch on a date that had gone terribly wrong and once had chased down a tourist who'd tried to run out without paying his check.

Very slowly, very deliberately she climbed to her feet. Because David had told her not to look the moose in the eye, she found her gaze being drawn right to the beast's luminous brown eyes. "Now what?" she whispered.

"We retreat." He had moved to her side of the picnic table and placed himself between her and the moose.

Millie crept even closer to David's back. Leaning over him, she felt his back move with his breathing. "Maybe it's hungry," she whispered. "Maybe we should give it something to eat."

"Shhh," David said. "It's trying to decide what to do."

As if it'd heard, the moose lifted its heavy, gargantuan head and snorted. The sound blasted like a trumpet through the quiet woods, sending a shiver of fear down Millie's back. "I think it just decided," she whispered. "And it's not good news for us."

"Stay behind me," David ordered. He lifted the cross-country ski pole high into the air and placed his other hand on his hip, imitating a fencing position. "If it charges, run for the restrooms and I'll hold it off."

"David." Millie tugged his elbow. "You're holding a ski pole, not a saber."

"I'm going to count to three. When I say go, you run as fast as you can."

Millie tightened her grip on his elbow. "I'm not leaving you."

"We don't have time to discuss this."

"Give it some food, and then we'll both make a run for it."

"That's just going to make it madder," David whispered harshly. "One, two. . ."

"David, you cannot challenge that moose to a duel and think it's going to end well for you." She tightened her grip on his arm. "We both go, or no one goes." She took a small step backward and tugged at David's arm. Although he wasn't a lot taller than she was, he was significantly stronger. Moving him was like pulling at the branch of a heavy oak.

"Stop that," he hissed.

"I'm not letting you get killed by a moose," Millie said, planting her feet and pulling harder. Years of carrying heavy food trays and hours on her feet had given her pretty strong muscles. She felt his feet slip a little, but the few inches she gained were immediately lost as he caught his balance and snapped back into the same position as before.

"Millie—let go." He tried to break free of her grip, but she set her jaw and held on tightly.

The moose let loose another trumpet blast, stopping them both in their tracks. Over David's shoulder, Millie watched it stomp its front hoof and toss its head. It backed up a few steps as if giving itself more room to build up speed to trample them.

"Oh no," Millie gasped.

"Just go!" David ordered, pushing her toward the restrooms.

Just in case he had any crazy ideas about holding his ground, she grabbed his hand and held tightly as she fled for the building. It was less than a dozen strides away, but they were knee-deep in snow, and it felt like a dozen miles. David's voice burned in her ear, encouraging her to go even faster. She didn't dare glance in the moose's direction for fear that she'd see it charging to intercept them.

They skidded around the privacy wall and slid into the ladies' room. Millie came to a screeching stop in front of the sinks. Wheeling around, she saw David right behind her, snow dripping off his boots and his brown hair standing nearly upright. His nostrils were slightly flared, his eyes were a flinty blue, and the plume of his breath hung visibly in the cold air.

He spun around and used his body to block the exit. She read his intent to fight if it came down to it in the taut lines of his body. She found herself staring at the breadth of his shoulders, the way the muscles in his thighs strained against the fabric of his snow pants, and felt something very primitive, very cave-womanish tingle inside her.

When he turned around, she was aware just how small the room seemed. There were only two stalls and two sinks. The two of them could easily have joined hands and spanned the width of the room. In the soft light filtering from the skylight in the roof, she studied the shadows on his face.

"We're safe," he said, and her eyes watched in fascination the rise and fall of his chest, visible beneath his unzipped parka. It almost, but not quite, distracted her from the more immediate problem of the moose.

"You think it's gone?" she asked.

David shrugged. "I'm not sure. Probably."

Probably meant possibly. She leaned back against the sink. There wasn't even a window they could look out to see if the moose had left. "There's no cell signal out here either," she said. "I wonder how long it'll take the rangers before they come looking for us."

"We won't be here that long," David said confidently. "It's probably long gone. Most wild animals are much more afraid of humans than we are of them."

Millie folded her arms. "They obviously didn't count me in that survey."

"Don't worry," David said. "I'll just go take a quick peek around the privacy wall."

"What if it's just waiting for you to do that? Don't be like the person in horror movies who investigates the scary noise in the basement and then gets killed."

He just laughed. "Millie, I'll just be a second."

When he returned moments later, he wasn't smiling. "You're not going to believe this," he said. "But there's two of them now. A male and a female."

Millie blinked. "You've got to be kidding."

"I wish."

"So we're stuck here, in the ladies' room, in the middle of nowhere, being held hostage by two moose."

"Basically," David agreed.

Millie shook her head. "I can't believe this is happening."

"At least we have shelter," David pointed out. "And I managed to grab our backpack, so we have a blanket and food."

"You think we'll be here that long?"

"No," David replied. "I'll look again in a few minutes, and if they aren't gone, I'll throw some snowballs and make some noise to scare them away."

"Maybe there'll be three of them the next time you look," Millie said glumly. "And the next time you go out there. . ." She lowered her head, formed antlers with her hands, and pantomimed a charging moose.

He smiled confidently. "Don't worry, Millie. I was first alternate on the fencing team at UCLA."

She nodded. "I'm sure you're very good at fencing, but I think we're better off with my plan."

"Which is. . . ?"

"Feeding it."

"Feeding it?"

"Yes. Once I realized that we were dealing with a moose and not your mother and Cynthia, I came up with the idea of distracting it."

An incredulous smile played along David's lips. "Hold on a second. You thought that moose was my mother?"

"Well, actually I thought it was your mother *and* Cynthia. And I thought they were both a little heavy on their feet."

David laughed. "How could you mix up my mother and a moose?"

"It was easy," she replied. "It sounded like two people tramping around in the woods. And who else would want to spy on us? I was not expecting a moose."

"I know. I was beginning to wonder if I was ever going to get you moving. You were stiff as a statue."

"I was trying to decide if we should give the moose the fruit chutney or the leftover carrot-cake muffins. But then you went into the fencing stance. I knew we had no shot of convincing it that we came in peace."

He walked a few paces closer to her. "You seriously thought throwing carrot cake at a moose would be taken as a gesture of friendship?" His eyes sparkled, and he was grinning hugely.

Millie lifted her chin a notch. "Offering food is a universal gesture of friendship. Think Pilgrims and the Indians."

"I don't think the Indians lobbed corncobs at the Pilgrims."

"Who knows? Maybe the history books have it all wrong."

David laughed. "I don't think so."

Millie didn't think so either. But the thought of the Indians standing on one side of a field and throwing corncobs to the Pilgrims who screamed and ducked for cover was so absurd that she started to laugh. Once she started, she couldn't seem to stop, and then suddenly David was laughing, too, and every time they looked at each other, they burst out in fresh humor. She'd never seen David's face so bright red, and the sound he was making was really funny—a string of *ha-ha*s that just kept going and going until it left him breathless and doubled over.

She hugged herself hard, but her ribs were shaking so hard she could feel the points jutting into her stomach.

After several failed attempts, Millie came up for air and managed to stop laughing. She didn't dare look at David and concentrated instead on wiping her eyes and blowing her nose. She was breathing hard from the exertion of laughing, but it felt good—like a poison had been cleared from her system. She couldn't remember feeling so light inside in a long time.

When she looked up, she caught him staring at her intently. She felt a tingle inside. A very definite tingle. She ordered the part of herself that was tingling to stop immediately. It didn't. She faked an easy smile. "Maybe we should check and see if the moose is still there," she said. "It's getting late, and we should probably head back before the park rangers get worried."

"We definitely don't want to be in the park after dark."

He returned a moment later. "Coast is clear."

After a brief and necessary pit stop while David waited outside, they gathered their equipment and headed out on the trail. The light was fading as they skied back to the rental shop, and Millie had to concentrate on following David's tracks. She wasn't scared though. She'd had an adventure—which was something she hadn't had in years. She couldn't wait to tell her mom about getting trapped in the restroom by two moose. Eva would laugh herself silly then say something like, "He defended you from a moose, Millie. How romantic!"

It was almost pitch black by the time they'd turned in their equipment and headed for the parking lot. Stepping down the stone steps from the building, David glanced sideways at her. "I'm really glad you didn't surrender our carrot cake. I'm kind of getting hungry again."

She punched him lightly on the shoulder. "Like you're getting the leftovers," she scoffed, but they both knew he was. They crossed the parking lot, almost empty now and lit by a smattering of tall light posts. A few thin patches of black ice gleamed in the darkness. They were hard to see, and it seemed the most natural thing in the world when David slipped his arm around her shoulders as they walked to the Lexus.

Chapter 14

Y our mother called twice," Aris said in greeting as David stepped through the garage door into the kitchen. It was just before six o'clock, and she jiggled her keys impatiently. "She wants you to call her immediately."

David threw his parka onto the back of a chair. "Okay. Thanks. How's Bart?"

Aris's face softened. "Doing well. He ate peanut butter cookies when he came home from the movies. That's a good sign." She gestured toward the oven. "Tuna casserole for dinner. I've got to run. Garden Club business."

She stuck her hat over her long silver braid and was out the door a moment later. David picked up the mail on the kitchen table and absently sorted through it. He saw the message light blinking on his phone but decided to call his mother back later.

"Hey, Bart," he called loudly enough to be heard over his son's music. "I'm home." In response the volume of the music coming from upstairs increased. The bass was so loud that it sounded as if at least a dozen heavy people were in Bart's room jumping up and down. Obviously his son was still angry at him about the breach of trust. David felt all the good feelings stored up from his date with Millie begin to fade.

Frowning, he started up the staircase. "Hey, buddy," he yelled, "turn it down." He paused outside his son's door. *Keep your cool,* David coached himself as he knocked. *It's going to take time to regain his trust.* He knocked a bit louder then, despite his determination to remain patient, tried the handle of the door. To his surprise, he found it locked.

This had never happened before. David knocked harder on the door. "Open. . .the. . .door. . .*now!*"

The music abruptly ceased, and the door swung open. "Dad," Bart said, blinking owlishly up at him. "I didn't hear you."

"Because you're playing your music at top volume." David put his hands on his hips. "It's time for dinner." He ordered himself to lower his voice. "I want to hear about your day."

Bart's face closed as if David had just asked him to divulge Batman's identity or the arm codes to the nation's nuclear weaponry system. His face said it would be a long time before he trusted David again. David squared his shoulders. He was Bart's father, and if this was what it took to keep his son safe, so be it.

In the kitchen, he pulled out the casserole and set it on the kitchen table. "Aris cooked your favorite again," he joked. "Tuna casserole." As he placed some on Bart's plate, he thought of the mini-muffins Millie had given him and perked up a little. Bart loved carrot cake.

Bart plunked down at the kitchen table and took a long drink of milk.

"So how was the movie?" David handed him a plate.

Bart poked at the mound with his fork and shrugged. "Good."

"Did your friends like it?"

"I guess."

"Did you see anyone else there you knew?" *Like GorillaGuy*

or that girl you like? David forced himself not to ask. After several unsuccessful attempts to draw out Bart, he changed the topic to his date with Millie. However, when he told the story about the moose chasing him and Millie into the restroom, it didn't sound nearly as funny. Although he laughed in the retelling, Bart didn't even crack a smile.

Twenty minutes later, David scraped the remains of tuna casserole into the garbage. He could have counted the number of words they'd exchanged during the whole dinner on his hands. At the sink, Bart rinsed the dishes and placed them in the dishwasher. The *clink* and *clank* of the dishes replaced conversation.

Finally, Bart turned off the water and wiped his hands on a dish towel. "Can I be excused now?"

David decided to grab the bull by the horns. "Look," he said. "I know you're upset about your privacy being violated, but you have to understand, Bart, that sometimes it's necessary."

"How would you feel if I spied on your date with Miss Hogan?"

"That's not the point. I need to know if anything else has happened at school."

"Why don't you just log on to my computer and read my e-mails?"

David blinked at the sarcasm. Had he ever spoken to his father like this? What would his dad have done? More like what would his mother have done? She was the disciplinarian.

His father had been more passive about discipline, more interested in teaching him how to play chess or tie a bow tie than he was in reprimanding David for not cleaning his room or for staying up late at night reading. His father had taken him on long hikes and taught him the names of all the trees. David realized that he wanted this same relationship with Bart. He'd thought he'd had it, too, until recently.

"One more word like that," David said, amazed at how calm his voice sounded when his heart thumped in his chest, "and you lose computer privileges for a week."

It was like telling his son that he was losing his right arm. Something like hurt flashed across his son's round face. "You'd do that?"

"Yes," David said, praying that he wouldn't have to. "I'm your father. You have to respect me even if you don't like what I tell you."

"Even when you spy on me?"

He hadn't spied on Bart; Aris had. But he refused to throw Aris under the bus just so Bart would like him. "Even if I have to do things that you don't like," David said. "I'm meeting with your principal on Monday, so if this boy has harassed you again, I need to know."

"You're meeting with the principal?" Bart's voice jumped up an octave. "Dad, you can't do that! Seriously—don't do that!"

"I have no choice."

Two splotches of angry red darkened Bart's normally pale cheeks. "I'm telling you. I'll handle this. I've got a plan."

David thought of Aris's plan to have an instructor teach Bart to chop-suey people. "I hope it's not taking karate classes."

The comment earned him a dark look. "It isn't, but I don't see why you wouldn't let me learn karate."

"It's not karate I mind," David said. "It's the fighting. You know how I feel about that. Violence doesn't solve anything. Bart, you need to tell me the name of this kid so I can talk to his parents."

Bart's chin came up a notch. "First, learning karate doesn't mean I'm going to fight someone. Second, I'm not five years old. I can handle this kid. He's just a cocky jerk. Third, I have a plan."

"Let's hear it."

"Well, you know how everyone in town is so big on the box sled race? If I beat this kid in that race, he'll leave me alone. I know it."

David frowned thoughtfully. "What makes you think he would even go in the race?" More likely, Bart would get stuffed in a locker for even asking the question.

"This kid likes to shoot his mouth off about how great he is at everything," Bart explained. "And last year he sort of won it. So when we're at lunch, I'll start talking about maybe entering it. I'm sure he'll start bragging about being the best to everyone—and that's when I'll challenge him to beat me."

"Bart, what if he takes you on your challenge and beats you? Won't that make things worse?"

Bart's face clouded over. "You don't think I'm good enough to win?"

David wished he'd expressed his fears differently. "Of course you can. It's just a possibility."

"All I have to do is sit in a cardboard box, Dad. Even I can handle that."

"It's more than that. I entered this race about twenty years ago, and my sled didn't even make it to the bottom of the slope. I had to get out and walk it down the hill."

"You don't have to design it," Bart pointed out. "I've been playing with some designs on the computer. All I need is a box, some duct tape, and paint."

David shook his head. "We need to let the principal know that a kid is bothering you."

"All that'll do, Dad, is make me look like a tattletale."

He sighed, caught between his need to protect his son and desire to please him. "How about we compromise? I'll talk to the principal, and you enter the sled race?"

"That's not a compromise," Bart pointed out. "A compromise would mean you gave something up—like talking to the principal—and I would give something up, like, say, trying to do everything on my own."

David's mind raced for a counterpoint. He heard himself say, "Well, that's the best you'll get. I'm your father, and I have your best interests at heart." It was lame, and he knew it. Yet he couldn't very well say, "I'm scared you'll get hurt."

Bart might be smart, but he was small for his size and had been a sensitive kid who cried easily. Until kindergarten, his best friends had been two girls who liked to play Barbies and watch Disney movies.

"What if I found someone who knows about building sleds and could help us? Would you agree to hold off on talking to the principal and let me enter the race?"

"My meeting with the principal is on Monday morning. I don't see how you'd find someone in time."

Behind his oversized glasses, Bart's gaze was rock steady. "But if I could, would you agree?"

"Maybe." He sensed a trap. "It would have to be someone I trusted."

Bart gave what sounded like an involuntary snort of triumph. "How about Miss Hogan? Her mother won the race awhile ago, and her sled still has the fastest recorded time."

David's expression froze. He couldn't very well say he didn't trust the woman he was supposed to be dating. Although he could still overrule his son and go to the principal, he hesitated. He was going to look pretty lame going to the principal without one shred of evidence or Bart to back him up. Besides, he couldn't protect Bart from everything—Lisa's death a case in point—and sadly his son already had figured this out. "You can ask," he conceded, "but if the Hogans say no, we do it my way."

Bart grinned as if it were a done deal and extended his hand for David to shake.

Chapter 15

Millie balanced the refrigerator box with one hand and tapped the garage door with the other. Behind her, her mother grunted as if in pain.

"Go on, hun," Eva urged. "Move. Before I drop everything."

"Stop pushing," Millie complained. "We can't move until David opens the garage door." It was late afternoon, and she and her mother had come to David's garage to begin work on the sled. She shifted her grip then nearly dropped the load as her mother gave another push.

The door rumbled then slowly rose. It had taken them a couple of days to find the exact right box. Several of the café's regulars had tried to help, but her mom had rejected box after box until finally Nelson Ridley had come up with the name of a friend of a friend who worked at Home Depot in Sioux Falls. A few phone calls later they were the proud owners of a Frigidaire side-by-side refrigerator box.

The garage door rumbled open, revealing what had to be the cleanest garage Millie had ever seen in her life. Tools neatly hung on Peg-Board, shelves held labeled plastic tubs, two bikes hung from the wall, and an enormous dry-erase board held a schedule for rotating tires and fertilizing the trees.

"Good grief, David," Millie said as she and her mother deposited their load in the middle of the floor. "You could operate in here."

David laughed. "When my dad needs to escape my mother, he comes here and organizes my garage."

"Well, send him over to ours the next time," Millie said. "But you'd better warn him that we have so many layers it's like an archaeological dig." She spotted Bart seated on the steps between the garage and the house. "Hi, Bart. You ready to build a box sled?"

Bart stood up and adjusted his glasses. "I guess," he said.

"Great," Millie said. "This is my mom, Mrs. Hogan—the current box sled record holder."

"Nice to meet you," Eva said. Instead of shaking the boy's hand, she simply enfolded him into her embrace and held him there, squashing him between her breasts. "We're going to build one heck of a sled, honey."

Bart emerged from her arms with his glasses askew and a look of dazed horror on his face. "Uh, nice to meet you."

Millie winked sympathetically.

"You look just like your dad when he was your age," her mother declared. "He and Millie were in a community play together. Remember, Millie? You and David were in *The Muffin Man*. David was Mr. Muffin, and you were Mrs. Muffin."

"Mom," Millie said. "That was like a hundred years ago."

"I've got pictures at home. Bart, you'll enjoy seeing your father dressed as a blueberry muffin," her mother said. "Oh, hold on a second. Almost forgot—one more thing in the car."

Her mother's absence seemed to leave a gap in the room. Eva was like that. She could produce a certain energy that attracted other people to her like a magnet. She couldn't go anywhere without someone stopping to hug her and talk. Her mother always had just the right word or touch. People laughed easily with her and walked away with a lighter step. Sometimes Millie studied herself in the bathroom mirror to see if her mother's spark could be seen in her own gray eyes. Other times she searched her reflection, afraid she'd see her mother looking back.

The silence lengthened. Both Denvers were studiously not looking at each other. Millie sighed and pulled at the thread of conversation her mother had started. "Your father was a really good singer in that play, Bart." Reaching into the box, she began pulling out supplies and handed Bart a couple rolls of duct tape. "You can stack these along the wall." She gave David a box cutter and a pair of heavy-duty sheers. "And he danced well, too—for a guy in a muffin suit."

"It wasn't dancing," David said. "We kind of ran around the stage a few times. I remember Karl Kauffman trying to trip me when I passed him."

"Karl was jealous because he wanted to be the muffin man," Millie said, continuing to unload the box. "Were you in any school or community plays, Bart?"

"I was the Stink Bug in our first-grade play called *Bugz*."

"He did great," David said.

"Dad," Bart said, "I stank."

"Wasn't that the whole point?" Millie met Bart's gaze, and they both smiled.

"Okay," Eva said, walking back into the garage with a blast of cold air through the side door. "This is for you." She handed Bart a white bakery box. "Go ahead," she urged him. "Open it. There's a batch of double chocolate brownies inside. I just made them."

They'd fought about it—Millie arguing that Eva would ruin Bart's appetite for supper. Eva had gotten red-faced and loud.

"Double fudge brownies are one of life's pleasures. Besides," she'd added more gently, "I want him to like me."

Bart tore into the box and wolfed down a brownie. "These are really good," he said as he chewed.

Eva helped herself to a brownie, looked at Bart, and said, "Ummm-umm—like I died and went to heaven."

Millie folded her arms as Bart helped himself to another brownie. "Hope we don't ruin Bart's appetite for dinner."

"Oh, it's fine," David replied. "We don't worry about that stuff."

"It's true," Bart said. "Our stomachs are really strong from digesting the food Aris makes."

"That's not being respectful," David said.

"Have one, David," Eva urged. "I separate the two layers of brownie with a thin coat of peppermint bark."

"Mom," Millie said, "maybe he wants to have one later."

"But they're still a little warm." Eva continued to hold the box out to David, who took one, bit into it, then grinned.

"These are fabulous." He smiled at her. "Almost as good as the carrot-cake muffins Millie made."

Millie smiled back at him. "Thank you."

"Millie," Eva said. "Aren't you going to have one, too?"

Translation: *Let me love you, too.*

"I know they're fabulous, but maybe later." Millie busied herself organizing the supplies they'd unloaded from the box.

"Next time I'll bring you chocolate éclairs, Bart."

Translation: *I like you a lot, Bart.*

"I love chocolate éclairs," Bart said.

"Me, too," David declared.

"Tomorrow," Eva promised and gave Millie a triumphant look. *You see,* her shining eyes said, *food makes people happy.*

Millie bit her tongue. "Let's get to work. What do we do first?" She directed the question at her mother.

"Well," Eva said, wiping her hands on her jeans, "we need to agree on a design. I sketched something the other night. It's in the red spiral."

Millie opened the notebook as David and Bart gathered around her. On the first page there was a pencil drawing of various rectangles that looked as if they'd been cut with pinking shears. Her mother had arrows pointing, half circles bisecting angles, and notes penciled in the margins. Millie turned the page. More crinkle-cut pieces—these looked like wings—and more incomprehensible notes. On the third page she saw a rough construction of something that might or might not have been a sled. The whole thing was very narrow, much narrower than the refrigerator box they'd brought with them.

"Mom?"

"Isn't she a beauty?"

"What exactly is it?" Millie didn't want to say that it looked like a coffin with funny cutout edges. "Aren't the sleds supposed to look like something—like a pirate ship or SpongeBob SquarePants?"

Eva sighed heavily and turned to Bart. "Millie nearly failed geometry. Couldn't do a proof to save her soul—but I blame the principal for moving the home ec teacher into the class after Albert Nevers had the heart attack. Idiot, spineless man, that principal. Spouted school policy without caring one bit about the kids. I'd like to have whacked him on the side of the head with my skillet."

Millie could laugh now, but at the time her mother's protective-ness had been a source of embarrassment. She hadn't wanted Eva flying to the school to argue a grade she'd gotten on an essay or challenge the teacher to defend the wording on an exam question. "What does my geometry grade have to do with the sled?"

Eva smiled at Bart. "She can't see what I've designed—but I think you can."

Bart looked up. Behind his glasses, his blue eyes were as clear as marbles. Millie could almost see the power of his considerable brain working away. "Is it a winged french fry sled?"

"Exactly! The wings fold in though. They're design elements."

"What?" Millie tried not to sound horrified and failed. "A french fry with wings?"

"I had a dream the night we talked about building the sled," Eva explained. "In my dream, there was a storm. Only instead of lightning bolts coming out of the clouds, it was giant french fries with wings."

Millie glanced at David, whose polite smile looked firmly frozen on his face. She didn't blame him. Her mother sounded like a lunatic.

"Now some people would say that dreaming about flying french fries was simply because I work in a café and we fry out a good hundred pounds a day, but I know the dream meant something."

"It means you went to bed hungry," Millie suggested.

Her mother shot her a dark look. "It was a sign," she insisted. "About the race. I think we're supposed to call the sled the *Flying French Fry*."

"Mom—that's a terrible name. Bart could get beat up for having a sled named the *Flying French Fry*."

"Nonsense," her mother replied with a dismissive wave. "We don't want anyone taking Bart seriously." She pointed her finger at Bart. "When people underestimate you, it gives you an advantage and you end up wiping the floor with them. I'm living proof of that. Everyone laughed at me for entering a sled shaped like a chocolate éclair— especially that cocky loan officer at First National. But he wasn't laughing when I sailed past him." She shrugged. "Of course it's up to you, Bart, what we name the sled."

"Uh, maybe we could brainstorm," David suggested. "How about *White Lightning*? That way we would use the object in your dream."

"I like the *Flying French Fry*," Bart immediately stated and shot his dad a challenging look.

Millie wondered if he only liked the name because David didn't.

Her mother grinned. "Good. It's all settled." She motioned to Bart. "Now I want you to lie inside the box so we can customize it to your measurements."

"Why didn't we just get a narrower box?"

Eva sighed at Millie's question. "We'll cut it so we can double the cardboard on the bottom layer. That way the sled will be stronger. The bottom will hold up when Bart has multiple heats."

"How am I going to see," Bart asked, "if I'm lying flat on my back?"

"Good question," Eva said approvingly. "You'll lie feet first. We'll bank the cardboard just a small amount to raise your head and lower the cardboard at your feet so you can see over the top. But we want you as flat as possible—that way you'll be more aerodynamic."

Bart lay down on the cardboard. As Millie's mom began to trace his body with a piece of chalk, he called out, "This is so cool. It's like a crime scene, and I'm the body."

"You'll be a body if you don't hold still," her mom said, but cheerfully. "You're the perfect size for this, Bart. You wait and see. You're going to win that race. Millie, please hand me the yardstick."

Eva made some measurements then referred to the sketch again. "We're going to need to take six inches off the width, graduate the slope of the sides, and lose about a foot off the top."

Millie hovered with a pencil, ready to mark the lines, but her mother waved her away. "I've got this," she said. "Relax. Talk to

David and have a brownie, hun."

In other words, *Go away.*

Her mother loved projects and could not be stopped from stepping in and assuming control. In high school, Eva had practically snatched Millie's projects from her hands. More than once Millie had awakened to find some model or poster-board project magically enhanced overnight. It was the same thing in the kitchen. Everything had to be done exactly as Eva wanted it. No variation to any recipe. Although Millie tried not to let it get to her, sometimes it felt that her efforts never measured up to Eva's.

Millie stepped back a few paces and folded her arms across her chest. Watching her mother and Bart banter back and forth made her a little uneasy. When she'd agreed to help build the sled, she hadn't pictured her mother and Bart bonding. He'd seemed too old for the infant her mother fantasized holding in her arms.

She noticed David squinting through one of the side windows and walked over to him. "What are you looking at?"

He drew back with a guilty look. "Just checking to see if she's there."

She, of course, meant Cynthia. Millie edged forward to look through the ice patterns etched onto the glass pane. The street was dark. Two cars were parked on the street. "Is she there?"

"No," David replied. "I think we're making progress."

Millie smiled. "That's great news." She lowered her voice. "We should probably go to the next step. I should give you something small but personal to display in your office." She thought about it. "A photograph of me—an eight-by-ten so she won't miss it."

David's eyes lit up. "Great idea. But how about two so I can put one in my office and one in my examination room? More people will see it."

"Perfect. And I'll need your photograph for my desk. Hold on. I've got another idea." She retrieved her cell from her purse then stood next to him. Holding out the phone, she estimated the center of the shot. "Smile," she said and snapped a picture. A moment later she held out her cell "Look—we're my new background."

Actually it was a pretty cute photo. She was snuggled comfortably against David's chest, and her smile looked genuinely happy. David had his arm around her, and his head tilted toward hers. His smile was open, his eyes crinkled at the corners. Studying the photo more closely, she noticed something different about his hair, too. He'd styled it differently. It was a little messier, a little more contemporary. She decided she liked it.

"You should send me a copy of that," David said. "I'll save it as my background as well."

Millie nodded. "The more evidence everyone sees of us together, the better. I should give you a Dosie's take-out menu. I've got one in my car. I'll give it to you before I leave."

"And I'll give you a magnet with my practice's information on it to put on your refrigerator."

"I'll need a couple. One for home and a few others for the café." She glanced at Bart, who was laughing at something Eva had said. They had their heads bent closely together. Eva was quoting some physicist Millie had never heard of, and Bart was spouting some mathematical equation at her.

"They're sure getting along," David commented.

"Maybe a little too well." Millie stuffed her hands in her pockets. "It might be a good idea to set a time for us to break up. You know, we don't want to give them too much time to get attached."

David nodded. "I've been thinking about that as well. What do you think about doing it right after the Winterfest Carnival?"

"I think that's perfect." Millie paused as the wind pushed a cold breath of snow beneath the garage door and frost danced across the floor then disappeared like a ghost. This would give her a little over a month to plan everything. Because after she broke up with David, she was heading for Los Angeles and auditioning for any acting job she could find. She looked over at her mother and wondered if she'd really have the guts to go through with this.

David seemed to misread her hesitation. "We could do it sooner."

"Oh no," Millie said. "I'm fine with waiting. One thing though." She inched closer to David and lowered her voice even further. "You're going to have to break up with me. And it has to be public. Preferably humiliating for me."

David frowned. "Can't it just be mutual? I really don't like scenes."

"Well, I'll have to cry," she explained. "But I'll keep it to a minimum—no screaming and thrashing around or breaking things. It'll be tasteful, I promise."

"I'd rather be dumped than the one to dump you."

Millie glanced over her shoulder to make sure neither her mother nor Bart were listening. "I'm sorry, but it has to be you. I won't bad-mouth you or anything. But you need to break my heart. That way everyone will understand why I need to get away. I'll just happen to pick California, and while I'm there"—she shrugged—"who knows what might happen? An audition, a small part in a movie, a spot on a reality television show. You just never know."

"You've been thinking about this a lot," David said quietly.

Millie kept her gaze steady on his. "Pretty much my whole life."

Chapter 16

David's mother dropped a black-and-white photograph of a weathered gray headstone onto his desk. "This is a photo of your great-great grandmother's grave." Another photo landed beside the first. "Now here's the marker for Cynthia's great-great grandmother." His mom's jeweled fingers tapped the first photo. "The two of them are buried right next to each other. So you see, David," she concluded triumphantly, "the bond between our two families goes back generations."

David raked his hands through his hair. All morning he'd successfully avoided his mother and her photos taken from the Saint Francis cemetery. Unfortunately, when the office closed for lunch at noon, his mother pinned him down.

"Mom, I'm not interested in Cynthia. I don't care if our families came over together on the *Mayflower*."

His mother laughed. "Who knows, maybe they did. You could discuss that over lunch. She happens to be free today."

"You should be encouraging her to see a counselor, not me." David picked up the photos of the headstones and handed them back to her. "Did I tell you that Bart is entering the box sled race at the Winterfest Snow Carnival? The Hogans are helping him build his sled."

His mother's smile thinned. "Is that really a good idea, David? Letting the boy get attached to that family will only hurt him in the long run." She fingered the long bead of pearls that hung atop her blue cashmere sweater. "I know you think you're too old to get advice from your mother, but relationships need a solid base. You get that through faith. Neither Millie nor her mother is a believer."

"You don't know what she believes," David said sharply. "It's not up to you to judge her."

His mother leaned forward. "David, they don't go to church."

"It doesn't mean they *won't* go to church."

"I love you, David," his mother said. "More than my own life. I want you to be happy. Cynthia is a good Christian woman. Our families have strong ties. She'd love you, David. She'd make a good mother for Bart."

His muscles tensed. "She's not the right woman for me."

"She could be if you'd give her a chance. You've been gone a long time, David. I'm not going to gossip, but there are things you don't know about Millie Hogan. I'd be very careful about how much time you let Bart spend with that family."

"The Hogans are good people." David found himself leaning over the desk. "Honest, caring, and hardworking—they're *exactly* the kind of people Bart should be hanging around with." He crossed the room in three strides, aware of the shocked expression on his mother's face but too angry to care.

He marched to the door. "I've put up with your silly matchmaking because I knew you were trying to help. But I *will not* put up with you insulting Millie. Is that clear, Mom?"

"Where are you going?"

Until she'd asked, he hadn't been sure himself. His only thought was to get away before he said something that he regretted. But now, looking at her, he knew. "To lunch. It's Thursday. The special at Dosie Dough's is meat loaf, mashed potatoes, and green beans."

His mother sucked in her breath as if he'd announced he was having lunch with the devil himself, but then David was out the door. He nearly knocked down Cynthia, who had her ear pressed against the door.

David steadied her with one hand then strode past her. Outside the January afternoon was painfully bright and clear. On the sidewalk, he took a deep breath of the cold, pure air, released it, took another, and then another.

He drove straight down Cumberland, clenching the cold steering wheel in his bare hands, past Ed's Market, the First National Bank, Unique Antiques, Monica's Beauty Salon, and Ready, Aim, Fire Hunting Supplies.

Small town, small minds. He'd never thought that way before; he had always been proud of Deer Park's Old World charm and was secretly grateful that it hadn't become as upscale as other towns in South Dakota that were closer to Mount Rushmore or the hot springs or all the amenities that Rapid City offered.

The biggest draw here was the Black Hills, which drew their share of vacationing families looking for skiing, hunting, or bargain shopping for gold jewelry that came from local mines. The tourism kept the town going, but it wasn't enough to make anyone rich.

The clock tower in the town square rang its hourly chime as he passed. As little as he liked it, his mother had spoken the truth. The Bible stated very clearly that a relationship between a believer and nonbeliever was doomed. Not that he intended to marry Millie— but it was the principle of the whole thing that bothered him. Every person had value. Every person was equally loved in God's eyes. People didn't crawl out of the womb praising Jesus. Following Christ was a choice. It was Millie's choice and not up to him or anyone else to judge her.

Soon the giant éclair on the top of Dosie Dough's roof came into sight. He found a parking spot on the street and headed for the building. A CLOSED sign hung in the dark window, and the front door was locked. Puzzled, David stood in the freezing cold and wondered what'd happened. His breath hung in the air, and he was aware of a bad feeling forming in the pit of his stomach. Getting back in the car, he turned back onto Mail Street and fishtailed a little on the sleety street as he headed for Millie's house.

She met him at the front door. Something inside him stirred at the sight of her in a pair of Levi's worn soft at the knee and a red flannel shirt that looked about two sizes too big. Without any makeup and her hair pulled back into a loose ponytail, she looked younger, almost exactly the way he remembered her in high school.

"David?" She blinked up at him, all big eyes and soft curves. "Is everything all right?"

"That's what I want to know. I went by the café. I got worried."

"Oh." Millie pulled the door wider, letting warm air escape from the house and with it the barest trace of the scent of something cooking. "Come in."

Stamping his feet free of a crust of snow, he walked inside. Millie raised her fingers to her lips, indicating for him to be quiet. "Mom's upstairs sleeping," she whispered and led him back to the kitchen.

"Have a seat." Millie gestured to the ladder-backed chairs that surrounded a battered-looking wooden table. Piles of mail and magazines, at least four cookbooks, and an assortment of prescription medicines covered half the tabletop. "Sorry everything's so messy," she said, clearing a spot for him. "I'm making chili. Can I get you some?"

"First tell me what's going on with Eva."

Millie sighed. "Her blood sugar went crazy." She moved a stack of books and papers next to an equally tall stack on the kitchen counter. "Last night it dropped to 45, and then it shot up to 250. We've been trying to stabilize it, but so far we haven't been able to."

"Shouldn't you call a doctor?"

"I already did. If she's not better in a few hours, I'll take her to see Dr. Wong."

David studied the dark circles under her eyes and the paleness of her lips. The scrubbed-down version made him feel like he was seeing a more vulnerable Millie. "What can I do to help?"

"Nothing—but thanks for asking."

"Are you sure it wasn't something she ate at our house? Or too much activity with building the box sled?"

Millie pulled a brick of yellow cheese out of the refrigerator and began to grate it. "Are you kidding? All she could talk about was how smart and cute Bart was and how much she enjoyed building that sled."

A small mountain of cheese appeared, but Millie continued grating.

"So when she came home, her blood sugar was fine?"

"Yeah, we tested it, and then she said she wanted to bake some red velvet cupcakes for Aunt Keeker—it's her half birthday today. I sat in the kitchen, working on my essay for *Chef's Challenge*—that's a new reality TV show on the Food Network."

She finished the last shreds of the brick and then, pulling out a white bowl from the cabinet, filled it to the brim with piping hot chili. Placing it in front of him, she asked, "How about some avocado or onions?"

David picked up the spoon. "This looks great. I don't need

anything else." He looked at her. "Aren't you going to have some?"

"I'm not that hungry," Millie said.

He took a bite of the chili. It tasted pretty great, but Millie was giving him a funny look. "It's excellent," he pronounced.

"Do you taste the cinnamon? I tried to hide it with extra cumin and chili powder."

David shook his head. "No," he said. "I like it." He spooned up another bite. "Does cinnamon have special meaning in your talking-with-food vocabulary?"

"No," Millie said. "Cinnamon is good for people with diabetes. But if my mother suspects that I'm trying to get her to eat healthier, she'll get mad."

As he put down another bite, his gaze fell on a piece of paper sitting on top of a *People* magazine. He realized it was an application for that reality TV show Millie had been talking about—*Chef's Challenge*. The printed handwriting covered every inch of the page. The lettering was slightly rounded, and he imagined her taking her time, trying to make it look as neat as possible.

"So you were working on your application and Eva was cooking," David prompted. "What happened next?"

Millie set down her mug of coffee. "I went outside and shoveled the driveway. By the time I finished, the cupcakes were ready to be frosted. We did that together then cleaned up the kitchen and went to bed. A couple of hours later, she knocked on my bedroom door and said she wasn't feeling so great."

"Did you see her take any medication?"

"Just the pills she took at dinner."

David watched the rooster clock on the wall twitch its tail with each passing second. Pictures stuck on the refrigerator spoke loudly of the closeness between Millie and Eva. He could see nothing that would have caused Eva's blood sugar to drop so unexpectedly. Nothing—unless. . . His gaze returned to Millie. "You don't think she could have doubled her medication by accident?"

Millie frowned. "No. She hates taking her medication. Usually I have to remind her to take it."

David stirred the chili. "You sure? Maybe she got overexcited building the box sled, or maybe she ate too many brownies and was trying to balance things."

Millie shook her head. "I'm sure. Her blood sugar was fine when she tested it before she went to bed. I saw her do it."

He chewed on another mouthful of chili. He couldn't accept that Eva's blood sugar had dropped so suddenly without there being a medical explanation. An accidental overdose seemed the most likely, but Millie felt the chances of this were extremely low, and he believed her.

His mind jumped to another possibility. What if Eva had deliberately overmedicated herself? He immediately rejected the possibility. Eva Hogan was not a stupid woman, and overmedicating herself was a pretty dumb thing to do. He would not even voice this thought to Millie.

And then his gaze seemed to go of its own volition to the application on the table. He wondered if Eva had watched Millie fill it out while she baked the cupcakes. If Eva had seen something in her daughter's face that said Millie wasn't as ready to settle down as Eva wanted her to be.

"Can I read this?"

"Sure."

He picked up the paper.

Hi! My name is Millie Hogan. I am thirty-one years old

and live in Deer Park, South Dakota. For most of my life I've worked at Dosie Dough's, which is a breakfast and lunch café. My mother owns the place. We sell a lot of burgers and sandwiches, but we specialize in breads and cakes. Once the Deer Park Reporter *gave us a four-star review, which is pretty good considering we don't advertise in that paper.*

I should be on your show because I am not afraid of any challenge. I think it would be fun to ice fish and then make a meal on a bonfire started from sticks and tinder. I would be happy to swim in a tank of eels or forage in the woods and create a gourmet meal out of berries and tree bark.

Education-wise, I took a few accounting classes at Sioux Falls Community College. Mostly, though, my education comes from the school of real life.

You want other qualifications? I was runner-up in the 1998 Miss Pronghorn Antelope beauty contest and played Blanche DuBois in my high school production of A Streetcar Named Desire.

In conclusion, you should pick me because I have restaurant experience, an adventurous spirit, and acting experience. I am including a three-minute audition tape and a recent head shot. I will be in the California area in mid-March and would be glad to come in for a screen test.

David read the short essay twice. His gaze remained fixed on the paper even after he finished reading. He didn't like what he was thinking.

"It's terrible, isn't it?" Millie stated. "I'm not much of a writer."

"It's fine. Great, I mean." He fingered the application. "You think she read it while you were out shoveling the driveway?"

Millie blinked. "Maybe. I didn't try and hide it. Why?"

David put down the paper. "Maybe that last line about you going to California upset her," he said as tactfully as he could. "Have you ever mentioned an actual date in your other applications?"

"No. But even if my mother read my essay and it upset her—which is a big if—I still don't think it would have caused her blood sugar to crash." She sipped from a mug with a big chocolate M&M on it. "My mother doesn't think I'll ever get selected to audition. Trust me. She doesn't believe I have a shred of talent and thinks it's a waste of time for me to even think about going to Hollywood."

"Maybe you've got it wrong," David suggested. "Maybe she's afraid that you'll go to California and be so successful that you won't come back. Or maybe she's just trying to keep you from getting disappointed." He thought, given the timing of Eva's attack, the former was more likely than the latter. However, he hoped Millie would make the leap to that conclusion herself. He was only speculating, and suggesting her mother was manipulative enough to use her diabetes as a weapon was a pretty strong statement. And it really wasn't any of his business.

He checked his watch. It was close to one o'clock. "I'm sorry, Millie, but I'd better get going."

"You haven't finished your lunch."

He was about to suggest she pack it up for him to eat later when a familiar voice said, "Going? I finally drag myself out of bed to say hello and you leave?"

Eva strode into the kitchen. She was wearing a thick fleece bathrobe the color of an eggplant. There were dark circles under her eyes of the same color, and her skin was puffy and blotched as if she'd been standing outside in the cold.

David jumped up to give her his seat. "I'm sorry to hear you had a bad night."

Eva dismissed his concern with a wave of her hand. "I'm fine now. What time can we come over and work on the sled?"

"Mom," Millie said firmly. "You need to rest. The sled can wait."

"I need to get off my duff," Eva corrected. "I'm really feeling much better. I made some extra cupcakes for Bart—and you, too, David."

"Let's see what your blood sugar level says." Millie unzipped a small black case. With the ease of someone who had done this hundreds of times before, she inserted a fresh lancet into the tester and wiped Eva's finger with a small pad of alcohol. Eva didn't flinch as Millie triggered the blade.

"You're still a little low," Millie said, reading the result. "I'll get you some orange juice."

"Thank you, honey," Eva said. "I don't know what I'd do without you."

"Oh you'd probably do fine, Mom."

The corners of Eva's mouth tugged slightly downward. "I think the Eskimos had the right idea. When someone got old and it was their time, they'd send them off on their own little iceberg. That way they were never a burden to their people."

"That was in the days before cable television," Millie joked, setting a glass down in front of her mother. "Now they just park people in front of the Game Show Network and turn up the volume. Have a sip, Mom. You'll feel a lot better after you've eaten."

"It's excellent chili," David added.

Eva gave him a penetrating look. "You sure? Last time she tried to make it healthier for me, and it gave me terrible gas. I'm telling you, David, I went *rat-a-tat-tat* for days."

Millie set a bowl down in front of her mother. "Just eat this and be quiet," she ordered, but David watched her squeeze her mother's shoulder affectionately.

"Well," David said, pulling his keys from his pocket, "anything I can do, just call." He grabbed his coat off the back of his chair and hesitated. Leaving suddenly seemed wrong.

He looked into Millie's large gray eyes. *Who looks out for you?* he wanted to ask and had to remind himself again that it wasn't his place to ask. But it still bothered him, and he found himself lingering at the front door. "If you need me, just call," he said. "I mean it, Millie—even if it's in the middle of the night."

Climbing into his Lexus, he thought about how tightly Eva clung to Millie and understood for the first time why Millie might dream of a different life. He had always thought of love as the best possible way to be bound to someone. Its presence alone was a God thing, something to be thankful for. Although Lisa's death had taught him that love could hurt, he'd never had to hurt someone else in order to be happy.

He backed the car slowly down the driveway. There really wasn't any other instinct stronger than the one to protect your children, and if Eva had deliberately taken the wrong medication, he felt sure Eva was acting out of love, possibly misguided, but love all the same.

He thought a parent could donate a kidney, empty a bank account, or step in front of a speeding car to save his child, and yet the hardest thing a parent might ever have to do was stand back and let go. When it came his time, he prayed Bart would never see just how hard this would be for him.

Chapter 17

It started to sleet as Millie drove with her mother to the café. A travel advisory was posted, and she gripped the wheel more tightly as small pellets pinged off the Subaru's windshield. The wipers swept rhythmically back and forth, noisy on a salt-splattered windshield.

"That was nice of David to stop by," her mother commented.

"Yes. It was."

Her mom snorted in agreement. "That boy of his is so cute I could just eat him up."

Millie tapped the brakes lightly so the car wouldn't skid as they came to a four-way stop. She hadn't planned to question her mother any further about the incident with her blood sugar, but the opportunity had presented itself, and she couldn't quite dismiss David's words. "Speaking of eating," she said carefully. "I've been thinking about last night—the way your blood sugar dropped so low. I was wondering if maybe you might have taken a double dose of Glucophage last night by accident."

"You think I'm that senile?"

"I'm just trying to understand what happened. It was busy last night. You could have been tired."

Her mother sighed. "Honey, just worry about your driving. Whatever it was, it's gone. I'm fine now."

Millie cast a sideways glance at her. "We don't want that to happen again. It's scary, Mom, when your blood sugar goes down like that."

"There's more danger that we're going to skid off the road if you don't look where you're going. I don't want to talk about this anymore."

Something in Millie wouldn't let it go. "Maybe we should keep that appointment at four with Dr. Wong. Run some blood tests and make sure you're really okay."

"I'm fine. I have an appointment in two weeks. We can talk about what happened then."

"Mom," Millie said, "if you don't go see him, I'm going to worry every night when you go to bed that your blood sugar is going to drop and you'll go into a coma."

"I'm not about to kick the bucket, so you can stop worrying. Besides, if I go, all Dr. Wong is going to do is run an A1C test and tell me that I need to be stricter about my diet, lose weight, and exercise more. That's all he ever says. And he charges a fortune."

This was true, but Dr. Wong also warned Eva that her casual approach to managing her diabetes was a big mistake, that with her disease came an increased risk for heart attack, stroke, and a host of other serious conditions.

Miles of wire fence line marked fields covered with snow. Millie sped past Burial Hill Road, which led to the cemetery where her grandmother was buried. After Grandma Gert passed away, she and her mother used to go there daily. That first summer, they planted black-eyed Susans in fat clay pots that flanked the small flat marker and lugged over gallon containers of water. While Millie tended the grave, her mother stared down at the plot with such grief in her face that Millie could not bear to look at her. No words could help, so Millie brushed dirt off the engraved letters, the weight of the vast blue sky bearing down on her shoulders. That summer, Eva's diabetes had required her to be hospitalized twice, and Millie remembered it as being the hardest summer in her life.

Dr. Wong had explained that grief could wreak havoc on the body and to expect fluctuations in her mother's health. He advised Millie to minimize any further stress and to watch for signs of depression. By the end of July, Millie was managing the café full-time and had decided to defer her admission to the University of South Dakota. The next summer, however, had been no better. Lightning had struck a tree, which had toppled onto the café's roof. Although insurance had picked up most of the expenses, Millie had needed to help her mother handle the paperwork and oversee the renovations. That fall Millie had started courses at the local community college, but caring for her mom and running the café proved to be more than she could handle, and she'd dropped out before the semester ended.

Ahead the hanging traffic light marked the entrance to Deer Park's business district. Cars and trucks parked in slanting lines filled both sides of the road. Stores stripped of their Christmas decorations now sported murals of ski hills, sleds, and banners advertising the coming Winterfest Snow Carnival.

She turned at the next light and pulled around to the back of Dosie Dough's. As she stepped out of the car, a gust of wind blew the sleet sideways, striking her face. She ducked her head into the collar of her parka and thought about how warm it must be in California right now. How people drove around in convertibles or sat at outdoor cafés sipping cool drinks and eating wraps made with sprouts and avocados. She pictured herself there, watching the world from behind a pair of dark glasses, an expensive silk scarf tied around her neck, the air warm and silky on her bare shoulders.

They came in through the back door, and Millie flipped on the lights. The stainless steel counters gleamed with near-surgical cleanliness, the twin refrigerators hummed in the background, and the vast grill sat empty and waiting, the fry basket sitting beside the covered tub of oil.

Millie tied on an apron then had to wrestle the forty-pound bag of flour from her mother's arms. "I've got this," she said. "You sit at the counter and supervise."

Eva shook her head. "I'm not a supervising kind of woman. I'm a doing kind of woman."

"Then work on the starter," Millie suggested as she emptied half the bag into an industrial-sized mixing bowl. A cloud of fine white dust rose into the air. "What kind of bread are we making anyway?"

"Sourdough," her mother said as if this were obvious. "We always have sourdough on Thursdays. Goes well with tomato basil soup."

She felt her mother's gaze as she gently stirred salt into the flour and then attached the dough hook to the machine. Eva was near fanatical in the handling of the dry ingredients prior to the addition of the starter sponge and water. She claimed overworking the dough made it tough and always watched to make sure Millie didn't stir too many times.

As a preteen, Millie remembered some of their worst fights had stemmed from baking bread. Eva had insisted she learn the proper way to bake, and Millie had been equally determined that she wouldn't. As her mother had gone over and over the way to knead the bread, round it, and proof it, Millie had let her mother's words flow through her brain like water down a drain.

Instead, she'd stared at Eva's broad face and mentally given her a makeover—a foundation so her skin would not look so pale and washed out and a concealer to hide the dark shadows beneath her eyes. She'd restyled her mother's thick curly hair into a neat, straight bob like the one her English teacher wore. She'd changed her mother's outfit from the shapeless black stretch pants and red sweatshirt with the oversized chocolate éclair into a sleek wrap dress. She imagined Eva as a slim, stylish mother who turned heads when she came to Millie's school plays, instead of the Eva who always was running late and more often than not showed up with her clothing dusted with flour or shirts stained with oil from the fryer.

Once Millie had told Eva that her appearance was an embarrassment.

"You're a teenager, and I'm your mother," Eva had retorted. "I'm supposed to embarrass you." And she'd laughed heartily at her own joke. But she'd stayed away at the next performance, and her absence had left Millie feeling gutted—like the jeweled bellies of the fish her mother slit open and emptied before baking them.

Eva walked over with the starter sponge and pitcher of tepid water. She began mixing the ingredients with a long, wooden paddle and the ease of someone who'd done it hundreds of times before. "This is nice—a quiet afternoon, no customers, no hustle and bustle—just you and me."

"It is," Millie agreed. The forming ball of dough smelled yeasty. She couldn't deny that there was something soothing about watching the hook chase the ball of dough around the metal mixing bowl and listening to the sound of sleet on the roof.

"I was thinking, after we finish the sourdough, maybe we could whip up a batch of apple tarts."

They were Millie's childhood favorite, and her mother had made them both to celebrate her accomplishments and console her failures. Today the tarts said, *Sorry I kept you awake most of last night. Let me make it up to you.*

Millie wiped her hands on her apron and left ghostly flour prints on the tomato-red fabric. *I don't want apple tarts,* she wanted to say. *I want you to tell me to go to Hollywood and do something amazing with my life—that you believe I can. I want you to look me in the eye and tell me that you don't need me.*

She bit her lip. Here she was again, still trying to remake Eva. She supposed it was impossible for her not to—just as Eva could not help trying to make Millie into the daughter she wanted.

"I don't need apple tarts," Millie began and was about to add that television cameras added ten pounds. But then she stopped at the look of disappointment that deepened the lines in her mother's face and killed the light in her eyes. Eva had essentially heard, *I don't accept your apology.*

Millie turned off the mixer and lifted the hook from the dough. "I don't need apple tarts," she repeated. "But you know I can't resist them."

Eva beamed at her. Apology made and accepted. "Excellent," she said.

Chapter 18

S o why did you become a dentist?" Millie lay in bed with the cordless receiver tucked to her ear and the down comforter pulled high around her. It was nearly ten o'clock, which was late for her to be awake, but ever since Eva's blood sugar had plummeted so inexplicably three days ago, David had been calling after he finished putting Bart to bed. *Just to check on you and Eva,* he'd explained.

Although initially Millie had bristled—she didn't need anyone checking on her—when David suggested that their talking on the phone was a natural part of the dating process, even if they were un-dating, she had agreed.

"I don't know," David's deep voice rumbled pleasantly in her ear. "I guess it seemed like a really cool job. I remember going with my dad to the office and him showing me the tools. I liked making the chair ride up and down."

Millie laughed. "But did you feel pressure to be a dentist because your father was one?"

"No. In fact, he wanted me to be a lawyer. An environmental lawyer so I could protect trees. He was very big on trees."

"Trees," Millie repeated, smiling. "Was it hard then, telling him that you weren't going to be a tree lawyer?" She pulled her knees up higher. In the very back of her mind, a small voice warned her that their phone conversations were getting longer every night, and these questions had ventured into personal waters.

"No. He said he understood. *His* father wanted him to be an architect. He said that God gave everyone a gift and a purpose and that to deny it was to waste it. And then he said he was proud of me, no matter what profession I chose, and that was it."

"Seriously? He didn't go into a decline?"

"No. But he sent me a ficus tree the day I opened my practice in Los Angeles."

Millie laughed then pressed the phone a little closer against her ear. "Tell me what it was like there," she said.

"Well, it was very nice, but not as nice as here."

The answer wasn't what she expected. "Why not?"

"It wasn't home," he said.

"In the old days," her mother explained, ripping a length of duct tape off the roll, "they used to let you use chicken wire to support the body of the box sled. But then they decided to simplify things and only use cardboard, duct tape, glue, and paint." She cut the tape. "If you ask me, the more people try and simplify things these days, the more complicated they get."

The propane heater warmed David's garage, chasing away the chill of a late-January afternoon. They'd discarded their coats and gloves and squatted on an old quilt near the cardboard carcass of what was slowly becoming the *Flying French Fry*.

Under the naked lightbulb hanging from the center of the garage's ceiling, Millie's mother's eyes sparkled, and her movements were fluid and purposeful. "Take the computer for example. Does anyone truly believe it's made their life any easier?"

"Maybe not easier," Bart agreed, "but a lot more fun. Have you ever played Sims?"

"Sims? What's that? Sounds like a respiratory disease."

Millie rolled her eyes and cut into a square of cardboard. "That's SARS, Mom."

"Sims is a cool computer game. I could teach you how to play it, Mrs. Hogan."

"Thank you, Bart, but you-know-where will freeze over before the computer makes any sense to me."

Millie and David exchanged smiles. Although her mother would never admit it, part of her dislike for computers came from her fear of pushing the wrong button. As if a single erroneous keystroke could take down the power grid in several states.

"You want some help?" David asked Millie.

She was cutting the cardboard in order to reinforce the hull, but the material was thick and hard to cut. She kept stopping to rest her hand.

David leaned over to pull the cardboard taut to make it easier for her to cut. The fabric of his wool sweater stretched over his lean torso. His face was close to her own, and she could feel the warmth in his blue eyes peering at her.

"If you tear the cardboard," Millie cautioned, "Mom will kill us."

"And bury you in the backyard," her mother confirmed and tapped her yardstick against her UGG boot like a military sergeant. "We don't want to compromise the integrity of the structure. Bart, have you seen the protractor? I'm wondering if we could shave off another degree or two from the front of the sled."

"It's in my pencil pouch in my room. Want me to get it?"

"Please," Millie's mother said. As the boy ran to retrieve it, she turned to Millie. "While you and David finish cutting the hull support, I'm going to discuss some race strategy with Aris."

"What race strategy?" Millie asked.

"You know," her mother said vaguely. "Ways we can help Bart." She was talking as she walked, and it was obvious to Millie that her mother was simply trying to give her an opportunity to be alone with David.

Millie snuck a peek at David to see if he realized. Of course he had. His blue eyes were laughing. "Take your time, Mrs. Hogan." He scooted a little closer to Millie. "Honey, let me help you with that."

When she handed him the scissors, their hands touched, and the heat of his skin sent a shiver through her. She glanced up to see if David had felt the same jolt. He hadn't moved, but the laughter had disappeared from his face. The easygoing, intellectual David was gone, and a man with a strong jaw and intense blue eyes was looking back at her.

Correction. Looking into her. It wasn't a staring contest kind of look at all. It was strong, and it was penetrating, and she felt it all the way to the tips of her toes.

She tried to remind herself of just why she'd given up men. Words like *trapped, dependent,* and *weak* floated through her mind as insubstantial as ghosts. His eyes continued to hold her, and the look was undoing something that had been tightly knotted inside her. She forced herself to look down, but it didn't help. The sight of his tapered fingers, the skin as pale as sand, made her skin burn.

The steps creaked. Startled, Millie's head jerked back. Her mother? She felt a flush of anger. Why was her mother standing there watching them? What was wrong with her? She clenched her fists, furious. *Go away*, she wanted to shout.

But she wasn't as mad at Eva as she was with herself. She'd wanted to kiss David—and that would have ruined everything. As soon as the door closed behind her mom, Millie released her breath. An instinct she hadn't known she possessed seemed to take control of her.

"You were amazing," she said. "The way you were looking at me just then was totally believable."

David flexed the scissors. His eyes said he wasn't fooled. "You were pretty believable yourself."

She didn't want to be reminded of any longings that he might have glimpsed in her eyes. "Well, you know me. I've had a lot of practice." She laughed as if this was funny, but David remained silent, and after a moment he began to cut the cardboard.

As the scissors hacked through the thick layers, Millie sat cross-legged, wondering why she'd felt the need to make herself sound cheap.

Beneath her lashes, she studied his profile. Usually she preferred tall, muscular men with craggy faces, steely eyes, and six packs. Her fantasy men were Navy SEALs, secret agents, and occasionally a Scottish laird with wide shoulders and a deep lyrical brogue.

She'd never fantasized about a dentist of average height and build.

To be fair, David had probably never dreamed of falling for a waitress. His first wife had been educated; they'd gone to dental school together. Millie had only a semester of college. Lisa had been blond, tiny, and beautiful; Millie was dark-haired, tall, and strong.

David finished cutting and placed the rectangle of cardboard inside the hull. Sitting back, he studied the sled. "One side looks a little higher."

Millie could have cared less. She still was thinking about her earlier remark and wishing she hadn't said it. She thought she might have hurt him, although this was more of a sense than a fact. She plucked at the fabric of her sweatshirt.

"I didn't mean that the way it sounded," she said.

"Mean what?" He picked up the yardstick and measured the lowest point of the sled.

He had to know exactly what she meant, and his politeness was only going to make it harder. She fingered the remains of a piece of cardboard. "Look," she said flatly. "I've dated a lot of guys, but. . ."

"What difference does that make?" David interrupted, studying the lines on the yardstick as if they were hieroglyphics that required immediate translation. "There's a quarter inch discrepancy between the sides. We should fix it." He picked up a pencil and marked the spot.

"One quarter of an inch isn't going to make a difference," Millie stated. "And I know I don't have to explain everything to you, but I want to."

He looked up. "Do you know that when I set a crown in a person's mouth, if it is as much as one one-hundreth of a centimeter off, the person's whole bite will be affected?" He picked up the scissors and cut the piece he'd just installed in the hull to make it fit better. "One side will bite down first. Every time that person chews something, he'll feel it. It could cause terrible problems down the road. TMJ for one."

"It's a sled," Millie argued, "not a dental appliance."

"It's an easy fix."

"That's not the point." Millie placed her hand over his, preventing him from cutting the cardboard. She felt the same tingle as before. She clenched her jaw. "David, I'm trying to tell you something about myself. Things maybe you need to hear."

"I appreciate that. And I'm trying to tell you that you don't have to tell me anything. I like who you are, and the rest doesn't matter."

The words stung in a way he probably hadn't intended. She lifted her hand off his and looked at him in astonishment. Why wasn't "the rest" important? "The rest" was her past. Wasn't he curious about the rumors he must have heard about her? Or was he trying to tell her that what happened in the past had no relevance because they had no future?

She wanted to ask but couldn't. She bit her lip and tried to find the way to express her feelings without actually risking anything. She couldn't get past the truth—that when they'd touched, she'd come alive in a way she never had before. And when she'd looked into his eyes, she felt him inside her.

At the same time, all this was terrifying. She'd always called the shots in the relationship. She always managed to stay at arm's length emotionally, if not physically.

What if she told David she wasn't just pretending to like him? What if he didn't like her back? And maybe, just maybe, she wasn't good enough for him.

Even scarier, though, was the thought he might like her in the same way she liked him. Where would that leave them?

In a relationship, she decided, that wasn't right for either of them.

Chapter 19

Millie played it cool when she kissed David good-bye. Walking out to the car, she straightened her shoulders against the frigid January night. Men complicated things. They made strong women vulnerable. If you let them, they would break your heart. If she had any doubt about this, she had only to look at her grandmother and mother, both single parents.

She backed down the driveway. In the passenger seat, her mother was uncharacteristically quiet. Eva looked out the window, and her profile was serious. Maybe old memories were kicking around in her head, too.

It'd been a rainy, chilly morning in April when Max Hogan had stopped being Millie's father.

She'd hurried down the stairs, grumpy because she'd overslept and was going to be late for school if she didn't hurry. She had a math test, which she was probably going to fail, and that would probably start another war with her mother, who thought she spent far too much time rehearsing the lines in her play and not enough time studying.

The house was uncharacteristically quiet when she walked into the kitchen. Eva was seated at the kitchen table with her head folded into her hands as if it were a weight her neck could no longer carry. She'd lifted her head long enough for Millie to glimpse her chalk-white face and scary red-rimmed eyes, and then her head crumpled back into her hands.

"What's wrong?" Millie whispered. She'd never seen her mother cry, and the sight was terrifying. "Mom?"

Grandma Gert padded silently into the room in her fluffy blue robe and slippers. "Your father's gone."

"Gone to work?" Millie asked.

"Gone," Grandma Gert repeated, and her face twisted. "I'm sorry, child."

Her mother made a deep guttural noise that sounded as if it had been torn out of her chest. Millie's skin turned to ice. Dad's dead. Impossible, she thought, I just saw him last night. But there was her mother, bent with grief at the table.

I'm never going to see Dad again. The thought sliced something wide open inside. Flinging herself into Grandma Gert's big chest, she closed her eyes and wept.

It was only later that evening, when she'd gathered her courage to ask Grandma Gert how her father had died, that she learned he had packed his suitcase and left in the middle of the night. In a way, this was worse, because it opened up all sorts of questions in her mind. Why had he left? Where had he gone? And why hadn't he asked her if she wanted to go with him?

She couldn't ask any of those questions though. Her mother stopped speaking and started spending long hours in the kitchen. When Millie came home from school, Eva would be at the speckled blue linoleum counter stirring a bowl of batter. Evidence of the day's baking would be lined up along the counter—German chocolate cakes with flaky coconut icing, heavy loaves of lemon pound cake drizzled in a raspberry glaze, and trays of brownies frosted in pink peppermint icing. Breads in various stages of rise battled for space with the sweet cinnamon rolls *topped with sticky pecan glaze.*

Each night Millie and Grandma Gert wrapped up the baking and gave it to neighbors. But when they awoke in the morning, the countertops were again filled with breads and pastries.

Eva couldn't stop, and as cakes and pies and cookies overflowed the kitchen into the dining and living room, out of desperation Millie wrote FREE PASTRIES *on a piece of poster board and stuck it at the end of the driveway. Word spread quickly, and it wasn't long before a steady stream of people came for the baked goods. Millie never charged anyone for the food, but people left money on the counters, under the front-door mat, and in the mailbox. It wasn't long before Millie began finding handwritten orders on scraps of paper, "a dozen raspberry Danishes," "an apple-strudel coffee cake," and "a Black Forest cake."*

Pulling into her garage, Millie turned off the car's engine and tried to push back the memories. She thought of her mother's brokenness—buried deep now but still part of her. Millie suspected it always would be.

She barely tasted the baked potato soup that Eva heated for dinner and hurried to her bedroom straight after dinner where she spent an hour on the PC, searching for auditions and cheap airfares to New York and California. At nine o'clock, she took off her makeup, brushed her teeth, pulled on her pajamas, and climbed into the cold bed.

A little after nine, she turned off the lights. She rolled onto her side so she wouldn't watch the clock. She wasn't sure if David would call or not, but if he did, she didn't plan on answering. She'd let him slip past her defenses just a little, but it had been a wake-up call. She needed to pull back before she lost control of the situation.

When the phone rang at 9:25, she jerked. Placing the pillow over her head, she waited as the phone jingled loudly once, twice, three times.

Finally, the answering machine kicked in, and the room went silent. She sat up, turned on the light, and fought back the panic that said maybe she'd done the wrong thing. Taking a sip of water from the glass on the bedside table, she tried to swallow the unexpected lump in her throat. Had the house always felt so quiet? Her room so tomblike? Her life suddenly seemed so inescapable, so dreary in its predictability, that she almost wanted to throw her glass against the wall just to see it break.

She didn't want to feel anything for David Denvers. She didn't want to miss the sound of his voice, the nightly conversations. She didn't want him in her head, her heart, or anywhere else. He did not belong in the life she wanted, and she certainly didn't belong in his. She turned off the light and laid her head on the pillow.

Suddenly there was a soft knocking on her door. "Millie?" Eva said, poking her head inside. "David's on the phone."

Millie concentrated on staying still and keeping her breathing smooth and even, although her heart was racing.

"Millie?" her mother whispered more loudly. "Are you awake?"

She clenched her jaw and lay corpselike on the bed. There was a long pause, and then the door clicked quietly shut. Millie heard the floor creak as Eva retreated down the hallway. She lay awake for a long time thinking about David, wondering if she'd done the right thing and what they might have said to each other if she'd picked up the phone.

Chapter 20

For years Gunderson Park had been a local hangout for teens. In the winter, the town roped off a portion of the lake and cleared the surface with a Bobcat. For ten dollars and a trip to the town hall, a skating pass could be bought for the season.

When she was fourteen, Millie had come here as often as she could find someone to drive her. It kept her out of the café and away from her mother. Millie didn't understand how Eva could be talking and giggling one moment, and the next she would be shrieking at a vendor or sitting at the counter too depressed to lift her head from her hands. Daily, it seemed, Eva was changing, gaining weight, and becoming more emotionally unpredictable. Grandma Gert whispered to be patient, but Millie discovered the only solution was to stay out of Eva's way as much as possible.

So it shocked her one sunny afternoon at Gunderson Park when Aaron Hughes skated up next to her. He was two years older and towered over her, although she was already the tallest girl in eighth grade. "Hi," was all he'd needed to say to start her heart thundering.

She kept her gaze firmly on the ice, because if she even glanced at his face, she'd have fallen flat on the ice.

"I was wondering," he said, "if maybe you'd like a hot chocolate."

Millie had practically swooned with importance. "Sure," she'd managed.

They'd wobbled their way up to the concession hut. He'd bought her a hot chocolate, and they'd stood beside a fire burning inside an oil drum and talked. It wasn't long before he said he wanted to show her something and led her to a grove of pines. He'd shaken the snow off the bough of one of the larger trees and pulled her beneath. Smiling, he'd looked down at her. "You're a really pretty girl. Did you know that?" he'd whispered and lowered his cold lips onto hers.

She hadn't liked the kiss, but she'd liked bragging to her friends about it. Although her relationship with Aaron hadn't lasted a week, Millie had discovered something about herself. She had power, and with a little practice, she began to know how to use it. By the time she was old enough to drive herself to the park, she was never without a boyfriend. And if other girls whispered behind her back, Millie ignored them. She liked the attention and wasn't giving it up.

Although Millie hadn't been ice skating in years, these thoughts were very much on her mind as David turned the Lexus into the entrance of Gunderson Park. She stiffened at the sight of the white van with the Methodist church bumper sticker. All her misgivings came rushing back, and she wished she hadn't given in to David's insistence that she attend the church's skating function.

Bart hit the ground running as soon as David parked the car. "Not cool to be seen with your father," David remarked wryly as they watched the boy speed toward the group of boys who were sitting on plank benches and putting on their skates.

Millie slung her skates over her shoulder. "We ditched our parents when we were Bart's age, remember?"

"I remember you had a white parka with a fur-trimmed hood, only you never wore the hood up. You had a white headband, and you wore your hair in the thickest, longest braid I'd ever seen."

She glanced sideways at him. Her eyes were nearly level with his. "You remember that?"

"Well it wasn't *that* long ago."

She felt her cheeks pink up as she remembered all those little trips behind the concession stand. David probably remembered them, too—although he was too polite to admit it. Plunking down on one of the cold plank benches, she pried open the ancient figure skates.

Sticking her foot into the cold, stiff leather, she crossed the laces tightly. Laughter and the sound of children yelling to one another filled the air. Knotting the laces, she sat up and scanned the ice and began recognizing people.

"Are you worried?" she finally asked.

"About what?" David finished lacing one skate and was working on the other.

Millie's stomach tightened as she continued to study the stream of skaters passing, circling the ice. She feared being judged and found not good enough to be dating David. "About being seen with me."

"You mean you're worried that people won't believe we're dating?"

She gave a small, brittle laugh. "No," she said, shaking her head. "The exact opposite. I'm worried that they will."

The ice was rock hard, uneven, and black as night. A slice of wind reduced Millie's eyes to slits, and her skates immediately began to rub her ankle. A group of kids whizzed past her, and she had to throw her hands out to catch her balance and ended up hitting David across the chest.

"Sorry," she apologized.

"Don't worry about it," he replied. "You want some help?"

"No, I think I've got it." Next to her, David barely needed to shift his weight to keep pace with her. "How come you look like this is easy?" she asked.

"It is. You just have to relax."

Relax? She'd never felt more uptight in her life. Over there was Henry Belltown, an ex-boyfriend. He was married now, as was Robert Sanders. She dropped her gaze, afraid of recognizing anyone else.

About halfway around the rink, it got a little easier. She made herself concentrate on how sweet the cold air smelled and the feel of her skates cutting across the ice. Her spirits lifted. None of the skaters they passed gave them anything but a friendly wave.

"You know, we should probably hold hands."

"Right." Her heart gave a little jump as her fingers inside her cashmere glove wove together with his leather-encased hands. It seemed all at once masculine and feminine—her softness to his strength—and it made her tingle.

They skated more closely together. He could have skated faster without her, but she appreciated the careful way he guided her around the rink. Glancing sideways at him, she started to thank him then found herself admiring the way the sunlight brought out the highlights in his dark hair and the clean, strong line of his jaw.

He caught her staring at him. She looked away so fast that it threw her off step. The blades of the skates clapped sharply against each other. David laughed a little. "You trying to trip me?"

"You're onto me," Millie deadpanned. "I was hoping to knock the wind out of you and then have my way with you in front of the members of your church. That way everyone will know I'm serious about you."

He shot her an amused glance. "I'm sure they'd enjoy that," he said. "Particularly Reverend Stockman." He gestured to the tall white-haired man in an oversized black wool coat who was skating a short distance ahead of them.

Millie groaned.

"He's a good guy—but maybe we should say hello to him," David suggested innocently, "before you tackle me. It'll make a better impression."

"David!" She hit his arm lightly with her free hand. "I was joking about tackling you, and I don't want to talk to Reverend Stockman."

"Why not?"

"Because," Millie murmured, unsure how to express what she felt. She measured the distance between them. It wouldn't be long before they intercepted the man. "I just don't want a lecture about Jesus, going to church, or the salvation of my immortal soul."

"He wouldn't do that," David stated firmly then shot her a sideways grin. "At least not on your first meeting."

Millie rolled her eyes. "I'll save him the lecture. Church isn't for everyone."

"You don't know that until you try it."

She gave him a hard sideways look. "I have tried it. My father used to be an usher in the church, remember? And it didn't stop him from walking out on my mother and me."

David's body swayed gently with the movement of his skates. "He might have done something wrong, but it doesn't mean you and your mom should stay away from church."

"You have no idea what it was like after my father left. People talked. It was awful."

"People can be pretty thoughtless, but I'd hate to see you give up on the idea of God and a church family."

"I don't want to talk about it anymore. And I really don't want to talk to Reverend Stockman. Whenever he comes in the café, he always looks at me as if he can see everything I've ever done wrong my entire life."

"He looks at everyone that way," David said dryly. "I think it's an occupational hazard."

Millie refused to see the humor in his words. They had almost caught up with the reverend. "Please."

He gave her a funny look but then cut across the ice and away from the reverend.

"Thank you."

"You're welcome."

She could have dropped it, but something in her felt compelled to add, "It'd hurt Eva if I went to church. It'd reopen everything for her. I can't do that."

"Sometimes the only way to heal something is to talk about it. Pastor Chris—he was the senior pastor back at my church in California—helped me a lot after Lisa died. I didn't want to talk about her, but he prayed with me and helped me understand that it was okay to be angry at God—the important thing was to talk to Him."

"I'm not saying that I don't believe in God, David. To me, God and church are two different things." She lurched a little as they hit a rough patch of ice, and he steadied her arm.

"So you believe in God?"

"Of course," Millie said. "I believe in heaven and hell and all the rest. I just don't believe in going to church." She didn't want to explain that she also felt that while God existed, she didn't think He loved her or wanted her to talk to Him. Like her father, God had long ago moved on to other people, other places. As a child, she'd learned to depend on herself. She didn't want to go to church with all its false hopes and phony promises.

"And Jesus—do you accept Him as God's one and only Son?"

Millie shot him an angry look. "Look—I avoided Reverend Stockman just to avoid a conversation like this. Don't try to save me, David." She skated a little faster, clipping the steel blade of her skate's edge against his in the process.

"I'm just trying to understand what you believe." David gripped her arm and used his body weight as a drag to slow them down. "Faith is important to me. I'm not judging you. I want to know."

She struggled against his arm and then against his weight slowing them down. Then she steeled herself to finish the conversation. Slowing to a stop, she turned to face him. The wind sliced across her cheeks, and she drew her hand through the hair that had fallen free and angled across her face. "It feels like you are—judging me."

His eyes were kind but steady, bright blue in the cold air. "I'm sorry it feels like that. But I'm not. I promise."

She crossed her arms. "Why does it matter what I believe?"

A group of kids whizzed by them so closely that Millie held her breath until they were safely past.

"It matters," David said when they were alone again, "because you matter." His gaze peered intently into hers. "I know we have a plan, so don't take this the wrong way, but the more I get to know you, the more I like you—as a friend of course."

She lifted her chin. "You mean the more you want to do your Christian duty and save me, right?"

"If you believe in Jesus, you're already saved," he said. "I just want to encourage you to give church another try."

Fat chance, Millie thought and shifted her weight. "It's just not for me. I'm sorry."

David nodded as if he understood, but his gaze stayed steady on hers. "I'm not going to tell you that everyone who goes to church is perfect and always does the right thing—but I will tell you that for me, after Lisa died, our church family were the ones who stepped in and helped. For weeks, maybe longer, I don't remember, I'd come home and someone would have cut my grass or left a basket with cookies on my doorstep. People invited Bart over for playdates or just called to ask how I was doing." He paused. "One of Lisa's friends—Lynn—bred English bulldogs, and she just showed up one Saturday morning with a little brindle puppy. It was the last thing I needed, but Bart's face—it lit up like a Christmas tree. The dog licked his face, wiggled all over, and then peed on him. Bart thought that was hilarious, and suddenly we were all laughing." He paused. "It didn't mean we missed Lisa less, but we felt loved. It helped. That's what a church family does."

His expression softened. "Just think about coming to church, okay?"

Millie shrugged and looked away from the hopeful look in his eyes. She didn't have the heart to tell him that the probability of changing her mind was low. More troubling to her was the snapshots that had formed in her mind of David's life in California, the obvious love he had for Lisa—perfect Lisa, whom Millie disliked without even meeting and for no good reason.

And why shouldn't David still love Lisa? Lisa was probably as beautiful on the inside as she'd been on the outside. Millie would probably look like a giant next to her, and there'd never been any question that God loved Lisa—that He'd chosen Lisa to be on His team. David had loved her deeply. She'd seen it in his eyes.

Millie clenched her fists. The truth was that she didn't dislike perfect Lisa as much as she was jealous of her. She drew an angry line across the ice with the blade of her skate. She didn't want to imagine David loving another woman.

Chapter 21

The mood had changed. Maybe David shouldn't have gone on and on about the church family and how good they'd been to him and Lisa. He'd seen something in Millie's face close down, and yet he'd kept talking, hoping that she'd reconsider her position on going to church. If she would only try it, she'd see for herself how it could be a source of comfort and strength.

The wind whipped off the ice. Millie shivered and hugged her arms around herself. She looked unhappy standing there, and yet he couldn't regret what he'd said. She believed in God—that was a good start. They'd continue the conversation later, and he would talk less, listen more, and hopefully address her fears.

"You want to get some hot chocolate?" he asked.

"Yeah, I'm ready for a break."

He steadied her by the elbow—not that she needed it, but it felt good to hold on to her as they wobbled off the ice, unlaced their skates, and put on their boots. At the concession hut, he bought them both cups of hot chocolate and then led her to one of the burning oil drums near the shoreline.

"Just as watered-down and lukewarm as it was fifteen years ago," David commented as they stood in the warmth of the flames and watched the parade of skaters glide past them.

"I'd be disappointed if it wasn't," Millie said. "It's part of the whole Gunderson Park experience."

David laughed. She was right. One sip and he was instantly transported to a nerdy, short teenager who played ice hockey every winter on the town's least competitive team. The games they'd won could be counted on one hand, but he'd had fun and made some good friends.

He remembered seeing Millie skating. She'd been tall and graceful and always surrounded by friends. He'd watched her because he couldn't help it and wished he was the one skating next to her. He sipped the hot chocolate and recognized the irony of the situation. Here they were, all these years later, skating together, and she was still just as unattainable to him.

"I was reading in the paper the other day about a new play opening up in Sioux City. It's a murder mystery, and the audience gets to vote on the ending. I was thinking maybe you'd like to go with me."

Millie's face lit up. "I'd love to," she said. "I know exactly what play you're talking about. It's about a woman who gets poisoned, and there's like five suspects and a twist. It's supposed to be fabulous."

"How about we make it a Valentine's Day date?"

Her eyebrows shot up. "Oh right—I almost forgot Valentine's Day is a week from Saturday. Get ready for something big and chocolaty."

David smiled. "You think everyone is ready for us to move on to the chocolate stage in our relationship?" He was partially teasing. He hadn't forgotten that in Millie's world food spoke a language of its own. Making him something chocolate had implications.

"They'll not only accept it," she said, "but they'll expect it. How do you feel about cake? Or are you a brownies kind of guy?"

"I'm not quite sure," David said, pretending to be serious and working to keep from smiling. "But if you made me both, I'm sure I could decide."

Her nose crinkled as she looked up at him. "You know, if I make you two desserts, people might jump to conclusions."

"What kind of conclusions?"

"That I'm chasing you."

David laughed. "I like that idea," he said and leaned even closer to her. "Now I definitely want the two desserts."

"Okay," Millie said, and her eyes were so clear and bright he could see the speckles of gray in her irises. "But be prepared—the aunts are going to razz the both of us about this."

She sipped her hot chocolate, and his gaze lingered on her lips. They were slightly more red than pink and invitingly full. His gaze lingered. He imagined himself moving closer, lowering his head, and kissing her. Immediately the heat burned inside him, as if he were already doing this.

Suddenly Millie frowned a little, and a small furrow appeared between her brows. "Uh-oh. Cynthia Shively, twelve o'clock. I think she sees us."

He started to glance over his shoulder, but Millie's hand on his arm stopped him just in time. "Don't look at her," Millie whispered. "Look at me."

He braced himself, dreading the encounter and wishing Cynthia would just go away so he could admire Millie's lips a little more.

"David, you're clenching your jaw, and you've stopped blinking. We're supposed to be having fun. Pretend to steal my hat or something."

When David did, Millie's curly hair tumbled to her shoulders. This was the way he liked her hair best, and for a happy moment he almost forgot about Cynthia.

"David," Millie prompted, smiling, "give me my hat."

It was a soft piece of red yarn with a large pom-pom. "Is this one of Aunt Keeker's hats by any chance?"

"It was my Christmas present from her," Millie admitted, standing on her tiptoes to reach for it. "The yarn is infused with the scent of forget-me-not flowers. When I wear this, you're not supposed to think of anyone but me."

David sniffed the hat and inhaled the smallest trace of something floral. He smiled and let himself look long and hard into her eyes. "It's working," he said, and although he'd meant to say it lightly, it didn't come out that way at all.

Millie's big gray eyes locked on his, and for a moment he felt something strong and real pass between them. He jumped when a hand tapped him lightly on the shoulder.

"Hello, stranger," Cynthia said brightly. "Feels like forever since I've seen you!"

He turned slowly and forced a smile. "Hello, Cynthia."

"Hi," Millie added.

Cynthia was dressed all in white—a fur-trimmed white parka, white stretch pants, and a white headband. The only color was her eyes, large and blue. "Well, Millie Hogan." Cynthia's smile widened. "I didn't expect to see you here. This is a wonderful surprise!"

Why wouldn't she expect to see Millie here? He and Millie were dating, and this was a family function. And then he saw the comment for what it was—a dig at Millie for coming to a church function when she wasn't a member. He slipped a protective arm around Millie's waist. "She's a pretty good skater."

"Well, I'm a little rusty," Millie said. "But I haven't taken out anyone yet." She smiled up at David. "Although we've had a couple of close calls."

Cynthia laughed. "I'm sure." She looked at David. "Have you introduced her to everyone? I know everyone will want to welcome her—especially Reverend Stockman." Her blue eyes sparkled as if they held a thousand secrets. "He loves meeting new people."

"Actually, I already know Reverend Stockman," Millie said.

"You do?" Cynthia looked at David as if to confirm this was true.

"Of course. My family were members at this church a long time ago."

"I didn't know that," Cynthia said.

"You were probably already at boarding school," David said. "Well, it's been very nice running into you, Cynthia, but Millie and I probably ought to get going."

She nodded. "Of course, but first, I was wondering, Millie, if I could borrow David for a few minutes."

Borrow him? He wasn't a book at the library that could be checked out. He restrained his irritation. "Maybe another time would be better."

"It's okay," Millie said. She flashed an encouraging smile at him and then gave him a quick kiss on the cheek. "Take your time."

It wasn't much of a kiss, but he smelled the very lightest trace of something floral—maybe it was the forget-me-not hat—and then she was gone. His gaze followed the sway of her hips as she walked up the hill.

"So I need your opinion, David," Cynthia was saying. "I'm thinking of taking on some volunteer work with the church."

This was what she needed to get him alone to ask? "That's great," he said.

"Well, it would mean I wouldn't have time to help your mom at the office with your files."

David tried not to grin and refrained from pointing out that she hadn't been hanging around his office in a while. "That's okay."

She frowned. "You say that, but you need someone." She pursed her lips hard, looked away from him, and seemed to wrestle with herself. "I could be that person, if you'd let me."

"We'll be fine," David assured her. "You go ahead and take that volunteering opportunity." He could hardly wait to tell Millie the good news.

"I will," she said. "One more thing—I don't know how to say this, but please be careful." Her voice was barely louder than a whisper. "She isn't one of us."

"You mean Millie?"

Cynthia nodded.

"What do you mean she isn't one of us?"

"You know what I'm saying."

"No, I don't."

She looked him long and hard in the eyes. "The whole church thing. If you aren't raised in a church, the chances that you will attend church as an adult are greatly reduced." Cynthia's eyes were flat and cold. "I didn't make that up, David."

"So what?" he snapped. "Not everybody gets to grow up in a churchgoing family. What are we supposed to do, ostracize those who aren't?" *Just the opposite should happen,* he thought angrily. *Just the opposite.*

"People are talking," she said. "I thought you should know."

"If people are talking, they should be saying how nice it is to see Millie here today—and they should mean it."

"You just don't want to hear the truth."

He planted his hands on his hips and then made himself count to ten. "The truth is that you need to get yourself another dentist."

"David—what?"

"Until you can be nice to Millie, we're done."

"You don't mean that."

"I mean it with every breath in my body," he said. Turning, he left her standing there and began making his way up the hill in the direction Millie had taken. He put his anger into each footstep and felt better as the distance between himself and Cynthia widened. Scanning the wooden plank benches, he searched for Millie's red parka.

She wasn't hard to find—she was in the back row, lacing her skates. All he could see was the fat knot of the yarn ball on top of her red hat. Something in him came alive, and he realized suddenly that he was no longer dating Millie because it buffered him from Cynthia or any other woman. He liked her for who she was—and those feelings were growing stronger. His step quickened. Despite Cynthia's warning, he felt strongly that being with Millie was a good thing, that he had not so much turned away from his faith as he had trusted it.

"Hey," he said and slid onto the bench next to her.

She looked up and smiled. "Hey, you survived the whole one-on-one with Cynthia."

"You had doubts?"

"Only a few," she said.

Chapter 22

Is there any more duct tape?" Eva asked from her spot at the hull of the box sled. "I'm still not satisfied with the strength of the hull. Racing can get ugly. People will ram you on purpose, Bart."

They were inside David's garage working on the sled, just as they'd done every night that week.

Millie handed her mother a thick roll of the silver tape then returned to outlining the winged french fries on the side of the sled. Next to her, David was cutting out a crinkle-cut piece of cardboard, which would serve as a rudder. Finishing the final cut, he held it up for Eva's inspection.

"Perfect," she declared. "But we'll want it double strength, so cut two. When you're finished, we'll wrap the pieces together with more duct tape."

"Maybe we should test to see if it'll fit in the hole first," Bart suggested.

He took the rudder from his father's hands. Crawling into the sled, he threaded it through a narrow slit in the cardboard right above where his head would be. "Cool," he said. "How does it look?"

"Perfect," David said. "Try moving it back and forth."

Bart managed to steer the rudder a few inches both ways.

"Now it looks like the sled is wagging its tail," Millie said. "It's a happy sled."

Bart sat up and peered over the edge of the cardboard. "It looks like poop," he said. "Like the sled is pooping a lightning bolt."

"Bart," David said sternly. "Please don't say things like that in public."

Millie giggled, earning her an equally stern look from David.

"I can't help it," Bart said. "And you know you're thinking the same thing."

"It'll look much better when it's painted," Eva promised. "You'll see."

They worked awhile longer, the topics ranging from Eva's advice on how to get the sled to slide faster to Bart's story about the sixth-grade teacher, Mrs. Mills, who had decided someone in class had stinky feet. "She made everyone take off his shoes, and then she smelled them one by one until she found the guy."

"Who was it?" David asked.

"Me," Bart admitted. He let everyone laugh for a moment, and then he said, "I'm only kidding. It was this kid, Roger Blanit."

Millie grinned at Bart. She liked his dry sense of humor and the ease with which he spoke to adults. He wasn't a bit shy, and she supposed part of it was because Bart was an only child. She wondered if, like her, being an only child was making him grow up a lot faster. Millie had only been a little older than Bart was now when Eva started turning to her to unburden herself. Millie remembered feeling extremely adultlike and proud during those discussions.

She also recalled the weight she'd carried. Millie had been her mom's friend, coworker, and at times, even a parent. This had been particularly true in the early stages of Eva's diabetes.

It would be different for Bart though. David was a very different sort of parent than her mother had been. Eva never would have let Millie handle this bully situation by herself. She would have assumed total control.

David's way was better. He was concerned but not hovering. Involved but willing to step back and let Bart help build the sled. David's confidence in Bart would give Bart confidence in himself.

"So, what do you say, Millie? You up for it?"

She jerked a little and studied Eva's face for clues. "Huh?"

"We're finished, and there's still a little time before dinner. The moon's out. And it's a perfect night for it."

Perfect night for what? Millie didn't want to admit she'd been in her own world, dwelling on Eva's shortcomings as a parent. "Do you want to?"

"Of course," Eva said.

"Then yes," Millie agreed.

"Super," her mother said.

Bart cheered, and even David looked pleased. "Let's get our coats on."

"Why?" Millie asked, wondering just how much of the conversation she'd missed and what she'd just agreed to do.

"We're going sledding," her mother answered. "We're going to help Bart practice racing."

The snow crunched under Millie's boots as David led them into the backyard. The temperature had dropped, and the air felt cold and wet against her skin. Her eyes teared as a gust of wind lifted a veil of snow from the ground and whipped it through the air.

Millie wiped her eyes with the edge of her mitten. She felt the deep quiet of the country settling into her bones. Lights twinkled from distant houses. As a child, she remembered walking past houses like these and straining for a glimpse of the families inside. Once she'd seen a father and daughter sitting at a kitchen table. They were bent over a book, and it was obvious he was helping with the girl's homework. Millie had stood for an hour watching them, longing to be that girl.

Beside her, David marched along, dragging the sled behind him. "My parents gave us the sleds for Christmas, but this is the first time I've gotten to try mine out."

"That's because you always say you're too tired, or you have to work, or the snow's too deep to be any good," Bart complained over his shoulder. He was walking next to Eva, who was dragging an aluminum saucer.

"Or you have to do your homework," David added unsympathetically. "Which you still have to do later."

Bart groaned.

"It's okay," Eva assured him. "We'll have plenty of time to get in some runs." She began walking more quickly, and they soon reached a fairly steep slope flanked by thick groves of ponderosa pines. The moonlight illuminated a sparkling blue-white hillside, unbroken except for the places where three large hardwoods had clawed through the surface and a scattering of prickly, waist-high bushes.

"You doing okay, Mom?"

"Just great." A touch of defiance edged into her mother's voice.

"When the *Flying French Fry* is done, we can test run it here," Bart suggested.

"No test runs," her mom stated. "It'll only weaken the structure. You build the sled the best you can, and then you have to have faith that it will be the fastest thing on the hill."

"Slow down, Mom," Millie warned. Her mother was noticeably huffing and puffing. "*You* don't have to be the fastest thing on the hill."

Her mother kept up the brisk pace. Despite her bulk, she climbed gracefully, her movements fluid and strong. Watching, Millie glimpsed a much younger, much more athletic Eva—an Eva that she'd seen in photographs but could not remember.

Moments later they all stood on the crest, breathing the thin, cold air and staring down at the climb they'd just made.

"Okay, Bart, I'm going to make a track now." Her mother placed the flying saucer at the lip of the hill and lowered her bulk into it. The snow crunched as the saucer sank into the snow. "Push," she ordered as the sled stalled.

It took Bart, Millie, and David's combined efforts to get the saucer started. However, once over the edge, the saucer began to slide. It immediately spun around so that Eva was facing backward as she slid down the hill. She began to laugh and shout. "Yell if I'm aiming for a tree!"

They watched her progress. It was slow but steady, and when she reached the bottom, Eva yelled triumphantly up at them. Bart sank to his knees and jumped headfirst onto his sled. Whooping, he pushed off and sailed down the hill. Millie watched him glide straight down, his knees bent toward his back to keep his feet from dragging. The Flexible Flyer moved much faster than her mother's flying saucer, and it wasn't long before he reached the bottom. They watched him jump off the sled and pump a triumphant fist in the air.

Millie gazed at the remaining sled then at David. "You go first. I'll go next time."

"That's silly," David said. "There's room for both of us."

Millie worried her bottom lip. Sled with David? That would mean being close to him, physically holding on to him—actually touching him. She felt her heart jump a little.

"You want the front or the back?" David asked.

It was easier to climb onto the sled than explain why she didn't want to ride with him. Sitting on the wooden slats, she wiggled forward as far as she could and put her feet on the steering bars. David climbed on behind her, and immediately the sled shrank. He moved closer and settled his boots on the outside edges of the steering bar next to hers. His chest pressed hard and solid against her back.

"You ready?"

"Yeah." His arms wrapped around her waist, fitting her against him. She wondered if he could feel the way her heart was pounding. Her head was almost level with his, and she knew if she turned they would be face-to-face. She wouldn't let herself do that, but the possibility of what might happen if she did seemed to crackle in the air between them. Her heart began to pound, and she was breathing faster.

David briefly released her to push with his hands. Their combined weight made the blades stick in the snow, and they had to rock the sled with their bodies to gain the necessary momentum to move forward. Finally, they managed to hop the sled to the lip. They paused. She didn't know why.

Far below, she could see her mother and Bart waiting for them at the bottom. They were small shapes, currently engaging in a snowball fight. Her mother ran behind a tree in an effort to avoid Bart's dead-on aim.

"Millie," he said, and his voice rumbled soft and low-pitched in her ear. "You smell really, really good."

"I baked chocolate muffins this morning," she said. Her voice sounded unfamiliar. She couldn't seem to help herself from leaning a little harder into him.

Start the darn sled, she turned to say, but his face was even closer than she thought. The words were lost as her mouth brushed the cold roughness of his cheek. He jolted briefly as if her touch had stung him, but then his lips lowered, grazing the corner of her mouth. She shifted a little, and on the next brush he found her lips.

Her hands seemed to rise of their own accord to wrap themselves around his neck. His lips moved lightly, unhurried, asking, making her heart beat faster. Her eyes closed. He was going so slowly, agonizingly slowly, and every pass was loosening something tightly wound inside her. Couldn't he feel the ache in her? Didn't he know each second the need got worse and worse?

He pulled her closer and finally deepened the kiss. She nearly groaned with relief and pushed herself more tightly against him. She was falling, tumbling through a dark tunnel, and she couldn't stop herself. But as long as she was holding on to him, it was okay. More than okay—it was as if she was coming alive in a way she never had before. All her senses sharpened, but she wasn't just Millie anymore.

Gripping him more tightly, she kissed him until she was lost to herself and there was only him and the growing realization that she'd been incredibly stupid. She'd thought she'd known what it was like to be kissed, how it felt to lose herself without losing her head, and how to walk away before things got out of hand. But kissing David, Millie understood how wrong she'd been. All these years, and it turned out she knew nothing at all.

Chapter 23

The next morning, Millie gave Mrs. Ellison caffeinated tea by accident then felt guilty when the librarian's hands shook so hard she dropped the change when Millie rang her up on the register. Millie also forgot to add the Tabasco sauce to Jeff Gulden's scrambled eggs and plunked down a jelly donut instead of a Bavarian cream in front of Lou Pinella's plate.

She mistotaled Chief Glugan's bill then snapped when Lillian accused her of daydreaming about David. By ten o'clock she had to flee to the ladies' room to avoid the speculation on the cause of her mental state. Staring into the mirror above the sink, Millie tried to make sense of the woman who gazed back at her—the one who couldn't stop thinking about David. The one who'd made a total fool of herself last night, practically whimpering in his arms for him to kiss her.

Do you really want to let yourself fall for a dentist—a guy who fights tooth decay and gingivitis for a living? The woman in the mirror looked steadily back. *Yes,* the woman said. *I'd follow him anywhere— to the ends of the earth. I'd climb mountains and ford rivers. I'd trek across deserts. I'd sleep in a tent or go hungry. Because when he looks into my eyes, when he kisses me, when I think about him—he's all I want.*

But what if being with him meant going nowhere at all? Would you stay here, in Deer Park, to be with him?

I don't know, Millie thought and watched the light die in the eyes of her image.

When the pink roses arrived at noon, she read the card then stuffed it in the pocket of her apron. At least a dozen times she picked up the phone to call him then hung up before the call went through.

She was relieved when finally the last customer left for the day. She locked the front door and turned the OPEN sign to CLOSED. As her mother cleaned the grill, Millie put the chairs up and mopped the floor. Aunt Lillian, who was waiting for Eva to finish closing up, had climbed up on a stool to close out the cash register. The sound of the clanking coins jangled Millie's nerves.

"I'm going for a walk," she announced, jerking her parka off its hook.

"That's fine," Eva called back. "Don't forget we're meeting David at six. Lillian can drop me off after we get our hair done."

"Be careful. It's supposed to sleet later," Millie warned. Lillian was known for having a lead foot and liked to joke that her van not only had been modified to accommodate a driver in a wheelchair, but also that its engine had a couple of extra cylinders.

"We're fine. Have a nice walk," Eva said.

Millie grunted a reply and stepped out into the gray afternoon. Stuffing her hands into her pockets, she began walking. She had two hours to herself and needed to figure out what to say to David about the kiss. He would have expectations now. It was always best to deal with these things head-on.

She walked with her head down, not looking where she was going and not particularly caring. It was her thoughts she wanted to get away from.

The distances between the buildings became greater. She kept walking until she found herself in front of the Methodist church, and she realized this had been her destination the entire time.

She studied the white clapboard building with massive oval-shaped double doors and a tall steeple with a bell that still rang each Sunday morning. People who worshipped here probably didn't doubt God like she did. They probably didn't wonder why He helped some people and not others. Why some prayers were answered and others seemed to pass through Him like wind through the trees.

She wondered if inner beauty was something you were either born with or not. If the purity of a soul was decided before birth, like height, hair color, or the shape of a person's lips. If this enabled some people to have faith while others would have doubts.

She thought about the night her father had left—if he had crept into her bedroom and tucked the blankets more tightly around her or whispered that he loved her. Or if maybe he'd stared at her sleeping face and seen something exposed that wasn't visible during the day. If in the stripes of moonlight slanting between the blinds and across her face, he'd seen an ugliness to her features that reflected the imperfections of her soul.

Why did he leave me, God? Was I so unlovable?

She flinched, as if she'd touched the tip of an inner pain so hot and fierce and deep it burned all the way to her soul.

Do You love me, God?

Why should He? She hadn't been to church in years, never read the Bible, and openly challenged Him when she wasn't doubting that He existed at all.

David believed. She was sure of it.

Millie clasped her mittened hands and thought of David with equal parts of longing and fear. Their relationship had come to a turning point, and from the way he'd kissed her, she was pretty sure what he wanted. But what if she opened herself completely to him? What if he turned out to be like her father, and once he knew her—all her faults and all her weaknesses—he couldn't love her? She didn't think she could handle that. You couldn't keep breaking a heart and have any hope left at all. And without hope, without dreams, what was left?

Nothing.

She felt the cold penetrating the warmth of her coat and knew it was time to head back to the café. It'd grown darker, but the light was still more blue than black as she picked her way over the snow-glazed sidewalk. She heard a car on the road behind her, and when it didn't pass, she glanced back over her shoulder and groaned. Karl had a black Ford Ranger truck just like that one. She hunched her shoulders and walked faster. The last thing she wanted right now was to deal with her ex-boyfriend.

The truck pulled alongside her, and the tinted window on the driver's side slid open. "Want a ride?"

Sure enough, Karl sat in the driver's seat. A smile softened his craggy features.

"No thanks." She waved him off.

He paced her a little longer. She tried to ignore him, and in the process paid less attention to her footing. When her boots hit a patch of ice, she slipped and just barely managed to catch her balance. Karl immediately pulled to the curb and got out of the truck. "You okay?"

She crossed her arms tightly around herself. "Yes." He was standing right in front of her, and when she tried to walk around him, he blocked her path.

"Millie," he said gently. "Let me drive you home."

He was a large man, older than her by a few years. He'd always reminded her of a grizzly bear with his thick muscular body, jet-black hair, and large, strong features. The first time they'd kissed, he'd lifted her off the ground and held her suspended as if she weighed nothing at all. She'd felt the strength of his arms and known he'd protect her to his last breath. She remembered that now.

"No thanks." When he didn't move, she added, "Come on, Karl. It's freezing."

"We could go somewhere warmer," Karl suggested. Although he was dressed in nothing more than a thick red flannel shirt and a pair of jeans that looked barely able to contain his muscular legs, he didn't seem cold at all. She remembered looking into the lines fanning out from his eyes and thinking that he wore his age well. She liked that he was older. It made her feel young, girlish—safe. She craved the feel of his arms around her even as she recognized that she didn't love him in the same way he loved her.

"Or not," Millie said.

"You're being silly," Karl stated calmly. "Just because we broke up doesn't mean we can't be friends. Haven't you been getting my notes?"

"The parking tickets?" Millie lifted her chin. "I'm seeing David now."

He looked around and lifted his eyebrows innocently. "I don't see him now."

Millie crossed her arms. The crooked smile on his face was getting to her. It also told her that he still had feelings for her. That with one word they could go back to how it was before. "Shouldn't you be on patrol?"

"Got off at three. What do you say I buy you a steak over at the Blue Moose?"

"Thanks, but I have plans."

"I miss you, Millie. Do you know that? Things didn't work out the way I hoped they would, but I accept that. What bothers me, though, is that you avoid me like the plague."

"Not the plague," Millie replied. "More like chicken pox."

He laughed. "I happen to know you had chicken pox when you were four years old, same as me. I'm not contagious." His voice softened. "Let's have coffee."

She shifted her weight, weighing her answer carefully. She didn't want to lead him on, but part of her wanted to say yes. It was cold. Coffee sounded good, and being around him reminded her that he was a good man. Besides, she'd broken up with him, hurt him, and now that she knew what it was like to care about someone, she realized how hard it must be to stand here now and ask for something as small as coffee, to be reduced to asking for scraps of friendship.

She checked her watch. There was time for a quick cup. "I'd like that," Millie said. She stepped closer to him and held out her hand. "I've been an idiot," she said. "There's no reason we can't be friends."

"Friends," Karl echoed, shaking her hand. The lines in his face seemed deeper, his skin reddened as if scraped by the cold. "Now let's go get you warm."

"I'm due at David's at six."

"I'll have you there in plenty of time." He walked her to his truck and opened the door for her. Offering his arm, he settled her protectively into the interior of the truck. Cranking up the heat, he tuned the radio to a rock station that she liked. She felt herself relax into the leather seats. He kept the conversation light, mostly about mutual friends Hilly and Tom Mengalo who had just bought a new Expedition. The car was a gas hog, Karl said, but with five kids in the family, there wasn't much choice.

Kids had always been part of Karl's picture of the future. She could tell by his tone they still were. She'd been far less enthusiastic about the prospect of motherhood. *"Why have kids when I've got Eva?"* she had joked.

They reached a four-way stop at the same time a taupe-colored Taurus navigated the intersection from the other direction. It wasn't until the cars crossed in the middle of the street that Millie recognized Mrs. Denvers at the driver's wheel. For a split second their eyes met. Millie ducked, but it was too late. Her heart sank at what David's mother must be thinking. For a moment, she thought of asking Karl to turn around or stop the car, but she didn't. The moment flashed past, and the ability to change anything slipped past her.

I'm only having coffee with him, she reminded herself and kept her mouth firmly shut and her eyes on the black strip of road in front of her.

David swung the door open and looked down into the warm brown eyes of Eva Hogan. All afternoon he'd been watching the clock, looking forward to seeing Millie. He wondered if she liked the flowers, if she'd been thinking about their kiss as obsessively as he had.

Eva Hogan stood on his doorstep. A puffy powder-blue coat the shape of a down comforter fell to her ankles. It made her seem almost as wide as she was tall, but when she smiled it was warm enough to take the sting out of the February night. The smile, he realized, was almost exactly like Millie's.

"Come on in," he urged, all the while peering over her shoulder at the empty driveway and wondering why there wasn't a battered-looking red Subaru parked in his driveway. "Where's Millie?"

"On her way," Eva said cheerfully. "Lillian dropped me off. Millie should be here any minute."

He pulled the door wider and motioned Eva inside. "Come on in. Did you get your hair done? It looks very nice."

"Oh." Eva preened, patting the tight white curls. "Thank you."

He took Eva's coat and asked if she wanted something to drink. As he walked to the closet, the down jacket felt bulky and too light in his arms. It wasn't cherry red with the fur trim, and it didn't have the faint smell of cinnamon. He shut the closet door with a deliberate click of the latch.

"Hey, Mrs. Hogan," Bart said, trotting down the steps. "I was surfing online last night and found this neat racing car blog that talks about calculating the slope of the car's hood in order to make it the most aerodynamic. We need to give our sled a 27.333 slope. We're at 34 degrees right now. We can glue another layer of cardboard in the back to raise it up."

"Hold on," Eva said, stepping forward and squeezing Bart's shoulder with affection. "Blog? What's a blog?"

"It's an online journal," Bart explained. "People set up a website where other people can read their journal."

"Why would anyone want other people to read their journal?" Eva's short white curls stayed firmly in place as she shook her head. "In my day, we kept diaries under lock and key and threatened to kill anyone who read them."

"Because it's fun," Bart replied. "You learn all sorts of cool stuff. Lots of kids my age blog." He paused to shoot David a significant look. "And they're all on Facebook. I've asked my dad, but of course my dad won't let me have my own page."

Eva patted his shoulder. "I don't know what those things are, but a blog sounds awfully close to *The Blob*, which was one of the scariest movies of the 1950s. It looked like a huge pile of sludge. It crept out of the darkness, slid across the floor, and ate people. I had to sleep with the closet light on for months."

"My dad and I watched *War of the Worlds* together," Bart offered. "The aliens were cool."

"Millie and I watched that, too. We had to hide under our blankets when the scary parts happened."

"You hide under blankets?" Bart asked with equal parts of skepticism and glee in his voice.

"Yes. We pull them over our heads so we can't see," Eva confirmed. "Then we argue about who has to look first to see if it's safe to come out. Usually I win."

David swallowed laughter. He would love to see that. Although he and Bart didn't watch scary movies often, when they did, they were of the man school, which meant that neither admitted to being scared. Other than an occasional involuntary grunt or flinch, both he and Bart made their way through scary movies with their lips tightly sealed and their hands securely wrapped around the respective arms of their chairs.

The stairs creaked under his feet as David led the way into the garage. He flipped a switch, and the room burst into light. The *Flying French Fry* lay on a tarp, its cardboard body looking more than ever like a baked potato wrapped in duct tape.

"It looks fantastic," Eva exclaimed. "Once Millie paints those french fries and stencils the name, it's really going to be a beauty." She tested the hood with her hand.

"What about the slope?" Bart's eyes were sparkling and focused behind his wire-rimmed glasses. "Are we going to bring it up to code?"

"Oh right," Eva said thoughtfully. "What were you saying about the extra cardboard?"

They settled into an easy work rhythm. Eva called out the orders, and David and Bart executed them like well-trained soldiers. Eva and Bart bantered back and forth, both seeming to enjoy the wide generation gap that lay between them. Bart had a good relationship with David's parents, but there was a certain stiffness, a formality that was absent with Eva. She had an unfiltered way of speaking that was relaxing. You never had to wonder what she was thinking about.

David stepped aside to give Eva and Bart more space. Standing beside the frost-etched side windows, he gazed out at the night. Where was Millie? He tried not to worry. The garage door rattled, and a whisper of cold air blew along the concrete.

He wondered if the kiss more than any errand or work at the café explained Millie's absence. He hadn't meant for it to happen, but she'd been scrunched up against him on that sled. His arms had been full of her soft curves, and when she'd turned her head, it'd just happened.

He hadn't kissed anyone since Lisa, but recently he'd been thinking a lot about it. About Millie, he amended. What it would be like. *Was it just me being lonely or ready, or was it something more?* He'd prayed about this, and again, having a relationship with Millie felt right. At the same time, he realized that faith-wise they were in different places. He really wasn't sure what she believed, and she wouldn't talk about it either. While he'd gotten angry at Cynthia and his mother for judging Millie, what if Millie never wanted to explore or deepen her faith? He couldn't see a future for them if this was the case. He needed to talk to her about it tonight if possible. He checked his watch.

It was nearly seven o'clock—an hour past when Millie was due to arrive. He glanced at Eva. "I think we should try calling her."

Eva nodded and rose heavily to her feet. She retrieved her cell from her purse and after squinting at the receiver, punched in some numbers. A moment later, the lines in her face deepened, and her lips tightened. She left a message then hung up.

When they still hadn't heard from Millie by seven thirty, David offered to drive around and look for her. "Make sure she didn't have a flat tire on the way."

"I'm sure she's fine," Eva said. "Maybe there was a problem with the meat delivery and she drove over to pick it up herself. Although why she can't pick up the phone is beyond me."

"Maybe she's in a noncell zone," Bart suggested. "We should go look for her, Dad."

David nodded. They left the supplies on the garage floor, turned off the space heater, and put on their coats.

It was a cold night, probably in the teens, but clear. Only a few flurries spotted the windshield as David wound his way through their neighborhood and onto Route 7. It was the way Millie would have come if she'd headed from town, and he was relieved to see there were no accidents on the side of the road. Eva sat in the front seat next to him, uncharacteristically quiet. He could feel tension radiating off her and tried to put her at ease by turning on the radio to the Christian rock station he preferred. "Maybe she went home and took a nap and is still sleeping."

"And maybe she got kidnapped by aliens," Eva snapped then sighed. "I'm sorry, David. I know you're trying to help."

They backtracked to Dosie Dough's. They saw Millie's Subaru parked in front, but she wasn't inside. "She's got to be somewhere close," David said. But where? Most of the stores around the town center had closed. All he could think of was the movie theater, the

CVS, and the grocery store. He glanced at Eva. "Let's ask around."

To his surprise, however, Eva shook her head. "She said she was going for a walk. I'm sure she just ran into an old friend and lost track of time."

It still didn't explain why she hadn't called. He found himself picturing car accidents, kidnappers, and muggers, although he knew none of these were likely. Wherever she'd gone, she'd gone on foot. "Maybe we should call the police."

"No," Eva said sharply. "I want to go home and phone a few of her friends. If you don't mind, David, I think you and Bart should go back to your place in case she shows up there. Whoever sees her first will call the other."

"You're all right being alone?"

"Oh yeah. It's Millie you need to be worrying about. When she comes home, I'm going to kill her for scaring us like this."

David gave one last peek into the dark interior of the car. "Call me," he said. "No matter how late it is, I'll be up."

Chapter 24

The lights were blazing in the house when Millie pulled into the driveway around ten o'clock. She hurried up the porch steps, but before she could stick her key in the lock, the door swung open. Eva stood in the doorway as if she'd been watching out the window for her to come home. Millie felt a flush of irritation. She wasn't a teenager breaking curfew.

"Mom," she said, unbuttoning her coat. "You didn't have to wait up for me."

Her mother folded her arms and glared at her. "Just where have you been? I've been worried sick all evening."

"Didn't you get my message?"

"What message? I've been calling you every hour on your cell."

Millie hung her coat on the rack. For the first time she noticed the haggard cast to her mother's complexion and the fatigue and worry in her brown eyes. "You didn't get a message from Karl Kauffman?"

"Why would I have gotten a message from Karl Kauffman when I was calling you?" Her mother's brows pushed together. "What's going on?"

"I ran into Karl, and we went out for coffee. We were having a good time, and time sort of got away from us. I tried to call, but my cell died." Millie kicked off her boots. "Karl left you a message. I heard him do it."

"I never got any message," her mother stated firmly. "And I checked my phone a hundred times. I even had David check in case I was doing it wrong." She planted her hands on her hips and stared at Millie unhappily. "Do you know how scared we were when you didn't show up at David's house? Do you know where we've been? Backtracking. Making sure you hadn't driven into a ditch."

Millie shook her head. There had to be some mistake. She'd seen Karl dial the phone, talk into it, and leave his phone number. It occurred to her then that he'd been pretending, purposely dialing the wrong number. "I'm sorry you were worried. I really thought Karl called you."

Her mother looked even more upset. "What in the world were you doing going out with Karl?"

"He needed to talk to me, Mom. I felt like I owed him." She had a quick flash of Karl's craggy face softened in the dim lights of the bar. "You don't look happy," he said. "Let's see what we can do to fix that." She hadn't protested when he'd drawn her onto the dance floor.

"I'm sure he wanted to *talk*." Her mother snorted in disgust. "All this time we've been worrying, and you were out gallivanting with Karl Kauffman?"

"Coffee, Mom," Millie said tightly. She bit her lip to keep herself from telling Eva to back off. It wasn't any of her mother's business whom she saw or what she did. Yet here she was, having to justify her actions.

Her mother shook her head and walked back toward the kitchen. "I've got to call David and let him know you're safe. He was worried, Millie. We all were. I don't know what was so important that you had to stay out until ten o'clock."

Millie stiffened. Another rush of anger burned through her. "Oh for Pete's sake, Mom, Letterman isn't even on yet."

"The point is that you stood up David and Bart. I thought I raised you better than that." She picked up the cordless phone, grimaced, and then cocked her arm as if she might hurl the receiver against the wall. "Why is it that every time something good starts to happen in your life, Millie, you sabotage it?" She lowered her arm and tried to punch numbers, but her hand was shaking, and she slammed the phone back into the cradle. "I can't stand it, Millie," she said passionately. "I just can't stand it."

"Stand what?" Millie snapped. "I had coffee with an old friend who wanted to talk. What's the big deal?"

But it was a big deal, and she knew it. She could give herself a hundred reasons for what she'd done, and it wouldn't change the basic fact that she'd messed up. She knew it. She didn't need her mother throwing it in her face.

Her mother pointed her finger at her. "David is the best thing that's happened to you in a long time. You're a fool if you let him go."

"Stop pointing at me." Millie dug her fingernails into the palm of her hands as she remembered the strength of Karl's arms holding her as they danced. She'd flirted with him, gave him her best smile, laughed at his jokes. For a couple of hours, she'd hid herself in the safety of Karl's arms. With Karl she didn't have to think too much or talk too much or feel too much. He never saw past the Millie she gave him.

"You call that man right now and apologize."

She had intended to do just that but wasn't about to admit it to her mother. "Have you checked your blood sugar lately?" It was a comment on her mother's behavior more than her health, and they both knew it.

Her mother's face turned dark red, and her arm sliced the air. "My blood sugar has nothing to do with what's going on. And I've had it up to here with you asking that." Her gesture accidentally knocked over a glass of water, which crashed to the ground and shattered into pieces. Millie started to clean up but then stopped. She was sick of cleaning up her mother's messes. She turned to leave, but Eva grabbed her arm.

"I married a man who spent his life looking out the window and wishing he were somewhere else. Nothing made him happy. All he could think about was what he was missing in a place that probably only existed in his imagination." Her chin quivered, but her gaze was steady on Millie. "I see the same look in your eyes, and it scares me to death. Be honest, Millie. You're planning to break up with David, aren't you?"

"If we're being honest," Millie snapped, "then maybe you should admit why you really want me to settle down in Deer Park with David. It's for your sake, not mine."

Her mother's head jerked as if Millie had struck her. "How can you say that? How *dare* you say that?"

There were tears in her mother's eyes, but Millie was too angry to back down. All the hurt and resentment had been bottled up for too long. "I say it because it's true." Her voice rose. "Tell me you've never used your health as a way to get me to stay in Deer Park."

"I most certainly did not," Eva shouted. "You're the one always harping on the diabetes. It's *my* health. *My* decision. I've never wanted to put that on you."

"But you have," Millie snapped. "You do. If I don't bug you about checking your levels or taking your medicine, you forget."

"So what? That's *my* business."

"And I'm what? Supposed to step over your unconscious body on my way to the car?" Millie heard her voice get shrill but couldn't seem to help herself. "You think I can just stand there and watch you kill yourself?"

A range of emotions washed across her mother's face—anger, fear, then simple resignation. In just those few short sentences, she seemed to shrink before Millie's eyes, aging almost visibly.

"Maybe I've been selfish," she admitted at last, "wanting you settled here in Deer Park. But what I've done for you, Millie, has always been done out of love. Your grandmother raised me by herself, and I've raised you by myself. Two generations of single parenting is enough. I want better for you."

Millie had heard this statement more times than she could count. "Mom," she said sharply. "Don't."

"Children are your guarantee." Her mother stared into Millie's eyes. "I haven't needed a man," she continued, "because I've had you. But when I die, what will you have, Millie?"

Normally Millie would have told her that she wasn't going to die for a very long time, and then she would have hugged her. Tonight the words coming out of her mother's mouth sounded like fingernails on a chalkboard. Her nerves jangled—they had since the moment when she'd realized she wasn't with Karl for his sake, but her own—to make her forget about David. But no matter how hard Karl made her laugh or how tightly he held her when they danced, it was David's voice she wanted to hear. David's arms she wanted to feel around her. She kicked a broken piece of glass and watched it skate across the linoleum.

"What am I supposed to say, Mom? That I'll live my life the way you want so you can die happy? I can't do that."

"No, you ninny." Her mother's voice rose in frustration. "You're supposed to *learn* from my mistakes. You're supposed to do *better* than I have." She scowled fiercely. "You're not supposed to throw your life away."

Millie felt a rush of hurt. She had dreams, but her mother dismissed them, just as she dismissed the idea that Millie had any talent other than waitressing. "Maybe someday I'll have an amazing career. You'll turn on the television to the Food Network and there I'll be on my own show—*Millie's Magnificent Meals* or *Marvelous Menus with Millie Hogan.*"

Her mother rolled her eyes toward the ceiling. "If you really believe that, then God help you," she said. "Because I can't."

For once, would it kill Eva to see things as Millie did? Would it be so hard just to say, "You'd be fantastic on a cooking show, Millie." Instead, her mother looked at her as if she pitied Millie for wanting something so far beyond her reach. Millie's heart pounded, but she couldn't tell if it was from rage or hurt. It didn't matter.

"You think I'm wasting my life dreaming about something that isn't going to happen. What about you?" Millie felt herself growing taller and taller until she seemed to tower over her mother. "Do you honestly think Dad is going to come back?"

Eva drew in a short, quick breath as if the mention of Millie's father had cut her to the bone. For a moment she just looked at Millie, and then she widened her stance and placed her hands on her hips. "I wouldn't take him back if he came crawling on his hands and knees." Her chin trembled, and she paused to steady herself. "The day he comes back is the day I take a skillet to his head."

Millie hadn't come this far to back down. "You've never dated since he left. You haven't changed anything in the house—if something breaks, you replace it with something that looks exactly like the one you had." She couldn't seem to stop herself. "And you overeat because you miss him."

"That is just hogwash." Her mother was breathing heavily, and her cheeks were flushed. "I eat because food tastes good, and I'm not going to let diabetes or anything else steal that joy from me." She pointed her finger at Millie. "I've made a good life for us here, and if you weren't so incredibly dense, you would see that. You wouldn't be so quick to throw it all away." She strode purposefully past Millie. "I'm going to bed." She glanced over her shoulder. "You call David. Tell him whatever you like, but remember there's a child inv—" The rest of her sentence was lost as her foot slipped in the puddle of water on the tile floor.

Millie jumped forward but couldn't catch her mother, who fell to the floor with a small cry and sickening thump. Kneeling, she leaned over her. "Mom!"

Her mother lay on her side, moaning.

"Mom!" Millie bent over her frantically, checking for injury. "Where does it hurt?"

Her mother moaned even louder, the deep guttural sounds coming faster and louder.

Dear, God, Millie thought, fighting panic. *She's broken something.* "Hold still, Mom. Everything'll be okay."

She didn't remember rising from the floor, but then the phone was in her hand. With hands that trembled so badly she could barely hold the receiver, she dialed 911.

Chapter 25

At ten o'clock there still was no word about Millie. David stopped pacing and paused in front of the kitchen window. Through the pitch darkness, he could make out the towering shapes of the trees and the lights of a neighbor's house. He didn't like waiting, and he didn't like feeling helpless. Ironically, it was precisely the combination of these two elements that reminded him there were a lot of things he couldn't control. He closed his eyes and prayed.

"Dad?"

David turned around. Bart was standing a few feet from him, and somehow he looked younger and more vulnerable as if each hour of the night had stripped a year from his son's face. "Hey, buddy. You finish your homework?" As if either of them cared.

"Yeah. It was stupid." He paused. "You hear anything?"

"No." Almost involuntarily David glanced at the telephone and resisted the urge to pick up the receiver, if only to hear the dial tone. "You should probably start getting ready for bed."

"I'm not tired," Bart stated.

"It's a school night," David reminded him.

"I want to stay up. I want to wait with you—make sure she's okay."

"You don't have to do that," David said. "I'm sure Millie's fine."

"What if something bad happened to her? Maybe someone kidnapped her."

David crossed the space between them to tousle Bart's hair. "Nobody in the history of Deer Park has ever gotten kidnapped. More likely she ran into an old friend and lost track of time."

Bart shook his head. "I don't think so. And I don't think you do either." He met David's gaze firmly, and suddenly Bart didn't seem so much like a little kid. "I'm not going to bed."

David considered enforcing his parental authority then realized he wasn't up for an argument. "Eleven, but no later."

Bart glanced at the clock and then nodded.

"How about some coffee for me and some hot chocolate for you?"

Bart shrugged. Although David felt the same ambivalence, it was an action. Neither of them spoke as David turned on the kettle, set out two mugs, and emptied cocoa mix into one and instant coffee into the other. There was something comforting about the presence of his son, and David found himself grateful that Bart had wanted to wait with him.

"Dad?"

He looked up from pouring the hot water.

"I know you weren't the person who spied on me."

"What?"

"Aris broke into my computer, not you."

David set the mug of hot chocolate in front of his son. "What makes you say that?" He poured himself a cup of coffee and anticipated Bart's response with a small amount of smugness—*because you trust me completely*.

Bart scooped a teaspoon full of marshmallows off the top of the hot chocolate. "Because Aris asked to borrow my cell, and I caught her checking my messages. I started thinking about how she's home more than you, and then it all made sense."

David groaned. "I'll talk to her again about snooping. I'm sorry, Bart. I know she loves you and is trying to help."

"I know." He stared into his hot cocoa. "I'm sorry I blamed you."

"It's okay." David wished his son would look at him. "You know you can tell me anything, right?"

"Yeah," Bart agreed, but his voice lacked conviction.

"I'm serious. You could have told me about the bullying. I would have listened."

Bart chased the melting marshmallows around the surface of the hot chocolate. "You were really sad in California, Dad, and then we came here and that woman started stalking you, and you got even more unhappy. You said if you had to handle one more problem you'd lose your mind."

David couldn't remember saying that, but it did sound a little like him. "I didn't mean it."

"And then you met Miss Hogan, and you started getting happy again."

David frowned. "What are you talking about?"

"You laugh more now."

"I do?"

"And you're funnier."

"I am?"

"Except for tonight," Bart pointed out. His gaze cut to the telephone. "Maybe you should call Mrs. Hogan and see if she's heard from her."

"In a minute," David agreed, registering that the leap from his improved parenting skills to the whereabouts of Millie had been a short one. "You like Miss Hogan, don't you?" What he was asking but couldn't bring himself to voice outright was whether it hurt

Bart to see him with another woman. If it was okay for his dad to like someone—to be with someone other than Lisa. He wanted permission, and yet he didn't want the giving of it to be another weight for his son to carry. He sipped his coffee with a casualness he didn't feel.

"She's funny," Bart said. "So is her mom. I like it when they pretend to argue."

"So you like Millie, I mean, Miss Hogan." He was pressing but couldn't seem to help himself. His gaze dropped to the contents of his mug in case the answer he wanted was obvious in his eyes. It occurred to him that now might be a good time to talk about dating relationships. How fragile they could be. How it didn't always work out. He realized, though, that he would be saying this for his own benefit, not Bart's.

He looked up. Bart shrugged. "She's cool," he said.

Cool was good. Maybe cool wasn't the answer he'd hoped for, but it was a good start. He drew a breath then folded his hands around the warm curve of his mug. Across from him, Bart copied his pose right down to the slight hunch of his shoulders. When their gazes met, David was surprised by the quiet strength reflected in his son's blue eyes. Despite his worry over Millie, he felt tremendous pride. He saw himself getting old and Bart gaining everything that David would lose as he aged. It was almost as if they each stood on one side of a scale that would always balance. He thought how God made the world like that and how right it was.

And then the telephone rang.

When David walked into Eva's hospital room, Millie nearly cried aloud in relief. His eyes locked onto hers, and she felt something inside crumble. She walked straight into his arms. All the tears she'd been struggling to hold back began to slide down her cheeks.

From the bed, her mother said, "Oh for heaven's sake. I'm not dead, you know. Where's the chocolate?"

David chuckled, and his arms remained tightly around Millie. "I'm a brave man, Eva, but not so brave that I'd bring you candy while Millie was around."

"Darn right," Millie confirmed, surreptitiously wiping her eyes before she let her mother see her face. "He'd end up in the bed next to yours, and you'd have matching broken bones."

Releasing Millie, David walked over to her mom's bed and kissed her cheek. "You don't look too bad, Eva," David commented, "for a woman with a broken hip."

"Thanks."

"What'd the doctor say?" David asked.

"Which one?" Eva shifted then grimaced. "Had a whole parade of them come through. Looked at me as if I were already lying on the autopsy table."

It wasn't true. While there had been visits from the attending doctor, the radiologist, and the anesthesiologist, all of them had been kind and respectful. Her mom was simply performing again, trying to make the whole situation seem funny so David would forget the reason that her mother was there in the first place.

"They need to screw her hip together," Millie explained. "She's scheduled for surgery at 8:00 a.m. tomorrow morning."

"Is it Dr. Irwin?" David asked. When Millie nodded, he added, "I've heard really good things about him. He'll fix you up, Eva."

"I'm more worried about Millie." Her voice was losing its normal vitality, and she seemed to gather herself with effort. "Would you please take her home? She looks like someone dug her out of the ground and propped her up."

"Thank you for that flattering observation," Millie said, "but I'm staying here tonight."

"Stubborn as a mule," her mother said, but her voice was hardly more than a mumble. "David, please make her go home."

"Just stop talking and rest." Millie locked eyes with her mom. She saw the deep weariness and the pain barely masked by the painkillers.

"How about a quick cup of coffee?" David asked Millie then turned back to Eva. "Why don't you rest for a moment? I'll take care of Millie."

Millie started to protest then saw the relief in her mother's eyes. She realized that if left alone, Eva would stop performing for everyone. She might even sleep a little while.

As they wound their way through the maze of corridors, Millie thanked David for coming. "I know it's late," she said.

"I know, but I wanted to make sure you both were okay."

They weren't—although Millie said they were. She was lost. Not only in the physical maze of the buildings, but also in the flow chart of decisions about her mother's care. Her mother had deferred almost every decision to her. All Eva wanted, she'd said, was to go home. "Too bad I didn't break a leg," she'd muttered when the X-ray results returned. "They could just cut it off then." The radiologist had laughed politely, but Millie had felt a crushing weight of guilt and worry settle over her shoulders as she directed her mother to sign one form after another.

In the cafeteria, as Millie was sipping hot coffee that tasted as if it'd been made out of ash, it occurred to her that it was after eleven and David had arrived alone. "Where's Bart?"

"Home with Aris. He wanted to come, but we figured they wouldn't let him upstairs. I got in with my medical credentials. But he'll be worried. I need to call him pretty soon." His voice softened. "What happened?"

Millie peeled an edge of the Styrofoam coffee cup. The memory of the accident was so fresh she couldn't speak for a moment, and she focused on ripping the cup until the liquid threatened to spill. Even then it felt like her throat was in a vise. "My mother and I were arguing, and she knocked over a glass of water. Both of us were too busy being mad at each other to clean it up. I said some things I'm not proud of, and then my mother started to storm out of the room and slipped on the wet floor." Millie's throat closed up. She'd never forget the sickening thud her mother made as she hit the tile floor. "It was totally my fault."

"It was an accident, and thankfully a broken hip can be fixed."

"I hope so." She continued peeling the Styrofoam and could not look directly at him. He didn't ask what they'd been fighting about or where she'd been earlier in the evening, and she was grateful for that. She owed him explanations for both, but she couldn't bring herself to tell him—not now. If she had to handle one more thing, she'd break into a million pieces, just like that glass that had shattered on the kitchen floor. *Later,* she promised herself. *Later.*

David covered her hand to stop her from mutilating the cup. "This is a good hospital, and they're going to give her the best care possible. There is one thing we can do for her though."

Millie looked up. "There is?"

"We can pray for her."

"Right now? Here?" Millie didn't like the sudden panic that shot through her. "I wouldn't begin to know what to say."

"That's okay. I'll do it for us."

Millie looked around uncomfortably as David reached for her hands. The cafeteria was pretty empty, but the lady at the cash register was in direct view—and so was that older man and what had to be his son and those doctors seated at nearby tables. She tried to tell herself that nobody would think anything of two people sipping coffee and praying, but she couldn't get her mother's warning out of her head. *"Be careful of people who lift their hands to the sky in public and every other word out of their mouth is 'Praise God this. Praise God that,' "* Eva had said. *"They hide behind religion, Millie. They hide their true ugliness and say and do horrible things. Trust me, Millie, I learned this the hard way."*

She felt the warmth of David's hands penetrating her icy fingers and wondered if he could feel her fear.

"Heavenly Father," David began, "we thank You for the doctors and nurses and all the people tonight who helped Eva Hogan. We ask that You lay Your healing hand on her and see her safely through her surgery and recovery. Please, Father, restore her to full health and let her know that You heal her through Your love and Your desire for her to know that love."

For a moment, Millie felt a small light struggling to penetrate the guilt and worry that clouded her thoughts and actions. As David continued to pray, she found herself leaning forward, absorbing every word, and feeling a small amount of comfort spread through her. Even as she held tightly to his hands, something inside whispered to keep up her guard. A long time ago she and her family had regularly attended church. She had been told that God loved her, that He would always be there for her.

But He hadn't. Neither had her father. Both of them had long since moved on, and Millie was on her own.

David said, "Amen."

Millie looked at her mangled coffee cup. David would be moving on as well when he discovered that she'd stood him up to be with Karl Kauffman. What had she been thinking?

Just for a second she felt a stab of regret and the sense that she had let something precious slip through her fingers. She tried to tell herself that she always would have been David's second choice—he'd said very bluntly that no other woman would ever measure up to his wife. But it didn't help. She would give anything to rewind the clock.

She felt the tears pool, and before she could stop them, they overflowed. Instantly, David came around the side of the table and put his arms around her. "Shhh," he said into her hair. "She's going to be fine."

He didn't realize how selfish she was. Her tears were not only for her mother, but also for herself—for the part of herself that had deliberately messed up and the fear that she'd fail over and over again and never understand why.

"It's okay. Millie, it's okay," David whispered. He said her name like a caress, and she felt it moving through her, gently soothing the aching places. She firmly silenced the voice that wanted to tell him about Karl Kauffman and told herself that truth could wait without going bad, that omission was not the same as lying. She let herself hold on to him and tried to believe it when David whispered that they would get through this together.

Chapter 26

The surgeon operated on her mother at eight o'clock the next morning. For the longest forty-five minutes of her life, Millie sat in a waiting room watching CNN. No matter how she tried to reassure herself, she feared there would be complications to the surgery. Eva might never fully recover, and it would be all Millie's fault.

David sat quietly next to her. He'd picked her up at six that morning and had insisted on waiting with her through the surgery. She shot a sideways glance at him, more grateful for his presence than she knew how to say. "It's taking a long time," she said.

"She's going to be fine," he said for probably the tenth time that morning.

"How do you know?"

"Because I heard her tell the doctor that if he messed up, she'd come back and haunt him."

This was true, but it didn't help. She flipped through a dog-eared magazine and replayed the argument with her mother over and over in her mind. She had been wrong, so wrong to think that going out with Karl would help her feel in control of her life. Instead, more than ever, she felt helpless and vulnerable. She sensed strength from David but was reluctant to lean on him too much. She didn't think she deserved it.

It seemed an eternity before the door between the surgical and waiting area opened and Dr. Irwin stepped into the room. His thin aristocratic features gave away nothing. Suddenly he was standing in front of her, and Millie was on her feet.

"She did great," Dr. Irwin said and smiled. He pulled out an X-ray and pointed to some scary-looking screws implanted in a grainy white shape that was probably her mother's hip. "Do you have any questions?" he concluded.

"Will she set off the alarm when she goes through security at the airport?" It was a stupid, stupid question. It wasn't as if Eva traveled.

Dr. Irwin chuckled. "Possibly."

About an hour later a nurse brought Millie into the recovery room. Eva's body was covered to the chin, and an IV dripped into her arm. Millie cautiously touched her mother's shoulder. "Hey," she said when her mother blinked groggily up at her, "you did it."

Eva murmured something unintelligible. Around lunchtime, they wheeled her to a semiprivate room where she continued to sleep. It was a restless sleep interrupted by bouts of moaning and half sentences. "You have to return it," Eva insisted. "You can't keep it. It's not right!"

Millie caressed her mother's forehead. "It's okay," she said. "You're just dreaming. Everything is okay."

Her mother opened her eyes and looked very clearly into Millie's. "I'm so, so sorry," she said. "I didn't know, Sarah. I swear I didn't know."

Sarah? Who was her mother talking about? Millie leaned forward. "Mom," Millie said gently, "you're in the hospital, and the doctor just finished operating on you."

Her mother blinked. "It hurts, Sarah." She turned her head away. "I hate what he did."

Millie charged to the nurse's station. "My mother is in pain," she told the nurse, who checked Eva's chart and saw that it was time for more pain medication.

When Millie returned to the room, her mother was semiconscious, twisting her head from side to side, and softly groaning. Leaning over the bed rail, Millie curled her fingers around her mother's. "Shhh, shhhh," she said. "The nurse is coming."

Eva's eyes stayed shut. "Please don't tell anyone."

"Tell anyone what?"

"I'm so sorry. I'll make it up. I promise."

Millie wished the nurse would hurry. "Mom, it's okay," she said. "Everything is going to be fine." A few moments later the nurse walked into the room.

Later, as Eva slept, Millie wondered who her mother had been talking about and why Eva had been apologizing. The only person she could think of was Sarah, the reverend's wife, who rarely came into the café. If Eva spoke of her at all, it was to dismiss the idea of going to church. Obviously the pain medication had confused her mother, and most likely Eva had been talking about someone else. Millie picked up another magazine. She wondered what David was doing right now. She'd told him not to come back after he finished work, but she couldn't help wishing he would.

Hours passed as her mother slept, rousing only when a nurse or doctor came into the room. Dinner came, but Eva managed only a few sips of soup. When Millie finally left to go home, she kissed her mother's pale face. "I'm so sorry," she whispered. "I'm so sorry for what I said."

Eva struggled to open her eyes. She smiled a little then went back to sleep.

Millie stroked back her mom's mop of white bangs. "Night, Mom. I love you, and I'm going to be a better daughter. From now on, things are going to be different." She kissed Eva's forehead. "I promise."

When Millie returned to the hospital the next morning, her mother was awake and eating breakfast. Her hair lay matted, but there was more color in her face, and her eyes were bright and focused.

"The eggs taste like cardboard," Eva complained. "And I've already been seen by two vampires."

"So you're feeling better."

"I'm telling you, Millie, it's a miracle anyone survives a stay in the hospital. They won't let you sleep for more than two minutes—and they've taken enough of my blood to start their own bank."

Millie smiled. For the first time in two days she could breathe again. A complaining Eva was a healing Eva. She settled into the chair next to her mother's bed. "So you're feeling better."

"You should go," her mother said. "Who's running the café?"

"It's closed."

Eva frowned. "Go open it, or people will think I'm dying."

"Shhh, Mom," Millie said. "The café can stay closed another day."

"I don't need a babysitter."

"I know. I want to be here."

Her mother lapsed into silence. The morning passed in a blur of game shows and talk shows. Eva perked up whenever a doctor or nurse came into the room. Almost instantly she would transform

herself into a lively entertainer who knew how to make everyone—
even the sour-faced physical therapy assistant—laugh. As soon as
Eva and Millie were alone again, however, the twinkle in Eva's eye
faded and her eyes returned to the television set.

By the end of the day, it was clear that her mother was doing
well but would need a few more days in the hospital before she came
home. They couldn't afford to keep the café closed—and Eva made
it clear she didn't want Millie's company—so the next morning at
3:30 a.m. Millie headed for the café. It was earlier than she and her
mother usually arrived, but without Eva, she'd be shorthanded, and
Millie intended to do most of the extra work before Lottie arrived.

Flicking on the lights, she glanced around at the tables carrying
their load of chairs and the gleaming stainless-steel countertops. Her
gaze slid over the walls with the old black-and-white shots of stiff-
lipped pioneers, saloon scenes from Deadwood, and prospectors
panning for gold in the shallow streams of the Black Hills. As she
moved to the kitchen area, she could almost feel people in those
photographs watching her reproachfully. It was her fault Eva wasn't
there, they said, and Millie was a poor substitute.

She pulled a bread starter out of the refrigerator and set it on the
counter to breathe. Retrieving supplies from the pantry, she began
adding flour, salt, and sugar to the industrial-sized stainless steel
mixing bowl.

As the mixer whirled, she thought of the countless mornings
when Eva had driven her crazy with her early morning high spirits.
How Millie would stare into the mixing bowl and wish she were
in Hollywood studying a script in preparation for a morning
audition. How daily she wondered if she would always live in the
shadow of her mother's exuberant personality. She thought about
the long recovery ahead for Eva and worried about her ability to

nurse her mother back to health. The house had no downstairs bedrooms or bathrooms. It would be difficult to accommodate a wheelchair. The thought of bathing her mother, of seeing her naked, scared her.

At the same time, she loved her mom. She knew that now clearer than ever before. Lifting the hook from the dough, Millie resolved to do whatever she needed to take care of her mother.

Millie set the rye dough in greased pans for the first rise. There was still pumpernickel, sourdough, and the baguettes to make. She glanced at the clock, worrying about the time, and wished she'd come earlier.

She was shaping baguettes when there was a knock at the front door. Wiping her hands on her apron, she hurried to the front and peeked out the bay window. Beneath the spill of the porch lights, David and Bart stood in cold morning darkness, rubbing their hands and stamping their feet in the frosty air. Tank was on a leash and sniffing the doormat.

She felt a rush of pleasure as she flung open the door and motioned them inside. "What are you guys doing here? Come in before you freeze to death."

"We figured you could use some help." David unzipped his parka and hung it on the rack next to Millie's. He was wearing glasses instead of his normal contact lenses, and the dark frames emphasized the sheen of compassion in his eyes. She felt her stomach twist. She really didn't deserve a guy like him.

"You really didn't have to do this," Millie said. "Get up so early and come here."

"Yes we did," Bart informed her. "Dad said that. . ." He stopped as his father shot him a sideways look of warning. "I mean, we wanted to help."

"We can stay until eight o'clock," David said. "Then I have to get Bart to school. By then Aris will be here."

"Aris?"

"She wants to help," David explained.

"She's bringing like a hundred cans of tuna fish," Bart said. "So she can make tuna casserole."

"Not a hundred, Bart."

"Well, that's really sweet of her." Millie remembered the night she'd eaten tuna casserole at David's house. The noodles had been soft and plentiful, and the sauce, although bland, had been creamy and dotted with peas. "It can be our special today."

"Great." David looked relieved. "She'll be thrilled."

"It'll be a big help," Millie said. She was suddenly conscious of her messy bun, her face bare of makeup, and the dusting of flour that coated her apron.

"So what can we do?" David prompted.

She thought quickly. "Well, could you build a fire? There's a pile of kindling stacked just outside the back door. And Bart, it'd be great if you would take down the chairs off the tables and top off the salt and pepper shakers."

It wasn't long before the fire roared cheerfully in the hearth and the chairs sat neatly beneath the wooden tables. Millie was pulling loaves of hot honey whole wheat bread out of the oven when David and Bart wandered into the kitchen.

"That smells awesome," Bart declared, coming over to inhale appreciatively as Millie set the pans on the cooling racks.

"Give it a few minutes, and then you can have some."

"Bart, we're here to work, not eat," David pointed out. He was standing in front of the grill, staring in fascination, as if he were studying the controls in the cockpit of a spaceship. "I could fry some bacon."

It was too early, but Millie knew he was itching to take the grill for a test spin. Plus he and Bart could eat it before they left. She pulled a slab of bacon out of the refrigerator. "But before you get started," she said, "you have to wear the official Dosie Dough's apron."

Bart snickered as David tied it over his scrubs.

"You, too, Bart," Millie said, handing him one. It reached his knees. "You both look pretty cute," she said and was rewarded with both Denvers males making faces at her.

As the bacon began to sizzle, Millie carried another sack of whole wheat flour out of the pantry. "Ever make bread before, Bart?"

"No, but I made a volcano erupt in science class with Diet Coke and Mentos."

"If you can do that," Millie agreed, "you can make bread." She smiled at the intense interest that formed in his eyes. David sometimes looked like that when he was thinking hard about something. "We're going to start from scratch and make a starter sponge."

Pulling out a small mixing bowl and measuring cup, she set both on the counter. Next she retrieved some honey and a container of yeast and turned on the hot water faucet. Testing it with her finger, she explained that the temperature should be warm but not scalding in order to activate the yeast, which was a live organism.

"It's going to eat the honey," she explained, "and come to life. It'll look like foam on the surface."

"Cool," Bart exclaimed and bent until he was eye level with the liquid in the measuring cup. "It's doing it!"

Millie laughed, and over the top of Bart's head, she caught David's gaze. He was grinning, and there were grease spots all over his apron and too much smoke coming off the grill. "You might want to turn that down a little," she said. "We don't want to start a grease fire."

"Dad likes to cook on high," Bart offered. "He blew up our grill."

"It was an old grill," David said, poking the bacon. "A very old grill."

"You should have seen it, Miss Hogan. It made a big whooshing noise and then *boom*!" He threw his arms open wide demonstrating.

"We'd had it in storage for a while," David said. "I probably had the propane turned up a little too high when I hit the starter."

"The neighbors called the fire department."

David's eyes crinkled at the corners. "I admit it wasn't my proudest moment."

"Well," Millie said, "usually the fire chief comes in for donuts and coffee. I think we'll be safe."

"He'd better bring the truck," Bart said, eye level with the foaming mixture.

When Millie turned, David was still looking at her. Her heart jumped in her chest. The expression in his eyes sent a wave of heat through her, and she laughed a little self-consciously. "Oh, we'll be fine. We've got plenty of fire extinguishers and good insurance." She slanted David a look. "Not that I think we'll need it."

He shrugged. "Just wait until you taste my bacon. You'll be whistling a different tune."

Millie glanced at the smoke starting to billow up from the grill and smiled. David looked manly and cute in the red apron. She couldn't remember—ever—a man being back in the kitchen working. Now she had two of them. That they were completely clueless about cooking only added to their appeal. She didn't care if David burned the bacon so badly it turned to charcoal. She'd eat it anyway.

Lottie arrived a little before six. She hugged Millie, asked about Eva, and then quietly set about the final prep work for breakfast. By seven o'clock when the first customers came through the doors, the coffee was hot; the cooling racks were full of warm, fresh bread; and a pound of bacon—only slightly singed at the edges—stayed hot beneath the heat lamps.

The aunts were among the first to come inside. Aunt Lillian glided into the café in her electric wheelchair. She was followed by Keeker, who wore an odd green cap that resembled a bathing cap with sequins, and Mimi, who marched inside with Earl Gray securely strapped to her chest in a baby carrier.

They swarmed Millie with hugs. "How's Eva?" "How are you holding up, dear?" "We're here to help you." "Don't you worry about a thing, honey."

"Quiet," Aunt Mimi ordered in the same tone of voice she'd used as a crossing guard. "Millie, honey, we've discussed this thoroughly, and there's going to be no argument. We're going to help you run the café until Eva is back on her feet."

"Before you all get too involved," Lou Pinella said from his seat at the counter, "could Millie please take my order?"

"Later," Mimi snapped at the portly owner of the movie theater. "We have more important things to discuss than bacon and eggs." She turned back to Millie. "Lillian can sit on the stool and work the cash register. Keeker and I will wait tables. You can fill in for Eva in the back."

"Thanks, but I can manage," Millie said, softening her words with a smile. The aunts, while good-hearted, had no idea what they might be getting into. Waitressing was very physical. "Why don't you all have a seat? I'll bring you some tea."

"Don't patronize us." Mimi's mouth puckered, and she drew herself up as tall as her four-foot-eleven frame would allow. "Eva is our dear friend. We're not going to sit back and sip tea when she needs us."

"We've got this, honey," Keeker said more gently. "I'm wearing my luckiest hat today. I was wearing it the night Roland called to tell me that he'd survived Pork Chop Hill—one of the bloodiest battles in the Korean War."

"We want to do this," Lillian insisted. "Please let us."

Millie looked around the room. Most of the tables were full, but she recognized almost everyone. She could almost predict what they would order. She glanced at the hopeful expressions on the aunts' wrinkled faces and sighed. "Okay," she said. "But if things get crazy, come get me." She paused. "And thank you."

"You're welcome, honey," Mimi stated firmly. "Don't worry about anything."

For the next hour, she put her head down and worked. She had taken her mother's place several times before but not in recent years. It felt strange to step into the bustle of the backroom, to see Lottie with her heavy legs braced in front of the sizzling grill, hands flying as she flipped pancakes and scrambled eggs. David was in constant motion, moving between the sink and the warming trays as he both washed dishes and monitored the ready food orders in order to block either Mimi or Keeker from carrying out any heavy trays. Bart bussed tables and was thrilled when someone left him a ten-dollar tip.

With working the ovens and helping prep the final orders, Millie barely had time to do more than thank David and Bart when it was time for them to leave. Aris arrived a short time later with two shopping bags of canned tuna. "There's more in the car," she murmured and set the bags on the counter.

Millie wondered just how much tuna casserole she was planning on making, but she had too many other things on her mind. Lottie wasn't quite as fast on the grill as Eva, and without David and Bart, Millie needed to help Mimi and Keeker serve. She thanked Aris, set her up in the kitchen, and then focused all her energy on running her mother's restaurant. When Eva came back, she would see that Millie had taken good care of everything. She would understand that this was Millie's apology to her, a way of showing her in a way that words couldn't how much she loved her.

All day Millie stored up things to tell Eva—the overwhelming smell of Aris's tuna casserole, the argument Mimi had had with Chief Glugan over the amount of mustard in his sandwich, and how Tank, the plump bulldog, had used a stool to jump onto the counter and eat two pounds of chicken salad before anyone noticed.

She was later than she'd planned, however, and the heels of her boots clicked on the tile floor as she hurried to the bank of elevators in the hospital lobby. The halls were quiet, and the nurses' station was empty as she slipped into her mother's room. The television was playing, but Eva's eyes were closed when Millie reached the bedside. The remains of Eva's dinner sat on an adjustable tray. The meat looked tough, and the potatoes lumpy. Millie resolved to smuggle her in food from the café.

Millie settled herself in the chair beside the bed. She watched her mother's chest rise and fall, the indent her head made in the pillow, and the double strands of plastic bracelets looped around her wrists. One strip identified her by name, and the other said she was diabetic.

The bands didn't say that Eva was a mother or a loyal friend or that she'd once won a box sled race. It didn't say that she celebrated the first snowfall of the year with coconut-iced cupcakes or that she got sad when it rained or that she feared big dogs and hated being helpless.

Millie stared at her, guilt-filled and sad. Despite what the doctor said, Millie feared her mother wouldn't fully heal, wouldn't be the same, and there was nothing Millie could do about it.

Nothing?

She almost dismissed the answer that came into her mind, but she felt a little desperate. She remembered how David's face had softened and recalled the sound of his deep voice praying. His faith had moved her. She knew she wouldn't be able to speak as if God were standing right next to her like David did, but something in her was urging her to try. She glanced uneasily at the doorway. When she was sure she was alone, she leaned her elbows on the hospital bed. Closing her eyes, she folded her hands and whispered the prayer her father had spoken every night. *The Lord is my shepherd. . . .*

Chapter 27

A few days later, Millie left Lottie in charge of the café and drove to the hospital. Her mother had been discharged from the hospital—or "kicked out" as she put it. Eva was in good spirits, high-fiving the nurses as she wheeled past them and inviting everyone within hearing range for free food at Dosie's. The smile on her lips died, however, when she eyed the distance between the wheelchair and the bucket seat in Millie's Subaru. Millie saw the fear in her eyes and stepped forward to help.

It took both of them straining and hauling to get Eva into the car. Afterward, they sat panting, both of them silently contemplating just how much everything had changed.

Millie drove straight to Lillian's apartment. Golden Sage was an assisted-living community. Lillian rented a two-bedroom apartment designed to accommodate a person in a wheelchair. Since there was no first-floor bathroom in Millie's house, Lillian had invited Eva to stay with her.

A nursing aide came every morning to help Lillian bathe and dress. When Millie had explained her mother's situation, the nurse had been happy to help out with Eva.

It had started flurrying earlier that morning, and as Millie stepped out of the car at Aunt Lillian's apartment, a thin layer of snow tinted the back window. Millie had the sudden urge to take her finger and write her name in the flakes, although she knew it would be covered up again within minutes.

"Be careful," Millie warned as she opened the car door. "The ground's getting slippery."

Eva stared at the two-story building ahead of them. Her face was stony. The silence disturbed Millie more than any complaint could have.

"It's not like this is forever," Millie said as she rolled the wheelchair to the passenger's side of the car.

Eva nodded. "I know."

"You'll be back to work before you know it."

"Yes," Eva agreed in a monotone.

Millie frowned. She hated seeing this look of defeat on her mother's face. "If you feel like it, tomorrow afternoon I'll take you over to David's and you can help us work on the sled."

Eva would not meet Millie's gaze. "Let's just go inside now, honey. It's cold out here."

"It's like she's an alien," Millie tried to explain to David a few days later. They were in the kitchen at the café, and as usual he and Bart had come early to help. "She's stopped complaining about everything. She says please and thank you."

"Maybe she's just trying to be a good patient," David suggested, turning a sausage on the grill.

Millie shook her head. She was mixing batter for apple cinnamon pancakes. "I know her," she said. "This isn't her."

"She's just been through a serious trauma. You need to give her time."

"Maybe." Millie put her spoon down and leaned against the counter. "It's just weird. You try to talk to her about anything and she just says she's tired and wants to watch television. She didn't even want to hear about the flowers you sent me for Valentine's Day."

"It could be the pain medication."

"She's watching the Game Show Network," Millie said dryly. "It means she's giving up."

"She might be a little depressed. Is she sleeping?"

"Not well."

"I'd give her a few more days, and if she doesn't improve, I'd call her doctor."

Millie heard herself agree, although part of her felt that David didn't fully understand the problem. Yes, Eva was upset about her hip, but it went deeper than that. Eva had never held back when it came to expressing her opinions to Millie. She spoke her mind, even when Millie wished she wouldn't. They bantered, argued, and talked about everything and anything.

It was all different now. It was as if not only had Eva's hip been broken, but the invisible bridge that had connected them, as well. Her mother didn't ask about Millie's day or anything else. All Eva wanted was her medication and to semidoze on Lillian's couch. Millie feared Eva's apathy was proof of her anger and disappointment in her. Her mother knew that once David found out about Karl Kauffman, he'd break up with her. Eva was effectively putting as much distance between herself and Millie as she could so that when the breakup happened, it wouldn't hurt so much.

"Lillian's also in a wheelchair," David pointed out. "Your mother probably relates to her pretty strongly right now. I wouldn't take it personally."

"It's more than that," Millie said, turning as the oven timer went off and pulling a tray of bread pans out of the oven. *Tell him,* a small voice said.

Immediately another voice in her head piped up. *Does he really have to know? It's not like anything big happened.*

She looked over at David. He had his back to her and was flipping the sizzling sausages. The Dosie's red apron was tied around his waist in a lopsided bow. His blue and gray finely checkered shirt outlined a strong set of shoulders that narrowed to a tapered waist. And beyond his good looks, he was the nicest person she'd ever met. He was the kind of man who understood right from wrong and never wavered, never let himself cross the line. She knew he wasn't perfect but also knew that he never would have done what she had.

How could she admit that she'd been so stupid and thoughtless? How could she make him understand what it felt like to be her?

She slipped another pan out of the oven and put it on the cooling rack. Maybe it was better that he never found out about her and Karl. Maybe she could pretend that it never happened. That would be a lot easier, but then if he ever found out from someone else—like his mother—it would make it much worse. She hesitated. Even if David's mother said something about seeing them together, she could always tell him that they'd gone out for coffee. She could leave out that little part about flirting with Karl— and kissing him. David would believe what she told him.

He never had to know, but what would it do to their relationship? Wouldn't she always have this small lie between them? Would it grow like cancer? She worried her lip, trying to quiet the voice that insisted she simply blurt out the truth.

She wiped her hands on her apron and watched him work. With her history, how could she ever make him believe that she truly regretted what had happened? That it would never happen again?

He turned around and caught her watching. "They're not burning."

Millie shook her head and managed a faint smile. "I know. They smell great." She paused, testing out words. *I'm an idiot. I made a mistake. I'm sorry.* Her throat felt squeezed. She swallowed hard.

"Then what?" He pressed gently.

Millie heard a voice in her head say very clearly that she should tell him the truth. Another voice argued that this wouldn't change anything. It would only hurt him. Confessing would be selfish. The voice said she deserved to carry her own guilt.

"I was just thinking about the meat order. I couldn't remember if I added enough ground beef." She forced a slightly brighter smile and felt the weight of her omission settle a little more heavily on her shoulders. She didn't like herself for lying, but she couldn't tell him either. Her choice had been made, and now she was going to have to live with it.

Later that morning, when Millie returned to the kitchen, she found Aris standing by the menu board. The older woman had her hands on her hips. "Why isn't my tuna casserole on the menu?"

The café had been serving tuna casserole for a week straight. Millie didn't have the heart to tell her that fewer and fewer customers had been ordering it or that an increasing number of feral cats had been attempting to breach the dumpster in the back. "Well," she said, "it is your recipe, only slightly modified."

"I don't think chicken tetrazzini sounds like tuna casserole." Aris's lips pressed together into a coral-colored line.

"We're just substituting chicken for the tuna and spaghetti for egg noodles."

Aris's eyes narrowed suspiciously. "That's it?"

"We'll brown a few onions when we make the sauce, but yeah, that's it."

"What about the peas?"

"We'll add them."

Some of the tension seemed to leave Aris's face. "I suppose we could try it."

Soon both of them were at the worktable chopping onions. Millie's hands flew over the cutting board. Tank lay at her feet. She found the dog's presence comforting.

"You know what the best thing about your mother breaking her hip is?" Aris commented.

"What?"

"Getting to know you," Aris said. "I'm impressed with how you're handling everything."

"Thank you. I couldn't have done it without your help."

A little pink color bloomed in Aris's thin cheeks. She looked up, and her eyes were bright with what looked like approval. "You're a very resourceful person. I like the way you've stepped up and taken over running the café. Your mom would be proud."

Millie warmed under the compliment. "I couldn't have done it without everyone's help. Yours especially," she added. "David's lucky to have you."

"I'm the lucky one," Aris stated firmly. "So. . .when's your birthday?"

"What?"

"I want to get to know you better. I thought your birthday was a good place to start. Were you born in Deer Park?"

Millie scraped the chopped onion to the side and picked up another. The question seemed strange, but she felt a little flattered at the older woman's interest. "Yes, at Saint Vincent's—the same place where my mother had her surgery."

"Date of birth?"

"Oh, not until July."

"July what?"

"The eighteenth."

"What year?"

Millie glanced up. Aris was watching her intently. "I'll save you the math," she said. "I'm thirty-one."

"Were your parents from around here, too?"

"No. They're both from Ohio." Millie sliced the onion in half. She didn't like the questions, but then it occurred to her that she had a few of her own. "How long have you worked for David?"

"Since before Bart was born," Aris stated, and her knife banged the cutting board as she diced the onion. "Tell me a little about your father. What'd you say his name was?"

Millie's hands stilled. "Max Hogan."

"Maxwell?"

"Maximillian, actually." She felt the small splinter of pain press into her heart at the mention of her father's name. She ordered herself not to overreact and calmly pulled out another onion. "What was David's wife like?"

"Lovely," Aris said without hesitation. "Classy and smart. Never heard her say one bad thing about anyone and was always helping others. She organized a mission trip to Africa to give children dental care. Imagine that!"

Millie didn't want to imagine that. How could she compete with someone who practically was a saint? She banged the knife down a little harder than necessary and sent a row of diced onion sailing across the cutting board.

"I want to know more about your father," Aris said. "What year did you say he was born?"

"I didn't," Millie snapped before she could help herself.

Aris retreated into silence, and Millie immediately regretted her sharpness. Aris, after all, was there to help. It was natural she'd be curious about Millie's past. She set down the knife. "Sorry," she said. "I don't like talking about him. The long and short of it is that my father abandoned me and my mother about twenty years ago."

"Did you ever try to find him?"

"No." She wouldn't admit how for years she'd clung to the idea that he would come back. How she'd loved him and hated him until she wasn't sure just what she felt at all. She thought about the night of her senior prom, how she'd pretended that it was her father's face watching her from the mirror in her vanity as she'd sat putting on her makeup. She imagined him looking at her with pride and approval. *"You'll be the prettiest girl there,"* he'd whispered in her mind.

She finished chopping the last onion and pushed it and the memories firmly aside. She no longer cared about or yearned for her father's approval. "As far as I'm concerned, Aris, he's dead."

Aris thankfully let the subject drop. But Millie pushed her sleeves up higher on her arm and poked at the onions with a little more force than was necessary. She was thankful the heat coming off the range could account for the flush in her cheeks.

Wherever her father was, Millie decided he could stay right there. He'd blown his chance to get to know her. Even if he begged her for forgiveness, she'd turn away from him. He would understand then what it felt like to be rejected by the one person who was supposed to love you. One day, she vowed, he'd regret what he'd done. She wasn't that old—it was still possible that she'd do something amazing with her life. One of these audition tapes could still hit, and she could be cast in a commercial or appear on a reality television show or land a role on a soap opera.

Her father could turn on his television, and there'd she be, filling the screen. It might take him a few seconds to recognize her, but he would. The shock would be overwhelming—he'd have to sit down. He'd realize that he made the biggest mistake of his life. He'd try to touch her face on the screen and give himself an electric shock. For once, he'd feel the pain of the years they'd lost together. He'd finally understand that he'd misjudged her, underestimated her potential. He'd be crippled with regret, and she'd be the one who felt nothing at all for him.

Chapter 28

On the way to David's house, Millie was thinking about chicken potpie. She had been running the café for almost two weeks now and was starting to play with the menu a little. As the Subaru purred through the early winter darkness, she went over the recipe in her mind. It was an old one—she'd come across it by accident in an old recipe book bound together with rubber bands. A heart and several stars had been doodled in the margins. Although the ink was faded and nearly illegible, she recognized her mother's writing. Obviously her mother loved this recipe. Millie pictured making it for her: Eva biting into the flaky crust and understanding everything Millie wanted to say but couldn't.

Lost in her thoughts, she almost passed the dark shapes half hidden in the shadows between the streetlights, but slight movement caught her eye. She slowed. Her first thought was that someone had fallen on the icy sidewalk and another person was trying to help. Pulling the car to the side of the road, the car headlights illuminated the situation more clearly, and she realized that one kid was facedown on the sidewalk and another was sitting on top of him. She pressed the car horn and held it there.

The kid sitting on top of the other kid got up and bolted. She glimpsed a shock of yellowish hair and a navy-blue jacket, but mostly her attention was on the kid who'd been tackled. He was just starting to get up, and her heart began to race as she recognized the familiar blue parka with the red trim.

"Bart," she shouted. "Are you okay?"

He didn't answer. She ran over to him, taking in the scrape on his cheek and the slightly dazed look in his eyes. Throwing her arms around him, she pulled him tightly against her. "Are you okay?"

For a moment, he stood still as a statue. His arms stayed at his sides, and the only movement at all was the uneven pull of his breathing. He was trembling a little, and she made soft, soothing sounds and stroked the short, silken hair on the back of his head. She felt him stiffen and remembered a little too late that he didn't like her to hug or touch him, and here she was fussing over him like he was a little boy. She just couldn't seem to stop herself. She was as shaken up by what had happened as he probably was.

His arms lifted. Something inside her sighed and prepared to let go of him. His hands, however, settled lightly, kind of tentatively, around her waist, and then he was hugging her hard. Something in Millie started to break. She held him tighter, silently promising him that everything would be okay. She wouldn't let anyone harm him ever again. She understood for the first time how parents could willingly throw themselves in front of a train if it meant saving their child. She bent her head so that the tip of her chin gently rested on the top of his head and breathed him in. "Oh Bart," she whispered.

It broke the moment. He pulled away and stared at her through eyes that shined a mix of embarrassment, pain, and a slight defiance. "I'm fine."

She looked him over again. There was a scrape on his cheek and a scuff mark on his jacket, but she understood his manhood was on the line. "Yeah," she said. "I can see that." She stepped back from him and assumed a brisk manner, as if she hadn't just found him helpless and flattened by a much bigger kid.

"He caught me by surprise," Bart added, straightening his glasses and then tentatively touching his cheek.

"Cowards do that," Millie said, longing to soothe away the red mark on his face but knowing better than to try. "They sneak attack you from behind. Not much anyone can do about that." She watched relief form in Bart's eyes. "He was a lot bigger than you, too, Bart."

The relief faded, and Bart scowled. "I would have been fine if my scarf hadn't gotten tangled under me."

His blue-striped scarf was hanging untied around his shoulders, but Millie nodded soberly and decided to change the subject. "What were you doing out here anyway?"

He shrugged. It could have been her imagination, but it looked like a little color came into his cheeks. "I missed the bus."

"You could have called me. I would have given you a ride." So would have David, or Aris, or Bart's grandparents. Something didn't make sense.

"I didn't have your number," Bart said and looked away. Both of them knew he'd walked right past the café on his way home.

Millie sighed and fished out her keys. "I want you to put my number in your phone," she said. "And I want you to feel free to use it anytime. No questions asked. You need me, I'm there."

Bart's eyes blinked behind his glasses several times. "Okay," he said and pulled out his cell.

She gave him the numbers and watched him program the phone. "You got it?" What she meant was, did he understand that she'd be there for him in any kind of situation? Even if he did something wrong?

He gave an offhanded shrug, but the way he held her gaze gave him away. "Yeah," he said. "I got it."

"I don't like this." David studied the small red scrape on Bart's face. Someone had hurt Bart, pushed him down and sat on him—his son, who wouldn't hurt a flea. Action had to be taken, but Bart was refusing to give him enough information to do anything. "Who did this?" he demanded for the third time.

Beneath the kitchen lights, his son's face was pale but determined. The stain on his cheek stood out like the map of Africa. "I don't know."

David's jaw tightened. If Millie hadn't been on her way to their house and stopped it, there was no telling what might have happened. "Come on, Bart. I know you know."

Something in Bart's eyes told David he was right. "Bart," he pressed. "Why are you protecting this kid?"

Bart's gaze slid away from him. "Because you'll just make it worse."

"I don't think that's possible," David snapped. He turned to Millie. "Tell me again. What did you see?"

She shook her head. "It was dark, David. All I saw was a tall, muscular kid with a blond crew cut and a navy parka." Her brow furrowed in concentration. "The hood of the jacket was partially unzipped, so it hung unevenly in the back. He ran away when I honked. I never saw his face."

"Dad"—a pleading note entered his son's voice—"you have to leave this alone. Nothing really happened."

"Nothing? You've got a scratch on your cheek and the front of your jacket is scraped up." He paused as a fresh swell of anger rushed up in him. "The next time this kid could seriously hurt you."

"He doesn't want to hurt me," Bart said, avoiding David's eyes and resting his gaze instead on Millie. "He just wants. . . Oh, just forget it."

"Wants what?" David demanded.

"Nothing." Bart's mouth turned down.

"I'm trying to help you," David said, but even he could hear the edge in his voice and tried to stamp down his anger and frustration. "We're going to stand right here until you tell me—even if it takes all night."

Bart widened his stance. "Fine."

David clamped down hard on his molars. He hadn't expected Bart to agree to his challenge, and now that he had, there was no backing down. He narrowed his gaze and settled in for the long haul. A touch on his arm made him jump.

"Listen," Millie said. "Let's all calm down."

"I'll calm down when he tells me the name of the bully."

"Maybe we need to ask why Bart won't tell us."

David didn't like being told how to handle his son. He moved his arm free of her touch and felt his already precarious grip on his temper slip another notch. He'd never argued with Lisa about Bart in front of the boy. That was the first rule of good parenting. A united front. "You should stay out of this."

"Maybe I should," Millie said, studying his eyes and frowning. "But I won't."

"This is my son. I'll handle this."

"I don't think a staring contest is going to end well for either of you."

"You don't have kids," David said tightly, keeping his gaze

pinned to his son. "You don't know what you're talking about."

"All I'm asking, David, is that you talk to him."

"I am talking to him."

"No, you're not. You're saying the same thing over and over. Only louder."

He turned to her. Part of him recognized the truth in her words, another part really didn't care. "Just stay out of this!"

"Don't yell at her, Dad," Bart said hotly. His round cheeks flushed a deeper red, and behind his glasses his blue eyes were dark and stormy.

"I'm not yelling," David snapped and watched Bart take a protective step toward Millie. He made an effort to tone it down. "I'm just trying to get to the bottom of this. You're not helping."

He directed this last remark at Millie, who drew herself to her full height and glared back at him. "Because you're not letting me."

"We'll talk about this later." When they were alone, he'd tell her that her place was to support him, be his second in command, not to question his parenting techniques.

"If you won't ask him, I will." There were twin spots of color in her cheeks. The pinched look of her mouth softened as she turned to his son. "Bart, please tell us why you won't reveal the name of the kid who's bullying you."

At Bart's silence, David shot Millie a triumphant look. "I told you he wouldn't answer."

Millie kept her big gray eyes firmly fixed on Bart. They were as soft and warm as gray flannel. David gave Bart credit for being able to hold out against that look.

"I know you're not afraid of this kid," Millie said.

"Of course I'm not afraid," Bart said with a snort. "I just don't want my dad calling this kid's parents." He pushed his glasses higher on his face in a gesture David recognized as one of his own. "I'm not a little baby."

"You're eleven," David stated.

"Almost twelve."

"You're birthday isn't until August."

"But I'm still older than eleven."

"The point is," Millie interrupted, "that you both want the same thing—to deal with the bully." Her voice softened. "Bart, what if we promise not to do anything? Will you at least tell us what happened today?"

"I'm not going to make that promise." David shot Millie a warning look.

Millie folded her arms and regarded him unapologetically. A lock of her dark hair had fallen onto her cheek, and as mad as he was at her, he found himself staring at that corkscrew curl, stubbornly defying the rest of her pinned-up hair. "The more we know, the more we can help Bart."

"We are not negotiating. We are parenting," David said firmly, pleased with how he'd put that, and then his smug feeling faded as he realized he'd used the plural instead of the singular about the whole parenting thing. Suddenly the theme to *Star Wars* jingled in the quiet room. It was Bart's cell. The boy took one look at the caller and bolted from the room.

"We're not finished," David called, stunned that Bart had disobeyed him and run away in the middle of their argument. He raked his fingers through his hair. When had his son become so defiant? Just that morning Bart had been eating Cap'n Crunch and they'd been debating if Superman or Spiderman was a better superhero. He started after his son, but Millie's hand pulled him back.

"Let him go," she hissed.

He pulled free. "I'm not letting him off the hook just because his cell rang."

"David, he had to take that call."

Scowling, he looked in the direction of the stairs. "What are you talking about?"

"It was a girl on the phone."

This stopped him in his tracks. "What?"

"A girl."

"How do you know?"

"His face, David. It was like he got hit by lightning. Guys do not look like that when another guy calls them."

David glanced at the open hallway for a second time. Bart was talking to a girl? A girl had actually called him? Possibly Lauren Mays?

"If you make him hang up," Millie continued gently, as if he were a patient lying rigidly in the dental chair as he explained a particularly extensive procedure, "you'll embarrass him. Let it be. Bart will be back when he hangs up."

David started to tell Millie that she wasn't Bart's mother and that he, David, knew his son better than anyone, but then he closed his mouth. At this very moment, Bart and a girl were exchanging sentences, sharing information, maybe even making plans to get together. His son was only eleven. Was this normal? How old had he been when he'd started looking at girls? Not much older, he realized. He looked at Millie and scowled.

"I know," she said. "I should stop telling you what to do. Sorry."

"That's right," he said, then added, "So what do we do?"

"Nothing. We wait."

It seemed forever before Bart walked back into the room. "Sorry,

Dad," he said in a voice a little deeper than it had been five minutes ago. "I had to take that call."

"Who was it?"

"Lauren Mays." Bart blushed to the tips of his ears but held David's gaze. "She had a question about the math assignment."

David suspected there had been more to the call than that, and when he glanced at Millie, he read the slight lift at the corner of her mouth and knew she thought the same. "We still need to talk more about what happened today."

Bart folded his arms and sighed loudly.

David sighed. "Asking for help isn't a sign of weakness; it's a sign of intelligence."

"Not at my school," Bart stated firmly. "Nerds are not cool."

"Your intelligence is a gift," Millie said.

"So far all it's done is get my hat stolen."

"Which we'll get back as soon as you tell us who jumped you," David said, but gentler than before. He glanced at Millie to see if she'd noticed.

"I really didn't like that hat anyway," Bart said. "It was itchy."

David sighed. "All right Bart, I haven't wanted to do this, but you're giving me no choice. Until you tell me the name of this kid, there will be no video games, no computer, and no television."

"What about homework? Sometimes I have to go on the Internet for assignments."

David exchanged looks with Millie. At this rate his son was going to be a trial lawyer. "You can use the computer for homework, but I will be checking your online history. If you delete that, I'll personally be supervising your computer time."

"Fine," Bart said, scowling.

"If you miss the bus," David continued, "you will call me. Understood?"

"Agreed."

"Secondly, I'm meeting with your teacher, the school counselor, and the principal. Obviously I can't tell them who is bothering you, but they need to know what's going on so they can keep an eye out for trouble."

"They won't do anything," Bart stated, scowling fiercely. "And if they ask me about anything, I'll just deny that it happened."

"They'll keep it confidential," David said.

"Can't you just wait until after the sled race?" A pleading note entered Bart's voice. "It's next Saturday."

"No," David said firmly. "I've put it off much too long as it is. Tomorrow I'm calling and making an appointment."

It was hard to feel good about doing the right thing when David saw Bart's shoulders sag. Millie didn't look so happy either. He saw the mute appeal Bart sent her and for a moment thought she would make one last appeal to him. She didn't, and while he appreciated this, a persistent feeling of doubt settled into his mind. He needed to be Bart's parent not his friend, but he wasn't completely comfortable with the role in which he had cast himself. Everyone said the key to good parenting was establishing boundaries then consistently enforcing them.

Bart's situation still weighed heavily on his mind as David climbed into bed later that night. Closing his eyes, he knelt by the side of the bed.

Please, Lord, keep Bart safe, he prayed. *Don't let this bully hurt him, and please help me to model Your love and tolerance for our enemies, because right now I'm not feeling either of those things. Please help us handle this situation in a way that brings glory to You. And, Lord, thanks for Millie being there today. I know things could have been a lot worse if she hadn't scared off that bully kid.*

The next morning, as soon as he got to the office he called the school and made an appointment to meet with the principal, counselor, and Bart's teacher at one o'clock that afternoon. However, at eleven o'clock, the school called and told him that he'd have to reschedule his appointment. There was a virus going around the school, and all three educators had gone home sick. She suggested scheduling the appointment for a week from Monday when classes would resume after spring break.

David countered by asking to meet with the assistant vice principal and was told the man was in a training class for the next several days. David, however, was welcome to meet with Miss Gibson, the substitute teacher for Bart's class. David actually considered it, even though he knew Miss Gibson was notoriously soft on the kids and probably wouldn't take him seriously. Only too well, he pictured her deciding to talk about Bart's problem in front of the class, which he knew would only make things worse.

Frowning, he considered his options then made the appointment for the first Monday after spring break.

Chapter 29

The population of Deer Park swelled as tourists streamed into town for the Winterfest Snow Carnival. Parking on South Main was impossible, and every time Millie glanced out Dosie Dough's front window, she saw a stream of people passing down the street wearing brand-new parkas and carrying shopping bags.

For the first time all season, customers had to wait for a table. They stood almost shoulder to shoulder near the front door, their faces rosy from the cold, their eyes reading the menu board eagerly. They had big appetites, and although Millie came in early and stayed late, she was having trouble keeping up with the demand.

She was glad for the fast pace though. When she was multitasking—running the kitchen and trying to help the aunts serve, it was easier not to think about David or Bart. She couldn't help but look at every boy about eleven years old and wonder if he was the one who'd jumped Bart.

In the kitchen, she grabbed an order from under the warmers. The race was just days away. Last night she, David, and Bart had put the final coat of paint on the sled. They'd made pizza from scratch in the kitchen and toasted each other with sparkling grape juice. She'd had to force herself to go home.

Later she'd filled the emptiness in the house by talking with

David. Lying in bed, she'd pressed the receiver to her ear and listened to the soothing deepness of his voice. She thought the last thing he'd said before she fell asleep was that he loved her. But she might have imagined that. Lately her dreams had been filled with him. Vivid ones, where she walked with her hand tucked firmly into the crook of his elbow and she was happy.

Pushing the swinging doors open, she wondered if it could be true—if David could actually love her. To be loved, didn't someone have to be worthy of it? What exactly did she bring to the table besides waitressing skills and a life full of unrealized dreams?

The front door jingled. A broad-shouldered man and a rangy, tall boy stepped inside. She recognized Martin Spikes and thought the boy must be his son. It was close to closing, and although most of the tables were full, there was no line at the counter. She set her tray down in front of the Dittmore brothers then hurried over to take the Spikes's order.

"What can I get you?"

"A Double Mountain Burger—well done—large fries, extra ketchup, and a black cow shake," Martin said. He had the same blond hair he'd had throughout high school, but the muscles that had seen him to a state championship in wrestling were going soft. He had a potbelly now and a receding hairline.

Millie nodded and turned to the boy. "How about you?"

"The same."

The boy had his dad's wide shoulders and short, close-cropped blond hair. He also had a navy coat. Millie's eyes narrowed. He was the right size, and the coat looked the same as the one she'd seen the bully kid wearing.

"So, Martin," she said, carefully keeping her face neutral as she scribbled down the orders. "Haven't seen you in a while."

"Been busy."

"Don't I know it." Millie flashed a smile at the boy. "How is your spring break going?"

"Great."

"What've you been up to?"

The boy shrugged. "Nothing much. Working on my sled for the box race."

"He's got a killer sled." Martin laughed. His brown eyes gleamed. "Gonna *eat* the competition, right, Dev?"

The boy laughed. "My cousin Thad helped build it. He's an aerospace engineer, and he says the thing can go faster than a bat out of—"

"Dev," his father cut him off. "Watch your language."

"You use that word all the time," Devon said, frowning.

His father laid his hand on his son's shoulder. "We're sorry to hear about your mother, Millie. Heard she was helping the Denvers's kid with his sled." He paused. "I sure hope her accident didn't interfere with that."

Millie's jaw tightened, and her suspicions raised another notch. They were digging for information about Bart's sled. "Thanks for your concern, but Bart's sled is all finished." She studied the pair over the top of her notepad. "So what's your sled like?"

"It's a shark. A great white shark," Devon said. Something malicious seemed to gleam in his small, dark eyes. "The side fins are designed to withstand sideways impact. My cousin Thad used—"

"All his knowledge to build it," Martin finished. "What's Bart's sled like?"

She blinked rapidly, considering. "Oh, nothing much. We call it the *Flying French Fry*."

"That's what he built?" Devon's jaw dropped open slightly, and he exchanged an incredulous look with his father. "No wonder he hasn't said very much about it at school."

Millie jotted something on the pad then casually added, "You wouldn't happen to be a friend of Bart's would you?"

"He's in my science class," Devon admitted. "Is his sled really a cardboard french fry?"

Millie's heart beat a little faster. She dropped her pencil deliberately, and when the boy bent to pick it up, she noticed the hood of his parka was partially unzipped and hung crookedly down his back. "Thanks," she said as Devon handed her back the pencil. "I'll go put your order in."

She rushed to the back room then leaned against the counter. Devon Spikes was the bully kid. He had to be. Why else the interest in Bart's sled? And his parka matched the one she'd seen. She frowned. She knew she ought to call David, but she also wanted to get a look at Devon's sled. She remembered Martin Spikes had cheated frequently in high school and wouldn't put it past him to have constructed his son's sled with illegal materials.

What she needed, she decided, was more information. The Spikes didn't live too far away, and while they were having their Mountain Burgers, she could get a quick look at the sled. Pulling her purse from the desk drawer, she fished out her keys. On the way out, she pulled Aris aside and asked her to cover for her.

Aris nodded. "Of course." Her thin face creased. "Is Eva okay?"

"Yes, she's fine." Millie started to make up a vague excuse for leaving but then had a better idea. "Look," she said. "I don't have much time to explain, but I think the kid that's been bothering Bart is at table six. He's been asking a lot of questions about Bart's sled, and he looks a lot like the kid I saw beating up Bart. Before I involve David, I want to get a look at that sled. Can you stay here and delay the Spikes?"

Aris's shoulders straightened, and her eyes narrowed. "That boy is here? I'll wring his neck for what he's done to Bart."

"No," Millie snapped. "That won't help. Besides, I could be wrong. What's more important is to look at that sled."

"Then I'm coming with you," Aris stated. "Keeker and Mimi can hold the fort." She read Millie's face then added, "I'm not letting you go there alone. You'll need a lookout."

Millie started to argue then saw the stubborn set to the older woman's face. "If you come, you'll have to stay in the car." When Aris nodded, she added, "I'll let the aunts know what's happening. They can mess up the Spikes's order then offer free ice cream to delay them."

"Good thinking. Tell them to make them big scoops." Aris's hazel eyes gleamed. "That kid might spill some good information if we get enough sugar in him."

David flipped on the overhead light in the garage. "There she is," he announced proudly. "Isn't she great? We put the final coat of paint on her last night." His gaze swung back to his mother in anticipation of her reaction. She hadn't seen the sled before, and he wanted her to be proud of it. He wanted her to see the Hogans in a new and better light. "Eva and Bart designed it. We all built it."

"Miss Eva taught me a little calculus," Bart added. "We used it to calculate the slope of the sled." He touched the shiny black hood. "Miss Millie said she's going to take a picture of me at the race and hang it in the café."

His mother stopped walking around the body of the sled and looked up at him with a crease of worry between her eyes. "Is that so?" she said.

"What do you think, Grandma?" Bart pressed. "Do you like it?"

They all studied the cardboard sled. David's gaze lingered on the giant winged french fry that covered the side of the sled. It was supposed to look like a flying, crinkle-cut fry, but if it wasn't for the lettering Millie had stenciled, nobody would have known. He suspected that Millie could have drawn the design a lot better than Bart, but instead, she'd chosen to let Bart do it and had praised everything he did. David remembered the glow of pride in his son's eyes.

"It's certainly unique," his mother said and then added, "But David, is it supposed to look like a coffin?"

"It's aerodynamic, Grandma," Bart said. "Miss Eva custom-shaped it to my body."

"Are those lightning bolts with wings?"

"Those are french fries," David explained. He glanced at his watch. Millie had said she might drop by later. He hoped he could talk her into going out for coffee. The race day was rapidly approaching and something had to be said about what would happen to their relationship. He planned to ask her if she'd like to date him for real and even had a little speech planned.

He checked his watch. Aris wasn't home either. Millie and Aris were probably still at the café getting a start on the morning's baking.

"Why is there a tail?"

"That's the rudder," Bart said. "It'll help keep the sled straight."

His mother circled the sled slowly then regarded David. "Are you sure this is a good idea? Bart entering this race? I remember when you did it—your whole sled fell apart."

David smiled but wished his mom wouldn't worry so much. "Bart'll be fine. Eva Hogan still holds the record for the fastest sled on the hill."

"I suppose." His mother's mouth puckered slightly, as it always did whenever David mentioned Millie or Eva. He straightened his back. "Will you and Dad be joining us at Dosie's after the race? I know Millie has invited both of you."

"Of course." His mother smiled but turned to Bart before he could read her eyes. "We're looking forward to meeting your friends."

Bart barely looked up. He was furiously texting—probably Lauren Mays. David had asked Bart to keep a low profile with Lauren until after he'd talked to the principal, but it obviously hadn't made an impact.

"Have I mentioned, David, that I'm going to help out with the charity ball at Saint Vincent's this spring?"

Last year his mother had helped raise a couple of thousand dollars for the children's wing of the hospital. "That's great, Mom."

"We're going to need some local business support."

"I'll be glad to do what I can."

His mother's face brightened. "We could use your input on a couple of things. Are you free Wednesday night?"

David mentally cringed at the thought of sitting around a table for a couple of hours discussing menus and venues, but then he brightened as it occurred to him that this could be an excellent opportunity to get Millie connected to the church. "Can I bring Millie?"

"Of course," his mother said, but then she added, "But I know she's awfully busy with Eva being hurt and all. She probably doesn't need one more thing on her plate." She smiled. "Maybe it would be better not even to ask her. That way she wouldn't feel obligated."

It wasn't hard to translate. His mother really was saying, *"I don't want her to come."* He bristled. "I'm sure Millie would be glad to make the time. She is a very generous person."

"Then by all means ask her." She hesitated. "But maybe I should clear it with my cochair first."

It took a second, but then he understood. "By any chance is Cynthia Shively your cochair?"

"I couldn't very well refuse her help when she volunteered, David."

He thought about the look on Cynthia's face at the skating rink when he'd walked away from her. He'd seen a new coldness in her face, a hardness in her eyes that bordered on dislike. Cynthia apparently hadn't mentioned their conversation at the lake to his mother. The whole Saint Vincent's plan had probably been hatched weeks ago. He turned to Bart, who had stopped texting and was watching them with undisguised interest. "Would you please give us a few minutes alone?"

As soon as Bart left, he said, "Mom, Cynthia and I are never going to date." He watched her body go very still as if she wasn't even breathing. "I would really like Millie to get to know our friends at the church. I'd appreciate your help in making that happen."

Beneath her carefully applied makeup, the lines in his mom's face seemed to deepen. "I'll do anything you ask me, David, but I think you should be very careful. I hate to see you getting serious with that girl."

"She's not perfect, but neither am I." David was fed up with people trying to tell him how bad Millie was. "Maybe if you stopped being so quick to judge her, you'd see that she's a good person."

"A good person doesn't act the way she does." She looked long and hard into his eyes. He saw the strength of the same woman who had grabbed him by the arm and bent him over her knee when he was a child and got into trouble. He watched her reach for the small gold cross that had hung around her neck for as long as he could remember. "I saw her a couple of weeks ago. She was with Karl Kauffman."

David made a noise that was something between a laugh and a snort. "So?"

"They were in his car. It was after dark. When she saw me, she hunched down like she didn't want to be seen." Her lips twisted. "I'm sorry, David. I didn't want to have to tell you."

His face felt strangely numb. He couldn't tell if he was smiling or grimacing, and when he tried to straighten his lips, he still couldn't be quite sure. "I'm sure there was a reasonable explanation."

But was there? In high school, Karl had been a jock, and a lot of girls had trailed him around wanting dates. Unhappily, he remembered that Millie had been one of those girls.

"She's two-timing you," his mother hissed. "That's what she does."

"She isn't two-timing me," he said firmly then heard himself ask, "When was this?"

"On Tuesday, February 10th. I remember, because it was bridge night at Gloria Kirpatrick's house."

It was also the night Eva had broken her hip. His stomach churned with the realization that Millie had been out with another man—and she hadn't told him.

"There's more," his mother added gently. "Aris did a little digging around into her background. There are things you need to know."

"What have you done?"

"I haven't done anything," she said. "Stop looking at me like I'm the bad person. I love you, but you blunder a curious habit of hiding your head in the sand. When there's something you don't want to see, you don't. I'm your mother, and I'll protect you with every breath in my body. You don't want to hear what I have to say? Fine. But ask her, David. She obviously didn't tell you about Karl

Kauffman—and there's more."

"Whatever it is, I don't want to hear it."

Her lips trembled as she fought for control. "You don't want Cynthia, and I'm willing to accept that. But don't ruin your life by trying to prove how wrong I am about Millie Hogan—because I'm not."

She left then, closing the door hard behind her and leaving a trace of her anger hanging as heavily in the air as her perfume. David listened to the sound of her car's engine as it roared away. He gripped his hands into fists. Right now he disliked her almost as much as he loved her.

He turned off the lights in the garage with more force than necessary. His mother had to be mistaken. She must have seen someone who looked like Millie riding in Karl Kauffman's car. If it had been Millie, she would have told him.

He stepped into the living room. What if he was wrong? Millie had never told him the full story of what had happened the night Eva had fallen, had she?

He didn't like the seeds of doubt that had taken root in his mind and seemed to grow stronger with every passing second. It all made sense. Millie had gone out with Karl Kauffman, and something had happened or else she would have mentioned it to him. He thought of another man holding Millie, kissing her, and a curious numbness seemed to settle over him. He walked into the kitchen, opened the freezer, and stood there as the chilled air spilled out. His mind turned the knowledge over and over but couldn't accept it.

There had to be an explanation that did not paint Millie in a bad light. He'd believed in her; he'd believed in them. He slammed the freezer door shut. He didn't want to think about it anymore. She could date whomever she wanted. It wasn't like they were exclusive—that had never come up in their plan, at least not that he could recall. They'd never talked about a future beyond the sled race, so it really wasn't a big deal. Only it was. He looked out the window in the living room and stared at the empty driveway. The numbness was wearing off, and this time when his mind pictured Millie with another man, it hurt.

Chapter 30

Fifteen minutes later, Millie and Aris arrived in the Spikes's neighborhood. Aris sat in the passenger seat, nose nearly pressed against the glass as she read house numbers.

"Remember," Millie said, "you're staying in the car. I'm taking a quick look at the sled, and then we're out of here."

"I know," Aris retorted. "While you're at it, though, keep an eye out for Bart's hat."

Millie doubted they'd see Bart's hat in plain view but kept this to herself. She gripped the steering wheel more tightly as they passed Karl Kauffman's house. He lived in this same neighborhood, and she hadn't forgotten the angry look on his face the night she'd broken up with him for the second time.

Her uneasiness increased as they pulled over to the curb in front of a modest raised ranch that was badly in need of a paint job. A Little Tikes plastic swimming pool was filled to the slide with snow, and a rusting Flexible Flyer leaned against the two-car detached garage. She started to get out of the car and saw Aris doing the same.

"What are you doing?"

"Coming with you." Aris slammed the Subaru's door and began to march up the Spikes's driveway.

"You were supposed to stay in the car," Millie hissed, drawing even with her.

"I lied," Aris stated unapologetically. "Let's see if the side door to the garage is unlocked."

It wasn't. But Millie bit her tongue and actually was glad to have Aris's company as they circled the structure and realized the windows were too high to see anything. They mulled it over then decided the only way to take a look was if Aris climbed onto Millie's back.

Soon Aris was sitting on Millie's shoulders. For a thin woman, she was surprisingly heavy and hard to balance. Millie struggled to keep her balance as Aris strained to see through the dusty windows.

"What do you see?" Millie hissed as the seconds ticked past.

"A lot of dust. Get closer." Aris leaned forward, nearly pulling Millie into the straggly bushes lining the garage wall.

"Hurry," Millie grunted.

"Ugh."

"What?"

"Piles of stuff. Boxes. Newspapers. It's like the town dump. Can you get me a little closer?"

She inched closer and slipped in the snow, nearly unseating Aris who grabbed Millie's head for balance. "Let go," Millie ordered. "You're almost breaking my neck."

The pressure under her jaw decreased a little, but Aris's legs clamped more tightly. "Would you look at that."

"Do you see the sled?"

"No, but there's a big roll of chicken wire."

Millie remembered Eva telling her that people had once used chicken wire to strengthen the structure of their box sleds. It was illegal now to use it. She braced herself against the increasing weight on her shoulders. "Maybe that kid is lining his cardboard with chicken wire."

Aris pursed her lips. "That's what I thought. Bend down. The sled isn't in here. We need to look in the basement."

Millie sighed in relief as Aris climbed off her shoulders. "Maybe we should just go."

"Just a quick look," Aris promised. "It'll just take a second. And it might help Bart."

Although Millie knew better, she silenced her misgivings and followed Aris around the side of the house. Beneath a wooden deck, a pair of glass doors opened to a walk-out basement.

Aris rushed up and pressed her face against the glass. "Look!" she cried.

At first all Millie could see was a large-screen television and a sagging green couch. But on the left there was a worktable, and sitting on top of it was a giant cardboard shark. It was painted black and white and had its mouth gaping open.

"It has teeth," Millie gasped. "And it's big." A lot bigger than the *Flying French Fry*. Whipping out her cell phone, she snapped a shot of it. "Is it even legal to be that size?"

"Eva will know," Aris stated. "Those teeth don't look like they're made out of cardboard either. Maybe they're lined with chicken wire."

"Martin did say something about eating the competition."

"You don't suppose they left the sliding door open, do you?" Aris's gloved hands were already on the handle. Leaning back, she slid the door open.

Aris was about to squeeze inside when a very deep voice said, "Hold it."

Millie recognized that voice. Her heart sank as her gaze slowly traveled up the gold stripe on long, blue pant legs to the ski parka with the Deer Valley Police Department badge. Swallowing, she struggled to put on a good face as her eyes took in Karl Kauffman's craggy features. "Hello, Karl," she said. "I can explain."

"Turn around slowly and put your hands against the side of the house."

"Karl, this really isn't necessary," Millie protested. "We're just looking. . . ."

"You were breaking and entering."

"We just wanted to see if anyone was home," Aris said. "Nobody answered the front door. . . ."

"Because you didn't ring the bell," Karl said. "I've been watching you."

"I can explain," Millie tried again.

"And you will explain, at the station."

"Karl—you know us—we're not burglars," Millie said.

He looked down at her and slowly shook his head. "I really don't know you at all." He motioned with his arm. "Get going."

The knowledge that Millie had lied to him was eating David up from the inside out. He had to know what else she was holding back from him, and yet he dreaded discovering what she might tell him. It was like waiting for biopsy results you knew would be bad.

He paced the living room. Every few moments he drew back the curtains and looked at the empty driveway. Why hadn't Millie talked to him about Kauffman? He felt a stir of anger. She had no problem telling him how to parent. And she'd had plenty of time. Eva had fallen weeks ago.

He waited as long as he could then did something he'd never done before—decided to leave Bart alone in the house. Millie's house was only fifteen minutes away, and he needed to confront her in person. He'd be back in an hour. Just as he started up the steps to tell Bart, he heard a car pull into the driveway.

He headed for the front door. Opening it, he was surprised to see Millie's Subaru in the driveway and Aris coming up the steps. She was barely through the door when he started firing questions. "Where were you? Why are you so late?" And then the question that ate at him. "Where's Millie?"

Aris pushed back loose strands of her silver hair and twisted her reddened hands together unhappily. "It's a long story."

David studied the haggard look of her face and the slight slump of her shoulders. "What happened? Is Millie okay?"

Aris wiped her nose with a crumpled tissue. "She's fine, but David, she needs your help."

"Just tell me where she is."

Aris's eyes darted slightly to the left. Then her gaze returned to rest unhappily on his. "Karl Kauffman took her to the police station. She's been arrested."

On his way to the police station, David thought about the story Aris had told him. He knew Kauffman wasn't going to charge Millie with anything. If anything, David suspected that Kauffman had a different objective in mind—like maybe what he and Millie had done the night David's mother had seen them in the car together. Something burned hot and deep in David's stomach. Would it always be like this? Every time a man looked at Millie in a certain way, was David always going to wonder just how well that man knew her?

To be fair, would Millie look at photos of himself and Lisa and wonder who David loved more?

He gripped the wheel tighter. *How do you do it, Lord? How do You start over? Build a life over a life?*

The answer was through faith in God—only it couldn't be just his. He had been encouraged by the way Millie had clung to him in the hospital when he had prayed for Eva. But now he doubted her. Doubted them. Maybe he'd been stupid to think that believing in God would ever be more to her than a concept. He'd even been vain enough to think that God might use him to help her personally know God.

Why didn't Millie tell me about him, Lord?

He listened hard, but there was only the hum of his Lexus's engine. His mind flashed through some of his conversations with Millie, confirming that she had had plenty of opportunity to tell him about Kauffman. He was the wronged one. And then his mind came to a screeching stop when he remembered the time in the garage when she'd tried to tell him of the men she'd dated. He'd shut her down, politely of course, but firmly.

"It doesn't matter," he'd said. *"I like who you are now."*

It had been the truth, but it wasn't the whole truth. He hadn't wanted to know about the other men. He didn't want to think about her with anyone else but himself.

He felt his chest tighten in the sudden realization that congratulating himself on being so much better than Millie was laughable. His intentions had been good, but somewhere along the line he'd let tolerance slip into ignorance.

He hadn't wanted to feel Bart's pain or loneliness, so he'd

distanced himself with work and taken Bart's good grades as a report card on the rest of his life. He hadn't wanted to deal with Cynthia's emotions, so he had used Millie to solve the problem.

Now that he knew this, there was no going back. No way of closing his eyes, of saying the world was one way when he knew it was another.

He accelerated down the quiet street.

It felt like days, not hours, had passed when Millie finally stepped out of the conference room at the police station. Karl had asked a lot of tough questions. *"Why did you flirt with me at the Blue Moose if you didn't want to get back together? Why did you dance with me? Let me kiss you?"*

Millie had shaken her head. She didn't know where to start or how to explain things she didn't entirely understand herself. It hadn't been about Kyle, she knew that much. It had been about her—about feeling afraid and confused and him being there. She apologized for misleading him and for hurting him. She'd felt small, telling him that she'd made a mistake kissing him, that there had never been a chance of them getting back together.

Karl shut the door behind them. She turned to say good-bye. "I'm *really* sorry for everything," she said. "I hope someday you can forgive me."

His response was to lift her off her feet and hold her there in a bear hug that she hoped was his way of accepting her apology. It wasn't very comfortable, but she didn't struggle, and after a long moment, he set her gently on the floor. "If he doesn't treat you right, Millie, just let me know and I'll arrest him for something."

Millie laughed and almost reached up to touch his face but stopped herself in time. "Thanks, Karl," she said. "Don't be a stranger at the café, okay?"

He nodded and then started down the hallway. Her gaze followed him until he turned a corner. He was a good man and in time would find someone to love and who would love him back. Someone much nicer than Millie. As she started down the hallway, her heart stopped when she saw a man in jeans and a blue sweater sitting on a bench just down the hall. "David," she said, hurrying over to him. "Am I glad to see you."

He stood slowly. "Are you?"

It occurred to her that he might have read more into that bear hug Kyle had given her than there was, but short of coming right out and saying it, she wasn't sure how to reassure him. "Of course," Millie stated firmly. "I was about to call you and ask for you to come bail me out." When he didn't smile, she added, "I hope Aris told you what happened?"

"She did."

"We saw chicken wire in the garage, David. Did she tell you that? And the sled is huge. It's a great white shark. I seriously think this kid is going to try something sneaky in the race."

"Right now I really don't care about the sled."

"You're mad that I interfered?"

David shook his head. He had an expression on his face she'd never seen before. "Let's just go," he said and began walking down the long, quiet corridor. He didn't offer his arm or speak as they walked out of the building. The freezing air stung her cheeks as they stepped outdoors, but the real coldness was coming from David, and Millie felt panic stir inside her. He'd gotten mad at her before, but it hadn't felt like this. She didn't understand it, but she feared it.

"David—I'm sorry."

The Lexus's engine jumped to life. David put the car in REVERSE and backed out of the parking spot. His gaze was fixed on the road in front of him. She sat silently wondering what to say. She'd already apologized. Couldn't he see that what she'd done had been for Bart?

"David," she said, "this is ridiculous. It's not like I robbed a bank or something."

He shot her a sideways look. "Why didn't you tell me about Karl Kauffman?"

Her stomach knotted, but she forced herself to smile. "Well, I didn't know he was going to arrest me."

She'd hoped for a laugh, but David didn't crack a smile. Her anxiety went up another notch.

She swallowed. "Look, there's nothing going on between Karl and me. I only came down to the station with him so he'd let Aris go home. And," she amended, looking down, "we had some unfinished business. That hug you saw—it was him saying good-bye to me."

They drove past the library with its flat, snow-carpeted lawn and towering pine, and then David turned unexpectedly and pulled into the parking spot behind the building. The streetlights had yet to come on, but the light was dim, and Millie had a sick feeling as he put the car into PARK and the sound of the running engine was the only noise.

"So what unfinished business did you have with him?"

Millie thought furiously. What was safe to say? How much should she tell him? "Well, you know we used to date." She paused. "He's having a hard time moving on."

"Are you?"

She laughed. "No. I want to be friends, but that's it."

"And is that why you went out with him the night you were

supposed to come to my house?"

She felt her expression freeze. *Oh God,* she thought, *he knows.* "We didn't plan it." She realized how bad it sounded. "It was nothing, David. He needed to talk to me, and I thought I owed it to him to listen."

"So why didn't you tell me about it?"

She shuffled her feet. "Maybe I didn't think you'd understand." How did you explain that sometimes going along with something was easier than fighting it? That she'd let Karl take the lead and closed her ears to the voice that knew she was making a huge mistake?

"Why don't you try me now?"

Because she was scared. She didn't want to hurt him, and she didn't want to lose him either. Yet once he knew that she'd basically lied and cheated, it would be over between them. There was no way he could forgive her, so why bother? She looked down at her hands. Short, blunt nails and a big, fake ruby ring. She considered simply opening the car door and running away.

"Have you ever done anything wrong in your entire life?"

"Of course," he said.

But he would never have done what she'd done, and the knowledge of this lay in her heart like a stone. What was wrong with her? Why was it so easy for some people always to do the right thing and others got caught in gray areas and messed up? It was hopeless. They should just call it a night. Yet deep inside, she didn't want to just walk away. David deserved better. Even if he ended up hating her, it was better to tell him the truth and not have to carry it around inside anymore.

Taking a deep breath, Millie told him about going for a walk and running into Karl. She told him how she'd gotten in his truck thinking they were going for coffee and then ended up at the Blue

Moose. "I had a glass of wine," she admitted, "and when the band started playing, I danced with him." She paused. "A few hours later, he walked me back to his truck, and I let him kiss me. I knew right away it was a mistake, and I told him." She looked into his eyes. "I'm so sorry, David."

He rubbed the back of his neck. "You kissed him."

"Yes. I totally messed up, but it won't happen again."

He was silent for so long she began to wonder if he was going to give her another chance.

She studied the dips and curves and contours of David's mouth. His lips were tight, serious, possibly disappointed. She swallowed. She'd come this far; she might as well finish what she'd started. She sighed. "Maybe you need to know why I kissed Karl."

Half expecting him to push her away, she reached to touch his face softly. He closed his eyes as she caressed his cheek and slid her hands into his hair. Leaning across the console, she lifted her other arm and placed it on his shoulder. He didn't move as she lifted her face to his. She heard him sigh as she kissed him, and then something seemed to release in them both, and he was kissing her back. His fingers buried themselves in her hair, and he supported her head, holding on to her as if he would never let her go. It was a kiss of apology, of acceptance, of an understanding that what they had between them was more important than anything that had happened.

Finally, they broke apart and looked long and hard into each other's eyes. "Do you understand now why I kissed Karl?"

His brow furrowed, but a hint of humor came into his eyes. "Not a clue, but I'm willing for you to show me again."

She almost laughed and gave in to do exactly that. However, as nice as kissing him was, she wanted him to understand why she had been vulnerable to Karl's advances. "It's the way you kiss."

"You don't like it?" His voice was low and private, but his eyes teased her.

"I like it very much."

"Then what's the problem?"

She held his gaze. The problem was that she couldn't kiss him like that and hold back part of herself as she did in other relationships. When she was with him, she was a different person, and it was very confusing. Folding her arms, she looked up at him and let her breath out slowly. "You scare me," she said very softly. "When you kiss me, you scare me."

"That isn't the reaction I'm going for," David said dryly.

"Maybe not," Millie said. "But you do. It's going to take me time to get used to it."

"When I kiss you, you don't feel very scared. You feel kind of wonderful, Millie."

"The scared part comes after," she admitted. "The first time you kissed me—that was the scariest because I wasn't expecting it. This time was better."

The corners of David's mouth tugged. "What exactly are you scared of?"

She shifted uncomfortably. Usually guys spilled their feelings to her—not the other way around. "For a genius guy, I can't believe you can't figure it out."

"I'm not a genius or a mind reader," he said mildly.

"And I'm not a girl who settles down," Millie said. "But when I kiss you, I kind of forget that. I guess I wanted Karl to remind me who I was."

"I know who you are, Millie Hogan, and you're a lot better person than you give yourself credit for."

"Thanks—but I'm not. I'm sorry I didn't tell you about that night."

"I'm sorry I scared you," David said gravely. "I didn't know."

Millie nodded. "My mother did. She was furious. She said I was trying to sabotage us, and she was right."

"It didn't work. I'm still here."

"Well, for now." Millie closed her mouth tightly. She'd meant to think that, not say it aloud.

He frowned. "What do you mean by that?"

She twisted her fingers together. "In my family," she mumbled, "the guy always leaves."

"I won't." He laced his warm fingers into her cold ones. "I'm not your father, and I'm not going to abandon you."

"You could get hit by a car tomorrow or have a heart attack like my grandfather."

"Or I could live to be a very old man and we could sit on the front porch in our rocking chairs together." The grip on her hands increased. "There are a lot of things we still need to figure out, but I have strong feelings for you, Millie. The past couple of weeks I've felt more alive and happier than I have in years. I feel like we're meant to be together."

"Me, too," she whispered then frowned unhappily at him. "This wasn't supposed to happen. I wasn't supposed to actually fall for you."

"I know."

"We had an agreement. With clear boundaries."

He started to smile. "I wasn't looking for this either."

"So what are we going to do?"

His smile widened. "I don't know, but I think we're going to need a new plan."

Chapter 31

Deer Mountain had its humble beginnings in 1936 when a group of skiers formed a club, built a rope tow, and used their wooden skis to trample a trail. It had been growing ever since with the goal of becoming the best family ski hill in the country. In the late forties, the owners of the mountain bought its first chairlift. Now the mountain featured a quad lift, three triple chairs, two doubles, and a J-bar for the bunny slope.

During the weeklong winter carnival, hundreds of tourists flocked to the races. Skiers of every age and level of ability could be seen schussing down the long white trails cut into the thick trees on the mountain. But what set Deer Mountain apart from other ski hills, and what brought people back every March was the box sled races.

This year's race day seems more crowded than ever, Millie thought as she squeezed her way through the people clustered on the second-story sundeck. It was not even eight o'clock in the morning, but the sun reflected off the snow, creating a shade so white the hill seemed to shimmer. Around her, people talked loudly, nearly drowning themselves out. She smelled bacon-and-egg sandwiches and the deeper aroma of coffee.

Eva, Aris, and the aunts were seated at a table reserved for handicapped people. It was nearest the wood railing and had one of the best views of the slopes.

"How'd it go?" Aunt Lillian asked as Millie walked up to the table. Lillian sat in her wheelchair with a thick wool blanket pulled around her.

"Bart's pretty nervous," Millie said. "But the inspection went fine. David is helping him bring the sled to the holding area."

"Come sit," Aunt Keeker offered, sliding down on the bench to make room. She was wearing a multitailed ski hat with bells at the bottom.

Next to Keeker, Aunt Mimi sat on a couple of blankets to give herself a little more height. Earl Gray sniffed for scraps atop the picnic table. Dogs probably weren't allowed, and Millie wondered how Mimi had managed to smuggle Earl Gray inside.

"Have some hot chocolate," Mimi ordered. "You look cold. This will warm you up."

"Maybe later." She glanced at her mother, but as usual Eva avoided her gaze. Although Eva had graduated from the wheelchair to crutches, their relationship felt as broken as ever.

On the side of the mountain, people were dragging their sleds to the top of the wide trail where the box sleds would race. Millie watched a father pull a little girl in a sled that looked exactly like Cinderella's pumpkin-shaped carriage. Behind Cinderella, a little boy wearing chaps and a cowboy hat sat in a cardboard Conestoga wagon. There was a dragon sled and a race car, all equipped with their miniature riders.

Millie's stomach tightened. Children. Would she want one with David? They hadn't discussed it yet, but they would. And soon. Bart was already eleven. And there was the whole church thing. David had made it clear it was important to him. So far she'd managed to use work as an excuse not to go, but the truth was that she was uncomfortable with the thought of everyone staring at her, congratulating David with their eyes for getting her there. She didn't want to open herself up to the conclusions they would draw.

She watched her mother sip her hot chocolate. "You warm enough, Mom?"

"Oh yes," Eva said. "Beautiful day, isn't it?"

"Yes," Millie agreed. "Aren't the little kids cute?"

"Adorable."

The old Eva would have said, *Look at that cute little girl. I want grandchildren. What are you waiting for, Millie? Instructions?*

"Did you take your pain pill?"

"Yes honey."

"Do you want to put your leg up?"

"No thank you."

Their exchange left a bad taste in Millie's mouth, as if she'd dumped way too much sugar into her coffee.

Someone tapped her on her shoulder, and Millie jerked. Aris bent over her. Her long silver braid was thrown over her chest like a sash. "I need to talk to you. In private."

The announcer's voice boomed over the loudspeaker, calling for the first heat of the peewee race. There was plenty of time before Bart's race, so Millie followed Aris into the lodge then down the metal stairs to the concession area. Nearly all the tables were taken, but when a family got up, Aris quickly slid into the seat. "I want to apologize," she began.

"For what?" Millie scoffed. "You didn't force me to drive you to the Spikes's house. And besides, Devon's sled passed inspection."

The older woman shook her head. Her eyes were downturned, and her skin was deeply wrinkled, tissue thin, and dotted with age spots. "Not for that."

Millie leaned forward. "Then what?" She wondered if the older woman had broken something at the café.

"I'm an interfering old woman, and I know it. But you have to understand that the Denvers are my family. I lost my husband in the Vietnam War. We had no children, and I was never close to my brothers. When I met Lisa and David, I was a cleaning lady who watched too much television and lived off frozen dinners and cans of soup." She sighed. "Lisa befriended me. Before I knew it, I was going to church with her, and my life started changing. It got even better when Lisa got pregnant and asked me to be Bart's nanny."

Millie sensed there was a purpose to the story, but she also was impatient to get back to the sundeck and watch the races. She had to bite her lip to keep from prompting Aris to hurry.

"So when you started dating David, I was curious about you. I love him, and besides, I promised Lisa to look after him and Bart." She twisted her thin fingers in her lap. "Remember all the questions I asked you that day I helped out at the café? I was getting information so I could research you. I had heard rumors, and I was curious about your father."

Millie felt herself go very still. "What?"

Aris's face seemed to fold into itself. "There's no excuse for what I did. You have every right to hate me."

"I don't hate you."

"You will when I tell you what I know."

Millie tried to swallow but found her throat had gone dry.

"I found him on the Internet." Aris reached into her purse and pulled out several sheets of paper. Sliding them across the table, she said, "It wasn't hard."

The pages were neatly folded and looked exactly like the cheap paper that came out of Millie's printer. She touched the edges gingerly then slowly lifted the papers.

The first thing she saw was a blue and red state seal, and then she read: *Salt Lake First District Court, State of Utah v. Maximillian Hogan.*

Her chest constricted as her eyes skimmed the page. Second-degree felony. Utah County. Embezzlement of funds. Salt Lake Christian Church. Guilty. A term not to exceed fifteen years in the state prison.

Her father was an inmate at the Utah State Prison. He was serving his sixth year.

Her father. A thief. In jail. She felt herself slump but didn't have the strength to sit upright.

Criminals were people she'd been taught to fear—the villains of the scary stories teenagers told in the dark, bad people who robbed, stole, and killed. They were the ones that made you test the lock on the doors at night.

"Millie?" Aris's voice seemed far in the distance. "Millie?"

She focused on Aris with effort. "There's got to be some kind of mistake." Her brain seized gratefully onto this possibility.

"There's no mistake. I'm sorry."

"There could be another Maximillian Hogan." Millie sat up straighter. Lots of people shared names and birthdays.

"I wrote to the First District Court of Utah County and got a copy of the judgment and commitment form. Everything matches."

"Maybe someone stole his identity."

"I don't think so," Aris said grimly. "I'm sorry, Millie. I wish I'd never poked my nose in your business."

Why did you? Millie was free-falling again. She shoved the pages at Aris then immediately wanted to grab them back. "It doesn't matter. He means nothing to me."

Aris pressed her lips together so tightly they disappeared and left a gash where her mouth should have been. Millie realized there was more bad news coming. "Tell me the rest," she said.

Aris sighed heavily. "I wasn't expecting to find out anything like this. Anything at all, really. And then when I did, I didn't know what to do with the information." She hesitated. "I went to David's mother."

"You what?"

"I couldn't go to David. I didn't think he'd be objective enough." She tried to touch Millie's arm, but Millie pulled away. "It was before I got to know you. And I'm really sorry I had to tell you this, but I think she wants to talk to you about all this."

"When?"

"Soon. Maybe today. I didn't want her to blindside you. She isn't a bad person, but she feels like David should know the truth."

Millie swallowed something bitter tasting. She supposed she should thank Aris for warning her, but the words wouldn't come out of her mouth. The weight of despair settled over her. She imagined Mrs. Denvers telling her that Millie was trash. That she wasn't good enough for David.

Millie bit her lip. Maybe Mrs. Denvers was right.

"Could I see that paper again?" Her hands trembled as she reached for the sheets. All this time she'd worried about turning into her mother and now this—this horrific news about her dad.

"Millie, are you okay? You're very pale. Let me get you a hot chocolate."

"I'm fine, Aris." She folded the papers and stuck them into the pocket of her parka. She forced herself to think. "Does anyone else know?"

"No. Just Mrs. Denvers and myself." Aris searched Millie's eyes. "It's not the end of the world. Everyone has a skeleton in the family closet. Some have quite a few rattling around." She laughed, but it ended in an awkward silence.

Skeletons maybe, but not criminals. Millie climbed to her feet. She thought of the money her father had stolen and wished he were dead. All those wasted years of dreaming of gaining his approval, of proving her worth so he'd regret leaving her. She felt sick to her stomach.

He's worse than nothing. And I'm his daughter, so I guess that makes me worse than nothing, too.

"You're upset with me, aren't you?"

I look out windows and dream about other lives. I've used and hurt other people. I'm exactly like him.

Millie struggled to speak past the interior voice grinding her into nothingness. "I'm not mad. I promise."

Anger would require emotion. She had nothing inside, nothing but this growing sense of shame and an awful voice attacking her, beating her down. She gripped her fingers into fists. Was there no way of stopping it?

She almost laughed. She'd dreamed of being famous, of people knowing her name, but never for something like this. Through the wall of glass, she could see the box sleds coming down the hill. She thought of David and Bart, and for a moment something warm and sustaining flickered through her. She thought of David telling her that he was in love with her.

A warm feeling started to fill the hollowness inside. She loved David. And love was not worthless. There was a strength to it. Inside, a new voice began to speak. *"Cling to Me,"* it said. *"I'm strong enough to hold you."*

But she couldn't. Loving David didn't give her the right to grab hold of him as if she were a drowning person and he were a life preserver. That would be selfish. That wasn't love. Love was selfless.

Despair washed through her again. Aris's mouth was moving, but Millie couldn't hear a word. She wanted to run and hide, find a dark hole and disappear. Just like her father. The realization that she wanted to run made her cringe.

She wouldn't run, and she would tell David about her father. Just not today. Today belonged to Bart.

Her mind made up, she climbed to her feet. She looked out again at the great white mountain and gathered her strength. She was going to have to pretend nothing was wrong in front of the people who knew her best. Well, she'd always believed that she was meant to act, and now it seemed she'd have a chance to prove it.

Chapter 32

R emember what Miss Eva said. If you hit a patch of heavy snow and your sled stops, sit up and use your body weight to rock it free."

Bart's ski goggles were perched on top of his head, and the boy squinted up at him through the bright sunlight. "I know, Dad."

They were standing on a relatively flat area at the top of the bunny hill. The junior girls' races had just finished, and the boys were just about to get started. Looking around at the other sleds—a pirate ship that was a clear nod to the *Pirates of the Caribbean* movie, a race car so detailed he could count the spokes in the wheel, and a spaceship the shape of a fried egg—David fought the uneasy feeling in his stomach. He hadn't forgotten how humiliating it'd been when his Huckleberry Finn raft had fallen apart and he'd had to walk his sled down the hill.

"If someone cuts you off, go around them," David coached. "You can use the rudder and your body weight to turn the sled."

"Dad," Bart said, "I had this conversation with Mrs. Hogan a million times. I know what I'm doing."

David looked at his son's round face and bit his tongue. The *Flying French Fry* wasn't nearly as fancy as most of the other sleds, and maybe it wasn't as fast either. He wanted to prepare Bart for the possibility of failure without making it seem as if he expected his son to lose.

"All I care about is that you do your best." David had already said this ten times, but what he was trying to say was that winning wouldn't change the way he felt about Bart. He squeezed his son's shoulder. "I love you, Bartholomew," he said as softly as he could and still be heard. "Remember, God is good—all the time."

Their gazes met and both nodded. As Bart shuffled off, David crunched through the snow to a spot a little farther down the slope to a free spot behind the orange safety netting.

It wasn't long before all the sleds had lined up. Inching even closer to the orange safety netting, David strained for a glimpse of his son's determined face.

"Racers—on your mark, get set, go!"

The line of sleds lurched forward. A sled shaped like a dolphin took the lead, followed by the bright yellow cylinder of a rocket ship.

"Go, Bart!" David yelled.

The *Flying French Fry* slid forward, not quite as fast as some, but better than others. A few remained stuck at the starting line and were just beginning to inch crookedly forward.

Eva had stated with clear confidence that Bart would win, but David hadn't believed her, not really. However, he couldn't deny that after a slow start, the *Flying French Fry* was picking up speed quickly.

David leaned over the orange safety net and yelled encouragement. He watched Bart navigate around the pirate ship sled, which had turned sideways and come to a stop. Next Bart passed the flying saucer ship, the race car, and one shaped like a mummy's sarcophagus.

Bart sailed down the hill and, to David's disbelieving eyes, took the lead. His gaze followed the *Flying French Fry* as it continued to put more distance between itself and the other sleds. A few heart-pounding moments later, Bart Denvers crossed the finish line and became the first qualifier for the box sled finals of the boys' junior division.

Millie leaned as far over the deck railing as she could, screaming her throat raw as Bart's sled crossed the finish line. She turned exultantly to Aunt Keeker, who was standing beside her jumping up and down and cheering so wildly that her hat flew over the side of the deck.

"He did it," they said at the same time, hugging and laughing. "He did it!"

"French fries rule!" Aunt Mimi shouted. She was dancing on top of the picnic table as Earl Gray bounced up and down next to her like a canine basketball.

"Oh my goodness," Aunt Lillian said. Her wheelchair was mashed up against the deck railing. "Did you see that?"

Eva leaned against the railing, eyes sparkling, her cheeks flushed with triumph. "I told you," she exclaimed. "I told you he could do it."

Their exultant mood, however, was tempered when in the next race Devon Spikes won his heat with the morning's best time.

"This isn't good," Millie said.

Eva shrugged. "The track is getting faster, that's all. Don't worry, honey."

But Millie couldn't help thinking of how big that kid was and how fast his sled had gone. By the time the seven finalists in Bart's category lined up, she'd bitten her nails down to stubs and was thinking about having a cup of her mom's spiked hot chocolate.

She searched the crowd on the sidelines for a glimpse of David, who surely had to be a nervous wreck. She wished she were standing next to him, but a voice inside said she didn't have the right to be there.

The finalists began to line up. The announcer introduced the racers by name and sled. Millie gripped the railing more tightly. *I don't know if You can hear me or not, but if You can, God, Bart could use some help.* Her mother squeezed her great bulk into the small space between Millie and Aunt Keeker. Millie found a small solace in the familiar feel of her body pressed against Millie's.

Leaning against the railing for support, Eva put her gloved hand over Millie's. "Here we go," she said.

The crowd roared as the sleds started down the hill. Millie leaned over the railing and yelled with all her might, "Go, Bart!"

The *Flying French Fry* slid forward. It was a faster start than Bart had had before, but not as fast as the rocket-shaped sled that slid into the lead. It was closely followed by a sled in the shape of a Wii controller. *Jaws*, the biggest sled on the hill, fought with a guitar-shaped sled for third place.

All around Millie people were screaming at the top of their lungs, and the combined weight of their excitement crushed her against the wooden railing. Millie's heart was in her throat as she watched the tight clusters of sleds progress down the hill. "Go, Bart," she screamed as he picked up speed and gained ground on the guitar and *Jaws* sled.

As if he'd heard her encouragement, the *French Fry* steadily accelerated and passed the guitar-shaped sled and the shark sled. She cheered as Bart drew even with the Wii-shaped controller.

A fat white flake plopped on her nose, startling her. It was starting to snow, and with dismay she realized the track would be slower. Some answer to her prayer, she thought as big flakes dotted the sky. Almost instantly the entire hill was veiled in a curtain of white lace.

Blinking, Millie strained to see the racers. In astonishment, she watched Bart close the gap between his sled and the rocket ship. They were almost dead even halfway down the hill. However, the *Jaws* sled was bearing down on them rapidly and moments later pulled up alongside Bart's sled.

"Come on, Bart," Eva bellowed. "Take him," she yelled in a more commanding tone of voice than Millie had ever heard before. "Take him down!"

But then Devon Spikes turned his sled into the *Flying French Fry*. It looked like the *Jaws* sled was trying to put the *Flying French Fry* in its mouth—or rather, push it sideways and out of the running.

She shouted a warning and tasted the icy flakes that spiraled into her mouth. She gripped her mother's arm without thinking what she was doing. "Bart's in trouble," she screamed.

"Use the rudder," Eva shouted so loudly it hurt Millie's ears.

The floor of the deck vibrated under the intensity of the cheering crowd as the *Jaws* sled increased its pressure and managed to alter the *Flying French Fry*'s course.

However, just as it seemed Bart's sled would be pushed completely sideways, the sled shaped like a Wii controller came up hard on Bart's right. It either couldn't turn or didn't have time because it slammed into the right side of Bart's sled. The blow straightened out the *Flying French Fry* and sent it flying down the hill.

Millie leaned as far over the railing as she could and screamed, "Go, Bart!" Her muscles strained as the *Flying French Fry* and the *Jaws* sled battled it out for the lead. Precious seconds passed. Millie measured the remaining distance to the finish line with her gaze and dug her fingernails into the wooden railing.

Seconds later, both sleds passed beneath the finish line. It was impossible to tell if it had been Bart or Devon who had won. A hush fell over the crowd as everyone waited for the results.

"I think I'm going to have a heart attack," Keeker said, fanning herself rapidly.

The silence was agonizing. Millie watched Bart get out of his sled. His gaze traveled around the crowd, probably looking for his father, but then it settled on Millie. A flush of pleasure shot through her when he grinned and waved.

"Ladies and gentlemen," the announcer's voice boomed over the ski hill. "We have the results of the closest finish today." There was a long pause. "After careful consideration, and thanks to Joseph Fairbranch photography, we have determined the winner." There was another long pause. "Setting a new record in the junior boys' division is. . .Bart Denvers and the *Flying French Fry*."

Millie jumped into the air and screamed. She high-fived Eva, hugged Aris, and leaned over to kiss Lillian's cheek. Keeker thumped her on the back.

"Never a doubt in my mind," Eva declared, beaming. She met Millie's gaze and gestured with her arm. "Now go on, honey. Don't wait for us. Go give that boy a hug."

Chapter 33

David grinned as Bart lifted the silver trophy above his head. Beside him, David's father fired off shots with a camera lens roughly the size of a canon. His mother had her cell pressed to her ear and was excitedly passing along the news to her sister in Wisconsin. A small crowd of kids Bart's age had formed a semicircle around them and were cheering. He spotted Millie in the back with Eva and the aunts and motioned for her to come closer, but she shook her head and gave him a big smile.

Bart had won. It hadn't quite sunk in yet. Nevertheless, there Bart was, trophy in hand, getting congratulated by Thomas Linklin, the tall, deeply tanned owner of the ski hill.

The award ceremony was short. Afterward there was handshaking and backslapping. Eva was triumphant and invited everyone within earshot back to the café for ice cream. Judging from the enthusiastic cheer that went up, it was going to be a big group.

Leaving Bart with the sled, David hiked to the back of the lot to get the Lexus. He planned to call Devon Spikes's parents that very evening and let them know that he was meeting with the principal and that he would not tolerate any further harassment.

His heart stopped as he pulled the Lexus to the snowy curb and saw Bart talking to the very kid he had been thinking about. He got of the car, started to march right over there, and then hesitated. Instinct urged him to wait, to give Bart a chance to work this out. Part of him screamed in protest as the bully kid, a full head taller, leaned over Bart, who kept pushing his glasses nervously higher on his face.

David's fists clenched. He'd give them two more minutes, and then he was marching over there and letting Devon Spikes know what it felt like when a much bigger person leaned over him.

More words were exchanged. The bully gave Bart a small push. David stepped forward. At the same time, his son's chin came up and his hands went to his hips. It wasn't a gesture David saw often, but when he did, it meant Bart was about to get very stubborn.

His son said something, and surprisingly the bully jerked as if in surprise. Bart said something else. The bully considered and then a moment later pulled off his ski hat (Bart's hat actually), threw it on the ground, and stormed off. Bart picked the hat off the ground, dusted it off, and stuffed it in his pocket.

David crunched through the snow over to his son. "Are you okay?"

Bart's eyes blinked at him from behind the thick lenses. "Yeah."

"What just happened? Did that bully threaten you?"

His son's cheeks were reddened from the cold, and his hair stood almost upright where the wind had riffled through it. Yet Bart didn't look as if he felt the cold at all. "He tried to push me around, but I handled it." He picked up the towrope to the sled. "We can go now."

"First, I want to know what he said to you—and what you said to him."

Bart seemed to think about this then nodded. "He wanted me to give him the money I just won, but I wouldn't."

David nodded grimly. "And then he threatened you?"

"Yeah, but don't worry, Dad. He won't touch me." Bart gave a small laugh. "Miss Hogan was right."

Frowning, David tried to remember what Millie might have said. "About what?"

"That I could outsmart him."

"How'd you do that?"

Bart stood a little taller. "Well, since I got the highest grade in my class on the last science test, I get to pick my lab partner for this week. It's a double grade, Dad. I told Devon that I would pick him as my partner." A smug smile appeared on Bart's face. "I told him that I had a 99 percent average and could fail the lab and still hold my A. I asked him what a zero would do to his grade." Bart paused. "At first he said it didn't matter and that he'd still beat me up. But then he figured out that if he was failing science he couldn't play on the ice hockey team." Bart grinned. "After that he was happy to let me keep the winnings and give me back my ski hat."

David grinned. "Brilliant. That was brilliant. I'm proud of you."

Bart shrugged, but his eyes gleamed. "You are?"

"Absolutely. It took courage to do what you just did."

Bart tipped his head but not before David glimpsed the pleasure in his eyes. "Dad," he said, "I've been thinking. Even though I can handle Devon, I want to go with you when you meet with the principal on Monday."

"What?"

"Devon's a bully. He might start bothering someone else, especially if we get a new student. I don't want them to go through what I did."

David rubbed his hand over Bart's spikey hair then snaked his arm around his son's shoulders, pulling him close. "That's a fine idea," he said thickly. "A very fine idea."

Chapter 34

Millie's arm ached from digging scoops of the rock-hard ice cream. "Here you go." She smiled and passed a double scoop of chocolate ice cream into the waiting hands of a skinny, dark-haired boy.

"Thanks, Miss Hogan." The boy flashed a brilliant smile, showing off a mouthful of silver braces.

"You're welcome." She pushed back her bangs with her shoulder. "Next?"

"Triple scoop of chocolate, vanilla, and strawberry," a tall red-haired boy said. He had a face full of freckles and a sunburn that marked the line of his ski hat. "And sprinkles. I love sprinkles."

"You got it," Millie said, putting some muscle into scooping.

As she handed over the cone, she spotted Bart and David talking with Mr. and Mrs. Denvers. David's mother smiled warmly at her. Of course Mrs. Denvers was happy. She had the goods on Millie.

Millie lifted her arm to wave back and felt cold drops of ice cream dribble onto her wrist. *Act happy,* she reminded herself. *Today is about Bart.*

At the table in front of the bay window, Millie's mother sat with the aunts. They were laughing even more loudly than the kids. For a moment, she soaked up the sight of seeing Eva so happy, and then her shoulders sagged. Her mother would have to be told about Max. She hadn't thought about that before.

Overwhelmed with this new worry, Millie asked Aris to take her place then excused herself to the back. Fleeing through the swinging doors, she wiped her hands on her apron. Unseeing, she passed the grill, the sinks, and the freezer. When she reached the back pantry, she jerked the door open and stepped inside. Without turning on the light, she shut the door and walked to the back of the room.

What do I do? How do I make this pain go away? I can't bear it anymore. I just can't. I just can't.

Covering her face with her hands, she made a keening noise. All these years, she'd thought she had star potential. What an idiot she'd been.

She pulled out the court papers from her apron pocket. It was too dark to read them, but holding them produced fresh agony. How could he have done this? Stolen from innocent people? Hard-working people who gave their money to the church.

Her father was the most heartless, selfish person she knew. And yet, even now, even holding the papers in her hands, she realized there was part of her that still loved him. As disappointed as she was in him, she still wanted to see what he looked like, to hear what he would say to her.

The door cracked open, and a wedge of light broke the darkness. David stood in the entranceway. She quickly swiped her eyes.

"Millie?" David stepped forward. "Are you okay?"

She grabbed a can off the shelf and plastered a smile on her face. "Oh sure." Maybe she'd never see Hollywood, but she could certainly act her way out of the pantry.

The lights flickered and then came on. He'd found the switch, and the sudden brightness was painful.

"We were running a little low on supplies, so I came back here."

"Yes," David agreed, "the kids would be very disappointed if you ran out of tomatoes." He glanced pointedly at the can in her hands.

Millie laughed. "Oh, right. I meant to grab the chocolate syrup. Guess I should have turned on the light after all." She gave another ridiculous little laugh. "So much for conserving energy."

"Millie," David said gently, "don't do this."

"Do what?" She flashed her best smile.

"Pretend. You're pretending with me. Don't." He studied her carefully. "You don't look right. You didn't at the ski hill either."

"That's not something you tell a girl." Millie pushed her hair out of her eye and batted her eyelashes. "No woman wants to hear she doesn't look good."

"I'm not saying that you don't look good. I'm saying that you don't look *right*. What's wrong?"

"Seriously, David. Nothing." She wasn't sure how much longer she could hold it together. "Let's get back to the party."

"In a minute. First talk to me."

Millie shook her head. "Nothing is wrong."

"Ever since the box sled race you've been avoiding me."

"I've been scooping ice cream," Millie said evasively. "I had no idea preteen boys could eat like that." She made sure her eyes crinkled at the corners when she smiled and wished David would stop giving her that doctor look—the one that said he saw right through her.

Her gaze dropped to her boots. Her good ones—the ones Eva said were too thin and too high-heeled. Stylish but impractical, they'd pinched her toes since the day she'd bought them. She wondered if her father wore orange sneakers to go with the orange jumpsuit.

"Are you getting goosey about us?"

She looked up. David stood about a foot in front of her. She felt the first domino in her heart trip, and she had to steel all her willpower not to step into his arms. "I don't think *goosey* is a real word."

"You know what it means."

Her shoulders sagged. He wasn't going to let her out of the pantry until she told him the truth. She opened her mouth, but no words came out, just a long breath that if visible would have been the color of shame. "Not now, David. Please. Let today be about Bart."

"I can't do that, Millie. Talk to me."

She shook her head. "Please."

"Was it my mother? If she hurt you, I want to know."

She folded her arms firmly across her chest and looked down.

"She said something, didn't she?" David's voice had an angry edge to it. "I'm going to go out there right now and tell her to apologize."

"Don't do that," she said. "She didn't say anything." At least not yet. Apparently Mrs. Denvers hadn't told David about Millie's father. But she would, especially if David confronted her.

He touched her hair. "You've been crying. Let me fix whatever is wrong."

She dug her fingers into the palms of her hands. "That's the problem. You can't." Shame was ugly. Private. Humiliating. "I'll tell you everything, but not today."

"This isn't how it works," David said. "I told you, I'm not the leaving kind of guy. I'm not leaving you alone with whatever problem you're facing. You're just making it worse because I don't know what's going on."

"Fine," Millie said then began to laugh. "You want to know?

Well, my father's a crook."

"So what."

She laughed again and realized just how close to tears she was. She was not a girl who cried, and the thought helped steady her. "I found out he's serving time. He's in a prison in Utah. Aris gave me these papers today." She thrust the pages at him.

His eyes skimmed over the papers. "This is it? This is what you're so upset about?"

Millie stiffened. "David, I just said my father is a criminal."

"I heard you."

"My father *embezzled* money from a church." She was having trouble keeping her voice down. "He's a *criminal*." She waited for his expression to change. "He's probably making license plates as we speak."

"I don't care."

"You should. He's my father—I'm his daughter."

"So? He's human and made a mistake. We all do."

"When was the last time you embezzled twenty-five thousand dollars?" As expected, he was silent. "Come on, David. There are good people in this world and bad. My dad falls into the latter category."

"You're oversimplifying," David argued. "People aren't all good or all bad. You can't heap them into two piles—one to be saved, one to be tossed."

She snorted. "You don't understand. Your father stuck around and raised you. He might have some annoying habits you don't like, but essentially you know who he is. You know who you are because of him."

David shook his head. "I don't downplay his role in raising me, but ultimately he doesn't define me." He hesitated. "Just as your father doesn't define you."

"You can look at your parents and see parts of yourself in them. How would you feel, David, if your father did something terrible? Wouldn't you wonder if you were capable of doing the same thing— or worse? Wouldn't you wonder who you were inside?"

David reached out for her hands. "I might. But I hope I would also turn to God and ask Him to save me, to define who I was on the inside."

Millie remembered her own unanswered prayers from childhood. *Bring my father home. Make my mother stop eating so much. Please don't let my grandmother die. Help me get out of Deer Park. Make me famous. Shorter. Thinner. Smarter.* "What if God doesn't want to?" She felt the hopelessness rise in her.

"That wouldn't happen." David's grip on her fingers tightened. "Your father abandoned you—that was a terrible thing—and I know it hurt you deeply." He leaned a little closer. "But you have a heavenly Father, Millie. He loves you, and He's never going to abandon you. You are His beloved daughter."

She jerked her hands free. "Beloved daughter?" She made a strangled noise. "He doesn't love me." She could feel a slow anger burning inside. How could David do this? Suggest her life could be changed by turning to God and simply saying, "Save me." "That's like throwing dental floss to someone drowning."

"God loves you, Millie. He is the Father you need."

She stood taller in her anger. "How could you possibly say that? You've never had the bottom of your world fall out."

He didn't flinch. "Yes I have. And it hurt. And I questioned. But in the end, I accepted." His blue eyes seemed to bore into her. "Sometimes it feels like you're completely torn apart, and you can't even breathe without it hurting. But you give the pain to God,

Millie, and He takes it, and then somehow—I don't know how—He finds a way of making things new."

"Just because God helped you doesn't mean He's going to help me. I wasn't going to tell you this today, David, but we're breaking up." She hadn't decided this until now, but she realized her mind was made up.

David just looked at her. "Millie, I know you're upset about this, but—"

"We're breaking up," Millie interrupted. She was hurting, and something unkind in her wanted to hurt him, too. She stuck out her hand. "It's been very nice, but it's over." It was her standard breakup line. Judging from the tightness of his jaw, he'd recognized it.

He ignored her outstretched hand. "Don't do this."

"We'll tell people tomorrow. Right along with my other big news."

"I'm not telling anyone we're breaking up—period. Because we aren't. Breaking up with me because your father is in jail doesn't make sense."

"Maybe not to you, but it does to me." She reached for a bag of marshmallows just to hold something in her hands. "Besides, it never would have worked anyway."

"How do you know that?"

"Because we're too different."

There was less than a hand's width of space between their faces. She could see the tightness of his skin and the storm in his eyes. She was getting to him, but the knowledge gave her no pleasure.

"What I see," David said in a very controlled voice, "is someone who's scared of getting hurt again. Your father hurt you when he left, and you don't trust easily. But sooner or later you're going to see that I'm not going anywhere. I'm not going to leave you."

Millie lifted her chin. "You won't leave me," she said. "But that doesn't mean I won't leave you." She saw his eyes flicker with surprise. "You and Bart could wake up one morning and I could be halfway to California. Maybe there's more of my father in me than either of us realizes."

Suddenly the pantry door opened, and Eva said, "Oh, sorry. I didn't mean to interrupt. I was coming back here for a box of those Social Tea Biscuits Lillian likes." She started to back awkwardly away on the crutches then paused as she took in their expressions. Her face seemed to deflate as she realized she'd stepped into the middle of an argument.

"Oh no, Millie," Eva murmured. "Don't do this. Don't break up with him."

"This is not your business," Millie said tightly. "Please leave."

Eva closed her eyes and shook her head. "Well, she may be dumping you, David, but I'm not. If you were my own son, I couldn't love you more."

"Thanks, Eva. The feeling is mutual. And by the way, Millie and I aren't breaking up."

"Yes we are," Millie said. "It's been fun, but now it's time for both of us to move on."

"My foot," Eva said. "I'll try to talk some sense into her, David."

"You're on his side?"

"Absolutely," Eva agreed.

"You're my mother," Millie pointed out. "You have to take my side."

"I don't have to do anything." She looked at David as if Millie weren't there at all. "What seems to be the problem?"

David just looked at Millie.

"The problem," Millie said, "is that David won't listen to me."

"I'm listening to you. I'm just not agreeing with you."

"Well, what is it that you don't agree about?" Eva's gaze swung back and forth between them. Her voice was conciliatory, as if Millie and David had been two kids squabbling over the same toy. "My vote can be the tiebreaker, and then we can all go back outside and enjoy ourselves."

Millie and David exchanged glances. She could see in his eyes that he wanted Millie to be the one to break the news about Millie's father. She wanted to disagree, but couldn't. "Mom," she said. "I think it's something we should discuss in private."

Eva frowned. "Whatever you have to say, you can say it in front of David."

"It's okay, Eva. Millie's right." He gave Millie a final look. "I'll just be outside if you need me."

It registered that as angry as he was with her, he was reluctant to leave her, and her fingers almost clutched at him as he released his grip on her.

As soon as the pantry door clicked shut behind him, Millie tore open the bag of marshmallows. "Here," she said. "Maybe you'd better have one."

"That bad," Eva replied, but made no move to take the marshmallow.

"Yeah," Millie said. She thought about eating the marshmallow but then dropped it back in the bag and set it on the shelf. She looked at a bar of semisweet chocolate but knew that no food was going to make this any easier. "It's about Dad. I found out some things about him today."

A stillness crept over Eva's features, and the color seemed to leave her face. "Max? What about him?" Her hand flew to her mouth. "He didn't up and die, did he?"

Millie flinched at the panic in her mother's eyes. "No," she said. "Unfortunately, he is very much alive."

"He's sick then—cancer?"

"No." She hesitated. "He's in jail." She paused. "He's serving time in the Utah State Prison."

"Prison?" Eva's jaw dropped, and her eyes widened. "I'll be darned. What'd he do?"

Millie braced herself for her mother's reaction. "Embezzled twenty-five thousand dollars."

"Oh no," she sighed. The lines in her face deepened. "Couldn't keep his hand out of the till, could he?"

"Apparently not."

"Who'd he steal from this time?"

Millie froze. "What do you mean, 'Who'd he steal from this time?' He did it before?"

Eva's face sagged. "Oh yes." She sighed. "Sometimes you close your eyes and tell yourself that things are fine. You know they're not, but you need them to be, so you make yourself believe they are."

"Mom, what are you talking about? What else did Dad steal?"

Her mother's face twisted. "I didn't want you to know, Millie. Swear to God, I loved that man, and I didn't want you to think less of him."

"Mom, please." Millie wanted to demand her mother answer her question, but her words came out barely above a whisper. "Tell me what happened." She waited a few moments then couldn't help herself. "Please."

Eva sighed. "It's a long story."

Chapter 35

Deer Park, South Dakota
Twenty years earlier

The tools clanked as Eva dropped the screwdriver into the tool chest. Wiping her hands on her jeans, she turned the dial to the spin cycle then stepped back to watch. The washing machine jumped to life. She listened as the spinner whirled inside the washer. She snorted in satisfaction as it moved smoothly through the cycle without cutting out once. All it needed was for her to tighten the drive belt.

Just how many housewives could fix a washing machine? *Saved us at least a hundred bucks,* she'd proudly tell Max when he came home from work.

She thought about rewarding herself with one of those butter scones her mother had made this morning, topped with the homemade strawberry jam, canned right from their own plants in the backyard, but a quick check of her watch confirmed that if she wanted everything just right before Max came home, she didn't have time.

"Success," she called out to her mother, who was sitting in Max's leather recliner watching a soap opera.

"Come sit for a moment, honey. You won't believe the acting—so awful. You can see them squinting at the cue cards."

Eva smiled and shook her head. "Gotta get dinner started and Max's shirts ironed before I pick up Millie from school."

Plus she needed to shower. Max liked it when she met him at the door with her hair freshly washed and styled, her makeup carefully applied, and the folds of her dress neatly pressed.

"I'll help." Her mother clicked off the television and heaved her bulk out of the chair. "I'll peel. You can chop."

Eva hid a sigh of relief. Max didn't like it when he came home from work and her mother was sitting in his chair. She didn't blame him. He worked hard all day. He had a right to his own recliner.

"So Millie's late today?"

Eva pulled out the cutting board. "Yes. Someone needs to tell that drama coach this is Deer Park, South Dakota. It's not like the kids are performing on Broadway."

Retrieving a bag of potatoes from the pantry, she pulled two peelers out of the drawer. She wished Millie would concentrate more on her academics and less on the fifth-grade play. She had a low B average, but Eva felt this reflected a lack of interest more than a lack of ability.

Soon the sausages were browning and the dumplings simmering in a creamy bacon sauce. She asked her mom to keep an eye on things and headed outside to grab Max's shirts off the laundry line. Pressing them to her face, she inhaled the aroma of sunshine and soap—and the barest traces of Max, traces that still had the power to make her heart race and her insides turn to jelly.

She steamed the shirts smooth, using just a whisper of starch and letting the iron linger longest at the cuffs and collars. Max took great pride in his appearance, and this small vanity had always appealed to her. With his thick, dark hair and smoky gray eyes, he attracted the gazes of other women. She and Max always laughed about it, and something inside bloomed each time he told her there was no one else but her.

There was no one else for her either. She'd been living in Centerville, Ohio, working at the Marriott as an assistant pastry chef in Dayton when Sandy had raced into the kitchen with the news that a hot guy at table nine wanted to meet the person who'd baked the German chocolate cake.

She was thirty years old and lived with her widowed mother. She'd been realistic about the future—she had the broad frame of her father and the plain, unmemorable features of her mother. She hadn't expected to look into the charcoal eyes of a tall, wavy-haired man with an easy smile and fall in love, but it'd happened. Even more miraculous, he'd fallen for her.

They'd been married six weeks later. He moved into their small two-story Cape Cod in Centerville, and Eva felt as if he'd swept back the curtains of her life and let the sunlight flood inside. He did silly romantic things like write in the margins of her recipe books—*add 100 kisses gradually; hug thoroughly before baking; dust with 50 grams of powdered love.* He wrote I LOVE YOU on the steam in the bathroom mirror and slipped rose petals between their sheets.

When he was fired from his job as a salesperson at Sears because the cash register hadn't balanced, she knew it was some kind of computer error. *"Let's see this as an opportunity to start fresh somewhere else. Deer Park, South Dakota,"* he'd said. *"A small town in the Black Hills. We could raise a family there. And who knows, I might find gold in the mountains, and then we'd live like kings. What do you say? Why be ordinary when together we're extraordinary?"*

He hadn't found gold though—just a job as a conductor on

the Black Hills Central Railroad line. The family they'd imagined hadn't exactly happened either. She'd had trouble getting pregnant. Increasingly she'd see him looking out the window. She tried her best to hold on to him by cooking his favorite meals, keeping the house spotless, and greeting him at the door with a smile and a funny story. Despite her efforts, he was restless. *"What are you thinking?"* she'd ask him. *"Nothing,"* he'd say. It was only a matter of time before he left, and she knew it.

And then Eva woke up one morning, looked into the mirror, and saw something different in her eyes. Something as fragile as the wings of a butterfly. Millie had been born nine months later.

"We're naming her after you," Eva had said, holding the precious bundle out to him.

"I don't think Max is a good name for a girl."

"You're a Maximillian," she said. "Millie's close enough."

It hadn't been the girl names they'd discussed. Hannah, Trudy, Emma—these names had flowed through Eva's mind like clear, fresh water. She'd spent hours dipping her hands into this beautiful pool of possibility, picturing the moment when she'd look into her baby's face and hand her the right name like a bouquet of flowers. But then, looking at the light in Max's eyes, she'd realized that she had finally found the one gossamer thread that would tie him to her forever.

Eva hung the last shirt on the hanger then trudged upstairs to their bedroom. The closet was crowded—mostly his stuff. She smiled at the line of blue and gray suits, the hangers all facing the same direction. Clothing for *someday*.

Until then, he wore them to church on Sunday. He was an usher, and she was proud of the way the minister knew them both by name. She liked watching Max move about the church, as at ease in the chapel as he was in his own home. People's eyes lit up when they saw him. She watched his lips move, the easy smile, the way he'd squeeze a man's shoulder in affection, hold out his arm to an elderly woman.

She made space on the wooden rod for the last shirt. Stepping back, she checked to see that they hung evenly and were sorted by color and style. Frowning, she noticed the flap on one of his suit coats sticking up. She started to smooth it flat and felt a bulge. Reaching into the pocket, her fingers touched something small and square. Without thinking, she pulled it out.

The envelope was small and blue and bore the name of the Deer Park United Methodist Church. There was twenty-five dollars in cash inside, and Eva's first thought was that Max had forgotten to put their offering in the plate the past Sunday. But then she remembered that she herself had dropped their envelope into the gold plate. So what was this one doing in Max's coat pocket?

She turned the edges slowly. There was spidery handwriting on the back—*Mr. & Mrs. Edward Hobbson*. She tapped the paper and wondered if Max had found the envelope on the ground and forgotten to turn it in. It made sense, but then she looked down the long row of Max's wool suits. He'd bought a new one just last week, and she'd worried about them being able to afford it. She didn't like the direction of her thoughts but couldn't seem to stop them. The one time she'd teased Max about his suit collection, he'd about taken her head off. *"Are you starving?"* he'd almost shouted.

Eva remembered feeling every one of the twenty-five pounds she'd gained since Millie's birth.

She bit her lower lip hard. What was she thinking—that Max funded his buying habits with church money? Max was no thief. She'd been watching too many episodes of *Matlock* with her mother. Replacing the envelope, she berated herself for doubting her husband. Max was a good man. He'd never said one word about supporting her mother.

The next day, however, she kept thinking about that envelope. When she checked Max's jacket pocket, it was gone. Something nagged at her, and she began searching Max's suit pockets every Monday morning as soon as he left for the railroad. She disliked herself for doing it but couldn't seem to stop. Weeks went by, and when she found nothing, she began to relax.

But then one Thursday night in April, the trash bag burst open as she carried it to the garage. Holding back an oath, she bent to clean up the mess. Her hands had faltered at the sight of little pieces of robin's egg–blue paper. Squatting on the cold concrete, she'd begun painstakingly sorting through the trash until she'd found every scrap. Slowly she began piecing them together.

When she was finished, she sat looking at the small puzzles around her. Together they formed the answer to a larger puzzle— the one that had nagged at her ever since she'd pulled the offering envelope out of Max's pocket a month ago. He was stealing—why else were there offering envelopes with other people's names on them in their trash?

Her hands flew to her face. What was she going to do about it? She had no college education and hadn't held a paying job in ten years. She had her mother to think about and Millie. How would she support them if Max went to jail? But if she said nothing, how could she live with him? With herself?

Looking at the piecemeal envelopes, she drew a shaky breath. *My God, what am I going to do?*

The air was very still as she ripped the paper into even smaller pieces then gathered them in her hands. Throwing them into the air, Eva watched her life fall down around her like scraps of confetti.

Chapter 36

Deer Park, South Dakota
The present

Dad was stealing from the church?" It wasn't so much a question as a statement, a way of getting the facts to sink into the dry earth of her brain. Millie looked into her mother's haunted brown eyes. She wondered what else her mother had kept from her.

"For five years. Maybe longer."

"How'd you find that out?"

"I couldn't sleep. I kept thinking about the people who were giving the church their hard-earned money and how Max was using it to buy himself nice things. So one night I confronted him about the envelopes. He denied it of course. But then I began reciting names off the envelopes. I told him I would call the church if he didn't do it himself. I was bluffing, but it was the only way I could get him to stop."

Where had Millie been when all this was going on? How could she not have known? She racked her brain for any arguments or signs of tension between her parents but came out blank. "But he wouldn't?"

Her mother shook her head and frowned deeply. "He argued

that he deserved to be paid for his work at the church. He said what he took came out to less than minimum wage."

Millie tried to reconcile this image with the soft-spoken man who had encouraged her to learn Bible passages. "That's crazy."

"Of course it was crazy, and I threatened to go to the church board. We went back and forth until finally I got him to agree to stop stealing and to repay the church. We sat up late with a yellow pad and figured out how much he'd taken. We were both a little shocked at how it'd all added up." Eva sighed. "The next morning, though, when I woke up, he was gone."

Millie remembered that morning all too well. She'd thought her father had died. "How could you have known he was a thief and not tell me?"

"You were ten years old. What good would it have done?"

Millie's response ballooned inside, and it took her a moment to get the words out. "Maybe I wouldn't have spent all that time wondering why he left. Maybe I wouldn't have missed him so much."

Eva shook her head. "You adored him—as I did. I wouldn't take that away from you."

"You should have told me. I had a right to know."

"You were a child, and I was trying to protect you. Bad enough that everyone in town knew he'd abandoned us—but it'd be worse if they knew he stole. He'd have gone to jail."

Millie's eyebrows shot up. "Maybe he should have. Covering up for him was wrong. You should have gone to the police."

Eva's eyes narrowed. "Don't be so quick to tell me what I should have done. You don't know what you would have done if you were me. Sometimes it's not a matter of right or wrong but simply survival. I did what I thought was best." She shifted a little on the crutches. "Besides, as much as I hated what he did, I didn't hate him." She gave Millie a long look. "He gave me you, Millie. And he tried to stick around. He just couldn't."

"What do you mean he couldn't? Were we that bad?"

"Ah, Millie, it wasn't about us. It never was." She sighed. "His father drank. And when he was drunk, he told Max that it was a good thing God made him attractive because he was stupid. He blamed Max and Max's mom for everything that'd gone wrong in his life. When people tell you something long enough, you start to believe it. So when Max's life didn't work out the way he hoped it might, he blamed us—just like his dad blamed his wife and child. He loved both of us, Millie, but he hurt inside. I guess he thought he would hurt less somewhere else."

"Yeah—the thought of paying back the church had to be unbearably painful."

"He wasn't all bad," Eva said sharply. "That's all I'm trying to say."

"Did he. . ." Millie hesitated then took a breath. "Did he ever write you. . .or try to contact you. . .or ask about me?"

Her mother shook her head. "No." The crutches clicked as Eva took a step forward and placed her hand on Millie's arm. "He loved you. I know he wouldn't have stuck around so long otherwise."

Millie made a scoffing noise. "If this is the way you treat someone you love, I'd hate to see how he treated someone he didn't."

Eva squeezed her shoulder. "Let it go, honey. For your own sake, let it go. Look at what you have, not at what you don't."

"What I have is a father in jail and a mother who hid the truth from me." Millie wiped her cheeks, furious with herself for showing this weakness.

"What you have," Eva corrected, "is a man who loves you and an opportunity to build a life together here. Let the rest go."

Millie didn't think she could let it go—even if she wanted to. "What about the people he stole from—should they let it go, too?"

Her mother's shoulders straightened. "I repaid every cent he took from the church. Took me ten years, but I did it."

Millie's jaw dropped. "You what?"

"I went to Sarah Stockman and told her everything. I mailed the church a check once a month."

Millie's hand went to her mouth. This was the Sarah her mother had been rambling about that night in the hospital. "How did you do this without me knowing about it?"

"I wrote the check out of my personal account, not Dosie's."

Millie thought about the way her mother held on to things— the furniture that was old and faded, the ugly green shag rug. Even her clothing was dated. As a child, Millie remembered cringing when Eva came to pick her up. She remembered wishing she was fashionable like her friends' mothers. It had never occurred to her that her mother simply hadn't had the money to put into the house or her appearance.

"I wish you'd told me," Millie whispered. "I would have helped."

"It wasn't your burden. And anyway, it's all paid off. Every last dime of it. With interest."

Millie's shoulders sagged. "All these years I never knew any of this. I always thought we gave up going to church because we felt judged. That you didn't like people looking at us and wondering what happened to Dad."

"Oh no, honey. It wasn't that at all. I couldn't go to church knowing what your father had done. I was too ashamed. I should have seen it sooner." She patted Millie's shoulder awkwardly. "I'm sorry, Millie. I've leaned on you harder than a parent should. And I've thought I've known what was best for you.

"But I want you to know that breaking my hip was a good thing. It's given me a lot of time to think about things. Lillian and I have talked about this, and we've decided that we make pretty good roommates. She's invited me to move in with her. So what I'm saying, Millie, is that we can sell the house. It's all paid off, and there should be enough profit to send you to Hollywood."

"What? Are you serious?" Millie shook her head. "I'm not leaving you—not with a broken hip and all this stuff about Dad. Who'd run the café? Who'd make sure you took your medicine?"

"You're not my keeper," Eva said firmly. "I am not your responsibility, and neither is this café. I guess there was part of me that always thought you wanted to be here, but I see now that you don't, and it's time for me to stop telling myself lies. I want you to be happy, Millie. I've always wanted that."

"I'm not abandoning you," Millie said firmly.

"We don't have to decide this today, but it's something to think about."

"I don't have to think about it. I'm not leaving you."

"Of course you aren't." Her mother's eyes filled with tears, and her whole face seemed to strain with the effort to hold them back. "No matter where you go or how far you go, you're still my daughter. And I love you."

Millie's heart tightened in her chest. Stepping forward, she bent her head and carefully pressed it into the curve of her mother's neck. "I love you, too." Hugging her carefully, she added, "We're the M&M's."

"Only you're not so plain, and maybe I'm not so nutty." Eva chuckled and began to stroke Millie's hair. "Now go on back there, and if anyone asks about your father, you hold your head high and tell them that he'd probably love a visitor. That ought to shut them up. Come on, honey, wipe your eyes and put a smile on your face. We've got a party going on out there."

Chapter 37

The house on Cherry Lane felt quiet and empty without Eva. In the kitchen, Millie made tea just to hear the kettle whistle then sat at the table with her hands wrapped around the warm mug.

She glanced at the telephone, hoping David would call and knowing that if he did, she wouldn't talk to him. She didn't understand this paradox in herself—wanting something she had decided to reject. As if she needed pain more than love.

It was an odd thought, and yet she had spent years responding to online audition calls and had never gotten anything except rejection. She had played out an endless cycle of hope and despair. Over and over she had confirmed in her mind that she wasn't good enough.

Standing, Millie dumped her cold tea into the sink. She strained to see out the window, but the glass was black and reflected only her own pale image. She touched the window, and the deep cold instantly penetrated her skin. *This is what aloneness feels like,* she thought. *A cold so deep it chills to the bone.*

It would be warmer in California, she assured herself. The air would smell of the ocean, and she would take acting lessons. She would go on casting calls and walk every day on the beach. She would stay too busy to be lonely.

The rooster clock clicked off the seconds. *Are you sure?* the sweep of its tail seemed to ask. *Are you sure? Are you sure?*

Millie took her palm off the glass windowpane. The smudge remained like a ghostly handprint. No, she wasn't sure of anything, and that was the problem.

A few hours later, Millie gave up trying to sleep. She pulled on jeans and a sweater and headed for her car. The Subaru cranked wearily in the cold night. With no destination in mind, she drove through the silent streets. She thought about simply driving until she ran out of gas or money or the will to keep going.

She stopped at a red light and rested her head on the steering wheel. She'd reached the intersection of Mill Road and Route 41. One direction would take her to the highway, the other into town. *If you don't go now, you never will,* a voice said inside her. *Stop using your mother's health as an excuse to stay here. The truth is that you've let her, maybe even encouraged her to depend on you, because as long as she needs you, she won't leave you.*

The light turned green. She wanted to deny that she'd had any role in enabling Eva to neglect her health, but she knew it was possible.

The light changed again, but she couldn't lift her foot from the brake. She thought of David and the things he had said to her. Did she really want him to remember her as someone who had snuck out in the middle of the night without even saying good-bye?

When the light changed again, she turned left toward town.

Inside the café, she flipped on the lights and walked into the kitchen. Her boots clicked on the tile floor as she trudged to the pantry. Lugging the twenty-five pound bag of wheat flour to the mixing bowls, she set to work.

For once she welcomed the physical work of lifting, kneading, pounding the dough into shape. Under her hands, the dough changed form and shape. She imagined her father's face, smashed it flat, and then formed it again.

The tears fell for all the years she'd spent thinking she wasn't pretty, smart, or good enough. She thought of all the men she'd gone out with—men who had given her attention and affection but hadn't been able to fill the empty space in her heart or make the pain go away for very long.

Her hands shook as she cut the dough into smaller parts and put them in bowls to rise. Placing them in the warming trays in the oven, she started the next batch. Emptying flour into the huge bowls, she wondered if customers would taste her grief in the loaves of bread.

By the time Lottie arrived, the morning's baking was finished and she had no more tears, only the sense of one more thing that needed to be done. Leaving Lottie in charge, she headed for her car.

As she climbed the stone steps, the steeple of the church seemed to tower over her. Two people in heavy winter coats stood in front of the thick wooden doors. Her smile felt numb as she took the program and stepped into the church.

Inside, it took a few seconds for her eyes to adjust to the dim, candlelit interior. The church was long and deep, the ceiling dark and high above her. There were rows and rows of polished wood benches, most of them filled. The organ was playing something slow and ponderous. Her gaze lifted to the stained-glass image of Jesus on the cross, and she swallowed with difficulty. She didn't belong here. And yet she couldn't bring herself to leave either.

She slid into the pew at the far back of the church. Bowing her head, she avoided making eye contact with anyone. As a pianist played softly, she ran her finger along the polished curve of the pew in front of her. As a child, she used to trace her name on the wood, as if she were writing in invisible ink and God alone could see it.

The light coming through the stained-glass windows was just the same, too. If she tried, she could almost picture her father ushering people down the aisle. Moving slowly until he'd seated someone and then striding back up the aisle as if he couldn't get to the next person fast enough. Eva used to poke her, and they'd laugh about this.

The piano music changed, and people jumped to their feet singing. Millie didn't know the words and stood silently, listening.

> *Rock of Ages, cleft for me,*
> *Let me hide myself in Thee;*
> *Let the water and the blood,*
> *From Thy wounded side which flowed,*
> *Be of sin the double cure,*
> *Save from wrath and make me pure.*

The old hymn moved along slowly, gracefully. The music filled the church. But the words, what did they mean? Why did they make her chest so tight?

> *While I draw this fleeting breath,*
> *When my eyes shall close in death,*
> *When I rise to worlds unknown,*
> *And behold Thee on Thy throne,*

Rock of Ages, cleft for me,
Let me hide myself in Thee.

Millie clenched her hands so tightly that her fingernails bit into the palms of her hands. Hadn't some part of her been looking for a safe place to hide? Wasn't that part of the whole Hollywood dream—to surround herself with thick walls of success? Earn her father's love by accomplishing fame?

Maybe it didn't have to be that way. She lifted her gaze to the stained-glass image of Jesus. The pull to Him was strong, and yet she felt herself resist. Her palms were damp, and she felt so tired inside.

Millie closed her eyes. David had suggested that God was the only Father she needed. But what if he was wrong?

The next hymn started. The words stirred more memories. She wanted to believe God still loved her, but she wasn't a child anymore. She wasn't sure she could simply will her heart to open. And yet wasn't there hope inside her? Hope that He existed—and that He could feel her reaching out to Him? Wasn't that why she'd come?

She pressed her fingernails a fraction deeper into her palms and warned herself that the higher her hopes took her, the longer and harder her fall would be. She tried to be angry at David. If it weren't for him, she wouldn't be sitting here right now. She wouldn't be feeling that her life could change if only she would let it.

Reverend Stockman began the closing prayer. A sudden panic washed over her. The moments were slipping away, and she realized with excruciating clarity that she didn't want to walk out of the church as the same person who'd walked inside.

Squeezing her eyes shut, Millie gripped her hands together. *Heavenly Father, I have doubts. I am the child of the man who stole from You. There's no reason for You to help me, but I pray You will. I don't want to live like I'm living anymore.* She drew a shaky breath. *Please, Father, be my Father and save me.*

She wasn't sure if the prayer worked. She was, after all, the same person when she opened her eyes. On her way out of the church, she paused to shake hands with Reverend Stockman, who stood in a long receiving line. Clad in his black robe and collar, he looked much more imposing than when she'd last seen him. But he returned her smile, and there was joy in his eyes when he shook her hand. "Welcome home," he said.

"Thank you," she murmured.

She stepped past him into the bright morning sun. *Welcome home,* the reverend had said. As if she belonged. Here. In this church where her father had been a thief and she and her mother had avoided for twenty years. She felt a small flutter of hope in her chest. He said she belonged here.

Millie was halfway to her car when someone shouted her name. She turned slowly. Squinting in the bright sunlight, she saw David hurrying toward her. His black wool coat flapped open, revealing his navy suit and the flash of a bright yellow tie.

She pushed her hands into her coat pockets and wondered what to say to him. It wasn't like one visit to a church could change her. And it certainly didn't change the circumstances. She squared her shoulders as he came to a stop in front of her. "Surprised to see me?"

"A little. You could have sat with us." The tug at the corner of his mouth told her it was an invitation, not an accusation.

"I didn't know I was coming," she admitted. "It seemed best just to sit in the back."

"I'm really glad you came."

She shifted her weight and looked around him to see if any other of his family members were there. The prospect of facing his mother still filled her with chills. "I'm glad I came, too," she said. A sliver of wind pushed a finger's width of hair across her cheek. "Yesterday— the things you said. You were right about a lot of them." She pushed the lock of hair away. "Part of the reason I wanted to be on television was because I wanted my father to see me and realize that I was somebody."

"You are somebody," David said. "You think I don't know how special you are?"

"It's hard for me to think like that," Millie admitted. "Part of me still thinks that I have to prove it." She let him see in her eyes how deep this belief ran.

"You don't have to prove anything to anyone—and especially not to me." It was his turn to push the hair from her eyes.

"Yesterday I said some things I didn't mean. I'm sorry."

"It's okay."

"How can you see the best of me when you know the worst about me?"

"Because I love you."

"David, Eva told me more bad stuff about my father. The crime in Utah—it wasn't the first time. He stole from our church a long time ago."

He nodded and looked very sad. "What he took from you was a lot worse."

She didn't know what to say and looked down at the ground. "I've made my own share of mistakes, but I'm trying to move forward." She smiled a little. "I'm not going to let him define me. I guess that's why I'm here."

"A very good decision," David confirmed. "Why don't we go somewhere and talk?"

Millie hesitated. She wanted to go with him, but she still felt a little raw inside. It wasn't as if it no longer hurt to think of the legacy her father had left for her. The last thing she wanted was to be the woman everybody thought wasn't good enough for David. At the same time, she knew she loved him. She might not think she deserved him, but here they were. She'd take it one step at a time.

"Coffee would be great," she said.

He grinned. "We have a lot to talk about."

He was right. The last time she'd seen him, she'd been trying to break up with him. She wanted to talk about the box sled race and about the after party at the café, where she'd seen Bart talking with a very cute dark-haired girl. She also wanted to know how Devon Spikes had handled losing to Bart.

"I know a great little café where we can sit for as long as we like and talk things through," she said. "The coffee is hot, and the pancakes are the best in town." She studied his face then added, "The aunts will stare and giggle, but they'll leave us alone. I promise."

"In that case," he said and offered his arm, "we should get going."

Millie slipped her hand into the crook of his elbow and leaned into him as they walked to his car.

Chapter 38

Myy mom had a nice lunch with you today," David said from across the table at Ben's where he and Millie had come to celebrate their sixth months of dating. "She raves about the tuna melt and mango-honey ice tea."

Millie laughed. "The tuna melt is really Aris's idea." Even after Eva returned to the café, Aris had remained on a part-time basis. This had allowed Millie more time to do other things—like take some night courses at the local community college and volunteer at Bart's school. Bart's sixth-grade class had produced their version of *The Mikado*, and both Lauren and Bart had had leading roles.

"To be honest, I think my mom enjoys your company even more than the food. She tells me word for word everything you talk about."

"I'm enjoying getting to know your mom as well."

Ever since Millie had started going to church, Mrs. Denvers had been coming to the café about once a week for lunch. At first Millie had found her presence uncomfortable. She feared any moment Mrs. Denvers would confront her about Millie's father. When she hadn't, Millie had finally mustered her courage. She'd set down the tuna melt in front of her and said, *"I know you know about my father."*

Mrs. Denvers had calmly cut off a piece of her sandwich. *"Let me tell you about your father."* She chewed slowly then wiped her mouth. *"A few days after my father passed away and everyone had gone on with their lives—the way people do—your father drove to my mother's house with a trunk full of rosebushes. He planted them in the backyard then sat with my mother. He laughed with her, and he cried with her. He knew that grief didn't end at a funeral and wasn't afraid to be around it."* She'd paused. *"It wasn't just my mother he helped either. He planted a lot of rosebushes for folks. Now, could you be a love and bring some vinegar for the fries?"*

That was the end of the conversation. Millie thought the story was a gift. It not only gave her another snapshot of her father, but also a new way of looking at Mrs. Denvers.

David lifted his water glass. "Happy anniversary, Millie."

She smiled as they clinked water glasses. "Happy anniversary, David."

As usual, nearly every table was filled. Across from them, a middle-aged woman wearing a hot pink dress and an expensive diamond necklace laughed at something the man sitting across from her said. An older couple—probably in their late eighties—was leaning toward each other as they ate.

How did they do it? Stay together all those years? More importantly, would it be David and her sitting there someday? She stopped herself. The old Millie worried about things she couldn't control. The new Millie trusted that things would work out as they were meant to be. Sometimes it was easy being the new Millie, and other times it was harder to put herself in God's hands. David said this was normal and that as her faith grew, she would trust God more completely.

She turned back to him. David was fiddling with the menu. She thought he looked a little nervous but couldn't understand why. "Everything okay with Bart?"

"Yeah, fine." He peered intently into the menu.

Millie stifled a little disappointment. She wanted him to be looking at her and thinking romantic thoughts, not wondering if he wanted the shrimp cocktail or a lettuce wedge. "See anything you like?"

"A couple of things." He handed her his menu. "Take a look."

This was odd—she had her own menu. She opened the cover. Instead of seeing the daily specials, she pulled out a piece of paper. "What's this?"

"An application."

"I can see that. But David, *The Newlywed Game*?"

"They're casting. I was thinking that we could include a videotape in our application. Something that would give people a flavor of our lives here in Deer Park. You know, interviews with your aunts, people at the café, Aris. . ."

"People would think we're crazy. David, this is really sweet, but you don't have to do this. I don't need to go on a reality television show anymore to be happy."

"But you'd like to, wouldn't you?"

"Of course." She still sent out applications, but she'd come to accept that if it never happened, it didn't mean God didn't love her. It just meant He had something else in mind for her. David and Bart were proof of that. And then it slowly registered. "Besides, David, aren't you forgetting something? We aren't married. You have to be married to be a newlywed."

"We can take care of that." He reached into his coat pocket and pulled out a small black jewelry box. Millie's heart started to pound with anticipation as he stepped around the side of the table and got down on one knee. "I love you, Millie. I want to be with you for the rest of my life. I want our lives together to be full of love and adventure. Will you marry me?"

Millie looked down at the top of his soft brown hair. "Are you asking me to marry you so you can go on a reality television show?"

David smiled. "I'm proposing because I love you, and if being on a reality television show is important to you, it's important to me." He smiled. "Millie, will you marry me?"

"Yes, I'll marry you. I love you, David."

Her hand shook a little as he slipped the diamond onto her finger. But then he looked at her and they both laughed, and somehow everything was all right. "I'm in shock," she admitted.

"Happy shock?"

"Extremely happy shock." Millie leaned forward to kiss him. "*The Newlywed Game?*"

His lips sealed the promise between them and sent a shiver of joy through her. "Yeah," he said. "I think we've got a great story to tell."

Epilogue

It would be a simple wedding. Neither Millie nor Eva had much money, and although David had offered to pay for everything, Millie hadn't wanted to start their married life that way. She and Eva insisted on paying for the wedding and reception. Millie did agree, however, to let David finance the honeymoon trip to Paris.

She and David wanted to be married as close to Christmas as they could, and Reverend Stockman said he'd be pleased to marry them on December 23rd. A reception would be held in the church's basement.

On their wedding day, at three o'clock in the afternoon, Fred Huey, who had a gift for all things mechanical and a passion for antique cars, picked Millie and Eva up in his Model T. Millie settled herself on the butter-soft leather and arranged the folds of her wedding gown around her. The full princess skirt filled most of the backseat, and she tucked it around her to make room for Eva. The dress was not the original one she'd ordered from the bridal shop in New York City. The store had sent her the wrong dress, but she'd fallen in love with it from the moment she pulled it from the box. When she'd called the store to straighten everything out, she'd been stunned to hear that the custom-made gown had been ordered for a woman who no longer wanted it. The sales associate offered her the dress at a highly discounted rate. Millie had been overjoyed to buy it.

As Fred backed the car out of the Hogan's driveway, Millie and Eva exchanged smiles. They were charmed by the antique engine's rapid *tick-tick-tick* sound.

"Did you ever think I'd be doing this?" Millie asked as the snow-lined streets moved past them at the rate of twenty miles per hour.

Eva laughed. "Oh yes," she said. "I just wish your grandma were here to see you. She'd be so thrilled to see you wearing her pearl earrings. You look beautiful."

Millie fingered the warm beads and felt the love of her grandmother fill her. "She's here."

It wasn't long before they reached the church. Fred opened the door, and Millie stepped into the frigid air. She shivered a little then pulled the veil over her face. It would be warm inside the church, she told herself, and David would be waiting.

As she stepped forward, several flashes exploded in her eyes. Blinking, she saw photographers lining both sides of the steps. She was a little surprised to see so many but also flattered.

It was only the sound of a helicopter circling that brought her feet to a stop. It was flying low and in a circular pattern around the church. She glanced at Eva. "What in the world is going on?"

Eva shook her head as another flash popped in her face. "Let's just get inside."

Sheila Abbott pushed a lock of her Tahitian-black, chin-length bob behind her ear. An ear-to-ear grin stretched across her face as she studied the footage coming in from South Dakota. She'd been the editor of the online celebrity magazine *Star Struck* for about two years now and was about to cement her reputation as the most influential editor in the industry. A year ago she'd broken the Matthew Langston and Katherine Heffner affair. And people were still talking about the way she'd had her cameras ready when four months ago Cleo Leonard had checked herself into rehab. Now she was about to make news once again.

For months people had been speculating when Monica Rayford and Derek Dunn—two of the hottest actors in recent years—would get married. She alone had figured it out and arranged media coverage. Her smile widened as she watched the bride—stunning, really, in the Carolina Herrera dress—make her way up the stone steps to the lovely little church.

The veil hid Monica's trademark ivory skin and huge blue eyes, but it was clearly the starlet. Who else had that elegant neck? That famous curvy figure? That slight tilt of her head?

Sheila clicked the keys that sent the video streaming live to the three networks who had already paid for the story. She'd let them edit what they wanted. She watched the train of Monica's dress disappear into that cute country church.

The dress had been the first tip-off. Sheila had been keeping her eye on Traditions, which was where the in-crowd shopped for wedding gowns in Manhattan. When Sheila learned Monica had bought a dress, she'd gone on high alert. With a little more digging, she learned that wedding invitations had been purchased from a high-end stationery store on the East Side. Although the clerk had been reluctant to give out the specifics, Sheila had gotten the clerk to admit a location and date. From there it'd been easy. There'd only been two churches in Deer Park, South Dakota, and only one wedding booked on December 23rd. Although the names had been changed, Sheila hadn't been fooled. Hogan was Monica's maiden name, and Derek Dunn had the same initials as David Denvers.

The first feed already had left her computer when her cell lit up with a text message. It was from Craig Watts, whom she'd assigned to cover the story. With a swipe of her finger, she opened the message.

IT'S NOT HER. PLEASE ADVISE.

Sheila's heart stopped. She typed, WHAT DO YOU MEAN IT ISN'T HER?

In response, a photo appeared on her screen. A bride and groom stood at the front of the church. The bride had lifted her veil, and while she was stunning, she wasn't Monica Rayford. The man, although handsome, had brown hair not streaky blond.

Sheila stifled a gasp of horror. Her brain whirled as she frantically tried to figure out what had gone wrong. In the next instant, she realized what mattered more was damage control. She tapped her fingers on the desk impatiently. A mistake like this could kill a career. She'd look like an idiot unless she came up with a new spin—and quickly. *A new spin.* . . Her mind whirled. *A new spin.* . . She thought hard, and then it came to her.

She'd turn this small-town wedding into a feel-good Christmas piece—a home-for-the-holidays wedding.

GET THEIR STORY, she typed. DIG FOR DIRT, BUT GIVE ME REDEMPTION.

Everyone loved a Christmas wedding story, she assured herself, especially when the bride was as beautiful as this one and was so obviously in love with the groom. It might be a little hick, but what was the alternative? Look like an idiot in front of her colleagues?

I can pull this off, she assured herself, then reached into her desk for her stash of M&M's. "Millie Hogan," she whispered as she popped one into her mouth, "you may not know it, but I'm about to make you a star."

Kim O'Brien grew up in Bronxville, New York. She holds a bachelor's degree in psychology from Emory University in Atlanta, Georgia, and a master's degree in fine arts from Sarah Lawrence College in Bronxville, New York. She worked for many years as a writer, editor, and speechwriter for IBM. She is the author of eight romance novels and seven nonfiction children's books. She's happily married to Michael, has two fabulous daughters, Beth and Maggie. She is active in the Loft Church in The Woodlands, Texas. Kim loves to hear from readers and can be reached through her Facebook author's page.

A Wedding
DATE
IN HOT SPRINGS, ARKANSAS

ANNALISA
DAUGHETY

Dedication

To Kelly Shifflett. God didn't give me a sister,
but He gave me you as a friend—and for that I am grateful.
Thank you for cheering me on and for offering insight as
I wrote this book. We've shared so many adventures together
and I have no doubt there are more to come.

Acknowledgments

Writing a novel can be a daunting task. Sometimes I learn
many more life lessons than my characters do. This book
in particular was hard for me on many levels and I am thankful
for those who helped make it possible. Thanks to:

My heavenly Father. You continue to bless me even though I
fall short time and again. Thanks for giving me the opportunity
to write, and I pray my stories always glorify You.

Vicky Daughety. If not for you, I'm not sure this one
would've gotten finished! Thanks, Mom, for "curbside
meal service" and for being my first reader.

Jan Reynolds. For brainstorming and critiquing—and for always
being honest about what is working and what isn't. It takes a
village to write a book, and I'm glad you're part of mine!

Kristy Coleman. You gave me input on this book—
and a ton of encouragement and prayers as I was trying
to finish it. I appreciate that more than you know!

Vickie Fry. For the prayers, encouragement, and input.
I love knowing that no matter how crazy my questions
are, you will answer willingly and honestly.

Megan Reynolds. For checking on me even when I'm in scary
deadline mode, and for always making me laugh no matter how
stressed I am. Thanks, also, for "taking one for the team"
and going with me to Hot Springs for a spa day.

Always be joyful. Never stop praying.
Be thankful in all circumstances, for this is
God's will for you who belong to Christ Jesus.
1 Thessalonians 5:16–18 nlt

Chapter 1

To: Staff@MatthewsLaw.com
From: Sampson.Matthews@MatthewsLaw.com
Date: August 17, 4:45 p.m.
Subject: Mandatory Meeting

There will be a mandatory staff meeting on Monday at noon in the boardroom. I look forward to seeing everyone there.

Violet Matthews was usually the last to arrive to the office. But not today. Today was a special day. A life-changing day. She'd started counting down to noon as soon as her feet hit the floor that morning. She'd never looked forward to a Monday before.

Her iPhone rang as she pulled into an empty spot in the parking lot of her Little Rock office. "This is Violet," she said, turning off the engine.

"Don't ever get married. Whatever you do, no matter how cute he is or how tired you are of checking that 'single' box, don't do it.

Your life will never be the same," Reagan McClure declared.

"Chad out of town again?" Violet grinned. Her best friend of-fered the same advice at least once a month, usually whenever her husband of ten years was traveling on business.

Reagan sighed. "Not only is he out of town. He's in Vegas. *Vegas.* For a week. He's at some conference, and as luck would have it, the kids are getting over the stomach flu. I'm pretty sure Dante may have had my life in mind in some of his writings."

"That bad, huh?" Violet couldn't help but chuckle. "I don't recall the staying-home-with-four-sick-kids-while-husband-is-away part of the *Inferno*, but it's been a few years since I've read it." It did sound pretty awful, but she'd never say that to Reagan.

"Don't make fun. I'm seriously losing it here. I don't remember the last time I had on something that was clean, and earlier this morning I scared myself when I looked in the mirror. No wonder Chad wants to be in Vegas."

Violet shook her head. "Chad loves you and the kids. I feel certain that he didn't arrange this trip to purposefully get out of helping you." She'd known Chad McClure since their freshman year of college. He'd doted on Reagan since he'd first laid eyes on her all those years ago, and from what Violet could tell, not much had changed.

Reagan groaned. "Don't you know you're supposed to be on my side even when I'm being unreasonable? Don't take up for him."

"I *am* on your side. I just hate to hear you so upset. Isn't there someone you can call to come over and help out?"

"My parents are too far away to help, and you know how Chad's mom is. Anytime I ask her to do anything, she uses it as an opportunity to point out all my failings as a mother and a wife."

Chad's mom was a piece of work, that was for sure. Violet had heard some of her "helpful advice" over the years, and it was no wonder Reagan didn't want to call her. "I'll do better, I promise. Do you want me to come over and watch the kids tonight so you can take a hot bath or go for a run or something?"

Reagan sniffed. "You're so nice. But no. The last thing you need is to catch whatever awful virus they have. Thanks though."

"The offer stands if you change your mind." Violet climbed out of her SUV and slung her bag over her shoulder. "I'd better run. Today's a big meeting, and I have a ton to do beforehand."

"I totally forgot this was the big day. Call me later and give me the details, okay? Although I'll never understand why you'd even want a promotion, seeing as how you don't like your job at all."

It was the biggest source of contention between them. Reagan had always thought she was crazy for not following her dreams, but Violet had opted for a safer route. "Don't be silly. I'm thrilled. Besides, I'm kind of far along the path to change course now, don't you think?" She said good-bye and hurried toward the multi-story building.

"Nice dress," Kelsey Klein said, giving Violet the once over as she entered the lobby. "But you look more like a forties pinup girl than a lawyer." She glanced around the tastefully decorated lobby with its neutral colors and back at Violet's emerald-green dress. "If it weren't for you, I swear I'd drown in a sea of beige." Kelsey had begun working as the office manager and receptionist after she'd graduated from the University of Central Arkansas in May. Only Violet knew she was biding her time and getting some experience until she could find a marketing position somewhere. "Where did you find that dress anyway? I could never pull off that look, but you sure do."

Violet smoothed the full skirt of her latest vintage find. "A little shop in New Orleans. I was down there last month for a conference and managed to slip out for the afternoon and go to a vintage store Reagan told me about." She grinned. "You're right about one thing, though. It's forties style. My favorite." She gave a little twirl, and the skirt flowed around her. "Can't you just imagine all the wonderful places this dress has been?"

Kelsey laughed. "You were definitely meant for a different time." She raised her perfectly arched eyebrows that were just a shade darker than her blond hair. "Any idea what the big meeting is about today? When your dad asked me to schedule it in the boardroom, I tried to get him to tell me what was going on." She shrugged. "He was totally closemouthed though."

Sampson Matthews was definitely a man of few words, at least until you put him in a courtroom. "I'm not sure." Violet almost shared her suspicion about the meeting with Kelsey, but thought better of it. The girl was nice and all, but she could give the town crier a run for his money. "Any calls for me?"

Kelsey shook her head. "Not so far. Want me to put them to voice mail?"

"Please." She needed a few uninterrupted hours to go over the stack of paperwork on her desk.

"Oh, wait. There was one call for you. Your mom. Since you weren't here, I sent her to your dad."

"What did she want?"

"She mentioned something about your grandmother, but I'm not sure what she was talking about."

Violet froze. Her only living set of grandparents lived in Hot Springs, a little more than an hour away from Little Rock. Surely everything was okay or else they would've called Violet on her cell. Still, though. They were in their eighties and not as spry as they used to be. "Okay, thanks. I'll call her soon." She stepped into her office and closed the door.

She sank into the leather chair behind her desk and picked up the framed picture she kept on her desk. It had been taken the day she'd graduated from the University of Arkansas School of Law. Grandpa Matthews had still been alive then, and he beamed in the picture, thrilled that his oldest granddaughter had followed in his footsteps. She'd promised him on that day that she'd someday move back to Little Rock and work in the firm he had founded.

She carefully put the photo back on the desk. It was hard to believe it had been seven years since graduation. After two years of living and working in DC, she'd followed up on her promise to her grandfather and joined the family firm. The past five years she'd worked hard, rarely even taking a sick day—much less a vacation.

And all her hard work would soon pay off.

Violet grinned with anticipation. Noon couldn't come soon enough.

Jackson Stratford had lost track of what the blond across the table was talking about. He forced himself to smile and nod at what seemed to be appropriate intervals, but mostly he just couldn't believe he'd let his life get to this point.

Maybe his rule of never dating a girl over the age of twenty-three needed to be reevaluated.

"Are you even listening to me?" Whitney asked.

He nodded. "Of course. You were saying something about your last trip to the lake." He took a stab, pretty sure he'd heard the words *lake* and *boat* at some point during the past twenty minutes.

She flashed a smile and a dimple. "Yes." She tossed her hair. "So anyway. Megan had brought her dog with us, and it was not okay with being on a boat." She rolled her eyes. "And I was like, are you kidding me? Your stupid dog is going to get all boat sick, and I just had it cleaned." Whitney sighed. "Megan said it would be fine, but then the dog got sick. Needless to say, we're not speaking now."

"You and Megan or you and the dog?" Jackson asked, grinning.

Whitney giggled. "Megan, silly. Dogs don't speak."

Jackson took a sip of his Dr Pepper as Whitney rambled on. He deserved this. At least that's what his friend Jeff would say. Jackson's dating habits might be the only thing the two of them disagreed on. That and their running Braves versus Cardinals argument.

"Do you?" Whitney asked.

Jackson furrowed his brow. "Do I what?" This time he had no clue what she might be talking about.

"Want to drive to Dallas next weekend? There's a really cool music festival going on."

Outdoor music festivals used to be one of Jackson's favorite things. But last year at Little Rock's Riverfest, his date had thrown up on his shoes and then a drunk guy in the parking lot had dinged his new Range Rover, and his opinion of music festivals had begun to change. In fact, Jackson felt certain he wasn't up for that kind of fun any longer. "I believe I'll pass."

Whitney frowned. "Are you sure? The weather is supposed to be great, and there are some awesome bands playing." She grinned. "Maybe even some that you've heard of. You know, like, from the eighties."

"Very funny." Both times they'd gone out, Whitney had been appalled at the preset stations on his satellite radio. "For your information, music today is not nearly as good as it was in the seventies or eighties."

"You sound just like my uncle. He's always trying to get me to listen to some big-haired eighties band. The other day he asked me if I'd heard of Cinderella." She giggled. "I totally thought he meant the Disney princess."

Jackson groaned. He'd been a Cinderella fan back in the day. "Just out of curiosity, how old is your uncle?"

"Way old. Like in his forties." She widened her blue eyes.

And that would about do it for this friendship. Jackson's next cake would have thirty-six candles on it.

"Do you have any aunts?" he asked with a grin.

Chapter 2

Violet Matthews: SORRY YOU'RE HAVING A BAD DAY. WHEN CHAD GETS BACK, LET'S PLAN A GNO. (Text message sent August 20, 11:48 a.m.)

Reagan couldn't remember her last girls' night out. Probably before the twins were born, which meant at least ten months ago. A night out would be fun, but what she'd rather have was a nap. And a shower that lasted more than five minutes.

She responded to Violet's text and tossed her phone onto the coffee table that had two little tooth-shaped chunks out of the corner, compliments of her oldest child, Izzy. Now that she was five, she no longer chewed on the furniture, but she found other ways to wreak havoc. Like last week when she finger painted a family portrait on the bathroom wall.

"Mommy, my tummy is grumpy." Ava Grace peeked her blond head around the corner. "And Scarlett is crying." She clutched her ever-present pink bunny. "But not Simon, he's sleeping." At three, Ava Grace was her mommy's eyes and ears. She watched her younger siblings like a hawk, always happy to report what they were up to. Reagan suspected that someday they'd call her a tattletale, but for now she was happy to have her daughter's reports.

Reagan frowned at the baby monitor sitting on the table. She hadn't heard any cries. Had it stopped working? "Okay, sweet girl." She picked up Ava Grace. No fever, so that was a good sign. "Do you want to eat a bite? Maybe some toast or crackers?" Izzy had been well enough to go back to school today, but the other three were still feeling puny.

Ava Grace nodded, her blond curls bouncing. "Goldfish."

Reagan put Ava Grace in her booster chair and poured some Goldfish on a paper plate. "Here you go, sweetie." She put the plate on the table in front of her daughter. "Do you want a drink?"

"Yes."

Reagan grabbed the Dora the Explorer sippy cup from the fridge and put it on the table. "Here's your drink. I'm going to run up and check on the twins."

Ava Grace nodded, her mouth already full of Goldfish.

Reagan picked up the baby monitor and held it to her ear. Silence. Great. Something was wrong with the monitor. Just one more thing to add to the list.

She hurried up the stairs to the nursery. She'd complained when they first moved into the house that the master bedroom was on the bottom floor and all the rest of the bedrooms were upstairs. But Chad had been sure it wouldn't matter much, and the house had been the right price.

Four kids later and Reagan was certain whoever had come up with the layout was somewhere laughing about the poor mothers having to go up and down stairs a million times a day to their kids' rooms.

She peeked into the nursery. Even though she'd hoped to redo it after moving Ava Grace into her own room, it was still the same pink it had been since Izzy was a baby.

Poor Simon. The lone boy in the family deserved a room filled with baseballs and boats. But she'd been too busy with Izzy and Ava Grace, and then she'd spent the last month of her pregnancy on bed rest for high blood pressure.

She'd hoped Chad would take some time off work to take care of it or at least hire someone to handle it. But no.

Violet had been the one to get Simon's crib bedding, and she'd chosen an adorable blue-and-green frog-themed set. It might clash terribly in the bubble-gum room, but Reagan loved it.

She reached down and smoothed her son's wispy hair. He didn't stir. If only she could sleep like that.

She crossed to Scarlett's crib and picked her up before she started crying again. Scarlett was a beautiful baby, with rosy cheeks and bright blue eyes. "Let's go downstairs and let your brother sleep." Reagan snuggled the baby to her chest and inhaled the sweet smell of her daughter. These would be her last babies, and she knew how fast they grew. They'd be little people before she knew it. It seemed like only yesterday they'd brought Izzy home from the hospital, and now she was in kindergarten.

Where had the time gone?

She nestled Scarlett against her and carefully maneuvered the stairs. It was her constant fear—that she'd trip while holding one of the kids.

"Are you finished with your Goldfish?" she asked Ava Grace once she reached the kitchen.

"Uh-huh." Ava Grace grinned. "All done."

"Good girl. Do you want to watch Dora for a few minutes?" She'd hoped to never be the kind of mom who encouraged TV, but some days it was a lifesaver.

She settled Ava Grace in the living room. "Just one show, okay?"

"Okay."

The phone buzzed against the coffee table. "Hello."

"Hey, babe." Chad's voice sounded muffled. "Just wanted to see how everyone was doing today."

"Izzy was well enough to go to school. She took the bus this morning, and Katie's mom is going to bring her home this afternoon so I don't have to get the other three out." It would be an absolute nightmare to load three sick children in the van.

"That's nice."

The distinct sound of water in the background caught Reagan's attention. "Where are you?"

"I'm at the hotel."

"*Where* at the hotel?"

Silence on the other end confirmed her suspicions. "Chad Michael McClure. Are you at the pool? Tell me that you are not at the pool in Vegas while I am at home with your sick children. And a busted baby monitor." May as well let him know that he'd be going out to buy a new one as soon as he got home.

"Don't middle name me like I'm one of the kids. My flight was delayed for a few hours, and I've already checked out of the room. What else am I supposed to do?"

She couldn't even form words.

"Babe. Come on. Don't be like this. I've worked long hours for the past month. If I get the chance to relax at the pool for a few hours before my flight, you should be happy for me."

"Yeah." She fought to keep her voice pleasant in front of the kids. "I've barely had a shower in four days. I haven't been out of the house except for Wednesday when I had to take the kids to the doctor. By myself. Do you have any idea how difficult it is to take four sick children to the doctor?"

"I'll make it up to you. I promise."

She'd heard that before.

The other line beeped, and she held it out to check the caller ID. "I've got to go. Izzy's school is on the other line." She hit the button. "Hello?"

"Mrs. McClure? I hate to call you so close to the end of the day, but we're going to need you to come pick up Izzy. I guess she isn't over that virus after all."

Reagan took a deep breath. "I'll be there as soon as I can."

She glanced down at her old T-shirt and maternity yoga pants. They'd never actually seen a yoga class, but they sure were comfortable. It would have to do. No way did she have time to change clothes *and* load three kids into the van.

All while her husband sat at a pool in Vegas and basked in the sunshine.

Her life certainly hadn't turned out the way she'd planned.

Violet paused outside of the boardroom and smoothed the skirt of her dress. She pasted on a smile and opened the heavy doors.

"Good of you to make it, Violet." Mom tapped her watch. "I was beginning to think you wouldn't be here."

Violet looked up in surprise. She'd had no idea her mother would be at the meeting. The totally unprecedented nature of her attendance confirmed her suspicions of the meeting's topic. "I'm not even late. It's not noon yet." She gave her mother a quick hug.

Julia Matthews waved a manicured hand around the boardroom. "But almost everyone else is here. It doesn't look good, dear, for the boss's daughter to be so lax about things."

I will not roll my eyes. I will remain calm. Violet had been coaching herself around her mother for so many years, it was second nature. "Sorry, Mom."

"Hey, y'all," Amber Matthews said, walking into the room. "Sorry I'm late, Mom." Violet's younger sister gave their mother a quick peck on the cheek.

"Oh, that's okay, honey. We know how busy you are with school."

Typical. Mom reamed her out for not being prompt enough but let Amber slide. Her sister was in her final year of graduate school and was dangerously close to becoming what Violet thought of as a professional student. She wouldn't be at all surprised if Amber announced she was going for a doctorate next. Their parents might be proud, but Violet suspected it was all a ploy to avoid getting a real job. "Glad to see you, Amber."

Amber smiled prettily. "You, too." Her eyes lit up. "Oh, there's Landry. He looks so handsome. I picked that suit out myself."

Violet followed her sister's gaze to Landry Baxter, Amber's boyfriend of three years. Violet and Landry had been friends in law school, and she'd been pleased when he'd joined the firm. She'd introduced him to Amber at the company Christmas party, and the rest was history.

She nodded at her sister and hurried to take an empty seat.

"Any idea what this is about?" Ryan Harpeth asked from across the table, a worried look on his face. He'd just started with the firm and had done his undergraduate work at Harding University, just like Violet.

She shook her head. "I don't think it's anything to worry about." She grinned. "So you can relax."

"I haven't been here long enough to know if these meetings are common or not," he explained. "But Kelsey was making a big deal about it this morning when I came in, asking if I'd heard anything."

Violet laughed. "She just likes to stay on top of things." More likely she'd wanted an excuse to talk to Ryan.

"Thanks for coming, everyone." Sampson Matthews always liked to make a grand entrance. Today was no different. He strode into the room and took his place at the head of the table. "I won't keep you long, but there is a bit of business to discuss."

Violet had always admired her father's ability to command attention. It was part of what made him such a great lawyer. He thrived on cases that went to trial. Violet had always preferred to settle out of court. She'd never been comfortable in her role, never felt as in command as her father always appeared. But she'd worked hard nonetheless and had a lot of success during her years with the firm.

"Everyone here knows the history of this firm. My daddy founded it right out of law school, and it was an honor to come and work for him once I completed my own law degree." He shot a smile in Violet's direction. "And I'm thrilled that a third generation of the Matthews family is part of the firm today."

Violet sat up straight. This was it.

"Legacy and history are important to us here at Matthews Law. So when it came time to add another partner, I didn't take the decision lightly."

Violet grinned.

"That is why it is with great honor that I announce Landry Baxter as the newest partner in the firm."

Applause rang out all over the room. Violet forced her hands to clap, but it was like banging two concrete blocks together. She couldn't believe her dad had chosen Landry over her.

"Thanks, everyone." Landry stood up, a huge grin on his face. "Of course, I'm thrilled to begin my new role here and am honored that Mr. Matthews is placing such confidence in me."

Another round of applause. Violet caught sight of Amber's gleeful face. She should've known her sister wouldn't be here for her. How could she have been so off the mark?

Once her father adjourned the meeting, Violet peeled herself off the chair and started toward the door. Maybe she could get out of here without having to speak to anyone, have Kelsey take messages for the rest of the day, and sneak out early.

"Violet," Mom called, waving her over. "Be at the house at six sharp tonight, okay? We're having a little celebration."

A celebration for Landry. Of course. "Oh, I don't know."

"Do you want Landry to think you aren't happy for him?" Mom raised an eyebrow. "You know how much he means to your sister."

Violet sighed. "Fine. I'll see you at six." She hurried out the door and to her office, wondering why the day had blown up in her face.

Chapter 3

Violet Matthews: You are not going to believe what just happened. Dad made Landry partner instead of me. I'm sure Mom and Amber put him up to it. I need chocolate. (Text message sent August 20, 2:46 p.m.)

Reagan McClure: No way. That stinks. If it makes you feel any better, my husband is sunning himself at a Vegas pool and Izzy is throwing up again. Trade lives? (Text message sent August 20, 3:52 p.m.)

Reagan put the final load of laundry in the washing machine and started the cycle. Few things satisfied her more than emptying the hamper. And with four small children, it was a rare occurrence.

"Anybody home?" Chad poked his head into the laundry room.

She nodded. "I'm always home. Unless I'm picking someone up, dropping someone off, or at the grocery store." If he hadn't had a sunburned nose, she probably could've kept her cool.

"Still mad?" He tossed a pile of clothes into the hamper she'd just emptied.

Reagan stared at her husband. He'd known her for fifteen years, since their freshman year of college. He should know her better. Shouldn't he? "I had to load the kids up and go pick up Izzy after I talked to you. She still has a touch of the stomach flu. The baby monitor isn't working. Ava Grace pulled Simon across the nursery by his leg, so someday when he doesn't walk right, it will be because I had to go to the bathroom and leave them alone for a second." She ticked off the highlights of her day. "And you hung out at a pool. Tell me what sounds fair about that?"

At least he had the decency to look sheepish. "Sorry you've had a tough time. But I'm here now." Chad grinned. "Didn't you miss me a little?" He raised his eyebrows up and down.

She shrugged. No reason to further emphasize how poorly she'd handled her stint as a single parent. "Did you miss *me*?"

"Of course. I wish you'd gone with me."

Reagan crossed her arms and leaned against the washing machine. "Easy for you to say, considering we both know that wasn't possible." She wouldn't be going anywhere anytime soon, or at least as long as the twins were still nursing.

"I can't win." Chad raked a hand through his blond hair. "There's no pleasing you these days." He jerked his chin toward the doorway. "Are the kids asleep?"

"Naps for all." *Except me.* There were precious few minutes to tackle the never-ending list of chores that needed to be done. Whoever had come up with the adage of sleeping when the baby slept must not have had other children to look after. Or a husband whose idea of helping out meant throwing his clothes in the hamper instead of on the floor.

Chad tugged on his tie. "I think a nap sounds like a great idea. Wake me before dinner, okay?"

She watched him go. There'd been a time not that long ago when he'd have suggested she join him, especially if the kids were napping. But not anymore.

Reagan glanced down at her stained shirt that couldn't hide the post-pregnancy belly that hadn't seemed to shrink as much as it did with the last one. Twins were harder on the body than she'd expected. Couple that with no makeup and hair that hadn't been properly washed and dried in what seemed like forever and it was no wonder Chad was content to nap alone.

She blinked back the hot tears that threatened to spill down her cheeks.

How had things gotten to this point? And more importantly, was there any way to keep them from getting worse?

Jackson poured himself a second cup of coffee and sat back down at his desk to look at the specs for a building he thought might be perfect for one of his projects. He'd been wooing a large appliance company for the better part of six months, trying to get them to open their new warehouse just outside of Little Rock. It would be a huge coup for the Arkansas Economic Development Commission to land the company, but Jackson was concerned. During their last meeting, he'd sensed some hesitation from the project manager. But maybe finding this building would satisfy the man. It more than fit their specifications.

His assistant's voice crackled over the phone's intercom. "Mr.

Stratford, there's someone here to see you."

He picked up the receiver. "I didn't know I had anyone scheduled."

"He says his name is Ricky Bobby, but that can't be right," Sheila whispered. "I think that's the name of a character from a Will Ferrell movie."

Jackson burst out laughing. "Send him in. I'll explain later." He and Jeff had used the same running joke for years. Always a different movie character name whenever they made restaurant reservations or just to mess with unsuspecting receptionists.

"Check you out," Jeff Galloway said from the doorway. "Cute assistant, big fancy office. Not that anyone would've expected anything different."

Jackson grinned. "Sheila's married with two kids, so don't get any ideas. And this office will do for now, but I'm hoping for bigger and better things down the road." He motioned toward a leather seat that sat opposite his desk. "Sit down and tell me what brings you here." Jeff and Jackson had been friends since they were assigned to the same little league team in the sixth grade. Even so, Jeff had never made an office visit.

"I've got news." Jeff leaned back in the chair. "Big news that I think you're gonna like."

Uh-oh. If Jeff's wife had another fix-up in mind for him, he'd be hard pressed to get out of it. A few years ago she'd insisted he go out with one of her coworkers, and the night had been a disaster. "Should I be nervous? Is Lauren in a matchmaking mood again?"

Jeff burst out laughing. "Are you kidding? After the way things went with you and Marie, I'm pretty sure she'll never let you get within ten feet of another of her friends."

"Marie. That was her name. I couldn't remember. She's a sixth-grade science teacher."

Jeff shook his head. "No. She's a first-grade music teacher. No wonder things didn't go well if that's as much attention as you paid her."

"We were a total mismatch to begin with. She was not impressed by me at all. Made no effort to hide it." He sighed. "Didn't help any when a girl I'd just gone out with ended up being our waitress."

"The way Marie told it, you were so busy ogling the waitress that you didn't even realize she'd left the table and called a cab."

"Pretty much sums it up." Jackson shrugged. He'd told Lauren he wasn't interested, but she'd insisted. "Left me with two plates of food to eat though." He grinned. "So what's the big news?"

"I'm here in an official capacity as a member of the Brookwood Christian School's board to let you know that you are going to be named our Alumnus of the Year at this year's centennial homecoming celebration."

Jackson shook his head. "Don't mess with me."

"I'm not. It was unanimous. Your family has such a legacy with the school, and your financial contributions mean a lot." He shrugged. "Plus you've volunteered a lot of time over the years, too."

A slow grin spread across Jackson's face. "My dad received that award when I was in junior high. The plaque hung on the wall in his office until last year." Walter Stratford's untimely death had been a shock to all, but especially to Jackson. "Now Mom has it hanging in the living room. She says it was one of his proudest achievements."

Jeff frowned. "How's your mom doing?"

"Still adjusting. We all are, I guess."

"That's to be expected." Jeff tapped his fingers against the arm of the chair. "I should get going. I just wanted to give you the news in person." He stood. "I'll e-mail you more information. The event is in mid-January, so it's still a few months off. There'll be a big dinner and silent auction on the Friday night before the homecoming basketball game on Saturday. We'd like for you to give the address that night. Talk about whatever you'd like." He turned to go, then turned back to face Jackson. "I do have one message for you from Lauren."

Jackson groaned.

Jeff laughed and held up his hands. "She wants you to call her. And if you don't, she will track you down." He grinned. "And she's the queen of tracking people down. If you don't believe me, ask her kindergarten best friend who she just found on Facebook. The poor girl lives somewhere in Wyoming and barely even remembers living in Arkansas when she was five."

Jackson told his friend good-bye and settled back at his desk. Alumnus of the Year. It didn't seem right that he was even old enough to receive such an award.

He did some quick math. He'd been fourteen when his dad received the award, and his dad had been. . .thirty-five. That couldn't be right. Could it?

He was thirty-five.

The same age his dad had been when he'd received the honor. Yet his dad had seemed so. . .settled. So grown up. He'd had a wife and two kids.

Jackson couldn't help but compare.

His dad had looked out at a table full of loved ones cheering for him when he'd given his speech.

Who would Jackson have?

The answer wasn't a pretty one.

Chapter 4

Amber Matthews: Vi, PLEASE DON'T BE LATE FOR LANDRY'S
PARTY. AND ALSO, DON'T WEAR ANYTHING GREEN. LANDRY
AND I ARE BOTH WEARING GREEN, AND I DON'T WANT ANYONE
ELSE TO WEAR IT BECAUSE IT WILL SPOIL THE PICTURES.
THANKS. (Text message sent August 20, 4:59 p.m.)

Violet pulled into her parents' driveway and turned off the
engine. At least the day couldn't get worse.

An older model Buick pulled in behind her. Mom hadn't
mentioned her grandparents would be at the party.

Violet climbed out of her SUV and smoothed her skirt. She'd
run home after work to let her dog go outside and to change into
something besides her new green dress. She had a feeling if she'd
been wearing blue today when Amber had seen her, it would've
been blue that had been prohibited tonight. It was too much
trouble to fight her sister though.

"Hey, Grandma." Violet hugged her grandmother as soon as
the elderly woman got out of the car.

Rose Wallingford smiled at her oldest grandchild. "I'm so glad to see you, Violet. I wasn't sure if you'd be here or not."

"If Mom had told me you were coming, I would've been a lot happier about being here."

Grandma laughed and patted Violet's arm. "Oh, honey. Julia told me that Sampson made Landry partner in the firm." She leaned closer to Violet. "Might be the best thing that ever happened to you," she whispered. "I have an idea we need to discuss."

Before Violet could find out what her grandmother was talking about, a sullen teenage girl climbed out of the backseat. Her Goth style startled Violet. What was this girl doing with Grandma?

"Violet, I'd like you to meet Shadow Simmons. You might remember her grandmother, Betty Kemp from next door," Grandma said.

Violet watched as Betty climbed out of the passenger side. "Nice to meet you, Shadow." She could see the teenager was pretty underneath the dark hair, dark eyeliner, and black clothes. "Hi, Mrs. Kemp," she said as the older woman came to stand next to Grandma.

"Hello, dear." Mrs. Kemp smiled. "I guess you've met my girl." She put an arm around Shadow, but the girl shrugged her away. "She's living with me and Oliver for the school year. It's so nice to have a young person in the house again."

Violet vaguely remembered that the Kemps' only daughter had been killed in an accident a few years ago. Shadow must be her daughter. "I'm sure it is." She smiled at Shadow. "How do you like living in Hot Springs?"

Shadow stared at her with dark-rimmed eyes. "You've been

there. It's boring. My dad sent me to live with them so he can focus on his new family." She frowned.

Mrs. Kemp didn't miss a beat. "That's why we're here tonight. To break up the boring week."

Grandma smiled at Violet. "Your grandfather couldn't make it tonight, so I was glad for the company." She motioned toward the house. "We'd better get inside. Julia and Amber will be wondering what's keeping us."

Violet followed them up the path. She couldn't wait to see Amber's face when an angry Goth teenager walked in to Landry's celebratory dinner.

It more than made up for not being able to wear her new dress. And then some.

Jackson stood outside of Main Street Bakery and waited for Lauren. He'd called her soon after Jeff left, and she'd asked him to meet her here on the way home from work.

"There you are, the second most handsome man to ever grace the halls of Brookwood Christian." Lauren grinned. "Actually, scratch that and make it the third. Bennett started kindergarten last week." She gave Jackson a hug. "Can you believe my baby is old enough to be in school?"

Jackson shook his head. "I sure can't. It seems like just yesterday we were there, doesn't it?" Jackson had known Lauren even longer than he'd known Jeff. She'd been in his class from the very start, way back when he'd worn Garanimals and carried a *Dukes of Hazzard* lunch box. Aside from his dad, Bo Duke had been his hero. Every now and then he still had the urge to slide into a car through the open window.

"Have you ever been here?" she asked, motioning toward the bakery. "It's one of our favorites. Jeff loves their buttercream frosting, and the kids think no dinner out is complete without dessert from this place."

Jackson held the door open for her, and the sweet scent of fresh-baked goods invaded his senses. "Nope. I've seen it on my way home but never stopped."

"Well you're in for a treat."

They ordered cupcakes and coffee, and Lauren led him to a table in the corner. "So how have you been?" she asked once they were seated.

He shrugged. "Okay. Busy with work. You know the drill."

"I do." She took a bite of her chocolate cupcake.

Jackson eyed her suspiciously. "What's this meeting all about anyway?"

"Can't I just get together with an old friend without raising an alarm?" she asked.

He narrowed his eyes. "No. Your husband comes to my office today to give me good news, news I'm sure you know about. For all I know, you're the one who nominated me. And he tells me I need to get in touch with you or you'll relentlessly track me down like you did to some poor girl in Wyoming." He grinned. "Who was it anyway? That weird girl who ate glue and accidentally got locked in the janitor's closet?"

Lauren laughed. "That was Suzy Jenkins. And for your

information, I didn't nominate you. Mrs. Chastain did."

"The librarian? I thought she hated me." Freshman year he'd put a fake mouse in one of the card catalogue drawers. Mrs. Chastain had made him sweep the library every afternoon for three weeks to make up for it.

"Guess not. Or maybe she's got a nice granddaughter she wants to fix you up with." Lauren grinned mischievously.

Jackson groaned. "Why don't you have your friend Marie have a talk with her. That'll nip it in the bud."

"I'm impressed that you remember her name."

He didn't have the heart to tell her Jeff had reminded him of it earlier at the office. "What do you think I am? Some kind of Neanderthal?"

She cocked her head. "Well. . ."

Jackson rolled his eyes. "Seriously. What's the deal here?"

"You won't like this much. But hear me out."

He already didn't like the sound of things. "What?"

"I talked to Kathleen the other night. She and I decided one of us had to have this talk with you." Lauren grinned. "And I lost."

"Great. What kind of scheme have you two cooked up this time?" Lauren and his sister had been inseparable growing up. Even though Kathleen lived in Memphis now, they still saw each other often.

"It's about the award. More specifically the dinner."

"If you're worried I'll say something off-color in my speech, don't worry. I'll be on my best behavior. Wouldn't want to let Mrs. Chastain down, after all."

She frowned. "That's not it. We're more worried about who

you're going to bring."

He crossed his arms and leaned back in his chair. "I won't embarrass the family, if that's what you're worried about."

"Jackson, you're a grown man. You'll be thirty-six in a few months."

"Easy now. Don't put me in the ground before it's my time." His joke fell flat.

Lauren took a sip of her coffee. "The last time you double-dated with me and Jeff, do you remember what happened?"

He might've known she'd bring it up. "Do we have to rehash this?"

"Yes." She raised an eyebrow and gave him a stern look. "That girl, bless her heart, was sweet. And very pretty. But let me just say that it's hard to take someone seriously as a real prospect for you when it turns out that I was her babysitter when I was sixteen."

It had been a nightmare. "She was only ten years younger."

Lauren shook her head. "It's not even about age. If you were going out with someone ten years younger than you who was a good match for you—who liked the things you do and could carry on an actual conversation—I'd be all for it." She shrugged. "But for some reason you choose to go out with girls you know there's no future with."

She had a point, but he wasn't going to give her the satisfaction. His lunch date with Whitney had really hit home with him today. "What exactly do you want me to do?"

"Think about the future. As far as I know, you've never been serious about anyone. You deserve more than that, Jackson. Jeff thinks so, too, but he'd never be so blunt as to tell you." She grinned. "He's lucky to have me, huh?"

Jackson chuckled. "I guess."

"So you promise? No bubble-headed girls at the awards banquet. You've got several months to find someone suitable. Someone you can be proud of to have at your table." She smiled. "Someone who cares about you for who you are, not the car you drive or how much money you make."

He'd never thought of himself as the kind of guy who had bad luck with women. In fact, he'd rather enjoyed himself over the years. He dated whenever he wanted, never got serious, and walked away unscathed. Not a bad way to live. "Fine. I promise to bring a suitable *woman* to the dinner. I'll leave the—what did you call them?" He grinned. "The bubble-headed girls behind for one night."

She sighed. "One night is a start."

It would have to be. Because while he might be able to admit that he was a little behind the curve on the "happily ever after" life that so many of his friends had found, that his dad had possessed when he was thirty-five, Jackson wasn't convinced it was the life for him.

Chapter 5

Reagan McClure: CHAD MADE IT HOME WITH A NICE
SUNBURN FROM THE POOL. NOW HE'S NAPPING WHILE
I COOK. WHAT IS WRONG WITH THIS PICTURE? (Text
message sent August 20, 5:28 p.m.)

Violet Matthews: SORRY. HANG IN THERE. I HAVE A GREAT
STORY TO TELL YOU LATER THAT INCLUDES A TEENAGE
GOTH, AMBER, AND SOME STINKY CHEESE. YOU'LL LOVE IT.
(Text message sent August 20, 7:02 p.m.)

Violet took a seat at the table between Grandma and Shadow.
"Looks good, doesn't it?" she asked. From the fresh flowers in
the center to the fancy china, it looked like Martha Stewart herself
had planned the party.

"It sure does." Grandma placed her napkin in her lap. "It isn't
every day I have such a fancy dinner." She took a sip of sweet tea.
"Your grandpa and I hardly ever sit at the dining table anymore."
She grinned. "Most of the time we eat on TV trays and watch

Wheel of Fortune. I guess we've turned uncouth in our old age."

Violet laughed. "I don't know about that."

"Are those. . .lobster?" Shadow asked in a disgusted tone when Amber placed a heaping platter in the center of the table. "Because I don't eat that."

Betty frowned at her granddaughter. "No need to broadcast it, dear." She lowered her voice to a still-audible whisper. "I don't either. We'll drive through McDonald's on our way back to Hot Springs."

"What's with the weird food they have?" Shadow whispered back. "Haven't they heard of normal stuff like chicken or pizza?"

Violet fought back a smile. Shadow had started out trying to be a good sport until Amber had insisted everyone taste the cheese she'd gotten at a gourmet food store. It stunk to high heaven. Amber had looked positively murderous when Shadow had declared it tasted like feet. "I promise you that I didn't grow up eating stinky cheese and lobster on a regular basis," Violet explained. "I'm guessing my sister planned the menu."

"Yes she did." Mom walked into the dining room in time to hear the end of Violet's statement. "And she's done an excellent job."

Once everyone was seated and Dad had offered thanks, Landry stood up. "Thanks so much for coming tonight to celebrate the second best day of my life."

Second best? If he said meeting Amber was the best, she might just gag.

Amber jumped up and grabbed his arm, a giant grin on her face. Her green sundress exactly matched his polo shirt.

"In fact, we have a little announcement to make," Landry said.

Amber thrust her left hand out and revealed a huge diamond.

"We're engaged!" she squealed.

Everyone around the table offered their congratulations, but Violet froze. She'd always assumed that as the oldest she'd be the first to marry. Of course she'd also assumed Dad would make her partner in the firm. Lesson learned: don't assume, even if it seems logical.

Grandma nudged her.

All eyes were on Violet, waiting for her response. She blushed. "Wonderful news!" She mustered up all the enthusiasm she possibly could. "I'm so happy for you both."

Amber smiled, appeased. "Thanks." She and Landry sat back down. "The wedding will be in December. I know it's quick, but we hate to spend another day apart. Right before Christmas will be perfect."

Of course. Violet had always hoped to have her own wedding around Christmas. Amber had always said she wanted a traditional June wedding. "Really?"

Amber's blue eyes flashed. "Really."

Violet turned her attention to the lobster. She really was happy for her sister. But seeing Amber's happiness and security with Landry only reminded Violet of what was missing in her own life.

Reagan turned on the sound machine in the nursery, and soothing sounds of the ocean filled the room. Scarlett must be the lightest sleeper in the world. Couple that with the world's loudest older sisters living down the hall, and the machine was a lifesaver.

"Everybody down?" Chad asked as she walked into the living room.

She nodded. "Yes. Thank goodness."

"Rough few days, huh?" Chad propped his feet up on the coffee table and flipped the channel to ESPN.

Reagan set the laundry basket on the couch. "Can you fold these towels while I go get the rest of the laundry out of the dryer?"

Chad didn't respond.

"Please?"

Nothing.

"I'm going to be out of town next week, and I'll need you to keep the kids."

Chad peeled his eyes away from *SportsCenter*. "Huh?"

She frowned. "Fold. The. Laundry." She enunciated every word and pointed to the basket. "Please."

He made a face but picked up a towel. "By the way," he said as she started toward the laundry room. "I fixed the baby monitor."

She stopped. "You did?" She smiled. "I'm surprised you remembered I'd mentioned it wasn't working."

He grinned. "It wasn't working because it was unplugged. Before you freak out about something being broken, maybe you should check to make sure it's plugged in."

Rookie mothering mistake. She should've thought to check that before complaining to Chad. He'd never let her live it down. "I'll bet Ava Grace is responsible. No matter how many times I tell her to stay away from outlets, she doesn't always listen."

"Great. One of our children is going to get electrocuted someday because they don't listen to you."

Reagan's eyes filled with tears. Stupid hormones. Why couldn't she just get angry without also being emotional? "Well I'm sorry you think they're so unsafe at home with a mother like me. Would you rather put them all in daycare? Because I'd be happy to go back to work."

He regarded her for a long moment. "You know that isn't what I meant."

"Sounded like it to me."

Chad sighed. "Come on, Reagan. Don't fight with me. I'm tired, you're tired. We'll just say stuff we can't take back."

At least they'd be talking. It had been months since the two of them had engaged in a conversation about anything other than the kids. "Just fold the laundry. I need to get the rest of the clothes out of the dryer and fix Izzy's lunch box for tomorrow. Hopefully today was the end of the virus." She watched as Chad haphazardly folded a towel. He didn't even make the corners match up. "I'll do that tomorrow." She took the basket from the couch. "Just forget it."

He shrugged. "Suit yourself." He clicked the OFF button on the remote. "I'm going to bed."

"Can you take Izzy to school in the morning?"

He stood up and groaned. "You know that puts me to the office later than I like." Chad worked as an HR manager for Baptist Health, one of the largest employers in the state.

"I hate to put her on the bus. Besides, I know she'd love the extra time with you on the way to school."

He shook his head. "Tomorrow is not a good day. It's my first day without an assistant, and my day is going to be crazy."

"What happened to Barbara?" The older woman had worked

closely with Chad since he started the position.

"She retired. I told you that."

Reagan shook her head. "I'd remember that. I would've taken the kids to say good-bye. She's been so nice to us." When Barbara found out Reagan was carrying twins, she'd brought several days' worth of frozen casseroles and made Reagan promise to use them on days when she was too exhausted to think about cooking. They'd been gone before she was halfway through her second trimester.

"I'll give you her home e-mail address. I'm sure she'd love to hear from you." He motioned toward their bedroom. "I'm headed to bed now." Chad disappeared into the bedroom before she had the chance to ask any more questions.

She tried to ignore the pang of uncertainty. It wasn't like him to forget to tell her something like that. And she didn't like the way he'd gone to bed in the middle of their conversation.

Her buzzing phone put a stop to her pity party.

"You are not going to believe this," Violet said.

Reagan cradled the phone against her ear and carried the basket into the laundry room. "What happened?"

"They're engaged. *Engaged.* Kill. Me. Now."

Reagan couldn't help but laugh. "I didn't realize it was so serious. I guess Landry being made partner makes more sense now though, huh?"

"True. But I was totally shocked. I wonder what it would be like to have the kind of sister you're close to, the kind who actually shares personal information with you instead of springing it publicly."

"As an only child, I can't answer that question." Even so,

Reagan hoped her girls grew up to be best friends, not just tolerate one another the way Violet and Amber did. "Maybe this will be good for Amber. Surely she'll grow up a little now that she's going to be someone's wife." Reagan had met Amber when she was just an annoying junior-high kid who used to sleep on the floor of the dorm room when she came for visits. Through the years, Reagan had watched her grow into a spoiled twenty-something who always managed to get her way.

"Let's hope so. Amber and I got along for the first twelve years of her life. Sometimes I wonder if we'll ever get back there."

"At least she has good taste. Your bridesmaid dress should be pretty."

Violet let out a laugh. "Oh, I didn't make the cut to be a bridesmaid. She actually said she felt like bridesmaids over thirty were kind of pathetic, so she'd rather I just serve the cake."

"Well that's just nuts. You'd make a beautiful bridesmaid regardless of your age. And everyone knows serving cake is the worst job. You can't enjoy the reception."

"Well, I might not be able to fully enjoy the reception, but I know one thing. I'm *not* going to that wedding alone."

Reagan grinned. "Does this mean you're finally ready to date again? I was beginning to think Zach had ruined you forever."

"Not to mention my best friend warning me against marriage all the time," Violet teased.

She deserved that. "Sorry. Want me to sugarcoat married life? Because I'd be glad to."

"Don't be silly. I know you don't mean it."

Reagan didn't have the heart to tell her that sometimes she did.

Sometimes being married with four kids seemed like the hardest job she could imagine. All the fairy tales and romantic comedies in the world couldn't prepare a girl for that. "So what's the plan? Join the church's singles group? Online dating?"

"I'm starting right out with the big guns," Violet said. "After I left my parents' house, I stopped at Main Street Bakery for a double chocolate cupcake. Up at the cash register, there was a stack of business cards for a matchmaker."

"A matchmaker? Seriously?"

"There's a money-back guarantee. My love life will be in someone else's hands. It's a great plan."

"I guess."

"Come on. What could be more perfect? I'll meet with them once, and then they'll do the work for me. They'll weed out the losers and find someone who meets my specifications. It's a no-brainer."

Reagan wasn't sure, but she'd muster up as much support as possible. "Sounds great." Despite her complaints about Chad these days, they'd had a lot of happy years together. She couldn't imagine having to date again.

Although it would be nice to have a date with her husband every now and then.

Dear Mama,

Is it weird to write to someone without an Earthly address? Maybe. Nana gave me this journal though, and I don't really know what to do with it. She also gave me your journal from when you were sixteen. I think she's just trying to keep me happy, but I don't know if that's possible. I miss my friends and my old room. But I'm not too sad to be away from Stephanie. She's always trying to act like she's my mom, but she isn't. It makes me so mad when she does that. Daddy tries to stay out of it, but I'll bet he's kind of relieved I'm not there now.

Nana is trying to introduce me to people here, but so far I haven't met anyone too interesting. We went to a party the other night and this girl named Amber got really upset because I spit out some kind of fancy cheese she'd bought. It tasted like dirty feet to me though! I don't think Amber will be inviting me and Nana to any more of her dinner parties.

Oh, and now that I'm in Arkansas, me and Axel broke up. Nana found his picture in the trash and asked me why I threw away a picture of Ozzy Osbourne. Ha ha. I'm surprised she even knows who that is.

Now she's trying to get me to dye my hair back to my normal color, but I don't know.

I love you and miss you.

Shadow

Chapter 6

To: Violet.Matthews@MatthewsLaw.com
From: rosewallingford@myinternet.com
Date: August 27, 10:33 a.m.
Subject: My idea

I didn't get the chance to tell you my idea last week
because of the wedding ruckus. I thought you might
like to know that the shop owner next to the Kemps'
antique store is moving to be near her grandkids down
in Louisiana. The place is adorable and would make a
perfect bakery. I don't want to interfere with your life, but
sometimes you have to take a leap of faith. Think about it
and then call me.
Love,
Grandma (Grandpa says hi, too)

Violet sat in the restaurant parking lot and stared at her
grandmother's e-mail. She had too much on her mind right

now to even consider opening a bakery. Besides, meeting her perfect match for lunch was enough of a leap of faith for now.

She'd been pleasantly surprised when Mimi Maxwell from Mimi's Matches had called her Friday to let her know that she'd found someone who met nearly all of Violet's specifications. Apparently he'd interviewed on the same day Violet had. Mimi assured her this was a good sign because it meant they were both at the same place on the journey to love.

Violet had fought back a sarcastic remark. She would be a good sport about this and believe matchmaking could work. Or at least work well enough that she wouldn't be dateless for Amber's wedding.

She climbed out of her SUV and grabbed her purse. If the late August heat was any indication, they were in for a typical Arkansas fall—hot, humid, and a few more weekends at the lake before the weather actually turned cool.

Violet took a deep breath. What kind of man had Mimi found for her? At least there were background checks done on the prospects so she wouldn't have to worry about meeting some criminal who'd steal her identity and credit cards.

She squared her shoulders and walked into Zaza, a popular eatery in the Heights area of Little Rock. She'd been here a couple of times and had always been impressed.

"I'm meeting someone here," Violet told the hostess. "Under the name Mimi Maxwell." Mimi had refused to give the name of her date. *"We don't want you Googling each other and jumping to any conclusions. Best to go in with an open mind."* Violet had laughed because that was the first thing she would've done if armed with a name. Even more than diamonds, Google was a single girl's best friend.

The hostess ran her finger down the list. "The other party is already seated. Follow me." She motioned toward the dining area.

Violet's heart raced. First dates made her nervous. But blind dates made her feel stupid. She hated walking into a situation without knowing what to expect.

She scanned the room, hoping to spot him before he spotted her. Her eyes landed on a handsome man at a table for two. He was engrossed in his phone, furiously texting.

"Here you go," the hostess said.

The man looked up from his phone and cast steely blue eyes on Violet.

Familiar blue eyes.

It couldn't be.

"Violet Matthews." He stood up, a grin on his handsome face. "You have got to be kidding me."

Jackson Stratford had been the bane of her existence her senior year of college. Handsome and charming, yes. But also conceited and spoiled and totally unreliable. And also the reason she'd graduated a semester late. "You." She shook her head. "No way that you are my perfect match."

"Well it's nice to see you, too." His blue eyes twinkled. "I mean, it's only been what? More than a decade?" He grinned and nodded toward her chair. "Have a seat."

Violet took in his expensive suit and stylish haircut. He was better looking than when they'd been in college. He'd filled out some over the years. She vaguely remembered that he'd been a couple of years older than the rest of their classmates. Something about a gap year in Europe before college. It still sounded as pretentious now as it had back then. "Eleven years. I guess I haven't seen you since that presentation we did for our Business Ethics class." Actually she hadn't seen him since they'd been called into their professor's office right after their disaster of a presentation, but surely he remembered that.

He frowned.

For a split second Violet wondered how she looked to him. She'd changed since college, too. Found her own sense of style and finally learned that her fair complexion wasn't suited for a suntan. And learned to embrace her sometimes wild hair. "So you're living in Little Rock now?"

Jackson nodded. "I've been here for a year. I work in economic development. I spent the past several years living on the Gulf coast."

Too bad he hadn't stayed there. Then she might've met a real match today. "That's nice."

The waitress stopped by their table. "Can I get y'all something to drink?"

"Sweet tea, please." Jackson grinned at the waitress.

Violet shook her head. "Nothing for me. I won't be staying."

The waitress raised her eyebrows but didn't say anything.

"Can't we let bygones be bygones?" Jackson asked once the waitress was gone. "You're here, it's lunchtime. You may as well stay and eat. Just two old friends catching up."

They hadn't exactly been friends, but she hated to point it out. "I don't think so. This wouldn't be a good idea."

Jackson shrugged. "Suit yourself." He picked up his iPhone and swiped the screen.

It certainly hadn't taken him long to lose interest. "Have a good lunch." She clutched her bag and stood.

He looked up and locked his blue eyes on her. "I'm sorry I wasn't what you were looking for, Violet. I didn't know what to expect from a matchmaking service, but it certainly wasn't you." He sighed. "But it was nice to see you again, regardless. I wish you the best, and I really am sorry for any trouble I caused you in college."

She paused. He sounded almost. . .sincere. That couldn't be right. Still though, now she felt bad. It wasn't like her to be rude. "It was nice to see you, too." She smiled. "The truth of the matter is that I'm really just looking for a date to my sister's wedding. Not a real relationship. So this would be a waste of your time." There. That should do it. Now she could have an excuse for leaving other than not wanting to spend time with him.

"Really?"

She nodded. "Yeah. So there's no point in staying here and having lunch with you like a real date. I expected to just meet some nice stranger and hit it off enough to take him to the wedding. But I'd never do that to you." She raked her fingers through her hair. "You deserve to find someone who is looking for the same thing you are."

The jubilant grin on his face set off warning bells.

And the smolder in his eyes told her to run.

But she didn't.

Jackson wasn't easily surprised. His years in business had taught him to expect the unexpected. But when Violet Matthews sashayed into Zaza, he could've been knocked over with a feather.

Those piercing green eyes and that dark red hair were the same he remembered from college. But she'd definitely blossomed in the years since he'd last seen her.

And in a good way.

She wasn't one of those petite girls who looked like the wind might carry them away or one of those super-skinny girls who never ate in front of anyone. Her simple yellow dress showed off the kind of curves women would kill for and men dreamed about.

"I think you should sit back down." His eyes grazed her slightly upturned nose and full lips. She'd been pretty in college. But now she was a knockout. He couldn't wait to walk into his awards banquet with her on his arm.

"Didn't you hear me?" she asked. "I said I wasn't really looking for a match. Just a date. Not a relationship."

He couldn't hide his smile. "Oh, I heard you. And I think you're going to want to hear what I have to say."

She tentatively perched on the chair. "I'm not eating."

"Suit yourself."

The waitress placed a glass of tea in front of him. "Are you ready to order?"

"Bring us a Petit Jean Ham and Pineapple Pizza. And a water for the lady." He fought back a grin as Violet scowled.

The waitress hurried off.

"I thought you might at least want a slice of pizza and some water while you hear me out." He grinned. "It's the least I can do."

"I could've ordered for myself." She ran a hand through her wavy hair. "You haven't changed much since college."

"I beg to differ. But we can discuss that later. Right now there's something I'd like to propose." He took a sip of his tea. "Bet you never thought I'd be proposing to you."

Violet narrowed her eyes.

"Fine. You don't like my jokes." He shrugged. "I can live with that."

"What do you have in mind, exactly?" she asked.

He leaned back in his chair and regarded her for a long moment. If he put this out there, he'd have to stick with it. All in. "I visited Mimi's Matches for much the same reason as you. I'm receiving an award at a banquet in a few months and am delivering the keynote speech. I'd like someone with me who isn't a bubblehead." He raised an eyebrow. "What do you do for a living?"

"A bubblehead?" She seemed offended. "I'm a lawyer."

"Perfect."

She glared. "What are you saying, exactly?"

"I'm saying, let's forget Mimi and avoid any other awkward encounters with well-meaning people who might be looking for something more than what either of us is interested in finding. Let's pose as each other's significant other. We have a history— albeit a rocky one. It would be easy for people to believe that we reconnected and are in a relationship." He let his idea sink in. It was the ideal situation. All he had to do was get her to agree.

And from the look on her face, that might be tough.

Chapter 7

Violet Matthews: APPARENTLY MY PERFECT MATCH IS
JACKSON STRATFORD. REMEMBER HIM? I'M JUST GLAD
MIMI HAS A MONEY-BACK GUARANTEE. (Text message sent
August 27, 2:02 p.m.)

Reagan McClure: FROM COLLEGE? SERIOUSLY? MAYBE MIMI
CAN FIND YOU SOMEONE WHO DIDN'T CAUSE YOU TO MISS
GRADUATION. . . . (Text message sent August 27, 2:17 p.m.)

Reagan stopped the van at a red light and flipped on her blinker.
They weren't even out of the neighborhood yet and all three
kids were screaming. "Ava Grace, let's sing 'Jesus Loves Me' for the
twins."

"I don't want to sing. I want my Bah." She let out a wail, and
the babies joined in.

Reagan took a deep breath. How had they managed to leave
the pink stuffed bunny at home? For three years that bunny had
gone everywhere Ava Grace did. Yet somehow they'd loaded up

without it today. "Bah is probably taking a nap at home. When we get back, he'll be nice and rested and ready to play."

Ava Grace continued to sob.

Sometimes leaving the house just wasn't worth it. "Can you be a big girl and sing for Simon and Scarlett?"

"No. I need Bah." Ava Grace's wails grew louder.

Reagan turned on the radio. There was no reasoning with Ava Grace right now. Maybe the twins would be lulled to sleep. "We're just going to drive through the pharmacy and then to school to get Izzy, and then we'll be right back home to Bah."

She'd asked Chad to pick up the prescription yesterday, but he'd forgotten. Even though loading up the kids was hard, sometimes it ended up being easier than trying to get Chad to handle an errand. Inevitably he forgot or got the wrong brand of whatever item was needed.

Once she'd picked up the prescription, she headed toward Izzy's school. They were actually running ahead of schedule. She glanced in the backseat. The twins had fallen asleep, and Ava Grace's wails had been replaced by pitiful whines and sniffles. Reagan would take that over loud cries any day.

She flipped on her turn signal. What she needed right now was Starbucks. They were out of creamer at home, and the thought of coffee with plain milk hadn't been appealing.

Reagan turned into the Starbucks entrance and glanced at the patrons sitting outside on the patio without a care in the world. One young woman had her head tilted up toward the sunshine. A man walked to her table and handed her a drink, and she laughed at something he said.

Reagan looked in the rearview mirror. No one behind her. She tapped the brakes and peered closer at the scene unfolding on the Starbucks patio. The woman tossed her dark, glossy hair and took a sip of her drink. The man finally took his seat so Reagan could see his face.

Chad.

Her husband was enjoying an afternoon coffee with a gorgeous woman. A woman Reagan had never seen before, except maybe in a Pantene ad.

A horn honked behind her.

Reagan pressed the gas pedal and drove past the drive-through. She didn't want coffee any longer.

She just wanted to get out of there.

Her eyes filled with tears as she pulled onto the main road.

Fifteen years, ten of those as husband and wife.

Four kids.

Did that mean nothing to him? Did she mean nothing to him?

Reagan wasn't sure she wanted to know the answer.

Violet closed her office door and sat down at her desk. What a disaster of a day. She picked up her phone and punched in a number. "Mimi?" she asked.

"Yes."

"This is Violet Matthews. You had me meet a Jackson Stratford today at Zaza." Her mind still reeled not only from the surprise of seeing Jackson, but also from his preposterous idea.

"How did it go? Did you two hit it off immediately?" Mimi trilled.

Hardly. "That's the thing. Jackson and I actually know each other from college. We aren't exactly compatible."

Mimi giggled. "I beg to differ, dear. You both fit the bill almost perfectly for what the other is looking for. I rarely make a match like that."

"Maybe on paper. But not in real life. In real life we'd kill each other." Violet drummed her fingers on her desk. "Please tell me you can find someone else for me. And fast."

The sound of fingers clacking away on a keyboard came through the line. "I'm looking at all of your available matches right now."

"And?" Violet held her breath.

Mimi giggled again. "And there's exactly one. Jackson Stratford."

Violet let out a loud groan. "This is ridiculous. There's got to be more than one man in your whole database who is a match for me."

Mimi clucked her tongue. "You forget, dear, that you also have to be a match for him. And only one person in my database fits that bill for you. Jackson Stratford."

"Stop saying his name." Violet pushed a strand of hair out of her face. The situation bordered on insane. "Surely there is another option."

"I offer a money-back guarantee. If you aren't satisfied with your encounter with. . .*him*, then I'll be happy to refund your money."

"Then what am I supposed to do?"

"I can't help you there, dear. There are other services out there, but I can't speak to their success rate. I can only tell you that according to the questionnaire you two filled out, as well as what I saw in your personal interviews, the two of you are—in my professional opinion—very well suited for one another."

"But why, exactly?" She couldn't imagine what she and Jackson had in common. He was probably a cat person who hated the outdoors and only ate takeout. He probably hated to travel and only listened to classical music. No way was he her match. No way.

Mimi sighed. "I encourage my clients to find that out for themselves."

Violet had had enough. "No thanks. I'll come by your office later in the week for my refund." She hung up the phone.

So much for that.

Her intercom buzzed. "Violet?" Dad's voice boomed through the office. "Can you come in here please?"

"Sure." She smoothed her yellow dress and hurried down the hallway. She smiled widely as she walked into the ornate corner office.

"Have a seat." He motioned toward the leather couch.

Violet sat down and waited for him to talk.

Dad paced in front of his desk.

"Is everything okay?"

Dad stopped pacing and looked at her. "We need to talk about the amount of pro bono work you do."

It was a fight they had about once a year. "You know that's important to me."

He leaned against his desk. "I know. And I'm proud of the work you do. It's just that over the past year, that has been the bulk of your workload."

"And you want me to find a better balance."

Dad nodded. "Sometimes we don't always get to do what we want to do. Sometimes we have to think of the good of the firm."

Violet hadn't done what she wanted to do in years. She'd dabbled in art in college and taken some creative writing classes. But her liberal arts degree wasn't too helpful in landing a job, so she'd chosen law school out of desperation. "I know. It's just that those are the only cases I enjoy."

Dad frowned. "Violet, you're not always going to enjoy every minute of your day. It isn't possible."

"I disagree. I think there are a lot of people who enjoy every minute of their days. You do, don't you?"

He shrugged. "I'm a different kind of person. I wanted to be a lawyer since I was a little boy and your granddaddy would let me come with him to the office."

She'd never felt that way. Not once. She'd wanted to be partner because it seemed like the kind of accomplishment she could be proud of, that her parents could be proud of. But not because it was fulfilling some kind of lifelong passion. "I want to be the kind of person who is happy with every minute. We're only given so many minutes to live."

Her eyes filled with tears as she realized what she had to do.

Jackson couldn't concentrate on work. He'd like to think it was just a bad case of spring fever, but he had an idea it was because of his redheaded lunch date. Or nondate, as she'd been quick to point out.

His cell phone buzzed against his desk.

Kathleen.

"Hey, sis. What's going on?" She was his only sibling, and despite past differences, they were great friends now.

"Oh, you know. Trying to find my Superwoman cape, but I keep losing it."

He chuckled. "How are Andy and the kids? Everyone well?"

"Andy is busy with work. Olivia and Tyler are both playing soccer this year. You'll have to come to a game."

Jackson nodded. He loved his niece and nephew dearly. "I'll be there. Send me a schedule." The drive from Little Rock to Memphis wasn't a bad one, and he tried to visit at least monthly.

"They'll be thrilled. And you know Andy and I would love to see you any time."

"Thanks."

Kathleen cleared her throat. "Have you seen Mom lately?"

"Sunday at church. Why? Is something wrong?" Since their dad's death last year, Kathleen and Jackson had been monitoring their mother closely.

"Not exactly." She sighed. "She called yesterday and seemed awfully chipper. After we talked for a few minutes, she told me she was having dinner with a man from her Sunday school class."

"What?" Jackson hadn't expected this news. "That's crazy."

"Not really, if you'll just keep an open mind. Daddy's been gone for a year. I kind of expected it to happen eventually."

"It's too soon." Jackson raked his fingers through his hair. "Way too soon."

"I had a feeling you might have that reaction, so that's why I wanted to give you a heads up." Kathleen had always been the calm one. "Don't overreact though. She's only fifty-six. Not exactly over the hill, you know? It's perfectly normal for her to want to date."

Jackson wanted his sister to be as outraged as he was. Clearly that wasn't happening. "I still say it's too soon. And what does Mom know about dating these days? Things have changed since she and Dad got together."

Kathleen laughed. "Mom is a smart woman. She'll figure it out. Does she text you as much as she does me? She loves her new iPhone so much that she wants an iPad for her birthday."

Jackson hadn't even gotten an iPad yet. "She texts sometimes. And I know she's a smart woman. That's why I'm surprised she's starting to date."

"Do you expect her to stop living? Relationships are an important part of life." Kathleen paused. "Speaking of. . . Did Lauren talk to you yet?"

He groaned. "Yes. She made her point—your point—very clear."

"We're just worried about you. Life can be more fun if it's shared."

"I've gotten along just fine over the years."

She laughed. "Let me rephrase. Meaningful relationships make life worth living. You're getting too old to keep playing games."

He loved his sister, but between the bombshell about Mom's newfound dating life and the analysis of his own love life, he'd heard enough. "I'd better go. Thanks for the info. E-mail me the kids' ball schedule."

Jackson hung up the phone and tried to concentrate on work.

But Violet's yellow dress and pretty face kept flashing through his mind.

Chapter 8

Violet Matthews: I JUST QUIT MY JOB. (Text message sent August 27, 4:22 p.m.)

Reagan McClure: I THINK CHAD IS HAVING AN AFFAIR. (Text message sent August 27, 4:24 p.m.)

You win." Violet clutched the phone to her ear as she boxed up her personal belongings from her office.

"Actually just the opposite. I lose. Big time." Reagan's hiccup gave away her recent crying jag.

Violet crammed some framed pictures into a box. "Tell me what happened." She listened as Reagan described seeing Chad and a woman having coffee.

"It's no wonder. I'm just a big old blob. I'm always covered in pee and poop and vomit. And I'm cranky. Not exactly the kind of woman a man wants to come home to."

Violet stopped what she was doing and sat down in her chair. "First of all, you aren't a blob. You look great considering you had twins just a few months ago. And who can blame you for being cranky? You haven't had a good night's sleep in forever. Let Chad get up with the kids all night and I'll bet he is a little cranky, too."

Reagan snorted. "Like that will happen."

"Seriously. Don't sell yourself short."

"Do you see those Hollywood actresses on the cover of *People*? Four or five days after they give birth, they're back in their size twos and strutting on a red carpet without a care in the world."

Violet let out a chuckle. "Come on, Reagan. First of all, I'm sure Photoshop is hard at work on some of those pictures. And second of all, I'd definitely put you on my list of hot mommies that I know."

"Shut up. I am *not* in that category at all."

"It's probably like ninety-percent attitude. Cut yourself some slack. It isn't exactly like you've had time to focus much on yourself during the past several months."

"True. And now Chad is off cavorting with some woman at Starbucks."

"Seeing him at Starbucks with a woman isn't exactly proof of an affair. Chad is in HR. He interviews people all the time and not always in the office. You know that."

"An interview? You think that's what it was?" Reagan asked.

"Until you know otherwise, that's what I'd guess. Try not to jump to conclusions, okay? I know things haven't been perfect lately, but try to keep calm."

"Calm." Reagan let out a laugh. "My life hasn't been calm in ages. I mean, I managed okay with just two kids. There were two of us and two of them. I wanted to wait to try for a third. I told

Chad I really wanted Izzy and Ava Grace to be a little older. But he wanted a boy so badly, and then when we found out we were having twins. . .well, I guess that's the last time I was calm." She sighed. "I love them all dearly. I'm so blessed to be their mama. And I know this part flies by so fast that I'll look back and wish I had it back."

"Still though. You're overwhelmed. Have you thought about calling your mom and seeing if she can stay with you for a couple weeks? Maybe if you have an extra pair of hands for a little while it will help you get a handle on everything."

"She and Daddy just got settled in their new place in Branson. He's finally feeling better, but I know he depends on her a lot. I hate to even ask because I know she'll come over right away. It would be different if Daddy would come, too, but I know he'd rather be at his own house." Reagan's dad had a variety of health problems, and her mother served as his primary caregiver.

Violet emptied her top drawer. "Isn't there someone who could look in on him for a little bit so she could come stay with you? And I know you don't want to consider this, but Chad's mother isn't too far away. Can you put up with her if it means preserving your sanity?"

Reagan didn't say anything for a long moment. "Maybe." She let out a huge sigh. "But I'm still not sure what I saw today. They were talking and laughing. It definitely didn't seem interview appropriate."

"So ask him. Tell him you thought you saw him there and see how he reacts. Just don't jump to the worst conclusion possible until you have some facts. Okay?" Violet hated the situation Reagan was in, but sometimes looks could be deceiving. Lots of interviews probably took place every day at Starbucks. Of course lots of affairs probably started there, too, but she'd keep that to herself.

"You're right. I'll ask him. Now what's this about you quitting?"

It was Violet's turn to sigh. "I resigned. Is that the craziest thing you've ever heard? First I learn that Jackson Stratford is the only man in the state of Arkansas that I'm a match for, and then I up and quit my job without even having a plan in place." Her dad had tried to talk her into staying put until the end of the year to give her plenty of time to find a new firm, but she'd asked for an immediate release.

"I can't even process all of that. The job first though. What happened?"

Violet filled her in on the conversation she'd had with Dad. "I normally take a ton of time in making big decisions like that. I pray about them, and I think about them. But in that moment in his office, I knew there was only one thing I could do. And that meant quitting."

"What will you do now?"

Violet finished filling the box. "I have no idea." She sighed. "I *could* interview for another firm, one that's more focused on pro bono work." She hated to tell Reagan about the other possibility.

"This is an important decision for you. You haven't been happy with your job in years. Ever, maybe. You could reevaluate."

"And what? Start a new career?"

Reagan sighed. "I'm just saying. Once upon a time in a land far, far away, I had a career that I loved. Adored. I was happy at work. Fulfilled." Reagan had worked as a graphic designer and had dabbled in photography. She'd given it up when Izzy was born, and she and Chad had agreed she'd stay home until the kids were all in school.

"I know. And you were good at it."

"So find what you're good at. Find your passion. I've been telling you for years that you should rethink your career."

It was the truth. Violet's favorite thing about being a lawyer when she'd gotten out of law school had been living in DC. Not her career. And when she'd moved back to Arkansas to join the family firm, she'd always thought she'd find the joy, but the only time she'd come close was doing the pro bono cases where she felt like she was actually making a difference. "Well. . .there is one thing I'm considering." She paused. "But it's totally crazy."

"Sometimes the best ideas are, don't you think?"

"Grandma e-mailed me this morning to let me know the shop next to Mrs. Kemp's is available."

"I'd forgotten about Mrs. Kemp's shop. What's it called?"

"Aunt Teak's." Violet smiled. "There's a shop right next door that used to be a sandwich place. Grandma thinks I should consider finally opening my own cupcake place."

Reagan let out a squeal. "Oh, Violet! You've always wanted to do that. And I have to say, every time we have a birthday party everyone always wants to know what bakery I use." She laughed. "Of course, now I'll have to start paying you."

Violet giggled. "Let's not get ahead of ourselves. This would be a gigantic decision. I mean, moving to a new city is a huge deal, even one as nearby as Hot Springs. Not to mention launching a store."

"I could design your logo. And website. And come in and do some pictures." Reagan's voice grew more animated than Violet had heard in a long time.

"I'll keep you posted on my decision. I need to go home and really think things through and look at my finances. I might go to Hot Springs soon though, just to look at the space." She couldn't believe she was saying this out loud.

"Well I, for one, am totally supportive. Even though it would mean you'd be an hour away."

Violet smiled. She could always count on her friend for support. It was just one of the many blessings in her life. "Thanks. If you want to pray for me to make a good decision here, I'd appreciate it."

"And if you want to pray that Chad and I can get on the right track, I would, too."

"Done." Violet hung up and picked up her box. She wanted to leave before Dad came to see her. He'd been pretty upset.

She hated disappointing her parents. But maybe it was time to start living out her own dreams.

Dear Mama,

Did you really like working at Aunt Teak's? Because I'm totally bored being around all that old stuff all the time. Nana says you liked it, but so far I haven't found anything in your journal to back her story up.

I'm trying to talk them into letting me get an after-school job somewhere a little cooler than an antique store, but so far I'm not having much luck. Nana's friend from across the street told me that her granddaughter might be opening a bakery next to Aunt Teak's. I haven't told Nana yet, but if that happens, I'm going to get a job there.

I met a cute boy at church on Sunday. His name is Chase, and he plays tennis. He invited me to play sometime, so I've been practicing by playing Wii tennis with Granddaddy. I don't think it's going to help much, but we're having a good time.

I miss you.
Love,
Shadow

Reagan put the last of the dirty dishes in the dishwasher and closed the door. Maybe they should start using paper goods. It would be bad for the environment, but it might save her sanity.

She glanced at the clock. Almost nine. This was getting ridiculous. She'd tried all day to put the scene from Starbucks out of her mind. Of course Violet was right. It was probably an interview. But each time she'd texted Chad after she got home, he hadn't mentioned it. Only said it was a hectic day and he'd be home late.

So once again she'd been alone to feed, bathe, and put the kids to bed.

"The door was unlocked," Chad said.

Reagan jumped at the sound of his voice. "I didn't hear your car."

"I was driving my super stealthy silent car tonight." He grinned. "But seriously, you should lock the door. Do I need to put that on your list?" He opened the fridge and took out a Coke.

She stopped wiping the counter and glared at him. He'd made fun of her list for months now. "I have a lot on my mind. You try getting out of the house with four kids and see if you can remember everything without looking at the list." She'd written all the necessities on a Post-it and stuck it next to the back door. One trip to church with no diapers in the diaper bag had been one too many.

"Easy there. I was only being helpful."

"You sure are in a chipper mood for someone who just worked a twelve-hour day." Did his Starbucks outing have something to do with it? "What's going on?"

"I wanted to wait until it was a done deal to tell you the news." Chad grinned.

"Please tell me you inherited a million dollars and we're hiring a nanny. And a housekeeper."

He rolled his eyes. "I'm being serious."

"So am I." She crossed her arms and leaned against the counter.

"I officially hired a new assistant today. And she won't be like Barbara and just answer the phones and make appointments. I've restructured things so the new position will actually handle some of the things I used to handle." He looked positively gleeful.

A sinking feeling washed over Reagan. "I meant to tell you that I think we saw you at Starbucks today."

Chad nodded. "You probably did. I wish you'd called. You could've stopped and met Reese. You'll love her."

Reese. Even the name made her blood run cold. Coupled with that perfect hair and nice figure and it was enough to make Reagan want to cry. "Reese, huh? How old is this Reese person?"

He frowned. "It's kind of illegal for me to ask that in an interview. But based on the years she graduated from high school, college, and graduate school, I'd say she's about twenty-six."

Of course she was. "Is she from here?"

Chad took a sip of Coke. "She's from a small town in northeast Arkansas. Went to college in Fayetteville and got her MBA from Vanderbilt."

Fancy. "Well that's just great."

He furrowed his brow. "What's wrong? I thought you'd be pleased that I'm going to be able to transfer some of my responsibilities. It should mean more free time and less late nights."

Right. Until he figured out how much more fun it was to stay late at the office with some hot twenty-six-year-old than it was to come home and wrestle four kids through dinner, baths, and bedtime. "So what does her husband do?"

Chad finished his Coke and tossed the can into the garbage. "She's not married. I know that because she mentioned today that she didn't know anyone here. She just moved from Nashville."

"Why exactly was your meeting at Starbucks? Why not at the office?"

He shook his head. "I do a lot of interviews out of the office. You know that. She had another appointment on that side of town, so it just made more sense for me to meet her there."

Reagan rolled her eyes.

"What is your problem?"

She knew that nothing she could say would make him understand. Anything negative about Reese and her shiny hair and perfect body would only make Reagan look stupid and insecure in comparison. And right now she had nothing to compete with but an extra fifteen pounds of baby weight and a belly that would never be totally flat again. "I don't have a problem. Let's just go to bed."

"You go on." He motioned toward the living room. "I'm going to catch up with the DVR."

Reagan closed the bedroom door behind her and went into their bathroom. She stood in front of the mirror and took a long look. Her ill-fitting clothes made her look even lumpier than she felt. Her blond hair hung limply around her makeup-free face. She leaned closer to the mirror. Dark circles beneath her blue eyes told the story of the past months.

And now Chad would be going to work every day and spending time with some single twenty-six-year-old.

She could let the news knock her down. She could let her insecurity squash the last embers of fire from her marriage. But she wouldn't go out without a fight. And if that meant taking some time to focus on the way she felt about herself, then that's what she'd do.

So starting tomorrow Operation Hot Mommy would begin.

And Reagan was ready.

Chapter 9

Kathleen Morgan: MARK YOUR CALENDAR. WE'RE COMING TO THE LAKE HOUSE IN TWO WEEKS FOR ONE LAST BIT OF SUMMER. (Text message sent September 4, 2:43 p.m.)

Jackson Stratford: SOUNDS GREAT. CAN YOU BELIEVE I HAVEN'T BEEN THERE YET THIS YEAR? P.S. MOM INTRODUCED ME TO HER DINNER DATE SUNDAY AT CHURCH. I'M NOT OKAY WITH THIS. (Text message sent September 4, 3:16 p.m.)

Jackson pulled his Range Rover in front of a small bungalow-style house. Thanks to Google and White Pages, he'd tracked down Violet's address. Did this make him some kind of stalker?

He shrugged off the feeling of uncertainty and hurried up the path that led to the front door. He squared his shoulders, feeling a bit like he might be headed into a war zone.

One more shot.

After being unable to get Violet off his mind over the weekend, he'd decided to give it another try. She really would make the perfect date to his event, and besides that, she was the kind of woman who would show Kathleen and Lauren that he could date someone they'd approve of. He knocked on the door.

A dog barked inside.

After a few seconds, the door swung open and Violet stood on the other side. Her red hair was twisted into a messy bun, and she wore an apron emblazoned with bright flowers. Her eyes widened at the sight of him. "What do you want?" she asked with a frown. "No, a better question would be how did you find me?"

Jackson grinned. "Southern hospitality must be a thing of the past."

"I'm very hospitable to invited guests." She glanced down at her apron. "Clearly I wasn't expecting company."

"This will only take a second."

She sighed. "Fine. Come on in."

He stepped into her house and inhaled. The sweet scent of vanilla permeated the air. "Smells good in here." It reminded him of summers spent at his grandparents' house.

A tiny smile played across her face. "Cupcakes. I'm baking." She motioned for him to follow her. "You can talk while I finish icing."

He stepped into her kitchen. Red appliances stood out against the white walls. It suited her. Bright and cheery. "Looks like you spend a lot of time in here." He sat down on a red barstool that looked like it belonged in a fifties diner.

"I bake when I'm upset. Or happy. Or confused." She smiled and picked up a tube of icing.

He watched as she expertly iced a cupcake. It smelled heavenly. "So which is it today?"

She glanced up and locked her green eyes on his. "Which is what?"

"Upset, happy, or confused?"

Violet sighed. "D. All of the above." She held up a cupcake. "Want one?"

"Do you even have to ask?" He grinned.

She put a cupcake on a small red plate and placed it in front of him. "Something to drink? Water? Milk?" She motioned toward a red coffeemaker. "Coffee?"

"Milk, please." He touched his tongue to the chocolate icing. "This is so good. You should open a bakery."

She laughed. "Here you go." She put a glass of cold milk next to his plate. "Enjoy."

Jackson bit into the cupcake. It was moist but not undercooked. Perfection. "Seriously. This is better than I had last week at some fancy shop in the River Market." Little Rock's River Market district was a hodgepodge of shops, restaurants, and nightclubs along the Arkansas River.

"Thank you. My grandma and I worked together on the recipe. It's many years in the making." She returned to her icing.

"So I was serious earlier. What's got you upset, happy, and confused?" He knew he was prying, but he sensed a melancholy air about her that hadn't been present at lunch the other day.

She shook her head. "Just some big decisions to make."

"I know you don't like me much, but I'm good at decisions." He smiled. "I'm very practical."

Violet rolled her eyes. "I'm sure you are. But I think this is a decision I have to make alone."

"Fine. Just trying to help." He popped the last of the cupcake into his mouth.

She regarded him for a long moment. "I quit my job last week. Aren't you glad I didn't agree to your stupid plan now? You wouldn't be able to pass me off as a lawyer anymore."

Jackson took a drink of milk. "So you'll find another job. Law firms are a dime a dozen."

Violet didn't say anything. She turned her attention back to her baking. Finally she looked up at him. "I don't know if I'll go back to a firm."

"So start your own practice." It's what he would do if he were in her position. Jackson had always wanted to be his own boss. He'd given thought to opening his own small business but had never settled on what kind. Plus he enjoyed his work in economic development. There was something very satisfying about bringing in new industries and businesses. Sometimes one industry could breathe new life into a stagnant town.

Violet pulled a fresh pan of cupcakes from the oven. "Why are you here again?"

The words from anyone else would've offended him. But not her. She had every reason to be suspicious of him, every reason to dislike him. He'd earned it after the way he'd treated her in college. "I came to discuss our lunch meeting last week. But that can wait."

"Good. Because I don't see that there's anything to discuss. It was a fluke."

A fluke his foot. It was the answer to what they were both

looking for. No strings. No complications. A believable solution. But she'd have to come to that conclusion on her own. "If you say so." He picked up his plate and carried it to the sink. "Want me to wash this?"

She shook her head. "Just put it there. I'll get to it later."

"So why did you resign anyway?" His curiosity got the better of him.

Violet stopped icing the cupcake she was working on. "Did you ever think maybe you were going down the wrong path? And you were going downhill and the only way to stop was to jump?"

Oddly, he understood. "Yes."

"That's kind of what happened." She gave him a tiny grin. "So I jumped."

Violet couldn't believe she was spilling her guts to Jackson, of all people. She'd sequestered herself to her house for the better part of the past week, only leaving to get groceries and go to church on Sunday. The rest of the time she'd baked and prayed and cried and paced. And ignored the barrage of calls from her mother. "When I was in college, I always admired those people who knew what they wanted to be when they grew up." She perched on one of the bar stools and dipped her finger into the icing for a taste.

"You seemed to turn out okay," Jackson said.

She shrugged. "I wasn't one of those people. What I was going to be depended on which day of the week you asked me. An author, an artist, a dancer, an archaeologist." She sighed. "I had a lot of interests. And I wished I were one of those who'd always known their path."

"Sometimes it's more fun to figure it out as you go."

She shook her head. "Not if you're me. My younger sister can get away with that. But everyone has always expected more from me. So when I graduated with the broadest liberal arts degree possible and wasn't really qualified to do anything but pour coffee. . ." She trailed off.

"You went to law school," Jackson finished for her. He grabbed another cupcake.

Violet nodded. "Yep. How nuts is that?" She held up a hand. "No. Don't answer that."

He grinned. "There are crazier things to do than become a lawyer."

"My grandfather started the firm when my dad was a baby. They were so pleased when I became the third generation to work there. But I hated it. Every single day I hated it."

"What prompted you to finally own up to that?"

She shrugged. "Have you ever taken a long look at your life and not been happy with what you saw?"

Jackson's blue eyes met hers. "I sure have. More than once."

"A few weeks ago my dad made someone else partner. At first I was really hurt. Outraged even. But then I realized it wasn't even something I wanted in the first place. Just something I thought I *should* want."

"So what do you want to do now?"

She lifted up a cupcake. "Something I'm passionate about. Something I love. And something that will pay the bills."

He grinned. "I'll be a customer."

Violet filled him in on the possible bakery in Hot Springs. "Moving and opening my own business just seems like such a leap of faith."

"But given the alternative—joining another firm and continuing to do something you have no desire to do—how can you not take it?"

"It isn't that simple."

"It never is."

She regarded him for a long moment. It was the closest to a civil conversation she'd ever had with Jackson. He must be up to something. "So that's my story. And the reason for my baking marathon."

"And now you're headed to Hot Springs for a few days to check out the place?" he asked.

"Just for a day." She pointed out the kitchen window where a boxer-mix dog lay in the sun. "That dog in the yard is Arnie. I put him outside before I opened the door for you, otherwise we would have had to endure a barking fit." She grinned. "He's old and nearly deaf, but he's still pretty protective of me. I can't take him with me because Grandma is allergic. So that means I'll need to make a quick trip."

Jackson pulled his keys out of his pocket and removed one from his key ring. "Here." He handed the key to her.

She furrowed her brow. "What's this?"

"The key to my lake house. Right on Lake Hamilton." He grinned. "It's the most peaceful place you could ever hope for. And dog friendly. My sister's family never visits without their dog, Max."

Violet stared openmouthed. "Oh, I couldn't. Really." She thrust the key back at him.

"Come on. It's empty. I haven't used it all summer. And you could spend a few days there making your decision." He grinned. "Maybe this would make up for you graduating a semester late?"

She rolled her eyes.

"Okay. Maybe not. But consider it this way—you'll have a home base while you get things figured out. You can take your time and make your decision. No need to rush back." He shrugged. "Just trying to help."

Violet thought for a minute. She didn't want to be in his debt. At all. He'd been a charmer in college, and she knew he hadn't changed. There was always something in it for him. "What do you get out of this arrangement?"

An indignant expression flashed across his handsome face. "Give me a little credit, okay? I'm not such a bad guy."

That was debatable. But she was sort of desperate. If she was going to move to Hot Springs and open a business, she needed to get the ball rolling as quickly as possible. "Okay. Well, thanks." She smiled. "Really. Thanks."

Jackson wrote down the address and security code on the back of a piece of junk mail. "And here's my phone number in case you have any questions about anything." He pushed the paper across the counter to her. "Stay as long as you need." He grinned and picked up another cupcake. "One more for the road."

Violet followed him to the front door, not sure what to think.

Jackson waved and headed to his car.

She watched him climb inside and drive away.

What had she just gotten herself into?

Chapter 10

Violet Matthews: I AM AT JACKSON STRATFORD'S LAKE HOUSE IN HOT SPRINGS. CAN YOU SAY "PLACE I NEVER EXPECTED TO BE"? (Text message sent September 6, 10:23 a.m.)

Reagan McClure: WELL I'M AT A GYM. ME. A GYM. WHO HAVE WE TURNED INTO? AND I'M GOING TO NEED SOME DETAILS ON YOUR LAKE ADVENTURE. . . . PLEASE TELL ME JACKSON ISN'T THERE. (Text message sent September 6, 11:16 a.m.)

Reagan glanced around her. She couldn't remember feeling more like an outsider. These women were fit, tan, and looked about twenty-two. And the men were either beefy or elderly. But the reviews she'd read online had been good ones, plus they had a daycare area for kids. Ava Grace hadn't been super happy about it until she'd spotted a Disney princess dollhouse.

The three college-aged girls watching the children had oohed and ahhed over the twins. Even though Reagan wasn't used to leaving the kids with anyone, knowing she'd be right across the hall made her feel better. Besides, after a week of trying to force herself to exercise while the kids napped, she was ready to admit she needed professional help.

A gym employee waved her over. "Would you like your personal training consultation now? It comes with your membership."

Reagan peered at the perky girl's name tag. "Thanks, Heather. What all does that entail?"

"Oh, you know. Weighing, measuring, determining your BMI. . .you know, just stuff like that."

"BMI?"

"Body mass index." Heather smiled. "We also do a complete nutritional evaluation where we help you to make better choices when it comes to food."

Reagan shook her head. "I think I'll wait on that. I'm just interested in starting slowly."

Heather nodded. "Okay, great." She pointed to a set of double glass doors. "That's the weight and exercise room. Ellipticals, treadmills, exercise bikes, and all the strength-training equipment you need is in there. Look for James. He'll have on a blue shirt just like mine. He can give assistance on any of the equipment." She handed Reagan a sheet of paper. "This is our class schedule. We offer pretty much everything. Aerobics, Zumba, yoga—you name it." She grinned. "There's also a pool for swimming and water aerobics."

Reagan felt so overwhelmed. This was much more complicated than she'd expected. Right now she mostly wanted to curl up on the couch with a Sam's Club-sized tub of cheese balls and watch mindless TV.

"Ma'am?" Heather asked. "Are you okay?"

Reagan looked up numbly. This had been a mistake. She turned to go, clutching her schedule. She'd get the kids and leave. She could cancel her membership over the phone. No one would ever have to know. She hadn't even told Chad what she was doing in case she failed.

"Overwhelming, isn't it?" A woman in a navy sweat suit asked as she filled her water bottle with water from the fountain.

Reagan nodded. "Very."

"I'm Maggie. I've been a member for about six months." She patted her stomach. "Lost ten pounds."

"That's great." Reagan smiled and introduced herself. "I haven't exercised in years. But after I had my twins, I've had a hard time getting rid of the extra weight."

"Twins!" Maggie exclaimed. "How old?"

"Nine months."

"Girl, you look great." Maggie smiled broadly. "You have any more kids?"

Reagan told her about Ava Grace and Izzy. "I never expected to have four. And can you believe my husband thinks we should try for one more? Says then he'll have enough for a basketball team."

Maggie clucked her tongue. "Why don't you wait and make that decision after you've had a few full nights of sleep?"

Reagan laughed. "Is it that obvious?"

"Honey, I've been there. Not enough hands, not enough hours in the day to get it all done. Little people depending on you for everything, and you start to feel like a nonperson. A husband who comes home from work late and tired and has no idea that your job is a job, too."

That summed it up exactly. "It's like you live at my house." She smiled. "But I love them dearly. I wouldn't trade it for anything."

"But you don't know who you are anymore. It's hard to tell if you're coming or going."

Reagan nodded.

"Well I think you've done a good thing by joining here. A little time for you." Maggie smiled. "Want me to show you the ropes?"

"Please. I don't have much time before we need to get home for naps and then go pick Izzy up from school."

Ten minutes later, Reagan had decided the treadmill was where she should start. "Thanks for your help."

"No problem." Maggie smiled. "I usually take the Tuesday and Thursday morning Zumba class. You should give it a try sometime."

Reagan shook her head. "I'll stick to walking for now. But you never know." She stepped on the machine and hit the START button. She should've thought to bring her earbuds so she could listen to music. Maybe next time.

Next time.

She was really doing this.

Maggie was right. She'd desperately needed to do something for herself.

So she ignored the guilt over all the things she could be doing for her kids, her husband, or her house, and she walked. It might be a slow pace, but it was something.

Operation Hot Mommy had begun.

Violet stood on the deck of Jackson's lake house and took in the view. The spectacular view.

She'd always hoped to have a house like this, right on the water with a sunny garden area and a hammock in the backyard. Not to mention the to-die-for kitchen.

She enjoyed one more second of sunshine before hurrying toward her car. Arnie was sound asleep on his bed in the family room, and Violet was confident he'd sleep most of the afternoon. Now that he'd lost most of his hearing, he could sleep through just about anything, including the sound of boats zooming past the dock at the edge of the yard as lake lovers took advantage of the last few hot days before fall set in.

Violet got in her car and drove toward downtown Hot Springs. Ever since she was a little girl, she'd loved visiting the town. Hot Springs was steeped in history, and people had been coming to bathe in the natural hot springs for hundreds of years.

Traffic along the main drag between the historic Arlington Hotel and Bathhouse Row was terrible. Violet slowed for a group of pedestrians and finally found a parking spot not too far from Aunt Teak's.

"There you are," Grandma called. "I was beginning to think you were going to stand me up."

"Not a chance." Violet grinned and pushed a strand of red hair from her face. "It took me a little while to get to the lake house and then back here."

Grandma gave her a quick hug. "Is Arnie okay?"

"He's hanging in there. The vet says he's doing well considering his age, but I don't know." The dog would be fifteen later in the year, and Violet knew the time he had left was short. "He's my longest successful relationship, you know."

Grandma joined in her laughter. "He's a good dog, dear. I'm just sorry you couldn't stay at my house for a few days because of my allergies." She smiled. "But if I ever were going to let a dog inside the house, it would be him."

Violet linked arms with her grandmother, and they walked toward Aunt Teak's. "Is Mrs. Kemp planning on staying in business?"

"Oh yes. She and Oliver adore the shop. Me, I like retirement. But they seem really happy." Grandma had taught kindergarten for thirty years before retiring.

Violet paused to look at the exterior of the building. "It's really beautiful." The first story of the Victorian-style building was a glass storefront, but the upper floor revealed large bay windows and turrets.

"I think you could have a wonderful little business here," Grandma said. "No pressure though. The Realtor left a key with Betty. You can look around and decide if this is something you want to pursue." She held the door open to the antique store.

"Good afternoon, Violet." Mrs. Kemp smiled from behind the counter. "It's been a long time since you've been in. There are some new items that you might like to see."

Violet adored things with a history. Her love of vintage clothes was only the beginning. "Every time anyone comes in my house, they want to know about the typewriter." She'd purchased a green Optima Super model typewriter from the store a couple of years ago. "I love thinking about the stories and letters that machine must have typed back in the fifties."

Mrs. Kemp nodded. "I'm sure it looks wonderful in your home. Rose showed me some pictures she took the last time she was there of some books you'd gotten at an estate sale."

"I love hardback copies of classic books," Violet explained. "I think they look so pretty on the shelf, not to mention how they smell."

"You like the way old books smell?" Shadow asked.

Violet hadn't noticed her sitting in the corner on a plush footstool. "I sure do."

The teenager made a face. Gone was the all-black attire and inky hair, and in its place was a tennis dress and light brown locks.

"I like your hair," Violet said.

Shadow absently touched her ponytail. "I'm not sure about the color, but it will do for now." She stood up and picked up a tennis racket. "I'm walking to the courts. I'll be back soon."

Mrs. Kemp nodded. "Don't be late. We'll leave here promptly at five to go home. Your granddaddy wants to go eat barbecue tonight at McClard's."

Shadow shrugged and walked out.

"Teenagers." Mrs. Kemp sighed. "That girl is her mama made over."

"How's she adjusting?" Grandma asked.

"She won't talk to us, so I don't know. She's struggling try-ing to fit into a new school. But she met a boy at church last week, so maybe that's a step in the right direction." She grinned at Violet. "I saw a picture of her last boyfriend, and he had so many piercings sticking out of his nose and lip, I'll bet he has a hard time going through airport security."

"Well, at least she's moved on," Grandma said.

Mrs. Kemp nodded. "I just wish I knew how to reach her. These past years have been tough. First Jenny's accident and then Stuart remarrying. I guess it's no wonder Shadow is having a tough time finding her place in the world."

Violet understood something about that. She hadn't experienced the tragedies Shadow had, but she'd never felt like she was on completely solid ground either. "Maybe I could talk to her sometime," she offered. "Take her out to eat or shopping or something."

Mrs. Kemp's face lit up. "That'd be wonderful. You are only a couple of years younger than her mom would've been. She and Stuart married so young—right out of high school. Shadow came along a couple of years later. I always said she and her mama grew up together."

Violet froze. It was hard to comprehend that she could be nearly old enough to have a sixteen-year-old. And here she'd not even started on a family. "I have no idea if she would open up to me. I'm good with small kids, when just giving them a stick of gum or a lollipop makes you automatically cool." She grinned. "But I'm pretty sure a teenager might think I'm kind of lame."

"You're no such thing." Grandma patted her on the arm. "*I* happen to think you're very cool if it's any consolation."

Violet giggled. "Thanks, Grandma. You're pretty cool yourself."

"Are you ready to go next door?" Mrs. Kemp asked. She fished around in a drawer beneath the cash register. "Here's the key."

Violet took it. Would this turn out to be a blessing or a waste of time? Only one way to find out. "I'm ready."

"I'm going to let you go over first," Grandma said. "See what you think without me butting in." She smiled. "But then I'll come over and give you my opinion."

Violet laughed as she walked out into the September humidity. It was a nice spot for a shop. She could see Bathhouse Row from where she stood. Tourists from all over would pass by and might be unable to resist a cupcake. She unlocked the door to the empty building and stepped inside.

The sparsely decorated space had a lot of potential. Violet could already imagine how it would look with a fresh coat of paint and maybe a mix-and-match set of tables and chairs. Reagan could help her with the design.

She ran her hand along the counter and peered into the glass case that likely had once housed sandwiches and salads. But it would look even better with her cupcakes inside.

She sat down in a lone wooden chair in the corner and the wobbly leg explained why it had been left behind. Could she do this?

It would be a lot of work. A business plan, marketing, financing. She knew a little about those things but not a ton.

And baking for real customers scared her. She'd loved to bake in law school. Her favorite part of study groups had been baking goodies to get her group through the long nights. Making cupcakes and cakes for friends' birthdays and special occasions was one of her favorite hobbies.

But could she pour herself into a business venture without knowing what the outcome would be? It all seemed so scary.

Lord, am I crazy? No. Don't answer that. Just help me make the right decision. Please show me the path to take and give me the courage to take it. Amen.

She opened her eyes as Grandma walked inside.

"Well? It's perfect, isn't it?"

Violet nodded. "More than I ever could've imagined."

Grandma walked around the space. "So much potential. Don't you love the high ceilings? And that bead board wall? A little paint on that and it would look so pretty."

"It is my style, that's for sure." Violet stood up. "Let's go look at the kitchen."

She followed her grandmother into the good-sized kitchen and could immediately picture herself there. Baking. Icing. Creating new recipes.

Happy.

"Change has never been easy for me," she said.

Grandma nodded. "It isn't easy for anyone. And if they say it is, they're pulling your leg."

"What if I fail?" Violet whispered.

Grandma put an arm around Violet's shoulders. "I can tell you this. You'll never succeed if you don't try. And to me, that would be the real failure."

Violet considered the advice. "I'm going to sleep on it."

"I'll be praying."

Violet hugged her grandmother. "Me, too."

Dear Mama,

Well, I'm in trouble with Nana. As usual. I texted her to let her know I'd be back to the store a little later than I was supposed to be, but instead of waiting there for me, she drove her big old Buick to the tennis courts. It was so mortifying. Chase thinks I'm a total baby now because my grandmother came and made me get in the car so we could go home.

I have my driver's license. I don't understand why they treat me like a baby. Granddaddy told me that I'd have to prove to them that I was responsible enough to borrow the car and that so far I hadn't because I kept missing curfews and not doing chores. That's really only happened twice, and I said I was sorry. They make a big deal about nothing. Daddy didn't care about stuff like that. I wish I could just go back to Texas, except that I'm an outsider there, too, now that the new baby is here.

Did you ever feel like you didn't belong anywhere? That's how I've felt ever since you've been gone. I'm living up to my name and turning into a shadow that no one even notices or listens to.

What if I never fit in anywhere and have to live in some hut in the woods like Thoreau? (See, I was paying attention in lit class last year despite what Mr. Baker said on my report card. . . .)

Ily,
Shadow

Chapter 11

Mom: THIS NONSENSE HAS GONE ON LONG ENOUGH,
VIOLET. IT'S BAD ENOUGH THAT I HAD TO HEAR ABOUT
YOUR RESIGNATION FROM YOUR FATHER, BUT NOW MY OWN
MOTHER INFORMS ME THAT YOU'RE IN HOT SPRINGS. AND
YOU WON'T ANSWER YOUR PHONE. EVER. WHAT IS GOING
ON? (Text message sent September 7, 5:02 p.m.)

Violet Matthews: I LOVE YOU, MOM. I'LL FILL YOU IN
SOON. DON'T WORRY. (Text message sent September 7,
6:11 p.m.)

Violet sank into the comfy deck chair and leaned her head
back. She'd called the Realtor this morning, and the man had
graciously offered to give her one more day to consider things.

Grandma and Grandpa had tried to get her to go to dinner
with them, but she'd declined. It was best that she stay focused.
She'd made endless pro and con lists throughout the day and still
came up uncertain.

She took a sip of water and stared out at Lake Hamilton. It was so beautiful here. A definite pro. She loved the outdoors, and moving to Hot Springs would give her endless opportunities to hike, fish, and water ski.

But would she really be happy here?

The distant sound of a doorbell interrupted her thoughts. Surely Mom hadn't found out where she was staying and driven over. She'd made it clear through her barrage of texts and voice mails that Violet was crazy for resigning and was clearly just going through some kind of "my little sister is getting married instead of me" brand of crisis.

As if.

Violet hurried through the house and banged her knee on an end table.

The bell rang twice in succession, followed by a series of knocks.

"Just a minute." She rubbed her knee. She just wanted peace and quiet. She peeked through the peephole and jumped back.

Jackson Stratford.

She glanced in the mirror above the offending end table. Her hair had air dried that morning, and it curled around her face like a lion's mane. Big hair might be her special talent. She hadn't bothered with makeup either.

The doorbell rang again. "Violet?" he called.

It irritated her that she looked so disheveled. Not because she wanted to impress Jackson, but because she hated to give him the satisfaction of seeing her less than perfect. She needed to be on her toes to deal with him, and looking all bare-faced and wild-haired put her at a disadvantage.

A girl needed her confidence to face someone like him.

Oh well. Violet opened the door. "Yes?" She crossed her arms.

He grinned. "Sorry about showing up like this. I called the house a couple of times, but you must not have heard the ring."

"Oh I heard it. I just didn't think it was my place to answer it." She'd had a suspicion it might be him calling to check in on her, but hadn't wanted to speak to him. Which, come to think of it, was probably a little rude considering he was letting her stay for free. "Sorry about that."

"Can I come in?"

She managed a smile. "It's your house. It's not like I could say no, could I?"

He chuckled and walked inside. "Well, I know I promised you peace and quiet."

"I've definitely had that." She narrowed her eyes. "Until now anyway."

Jackson didn't even have the decency to look sorry. Instead he grinned. "Come on now, you were probably ready for some conversation."

She ignored his comment. "It's an amazing space." She motioned to where Arnie slept on his bed in a corner. "Arnie sure thinks so."

Jackson nodded. "I see." He pointed at a closed door. "The vacuum is in there in case you want to make sure there's no dog hair left behind." He grinned. "If I were going into politics, that'd be a program of mine. No dog hair left behind."

"Ha-ha." His jokes were as corny as ever. "I'll have you know that Arnie doesn't shed like some dogs." She bent down to give

Arnie a pat on the head. "But I'd be happy to vacuum before we leave just the same."

"Thanks. I hate the thought of dog hair on the floor." He smiled. "The way I'm always vacuuming and sweeping drives my sister crazy every time her family visits. She always accuses me of being OCD about stuff like that. It's why I'd never have an inside dog."

"Never?" She couldn't imagine life without a dog in the house.

He shook his head. "Nope. Way too much trouble. Plus they'd dig up the yard."

"And provide unconditional love and companionship. Or is that something you don't know anything about?" She couldn't help it. He was crazy.

Jackson held up his hands. "Whoa there. I'm just telling you my position on inside animals. Don't get defensive."

"I'm sorry. I'm just offended on Arnie's behalf. He's a great dog. I can guarantee that your life would be more complete with a dog like him in it."

"Yeah. Completely full of dog hair." He snickered.

She glared. "You're impossible."

"I could say the same thing about you."

Violet sighed. The last thing she wanted was an argument. "Listen, if there's a problem with me and Arnie staying tonight, we can pack up. No big deal." There was surely a pet friendly hotel nearby. Or she could just drive home and come back tomorrow if she needed to.

"Don't be silly. I'm just giving you a hard time." He plopped down on the leather couch. "Besides, I need to talk to you."

She eyed him suspiciously. What was he up to? "What about?"

He pulled a folded piece of paper from his pocket. "This." He tossed it on the coffee table.

She scooped it up and unfolded it, quickly scanning the scrawled words. "A dating contract? You're crazy if you think I would ever agree to this." She couldn't believe he still thought she would agree to be his faux girlfriend. She thrust the contract back at him.

"It's more than fair." He smiled. "Besides, it's already September. Isn't the wedding in three months? Do you really think if you open a business and move, you're going to have time to find a suitable date?"

Violet scowled. Amber had texted her this morning to see if she wanted her invitation to be for "Violet Matthews and guest" or not. "First of all, I haven't made up my mind about moving. And second of all, what makes you think you're so suitable?"

He laughed. "Man, you really don't like me." He raked his fingers through his hair. "Don't you think we could let bygones be bygones, at least until January? I mean. . .we're in the same age bracket, both intelligent, reasonably attractive, and neither looking for a real relationship. What more do we need?"

"Reasonably attractive?" She couldn't decide how offended to be.

He gave her a sideways glance. "You fishing for a compliment?"

She didn't respond. How bad would the next few months of her life be if she agreed to this? She wasn't sure they'd make it through without killing one another. "Not at all. I assume you were talking about yourself when you said *reasonably* attractive."

Jackson grinned. "Come on. It will be one less thing you have to do. And frankly, one less thing that I have to do. My sister and friends are on my case. If I could just get them to back off for a few months, I could breathe easy."

"And then what?"

"We stage a breakup. Nothing that makes either of us look bad though. Maybe we don't see eye to eye on something important." He motioned at Arnie. "Like what to do with your inside dog."

She thought for a moment. "Fine. Let me see the contract." She held her hand out.

"It's pretty straightforward," Jackson began. "Four months. Thirty dates."

"That's too many."

He sighed. "Twenty-five dates and three weekend trips."

She widened her eyes. "Trips? Seriously?"

Jackson nodded. "We want to make this believable, right? One trip to Fayetteville for a Razorback football game. One trip to Memphis to see my sister." He grinned. "The other can be your choice."

She shook her head. "Twenty-five dates and a football game in Little Rock instead. Then one trip to your sister's."

"Tough negotiator."

"I'm a lawyer." She tapped the paper. "And what is this about professional events?"

"My office Christmas party in early December. And I'll attend one event of your choice."

She met his gaze. "Fine. What else?"

"Holidays. Specifically Christmas and Thanksgiving. We'll do Thanksgiving with my family. Christmas with yours."

She shook her head. "Yes to Thanksgiving. No to Christmas. It would be too soon for me to take a guy home for Christmas."

He stood up and grabbed a pen from the end table. "Fine." He took the paper from her and scribbled a note in the margin. "Now for the fun one."

She raised an eyebrow. "What's that?"

"Time to negotiate our physical relationship." He grinned.

Violet's face flamed. If Jackson Stratford thought they were going to have any kind of physical relationship, he was dead wrong. "There is nothing to negotiate."

His blue eyes danced. "That's where you're wrong."

Jackson couldn't believe she'd gone for it. He'd fully expected his plan to be rejected again. But she'd at least semi-agreed. "No couple who dates for four months isn't going to at least hold hands and kiss a little. We aren't Quakers."

She crossed her arms. "Not a chance."

Jackson sighed and walked over to where she stood. "Come on, Violet. Hear me out. I'm not proposing we make out like teenagers every chance we get. This would be very dignified and would only make our relationship more believable."

Violet shook her head. "No way."

"Five kisses. One at each of our big events and three just for fun." He grinned at the scowl on her pretty face. She was so much fun to mess with.

She rolled her eyes. "I don't kiss for sport."

"Fine. Three. One at each event and one that can be our first kiss story. You know. . .to keep it legit."

Violet's green eyes flashed. "You are incorrigible."

"Do people really use that word in sentences?"

"I just did, so I guess so. Why? Do I need to get you a dictionary? I know you're used to dealing with bubble heads, so maybe I'm too advanced for you." She smiled. "I'll try and dumb it down from now on."

"You exasperate me." He winked. "See what I did there? Maybe I don't need that dictionary after all."

She glared. "Do you have no concept of personal space?"

Jackson hadn't realized it, but he'd been moving closer and closer to her. He took a long look at her full lips. He could just kiss her now. Take her by surprise. Of course she'd probably hit him and toss him out. "Guess not." He smiled and took a step back. "Seriously though. I'm not just being some typical guy, trying to take advantage of you. I'm just saying, if we're going to pull off a faux relationship, we're going to have to make it look real. That means holding my hand and hugging me sometimes. I know it repulses you, but surely you can handle it." He didn't want to mention that he was kind of looking forward to knowing if her lips were as soft as they looked.

"So this relationship would have everything but—"

"But feelings." He cut her off. "No strings. No commitment after January. We'll just mutually part ways and continue along our separate paths." He grinned. "But we agree not to tell anyone. At all. No one."

She frowned. "So I'm supposed to let my best friend think this is real?"

"Only way it works is for us to keep it between the two of us. Oh, and I'll need you to change your Facebook relationship status."

She groaned and sank onto the couch. "I can't believe I'm considering this."

Jackson sat down next to her. "There's nothing to lose. You and I are a terrible match, and we both know it. For one, I'd never have an inside dog." His eyes landed on a pile of notebook paper she'd scribbled on and an empty Dr Pepper bottle. "And I'm much neater than you are."

"There are plenty of things I don't like about you, too. Don't think I've forgotten what happened in college. And I don't care if it was eleven years ago. You made a fool out of me. Not only did I graduate a semester late thanks to the incomplete we got on that project, but Clay Wells broke up with me because of you."

Jackson had hoped she'd forgotten that. "I was a jerk and I know it." He put a hand on her arm. "And if it helps, you dodged a bullet with Clay. I heard he lives somewhere out West and is a rodeo clown."

She raised her eyebrows.

"I'm not making it up." He chose not to mention that Clay was also a doctor by day. "I'm not the guy I used to be. I've learned a lot of lessons since then. Just give me a chance." He grinned and hoped his charm still worked. "I'll be the best fake boyfriend you could ever hope to have." He stuck a hand out. "Do we have a deal?"

Violet hesitated, the uncertainty flickering in her eyes. "Add moving to the list."

"What?" he asked.

She tapped the paper in his hand. "I think my fake boyfriend will be glad to help me move all my stuff from Little Rock to Hot Springs. Especially the heavy stuff."

He was pretty sure he saw the hint of a smile in her eyes, but couldn't be positive. "Fine. So, deal?"

Violet took a breath. Finally, she extended her hand. "Deal."

Jackson took her hand and shook it firmly. This might go down as the greatest idea he'd ever had.

He ignored the niggling thought that it could also be a disaster.

Violet would help him get Lauren, Jeff, and Kathleen off his back. And maybe she'd help take his mind off his mom's newfound dating life.

Only time would tell.

Chapter 12

Reagan McClure: JUST LISTENED TO YOUR VOICE MAIL—
OR WAS THAT SOMEONE PRETENDING TO BE YOU? MOVING.
DINNER WITH JACKSON. WHAT HAPPENED TO THE VIOLET
I KNOW??? (Text message sent September 9, 2:23 p.m.)

Violet Matthews: I NEEDED TO TALK IT OUT WITH YOU,
BUT COULDN'T GET YOU ON THE PHONE. SORRY FOR THE
FRANTIC MESSAGE. I DECIDED TO GO FOR IT WITH THE
BAKERY! AND I FOUND AN AWESOME HOUSE FOR RENT.
DINNER WITH JACKSON WAS A FLUKE. I THINK. (Text
message sent September 9, 2:39 p.m.)

Reagan used to be the kind of person who never missed her
Sunday afternoon nap. But it had been a long time since she'd
had that luxury. "Good lesson at church this morning, don't you
think?" she asked Chad once the kids were down.

"Sure was." He grinned. "Do you remember when I wanted to
be a preacher?"

She nodded. "You would've been great."

Chad sat down on the couch and patted the seat next to him. "Want to watch a movie or something?"

She knew if she sat down, she'd never get up until one of the kids woke. After two trips to the gym, she was so sore she could barely move. "I need to start on the laundry, and it would be great if you could stay here with the kids for an hour or so while I run to the grocery store."

Chad groaned. "Why don't you stay here now and go to the store later in the week?"

She put her hands on her hips. "Have you ever gone to the store with three kids? They take up most of the room in the cart, not to mention the inevitable meltdown Ava Grace has in the cereal aisle."

"My mom would be glad to help out." He raised an eyebrow. "You could call her to watch the kids while you go to the store."

They had the same argument at least twice a week. "Or you could just stay with them for a little while today and let me go get the errands done. Then we won't have to worry about it for at least another week."

Chad clicked on the TV. "Fine."

She grabbed her list and her purse and headed out the door. There had been a time when Sunday afternoons were for the two of them. Back when Izzy was a baby, they'd put her down for a nap and then lay on the couch and talk. No TV or anything. She couldn't remember the last time she and Chad had only focused on each other.

As she backed out of the driveway, the phone buzzed against the console. She glanced at the caller ID and hit the SPEAKER button. "I guess congratulations are in order," she said.

"You think I'm crazy, don't you?" Violet's voice filled the van. "Do you think it's a mistake?"

Reagan laughed. "Not about the bakery. Maybe about dinner last night with Jackson Stratford." The guy had done such a number on Violet back in college. Not only had his halfhearted effort on their project caused real problems for her in class, but he'd also insinuated that there was something going on between the two of them. Violet's boyfriend at the time had totally bought it and dumped her. It had been a terrible summer for Violet as she made up the class and dealt with a broken heart. "I'm not sure I trust him."

"It was just dinner," Violet said. "I think maybe he's trying to make up for some of the dumb stuff he did. Besides. . .people can change, right?"

Reagan didn't like the direction this conversation was headed. Was Violet seriously interested in the guy? "I know that matchmaker said y'all should give things a shot, but she wasn't there for you back when your world exploded and your heart was broken. I was. I'm just not sure it's a smart move, that's all."

Violet didn't say anything for a long moment. "But how about the bakery? Do you think that's a good idea?"

"That one I'm totally behind. In fact, I'm very proud of you for going after your dream. It's been a long time coming. And my offer to help with the logo and some of the design work stands." She flipped on her blinker at the red light next to Sam's Club. "Of course, you might have to house me and four kids for a few days while we work on things."

Violet laughed. "Y'all are welcome to stay. Grandma would be happy to help with the kids. And Mrs. Kemp's granddaughter probably would, too. She's going to work in the bakery once it opens. I talked to her about it today after church. I think she's super excited, but she's too cool to show it."

"The Goth girl? Are you sure that's going to be good for business?"

"Oh, she's not Goth anymore. Now she's all sporty. Wears tennis skirts and ponytails. She even lightened her hair some."

Reagan pulled into a parking space and turned off the van. "That's quite a change, huh?"

"I can't quite figure it out. She seems kind of lost. Drifting. I mean, my mom and I have certainly had our differences, but I can't imagine having grown up without her."

Reagan's eyes filled with unexpected tears. The thought of her kids growing up without her guidance filled her with sadness. There were so many things she hoped to teach them someday. So many milestones she looked forward to sharing with them. "That's tough. What about her dad?"

"Remarried, new baby. I get the impression that he doesn't know what to do with her, and the stepmother tries too hard to be her friend and not an actual parent."

Reagan hurried into the store. She figured she had thirty minutes before one of the kids woke up and Chad called to tell her to come home. "Maybe it's good that she'll be working with you. Sounds like she could use a good role model."

Violet laughed. "I wouldn't call myself that, but I did tell Mrs.

Kemp I'd spend some time with Shadow—take her shopping, that kind of thing."

"Sounds like a great plan. So what's the deal with the bakery?"

"I can't wait for you to see the place. It's perfect. I'm working on a business plan right now, just trying to figure out what all needs to happen between now and an opening. I want to move on things as quickly as possible."

"It does my heart good to hear how excited you are. I know how frustrated you've been, career-wise."

"This might fail. It might be the worst decision ever. But I would always wonder what might've happened. You know? I've recently spent a lot of time praying and thinking about this, and I really feel like this is the best plan for me."

"I'm so glad. And I'm excited about helping. I think it will do me some good to feel useful."

"You are already useful and you know it. Your husband and kids would be lost without you."

"You're sweet to say so, but I don't always feel that way." She put a package of paper towels in the cart. "But the gym is going well."

"What does Chad think about it?"

Reagan didn't say anything. She hated to admit that she hadn't told him yet. "He doesn't exactly know."

"You need to tell him. Secrets aren't good."

"I don't know how successful this will be. I'm so sore today, it's hard to walk. This morning I thought I was going to cry just trying to get Scarlett out of her car seat."

"I'm pretty sure Chad will be thrilled that you're doing something for yourself."

Reagan let out a bitter laugh. "Chad is at home right now on the couch. I'm at the grocery store. If he were too concerned, wouldn't he have offered to do the shopping?"

"No. You know that you have certain brands and certain ways you do things. Remember when we lived together and I bought the wrong kind of toothpaste? You'd have thought I'd committed a federal crime."

"I'm not that bad. I just know what I like."

Violet sighed loudly. "But wouldn't it be easier to let him help you rather than feeling like you have to do it all yourself? Couldn't you deal with a different brand of toilet paper or toothpaste if it meant your husband pitched in?"

Reagan didn't answer for a long moment. "Are you trying to say I'm a control freak?"

"Maybe a little. You've tried to be Superwoman for so long that I'm sure Chad doesn't think he could measure up to your expectations. Didn't you tell me that you got mad at him over coffee creamer a few weeks ago?"

Reagan winced. She'd forgotten about that. "He got the wrong kind. I like a certain flavor."

"Don't you think you could deal with the wrong flavor if it meant you didn't have to go to the store?"

"You don't understand. We've been married for ten years. He should *know* what kind of coffee creamer I like. That's the reason I get so upset. Because these things aren't rocket science. I'll bet you know my favorite coffee creamer flavor, don't you?"

"Hazelnut."

Reagan nodded. "Yep. How do you think it makes me feel that my husband can't even pay enough attention to me to get that small detail correct? I've been drinking my coffee the same for years. He just doesn't notice."

"I'm sorry. I wish you'd talk to him and y'all would figure out a way to work on things. Maybe a marriage seminar or something."

That would be the day. "I don't think we'd be able to find the time for something like that. I just have to hope that when the twins get a little older, things will get easier." It was what Reagan had to cling to these days. Because she couldn't deal with the alternative.

Dear Mama,

I'm trying out for the tennis team. Can you believe it? I've been working with Chase and think I might really enjoy it. He says he's going to play in college. Maybe I will, too.

And a woman named Violet is opening a bakery next door to Aunt Teak's. Nana says I can work there after school if I want to. I talked to Violet about it. She's kind of a funny person. Nana calls her quirky. She's always wearing these dresses that look like they should be in black-and-white movies. She even has a bunch of old books and a typewriter at her house. I think it's kind of weird that she likes all that old stuff.

I wish you were here. Violet told me that she remembered you from when you were teenagers and she'd come visit her grandmother. She said that one summer y'all worked together at Aunt Teak's. I guess I like her a little more now that I know she knew you when you were my age.

Love,
Shadow

Violet put the last of her belongings into a box and taped it shut. She'd passed being tired hours ago and was headed full into the land of exhaustion. But it was worth it. During the past few days, she'd moved from disbelief over her decision through panic and had finally arrived at excitement.

She was opening her own bakery. Her own bakery!

It had been her dream since law school, maybe earlier. Some of her fondest memories as a child included standing up on the barstool next to Grandma, stirring the batter or learning to make homemade icing.

Cupcakes made people happy. And making people happy gave Violet a sense of accomplishment. She liked to feel that she'd brightened someone's day.

The doorbell rang, and she jumped up to get it.

"I think you should reconsider. It isn't too late." Mom barged in as soon as Violet opened the door. "You don't know what you're doing. You've never operated a business. There's much more to it than just baking some cakes and wearing a cute apron."

Violet sighed. "I'm sorry I didn't include you in my decision, Mom. But this is just something I have to do. If it fails miserably, I can go back to a law firm."

Mom paced the living room. "But you belong in the family firm. I know you're disappointed that Landry was made partner. But there's no need for a knee-jerk reaction like this."

Violet picked up a box and added it to the stack in the corner. She'd found the perfect house to rent in Hot Springs with plenty of room for her stuff and a great yard for Arnie. The papers were signed, and Jackson had promised to be there with a truck first thing Saturday morning. She had to admit, having a fake boyfriend during a move was quite convenient—even if it was Jackson. "That's the thing. This isn't a knee-jerk reaction. And it honestly has nothing to do with Landry."

Mom opened her mouth to speak, but Violet cut her off.

"Or Amber. This isn't about not being made partner or my sister getting married. This is about me taking control of my life and doing something that I've always dreamed of. Did the timing of those things help push me? Sure. But this isn't something I just thought of—it's something I've wanted for a long time."

"Honey, I just want what's best for you. And I can't see that taking such a big financial risk is what's best."

So that's what it was about. Money. "I've always been a saver. You know that. I have money saved up, and I'm already in the process of obtaining a small business loan. I'll be okay. People start businesses every day."

"And they fail every day, too."

Violet blew out a breath. "Can't you just be supportive? One time. Support my dreams."

"Not when your dream has the potential to end in disaster. Not to mention—how are you ever going to meet anyone suitable if you're always holed up in a bakery? And you'll be wearing awful clothes and all covered in flour. Not exactly the most attractive way for a single girl to be."

It was time to drop her bomb. "For your information, I'm seeing someone." Violet wished she had a camera to capture the shocked expression on her mother's face. "He works for the state in economic development. In fact, he's helping me with my business plan *and* coordinating my move." Sweet satisfaction.

"And you didn't tell me?" Mom raised her eyebrows. "How could you leave something like that out? Is he your plus one at the wedding? Amber told me you'd requested two spots at the rehearsal dinner and reception, but I figured you were just hoping to have a date by then."

Violet had been on the fence all week over her arrangement with Jackson. But in that moment, she knew she'd made the right decision by agreeing to his contract. "That's right, Mom. He'll be with me at the wedding."

And then she'd go play supportive girlfriend at his speech. And the week after his speech, they'd go their separate ways. What a beautiful plan.

Chapter 13

Jackson Stratford: DINNER FRIDAY NIGHT? I KNOW YOU'RE ANXIOUS TO MARK SOME OF THOSE CONTRACTED DATES OFF THE LIST. . . . (Text message sent September 13, 1:12 p.m.)

Violet Matthews: DID YOU REALLY JUST ASK ME OUT VIA TEXT? JUST FYI, IF THIS WEREN'T A RUSE, I'D SAY NO. FRIDAY'S FINE. PICK ME UP AT 7. (Text message sent September 13, 1:17 p.m.)

Jackson walked past a FOR RENT sign on the way to Violet's front porch. He hadn't seen her all week, but they'd texted a few times. Mostly details about tomorrow's move. He knocked on the door and waited.

The door swung open. "Come on in." Violet ushered him inside.

The living room was littered with boxes and plastic totes. "I don't know if I could sleep in a house this chaotic." He grinned. "And you have so much stuff."

She made a face. "I'm sure you'd manage, Mr. OCD. I'm sorry that my chaos and clutter offends you so much." She grinned and motioned toward Arnie, who slept on a rug in between two stacks of boxes. "My super shedding dog doesn't seem to mind."

Jackson couldn't help but laugh. "Poke fun all you want."

Violet grabbed her purse and cell phone from the coffee table. "I won't make you stay in this mess any longer than necessary. Let's go."

"I've never seen you in jeans before," he said as they walked out the door. "What gives?" Not that he was complaining.

She grinned. "Well I didn't want to show you up by being the better dressed portion of a *reasonably* attractive couple."

He chuckled. "Are you always going to remember every dumb thing I say?" He opened the passenger door of the Range Rover, and she climbed inside.

"Probably. At least until the week after your speech." She grinned. "Then I won't care."

Jackson got in the car and glanced over at her. "So I was thinking. . ."

"First time for everything," she said with a laugh, cutting him off.

He pulled out of the driveway and headed down the street. "Very funny." He cleared his throat. "As I was saying. I was thinking that we should fast-track the whole 'getting to know each other' portion of things."

"And how do you propose we do that?"

"I'll text you a question. You answer it. You text me a question. I'll answer it." He grinned. "That way we can be a believable couple in a shorter amount of time."

Violet sighed. "Okay."

"I'll have you know that texting isn't my favorite form of communication, so I'm kind of making a concession here."

"How gallant of you."

Jackson merged onto the interstate. "Where do you want to eat?"

"Someplace where I can get vegetables. That isn't crowded. Or too expensive. How about Cracker Barrel?" She looked over at him. "And it just occurred to me that we haven't discussed money."

"Money?"

"This relationship is not real. I don't expect you to pay for dinners and things."

Jackson hadn't even thought about it. "It's four months. I'd go on at least twenty-five dates over the course of four months. So I'd be paying that money anyway." He shrugged.

"You'd go on twenty-five dates in four months? Where do you find these girls?"

"Jealous?" He grinned.

She laughed. "Hardly. I'm just mystified."

"For your information, I meet them everywhere. Starbucks. The gym. Work." He shrugged. "Church."

"You go to church?" From the incredulous tone to her voice, he may as well have said he met women on the moon.

Jackson was beginning to get irritated. "Yes. I go to church. In fact, I even teach the Wednesday night men's Bible class."

Violet sputtered. "Wonders never cease."

"There's a lot about me that you don't know. If you'd just throw out any preconceived notions you formed about me all those years ago, you might find that I'm actually a pretty nice guy."

Violet fell silent. Finally she cleared her throat. "I'm sorry. I didn't mean anything by that. It's just that I remember you as being something of a wild man back in college."

"I've done things I'm not proud of. But that was a long time ago." He gave her a sideways glance. "I've changed a lot." He frowned. "But you haven't."

He drove in silence the rest of the way to the restaurant.

Maybe this had been a bad idea after all. Violet might never see him as anything more than the guy he'd been in college. And even he could admit that guy hadn't been the greatest.

But didn't everyone deserve a second chance?

Violet was pretty sure she'd hurt his feelings. She'd just been so shocked at the thought of him teaching a Bible class that she'd not been able to control her mouth. "I really didn't mean to offend you," she said as he pulled into a space at Cracker Barrel. "I was just surprised."

Jackson turned off the ignition and turned to face her. "I'm not proud of the guy I was back then. I know I wasn't exactly walking on the straight and narrow. But I've done a lot of growing up since then." He gave her a tentative smile. "At least I own up to my mistakes."

She sighed. "Do you think I'm too judgmental?"

"I think maybe you just don't trust me." He took the keys from the ignition. "Yet." He shrugged. "And that's fine. There's plenty of time for that, and besides, in order for our plan to work, you don't have to trust me. You don't even have to like me."

"I just have to pretend that I do," she said softly.

Jackson nodded. "That's right. Let's see how good of an actress you are."

She laughed. "I was the lead in a play when I was in fifth grade. That's the extent of my acting experience until now."

Jackson opened the door for her and helped her out. He reached over and took her hand as they walked toward the restaurant.

She tensed.

"Easy there. I'm not going to bite. Just practicing." He dropped her hand at the door and held the door open. "After you."

Violet brushed past him, and her heart beat faster. Holding hands meant he'd be pushing for their fake first kiss soon. It had been so long since she'd kissed a guy. What if she'd forgotten how? Stupid Zach had really done a number on her.

"You okay?" Jackson asked once he'd put their names on the waiting list for a table.

She nodded. "Just thinking."

"Moving is overwhelming, huh? And starting a new business on top of it."

Violet smiled. "I'm overwhelmed, but in such a wonderful way. I've dreamed of doing this for such a long time. Now that I've made the decision, everything is just falling into place."

"God's plans are always better than we expect."

She looked into his blue eyes. Sincere blue eyes. "Aren't they though?"

Jackson smiled. "Once I finished my master's at Auburn I had the same kind of thing happen. I'd prayed and prayed that I'd find the job that was right for me. And then the job in Mobile came open, and it was perfection. Trusting that God would lead me in the right direction was hard, but once I opened myself up to things besides just what I wanted or what I thought was best, I ended up getting the perfect offer."

"I didn't know you had your master's."

He nodded. "Yep. I think that was really the time in my life when I grew the most. I wasn't at a Christian school any longer and wasn't surrounded by Christians. It was very difficult at first to make good choices, but eventually I found my own faith. There were some dark days, but ultimately I think it was the time when my Christian walk started—apart from what my parents believed or my friends believed. I searched and questioned and developed my own relationship with the Lord."

Violet was impressed by his candor. Maybe she'd under-estimated him. "That's an amazing story. And I know what you mean. It's easy to make good choices when you're surrounded by people who come from the same kind of background as you. I lived in DC for a little while after law school. I loved the city, but I was faced with things I'd never been faced with before. I'm glad, though, because ultimately it made me stronger."

"Skywalker, your table is now available."

Jackson took her hand. "That's us."

"Skywalker?" she hissed. "Seriously?"

He grinned. "It's a thing I do sometimes. Call me Luke in front of the hostess." He squeezed her hand and led her to the hostess stand.

She burst out laughing. Jackson might not be the uptight guy she had him pegged to be.

Come to think of it, he might have some layers to him that she hadn't expected.

Dear Mama,

Chase and I broke up. And right after I spent all my money on a fancy tennis racquet. The store won't take it back either.

Nana says I can sell it on eBay or something, but I'll never get my money back. And I made a C on my history quiz.

So I'm having kind of a terrible week. Daddy called to see if I'd come to Texas for Thanksgiving. To tell the truth, I don't really want to. Stephanie will try to be my BFF and take me shopping and stuff. But she doesn't understand me at all. She keeps sending me these e-mails that say she wants to be my friend and be involved in my life and wants me to come back to Texas and be a good big sister.

But I don't want to. It makes my heart hurt to be there because I don't understand how Daddy could forget about you. I haven't forgotten. So why did he?

Oh, and I met a guy in the library the other day. His name is Thomas, and he is on the Quiz Bowl team. He has the cutest glasses. I think he is going to ask me out.

I miss you,
Shadow

Chapter 14

Jackson Stratford: HOPE UNPACKING IS GOING WELL. WHAT'S YOUR FAVORITE BAND? (Text message sent September 18, 10:34 a.m.)

Violet Matthews: THANKS FOR HELPING UNLOAD. UNPACKING IS A PAIN. BE GLAD YOU AREN'T HERE FOR THE CHAOS. HA. AND U2. OR BON JOVI. THE OLD-SCHOOL STUFF FROM THE LATE '80S. YOU? (Text message sent September 18, 10:39 a.m.)

Jackson Stratford: REMEMBER THAT LESS IS BEST. WANT ME TO COME THROW SOME OF THAT STUFF OUT FOR YOU? I'M GOING WITH SOMETHING MORE CLASSIC: THE BEATLES. (Text message sent September 18, 10:42 a.m.)

Violet opened the back door and let Arnie run into the fenced-in yard. This place was perfect. Not too far from the shop, but in a rural area. She couldn't believe it had been for rent, and the

Realtor had told her if she liked it, there was a chance the owners might want to sell.

She adored everything about the place, especially the big yard and big kitchen—two of her must-haves. And while three bedrooms seemed like a lot for one person, she planned to turn one into an office and have a guest room set up so Reagan could come visit.

The Lord had certainly blessed her.

She glanced around the sunny kitchen. It would be easy to get overwhelmed by all the things that needed to be done. Not only did she have a house to put in some kind of order, but she also had to make a lot of decisions about the business. Starting with a catchy name.

Her phone buzzed.

Jackson.

She picked up on the third ring. "The Beatles? Really?"

He laughed. "I'm a classy guy. I appreciate the finer things in life, which includes really good music."

"I guess." She took the tape off of a box labeled KITCHEN UTENSILS and began to unpack. "So what's going on? You trying to break the contract already?"

"Not a chance. Actually, I was calling to see what you have planned for Saturday."

"I guess I'll be unpacking and organizing. Why?" She peeked out the window to check on Arnie. The sweet dog was wriggling in the grass.

"It's the Legends Balloon Rally. I thought we might go to some of the festivities."

Violet wrinkled her nose. "I don't know. I'm a little overwhelmed here, trying to get settled and starting to work at the shop. I'm planning on painting the inside pretty soon."

"That's exactly the reason we need to go to the festival. You'll need a break by then. We'll eat, listen to some music, and watch the hot air balloons. It'll be awesome."

She sighed. "I just have so much to do."

"Tell you what. I'll stay at the lake house on Saturday night so I can help you paint on Sunday afternoon."

Violet thought for a moment. "Can we count painting as one of the contracted dates?"

He chuckled. "You never stop negotiating, do you?"

"Nope."

Jackson let out a heavy sigh. "Okay, fine. Saturday night and Sunday will each count toward the twenty-five *if* we grab dinner on Sunday. We'll be rid of each other before you know it."

She opened another box. "Sounds like a plan. What time will you be here on Saturday?"

"How about late afternoon? That'll give us time to go to the festival first, and then we'll have dinner. Maybe five?"

"See you then." Violet hung up and put the phone back on the counter. She'd never been to a hot air balloon festival before, but had always heard about it. Inevitably, they would run into her grandparents. It had been forever since she'd introduced a guy to anyone in her family. Not since Zach.

Reagan shimmied across the floor trying to keep up with the beat of the music. Maggie had finally talked her into a Zumba class, and Reagan had figured if a woman Maggie's age could handle it, so could she.

She'd been wrong.

Her whole body hurt, and she was pretty sure things were jiggling that weren't supposed to jiggle. She avoided the full wall mirror at all costs so she wouldn't see how stupid she looked.

"You're doing great," Maggie called. "Isn't it fun?"

Reagan gasped for breath and nodded. "It's different, that's for sure."

The music ended. "Water break," the instructor called.

Reagan collapsed on the floor. "The last time I huffed and puffed this much, I was in labor with the twins."

Maggie laughed. "How is everything going now that you've had a few weeks of exercise? Is your head clearer?"

Reagan leaned back and stared at the ceiling. "I think so. I feel better and seem to have more energy."

"What's your hubby say?" Maggie asked.

Reagan sat up. "I haven't told him." She wanted to wait until she'd been a member of the gym for a month. By then she'd know if she was going to stick with it or not.

"Secrets are never good, but I guess this one is going to end up being a pleasant surprise."

"I hope so. I've lost five pounds so far, but you can't really tell." Reagan had been thrilled when she'd seen the scales. Her clothes were starting to fit better, but she still wasn't back to her old size. "It isn't really about the weight, though. I know Chad loves me no matter what."

"You know how men are," Maggie said. "They're visual creatures. I'm sure he appreciates the extra effort."

Reagan sighed. She still felt pretty invisible at home and tried hard to forget that cute, tiny Reese was at Chad's office every day. "I guess."

"Girl, what you need is a romantic date night. Get some of the spark back." Maggie smiled. "Me and my husband took a class at our church several years ago, and the guy who taught it was a marriage counselor. He said date nights were important."

"It's been a long time. But with four kids, it isn't that easy to get a capable sitter." She and Chad hadn't been out just the two of them since before the twins were born. How was that possible?

Maggie smiled. "Do you think sometimes God puts people in your path for a reason?"

"Yes."

"Did I ever mention to you now that I'm retired I work as a nanny? Right now I'm working for a family with two kids, a boy and a girl. They're three and four."

Reagan's eyes widened. She'd just assumed Maggie was retired and had never thought to ask if she had a job. "I didn't know that. Do you enjoy it?"

"I love it. I used to be an elementary school art teacher—got my early childhood degree from the U of A. But I think I might enjoy this more. I didn't get to stay home with my own kids when they were little. The kids I keep are so sweet. Tuesdays and Thursdays are the days their mama works from home, which is how I find time to come here." She grinned.

Reagan had often thought about going back to work part-time and hiring someone to come to the house to keep the kids. But she'd never broached the subject with Chad. He'd always been so traditional that she knew he'd balk at the idea. His mom had stayed home with him and his sisters, and he'd always wanted the same thing for his own kids. "That sounds really nice. I'll bet you're wonderful." How lovely it must be for the family Maggie worked for, especially the mom.

"We're starting again." Maggie stood up. "Come on. Ten more minutes."

Reagan slowly got to her feet and focused on the instructor. Even if she felt stupid waving her arms and shaking her hips, she had to admit it was kind of fun.

Thirty minutes later, she'd loaded the kids in the van and headed toward the house. There'd be enough time for the kids to get a nap and her to get a shower before they loaded up again to get Izzy from school. "Ava Grace, you sit with Simon while I get Scarlett inside." She unhooked Ava Grace's car seat. "Can you sing to him for a minute?" She got Scarlett out of her car seat.

"Hi, baby Simon," Ava Grace said, leaning close to her brother's face.

He cooed.

Reagan grinned as Ava Grace sang "Twinkle, Twinkle, Little Star" to Simon. There might be nothing sweeter than her babies loving on each other.

"Down you go." She put Scarlett in the Pack 'n Play in the living room. "Mama will be right back." Now that the twins were crawling, it made it much more difficult to maneuver. She refused to think of how it would be when they started to walk. Mass chaos came to mind.

As soon as she got Ava Grace and Simon out of the car, her phone rang.

"Hey, babe." She was pleased that Chad had called during the day. That happened less and less often.

"Everyone okay?" he asked.

"I'm about to put the kids down for a nap and jump in the shower." She put Simon in the playpen with Scarlett and turned on the TV for Ava Grace. "Watch Dora for a minute while I talk to Daddy," she whispered.

"Can you look at the calendar for next weekend?"

She walked into the kitchen to the magnetic calendar she kept on the fridge. "Next weekend." She ran her finger along the calendar. It was hard to believe it was almost October. Time sure went by fast. "Ava Grace has been invited to a birthday party for Collin from her Sunday school class. And it's the deadline to sign Izzy up for gymnastics." She peeked through the opening over the counter and checked on the kids. "Why?" She couldn't help but hope he was going to suggest something fun. Maybe he missed their time alone as much as she did.

"I have to go to Miami for a conference. I just wanted to make sure I wouldn't be missing anything big before Reese books my flight."

Reese. Booking a flight to Miami for *her* husband. The uneasy feeling rose through her body. "You won't be missing anything big. Just life with your wife and kids. That's all. Nothing big." She couldn't keep the bitterness out of her voice.

Chad groaned. "Reagan, you know I'd rather stay home. My boss asked me to go in his place."

She fought the urge to ask if Reese was going. That was a conversation she wanted to have in person. "I think I'll take the kids to Hot Springs if you're going to be out of town. We'll visit Violet and check out her new place."

"Are you up for a road trip with all the kids by yourself?"

The fact that he doubted her abilities angered her. Didn't he realize that she took care of the kids by herself most of the time? "I'm pretty used to handling the kids by myself. We'll manage fine." Her eyes filled with tears. Any stress her Zumba class had gotten rid of had come back and brought friends. "I've got to go." She clicked off the phone and leaned against the counter. What if the wedge between them kept growing? Where would that leave them?

There was a cry from the living room. Time to focus on the kids.

And not on her crumbling marriage.

Chapter 15

Daddy: I'M PROUD OF YOU, VIOLET. I'M LOOKING
FORWARD TO THE OPENING OF THE BAKERY. LET ME KNOW
IF THERE'S ANYTHING I CAN DO TO HELP. I LOVE YOU.
DAD. (Text message sent September 22, 8:34 a.m.)

Violet Matthews: THANKS! THAT MEANS A LOT. I'M
WORKING ON NAILING DOWN THE DATE FOR THE GRAND
OPENING. I HOPE YOU AND MOM WILL ATTEND. (Text
message sent September 22, 8:41 a.m.)

Jackson sat on the back deck of his lake house. It was still hard to
think of it as *his* place. His dad had always planned on leaving it
to him, but Jackson had always imagined that would be way down
the road.

After Dad died last year, Mom had wanted him to go ahead and
take ownership. She'd said it was what his dad would've wanted.

It was weird. In the months after Dad's death, lots of people
had speculated what he would've said or would've done or would've

wanted. But Jackson couldn't help but wonder how they could be so sure.

Thinking about his dad filled him with a sadness he hadn't known existed. The death had been so sudden and had come without warning. It had really made Jackson take stock of his life though. Was he the kind of man his dad would've been proud of? He tried to be, but knew he probably failed sometimes.

He pushed the thoughts from his mind and turned his attention to the evening's plans. He'd cooked up a surprise for Violet. Whether she'd like it or not was anyone's guess. She certainly didn't cut him any slack.

Jackson went into the airy kitchen and took stock of the refrigerator's contents. He still needed to get a few items, but for the most part he was ready.

He smiled to himself as he pulled the picnic basket from a shelf in the pantry. This had the potential to be a wonderful night.

His cell phone rang, and he picked it up from the counter.

Jeff.

"Long time no talk."

Jeff chuckled. "The beginning of the school year is busy for kindergartners and their parents. Did you know that?"

"Can't say that I did. What makes it so busy? Don't they just color and stuff?"

Jeff let out a whistle. "No way. Bennett's got homework. It's crazy the way things have changed since we were kids. He's already starting to read."

"I don't know about all of that," Jackson said. "Seems like there should be more time for a kid to just be a kid." He hoped to have kids of his own someday and wanted to make sure his offspring knew the same simple pleasures of childhood that he'd known.

"Bennett's adjusting pretty well though. He seems to like his classmates and teacher a lot, and we're getting ready for his first soccer game. It should be a hoot if it's anything like T-ball was over the summer." The fatherly pride in Jeff's voice was evident. "But that's not why I called."

"What's going on?"

Jeff sighed. "Lauren's been after me to check in on you and see how things are going. So. . .how are things going?"

Jackson laughed. "I'm surprised she hasn't called me herself. I'm happy to report that I have a date tonight. With a woman who knows who Luke Skywalker is and likes the big-haired version of Bon Jovi—not the sleeker, more modern version."

"Got it. I'll relay to Lauren that you're finally dating someone she'd consider age appropriate." He chuckled. "She'll be thrilled."

"In fact, how about the four of us get together sometime soon? I'd love for y'all to meet her." Jackson would have to run it by Violet, but as long as it meant she got to check a date off their list, she'd probably be on board.

"Does this mystery woman have a name? If I don't give a full report, my wife will mercilessly dis my investigative skills."

Jackson grinned. "Violet. Her name's Violet. She's a lawyer but is getting ready to open her own business." He liked saying it. It was a new experience to be proud of someone he was seeing. Even if his relationship with Violet was fake, he was still proud to be associated with a woman like her.

"Impressive. I'm sure Lauren will be impressed, too."

"Well I aim to please."

Jeff laughed. "And we'd love to get together. Just let us know when and where."

"Will do." Jackson hung up and turned his attention back to the refrigerator. He might not be a gourmet cook, but he thought he could win some points for effort.

And considering the way Violet viewed him, he could use all the extra points he could get.

Violet took one last look in the mirror. She'd fought hard to straighten her hair and was pleased with the outcome. Even her mother would approve—she always commented when Violet's hair was less than straight. After thirty-three years of critique, Violet figured she should be immune to it, but that day hadn't come yet.

She stepped into one of her favorite dresses. It wasn't exactly orange, more like tangerine. She loved the lace detail on the bodice and the way it made her waist look tiny. There was a time when Violet would've been afraid it clashed with her red hair, but she got so many compliments when she wore it, she'd decided it was definitely one of her "good" colors, no matter what the woman at Color Me Beautiful had said when Mom had taken her to get her colors done in high school.

The doorbell rang. Jackson was right on time.

She opened the door. "Come in," she said with a smile.

"Wow." Jackson walked inside and looked around. "It's looking good." He ran a hand over the typewriter she had displayed on an antique secretary table she'd found at an estate sale. "And this is very cool."

Violet grinned. "I guess you didn't see that during the move because I had it boxed up. I adore old things." She did a curtsey. "In fact, this dress is vintage. I found it in a little shop in Atlanta last summer."

"It's nice." He returned her grin. "Are you ready? I have some fun stuff planned."

She raised her eyebrows. "You do? More than just going to the festival?"

"Yes."

She waited for him to elaborate, but he didn't. "I'm ready." She knelt down to give Arnie a pat. "Bye, sweet boy."

"Why do you talk to him if he's deaf?" Jackson asked as they walked outside.

"Are you serious?"

He nodded.

She sighed. "Partly habit. I've been talking to him for nearly fifteen years. But also because I don't want him to think I'm upset with him."

"Upset with him?"

Violet shrugged. "I can't imagine how it must be for him to not hear anything now and not understand why. Sometimes I worry that he thinks I'm mad at him or something." She waited while Jackson opened the passenger door.

"I'm sure he doesn't think that," Jackson said once he was behind the wheel. "But I'm sorry it upsets you so much."

His words seemed sincere. "Thanks."

Jackson headed toward town. "How are you settling in? Have you gotten much done at the shop?"

"The house is coming together fine. And I've got the paint picked out for the shop—a nice, cheery yellow. My friend Reagan is going to design the logo." She glanced over at him. "You might remember her from college. Reagan Thompson. She married Chad McClure, so she's Reagan McClure now."

He was silent for a moment. "Blond girl? And Chad was one of those studious types who was in the choir?"

She laughed. "Yes all the way around. Reagan was in the choir, too. In fact, they say they fell in love during the fall choral tour our freshman year. Honestly, I think it was more like they fell in love as soon as they laid eyes on each other."

"Love at first sight, huh? Do you believe in that?" he asked. "I didn't peg you as the hopeless romantic type."

She grinned. "I believe in it for everyone but myself. And I'm *not* the hopeless romantic type. How about you?"

He quirked his mouth into a smile. "You'd be surprised. I think I probably am a bit of a softy. And I definitely am more romantic than most guys. I love the idea of that old-school, traditional romance. Picnics, sharing popcorn at a movie, dancing in the rain." He glanced over at her. "Stuff like that."

She couldn't hide her surprise. "I never would've guessed." She wondered why someone with that kind of outlook was still single, but didn't want to pry.

"Speaking of picnics. . .I've prepared one for us." He grinned. "Hope that's okay."

Violet couldn't believe it. She'd never expected Jackson to go out of his way to do something nice for her. "You didn't have to do that."

"I just thought it would be nicer than having dinner at a restaurant. We can see the hot air balloons. I thought we'd picnic up near the mountain tower. I know the perfect spot."

"Did you ever go up in the tower?" she asked. The Hot Springs Mountain Tower sat atop Hot Springs Mountain inside the national park boundaries. From the top of the tower, visitors could see nearly one hundred and fifty miles of beautiful scenery. It was a favorite during the fall when the colors were at their peak.

He nodded. "My family did a few times when I was a kid. We used to spend a lot of time here at the lake house." He grinned. "And my sister and I loved going to Magic Springs." The amusement park was a favorite vacation spot for families.

"I did, too." She laughed. "My cousin and I used to bug our parents to let us stay in Hot Springs at our grandparents' house just so we could go ride the rides. The log ride was my favorite, until it got to the top."

"Right before the free fall down into the water?"

She nodded. "Yes. I loved the slow pace of the ride so much that I'd always forget how fast and far it dropped at the end. And every time we'd make it up to the top, there was that guy whose job was to just sit there and say, 'Are you ready?' or something like that." She laughed. "Every single time I'd say no and beg him to let me get out of the boat."

Jackson laughed. "So you weren't much of a daredevil?"

"Not at all." She smiled at the memory. "I'd forgotten about that. I haven't been to Magic Springs in years. Not since they added the water park." Crystal Falls had opened in the midnineties and had the traditional water slides and wave pools that most water parks included.

"I went last year with my niece and nephew. It was pretty fun."

"So you're an uncle. That's cool."

He pulled the Range Rover into a parking space. "I enjoy it. I probably spoil them more than I should, but they're really great."

"Do you want to have kids of your own someday?" she asked.

He nodded. "I do. Not too many though. My sister and I were pretty close growing up, and I think that's a special bond. So I'd like to have at least two." He glanced over at her. "How about you?"

Violet sighed. "My sister and I are kind of far apart in years. She's nine years younger than me, and I think that's caused a little bit of a division. I grew up babysitting her, and now I think it's hard for us to relate to each other as equals."

"Is that why it's so important to you to have a date to her wedding?"

She nodded. "She's the kind of sister who takes every opportunity to take jabs at me. So I knew the wedding would be brutal. Between her and my mom, they'd probably announce to the world that I'm officially ready to be the new face of the Old Maid deck."

Jackson laughed. "Surely it isn't that bad."

She managed a tiny smile. "You'd be surprised."

He grabbed the picnic basket from the backseat. "There's a blanket behind your seat that we can sit on. Come on." He climbed out of the vehicle, and she followed him to a grassy spot.

Despite their rocky history, she had to admit that Jackson kept surprising her. One thing was sure—the next few months would definitely not be boring.

Chapter 16

Thomas Daniels: DO YOU WANT TO MEET ME TONIGHT
AT THE HOT AIR BALLOON FESTIVAL? THERE'S A POETRY
READING TAKING PLACE THAT I'D LIKE TO GO TO. (Text
message sent September 22, 5:45 p.m.)

Shadow Simmons: I <3 POETRY! I WILL SEE YOU THERE.
(Text message sent September 22, 5:46 p.m.)

J ackson pulled a sandwich out of the basket. "It's chicken salad.
My mom's recipe."

Violet took the sandwich. "Ooh, on a croissant. My favorite."
She grinned.

He hoped that meant he'd finally arrived in her good graces.
"I also made deviled eggs and banana pudding." He placed the
containers on the blanket between them.

"Wow."

"I know those things probably don't go together." He chuckled.
"But this is kind of the extent of my cooking skills unless there is a

grill or a frozen pizza involved."

She laughed. "This looks amazing. Seriously. I'm not used to anyone being so nice to me."

"Well you should be." Once he'd distributed the food, he handed her a bottle of water. "Hope this is okay."

"Perfect." She smiled. "Oh, look at that!" She stood up and pointed toward the sky.

Jackson followed her gaze. Hot air balloons in a variety of colors bobbed in the distance. "So cool. Too bad we didn't go up in one, huh?"

She shook her head. "I'd rather just see them while my feet are firmly on the ground. But they're beautiful."

She sat back down on the blanket. If a picnic beneath a sky dotted with hot air balloons didn't get him some bonus points, he didn't know what would.

"I'm glad you talked me into getting out of the house for this tonight."

Jackson nodded. "Thanks for coming. Although I suspect you have a countdown list at home you'll be checking off once the night is over."

She grinned. "Either way, if anyone ever asks if we had a unique date, we'll have one to share."

"True." He watched her for a long moment as she arranged the food on her plate. "Mind if I pray?" he asked once she was situated.

"Please."

Jackson bowed his head. "Thank You, Lord, for the chance to spend time getting to know one another. Please help us keep You in the center of our lives and show us the path You have for each of our lives. Lord, especially be with Violet as she makes this transition in her life. Bless her and be with her as she opens her business. Amen."

Violet caught his eye. "Thanks," she said quietly. "I can't remember the last time I heard someone pray specifically for me."

In that moment, Jackson couldn't help but wonder what had happened to her. She seemed so surprised—grateful almost—like he'd done something extraordinary for her. "Can I ask you a question?"

She took a bite of her sandwich. "Sure."

"Why are you single? I mean, you seem like the kind of girl who would've tied the knot years ago."

Violet daintily wiped her mouth with a paper towel. "I almost got married a few years ago. I met him right after I moved back from DC." She sighed. "It was one of those cases where I just refused to see what kind of person he really was. You know?"

Jackson wasn't sure if he did. "Was he a bad guy then?"

"He was a smooth talker. Always had a line. In hindsight, he'd probably make a great politician." She shrugged. "But he was a lousy boyfriend."

"I'm sorry."

"One thing I hate is being the center of attention. I hate for people to stare at me and to feel like they're judging me somehow. But Zach was always calling attention to us. He'd have the waitstaff at restaurants sing to me because he thought it was funny how uncomfortable I became. And he'd make a big production out of everything—from arguments to terms of endearment. It was like he needed an audience."

"Sounds like he was kind of a jerk."

"He didn't understand me either. I know I like things that are a little weird." She ran a hand along the hem of her dress. "He thought it was dumb for me to like vintage stores. And when I bought that typewriter, he made no effort to hide how archaic he thought it was to even have it in my house." She smiled. "And when he caught on to my weird attachment to old pennies, he couldn't make enough fun of me."

Jackson raised an eyebrow. "Old pennies?"

Violet burst out laughing. "I know it sounds crazy, but hear me out."

"My mind is totally open." He grinned.

She took a sip of water. "I collect pennies that are older than 1984."

"Because. . . ?" He hated pennies. He'd read somewhere it cost more to produce them than they were even worth.

She sighed. "I knew I shouldn't have told you. You probably think I'm as weird as Zach did."

Jackson shook his head. "Nope. Not a chance. I've never met anyone else like you before, but that isn't a bad thing."

"I have this theory that we were all really happier back then. Have you ever watched families today? The next time you're at a restaurant, take a good look. Everyone is looking at their phones. Texting, Facebooking, playing a game." She shook her head. "I'm pretty sure real conversation is on the decline."

Jackson had thought he was the only person who felt that way. "You're right."

"I just worry sometimes that we're so caught up in progress and convenience and technology that we forget what's really important. That's why I save those old pennies. They remind me of a simpler time and of how fast time passes."

"Because you have clear memories of 1984?"

She nodded. "I was five. I still remember my first day of kindergarten. And when I'd get home from school, I'd play outside. We didn't have a computer or a remote control. There was only one TV in the family room, and we didn't get that many channels."

"I remember those days fondly."

She shrugged. "I guess that's partly why I hang on to such old stuff. The clothes, the furniture, the books. . .the pennies." She grinned. "I even have a record player at my house because I think there's nothing quite like the sound of a real record."

Violet continued to surprise him, that was for sure. He'd just assumed she was a little bit quirky. He'd never guessed that there was more to it than that. "That's very cool. I haven't listened to a record in forever. Probably since I was in elementary school."

"Maybe I'll let you listen to mine sometime." She grinned. "I actually have some Beatles albums."

"You just might be the perfect woman." He realized as soon as it left his mouth how it must sound. "For someone, I mean."

"Someone who doesn't mind inside dogs and clutter."

He chuckled. "That's right." He scooped some banana pudding into a bowl. "So did you and this Zach guy just finally realize you weren't meant for one another?"

"If it had only been that simple." She gave him a wry smile. "He cheated on me. A lot. With more than one girl." She sighed. "I had no clue it was going on, but it seems that everyone else did. Finding out was pretty terrible." She shrugged. "That kind of thing does a number on your self-esteem. I haven't dated much since then."

He let out a low whistle. "I'm sorry. You didn't deserve to be treated that way."

"It's really hard for me now to believe I'll find someone who is really trustworthy. Plus I'm sort of scared I'll put my trust in the wrong guy. I've done it once; who's to say it won't happen again."

Jackson shook his head. "I don't have a magic answer. But I do think you deserve the kind of guy who'll treat you like a princess."

"Thanks. Maybe I should've found a fake relationship years ago. It's nice that there's no pressure to be anything but myself. I'm not usually this relaxed on a date." She grinned. "But since this isn't a real date, I can be totally honest."

Not a real date. Why did Jackson keep forgetting that? He smiled. "That's right. Nothing real here except the chicken salad."

"Do you want us to come help you, dear?" Grandma asked after church on Sunday.

"I'm awfully good with a paintbrush," Grandpa said. He winked. "Or is that nice young man we saw you talking to after Sunday school going to be helping?"

Violet blushed. She hadn't expected Jackson to show up at church this morning. They hadn't discussed it last night. "We're going to get the final coat of paint finished. Shadow helped me prime it earlier in the week."

Grandma smiled. "It's all coming together."

"Thanks to a lot of prayers by a lot of people." Violet hugged Grandma. "And you're sure you don't mind helping with Reagan's kids next weekend? They can be a handful." Violet loved them dearly, but each time she watched them for Reagan, it took her two days to recover.

"I'm looking forward to it. And I've got some reinforcements. Betty and Shadow are already lined up to help out." She patted Grandpa's back. "And I wouldn't be surprised if someone else showed up."

Grandpa grinned. "She can't bear to be away from me." He winked at his wife.

Violet hugged them both and hurried toward her car. She loved spending time with her grandparents. She hoped to have a bond like theirs with someone someday.

An hour later, she'd let Arnie have some backyard time and had changed into her painting clothes. She sure wouldn't win any awards today in an old T-shirt and yoga pants.

As she hurried up the sidewalk toward the bakery, she spotted Jackson sitting on a bench in front of Aunt Teak's, wearing a baseball cap and some faded jeans. "Ready to paint up a storm?" she asked, digging in her bag for the keys.

Jackson nodded. "I sure am. I'm even more ready for the kitchen to be functional so I can indulge in some more of those cupcakes."

She pushed the door open and laughed. "You'll be in luck next weekend."

"What's going on then?" He followed her inside and flipped on the light switch.

Violet dusted a speck of dirt from the counter. "Reagan is coming to help with some marketing stuff. One of the things she wants to do is take pictures of cupcakes for the brochure." She grinned. "So there'll be a variety of cupcakes to taste test."

"I like the sound of that," he said.

"Plus I really want to work on the menu. I'm getting really excited. I'm thinking I'll have some basic flavors that are always on the menu. You know—chocolate, vanilla, strawberry, maybe a red velvet." She grinned. "But then I think I might rotate other flavors out on a weekly basis."

"Keep the menu fresh, so people will want to stop in to see what's new." He grinned. "I like that. Smart business."

She blushed. "Just an idea."

"It's the kind of idea that will help make you very successful."

Violet sighed. "I hope so. The closer I get to the opening, the more nervous I get."

"I think we need to work on your self-confidence a little bit." Jackson took her by the shoulders and looked into her eyes. "You are brilliant. You're smart and funny. People are going to love to stop in here just to talk to you. Your cupcakes are amazing, and your sales are going to be off the charts."

She blinked. He really thought those things about her? "But what if—"

He put a hand over her mouth. "No buts. You need to believe in yourself and your abilities." Jackson removed his hand and smiled. "I believe in you. Your grandparents believe in you. Reagan believes in you. It's time for you to believe in yourself. Otherwise you're going to worry yourself silly trying to open this place and being too afraid of failure."

Tears filled her eyes. Was it really that obvious that she struggled with self-doubt? "Thanks for the pep talk," she whispered. "I guess I needed it."

Jackson grinned. "Anytime." He motioned toward the paint cans sitting on the floor. "Now let's get this party started." He opened a paint can and poured the creamy yellow paint into a tray. "That's going to be awfully cheery."

"I hope so." She picked up a foam paint roller. "I considered just painting it white, but decided a pop of color would be better."

"You definitely seem like the type of person who would do better surrounded by color. Plain walls just don't seem to go with your personality." He dipped a brush into the paint and climbed up on the step ladder. "I'll start cutting in, and you can roll behind me. Is that good?"

Violet nodded. "Works for me. I'm not that great at cutting in. You can always see my brush strokes." She watched him work for a long moment. "So I'm thinking about bringing my record player to use in the shop. What do you think?"

"That could be fun. Kind of a retro feel."

She laughed. "Plus then I'll have an excuse to look for records at thrift stores and yard sales. I might use some as decorations."

"Sounds like a plan." He concentrated on the corner. "And that girl we saw last night is going to work here?"

"Shadow. Yeah. Her grandmother owns the antique store next door and lives next to my grandparents."

"So she lives with them?"

Violet rolled the roller in the tray and let the excess paint drip off. "Her mom—their daughter—was killed in an accident a couple of years ago. Her dad remarried, and I think she's just had a really hard time adjusting."

Jackson let out a low whistle. "Such an awful thing for a kid that age to deal with." He stepped down from the ladder to dip his brush into the paint. "Really for any age to deal with."

"I can't imagine."

He looked at her with pain in his eyes. "I can. My dad passed away last year. It was completely unexpected. He'd always been the picture of health."

Violet put the roller down. "I'm so sorry to hear that."

Jackson nodded. "Heart attack. It's been a pretty awful year." He turned back to the wall. "And now my mom is dating again." He laughed bitterly. "I'm having a hard enough time coping with that—I can't imagine if I were still in high school."

Violet watched him work and couldn't help but feel an ache in her heart. Part of her wanted to hug him, to try and take away the pain he obviously still felt.

But it wasn't really her place. They were only together for show, not to be part of each other's lives.

So she kept quiet and turned her attention back to her painting.

Dear Mama,

This was an awesome weekend. I got to see hot air balloons and listen to Thomas recite some of his poetry. He's so cool.

Nana and Granddaddy would only let me meet up with him for an hour though. I'm tired of them treating me like a baby. I read in your journal that they didn't let you date until you were seventeen. Well, I'll be seventeen in five months. And I can't wait.

Thomas and I ran into Violet and her boyfriend at the festival. She wants me to start working regular hours at the bakery pretty soon! I helped her do some painting after school earlier in the week. I think she was surprised that I was actually good at it. I hope she'll let me put icing on the cupcakes once the bakery opens.

I got another e-mail from Daddy asking me about Thanksgiving. It seems like I don't really have much of a choice but to go.

I miss you so much, Mama. If you were still here, I wouldn't have such a big hole inside me. Thomas says I should draw on my pain to create poetry, but I don't know.

Ily,

Shadow

Chapter 17

Jackson Stratford: How does the paint job look today? And what's your favorite movie? (Text message sent September 26, 4:13 p.m.)

Violet Matthews: The paint job is fantastic. And I'm a John Hughes fan, so either The Breakfast Club or Sixteen Candles. Or Ferris Bueller's Day Off. You? (Text message sent September 26, 4:19 p.m.)

Jackson Stratford: You get more impressive by the day. Nice choices. I've got to go with Indiana Jones though. Either Raiders of the Lost Ark or Temple of Doom. Can't go wrong there. (Text message sent September 26, 5:03 p.m.)

Reagan paced the floor Wednesday night. They'd just gotten home from church and put the kids in bed. She'd hoped she and Chad would finally have the chance to sit and talk, but he was flipping through the channels.

Ever since he'd dropped the bomb about his trip to Miami, she'd been trying to figure out the best way to broach the subject. Except that she wasn't totally sure she wanted to know who all from his office would be attending the conference.

"So are you still on for Miami?" she asked, sitting down beside him on the couch.

He glanced up. "Yeah. I'll be leaving Friday afternoon and be back on Monday."

"What kind of thing is it, anyway?" She brushed some dirt from her pants. No telling where that had come from.

"It's a continuing education thing put on by SHRM. Nothing exciting, believe me." He grinned.

"Are you the only one that has to go?"

Chad furrowed his brow. "No. There are six or seven of us I think. And even that won't make it more exciting. In fact, I'm on a different flight than they are because I have a meeting Friday morning that couldn't be moved."

That set her mind at ease, at least to a certain extent. At least it wouldn't just be him and Reese. "How's your new assistant working out?"

"Reese? She's great. You should come by and meet her sometime. She reminds me a lot of you when you were that age."

Reagan froze. "When I was that age? What, like I'm some old lady now?"

Chad chuckled. "Of course not." He reached over and squeezed her knee. "But when you were in your midtwenties you were all about your career. She's like that."

His explanation didn't make her feel any better. "So is Reese going on this trip?"

"Huh?" He pulled his gaze away from the TV to glance at her. "Oh. Yeah. She's going."

No remorse. "Don't you think it's a little inappropriate for you to be heading to Miami with your single assistant?"

Chad clicked off the TV and glared at her. "What are you getting at? That I'm lying about having to be there and am instead planning some rendezvous?" He shook his head. "When did you get so paranoid?"

She should've kept her mouth shut. "I don't know. When you started working around the clock. When I found myself stuck in the house all the time taking care of your children while your life just goes on like normal. When you don't even notice anything about me anymore." She ticked them off on her hand. "Take your pick."

Chad stood up. "You're being ridiculous. I love you. I adore the kids. I'm the same guy I've always been. And the fact that you'd even insinuate that there might be something inappropriate going on between me and Reese is a huge insult." He tossed the remote on the coffee table. "I thought you knew me better than that." He jerked his chin toward their bedroom. "I'm going to bed."

Without another word, he walked out of the room.

Was it true? Was he the same guy he'd always been? And if so, did that mean she was the one who'd changed?

Reagan curled up on the couch and closed her eyes. *Lord, I need help. In a major way.*

Thursday afternoon the door to the bake shop burst open, and Violet looked up from the supply list she was working on. "Hi, Shadow. Thanks for coming by today."

The teenager nodded. "No prob." She put her backpack on the floor next to the counter and glanced at the walls. "It looks really pretty now. I love the yellow. It makes everything much brighter."

"Thanks. I'm really happy with the way it turned out." Violet admired the wall. "I especially like the way the yellow looks against that white crown molding."

Shadow nodded. "So what do you need me to do today?"

Violet took a good look at Shadow. "Those are cute glasses." She hadn't been wearing them last week when they primed the walls.

"Thanks. They're just reading ones."

After running into Shadow and a boy named Thomas the other night at the Legends Balloon Rally, Violet had a pretty good idea of what was going on. "And that sweater vest is adorable. Different from your normal style." But very similar to the way Thomas had been dressed on Saturday.

Shadow shrugged. "I like plaid."

"Argyle. It's Argyle."

"Whatever."

Violet fought back a grin. She didn't want to push the girl away. "I was thinking you could help me take inventory this afternoon. I had a delivery earlier today of some of the things we'll need during the next few weeks." She handed Shadow a list. "The delivery guy put the boxes in the storeroom. Just check to make sure everything on this list is there and in the quantity this paper says."

"Sure." Shadow looked at the list. "Have you decided when to open?"

Violet smiled. "My friend Reagan is coming to town this weekend, and she'll be starting on the logo and some marketing materials. Once she's got some of that figured out, we'll have a better idea. I'm hoping for Halloween though."

Shadow gave her a tiny grin. "Really?"

"Wouldn't that be kind of fun? We could wear costumes and everything. Plus we might be able to come up with some neat Halloween-themed cupcakes."

Shadow bit her lip. "Um. I'm pretty good at drawing stuff. Maybe I could help with some of the decorations."

Violet nodded. "Of course." As far as she was concerned, Shadow even showing interest in the bakery was progress. The first few times she'd been around the girl, she'd barely acknowledged anyone or anything. But Mrs. Kemp had mentioned that she thought Shadow was really excited about the bakery opening and about working there.

"I'll be out here if you need me," Violet called as Shadow went into the storeroom.

Her phone buzzed against the counter, and she glanced at the caller ID. "There's my favorite graphic designer. Are you ready for a weekend of chaos?"

Reagan laughed. "Have you forgotten who you're talking to? My *life* is chaos. Not just my weekends."

"True. Any idea when you'll be arriving?"

"Tomorrow afternoon. I'll pick Izzy up from school, and then we'll be on our way."

Violet couldn't wait. "We'll have so much fun. And by the way, Grandma, Mrs. Kemp, and Shadow are on board for a little Saturday afternoon babysitting. I think Grandpa might even pitch in as long as he can watch the Razorback game." Grandpa had called her yesterday to make sure she had ESPN. She hadn't pressed, but she figured he was trying to arrange his Saturday around his favorite team.

"You're kidding. They don't have to do that."

"Oh, but they do." Violet grinned. "Because not only will we be working on the design of the store logo, but I've booked us two hours at one of the spas."

"Time at a spa? You're going to make me cry."

Violet laughed. "You deserve it. A massage and a facial are probably just what you need. And I even booked us for the bath package."

"You did?" Reagan laughed. "What is it they used to call it? Taking to the waters?"

"That's right. The waters have healed and rejuvenated people since Hot Springs was discovered," Violet said. "So why shouldn't we partake in some of that therapy?"

"I'm game, especially if it will take my mind off the fact that my husband will probably be poolside in Miami this weekend with his twenty-six-year-old assistant." Her bitterness came through the phone.

"I thought you talked to him about it."

"I did. But what's he going to say? Of course he denied it."

Violet exhaled. "Please try not to worry. Just come to Hot

Springs and relax. Maybe just having a bit of a break will give you fresh perspective."

"Maybe." Reagan obviously wasn't convinced. "Or maybe I should just face the facts. Something is off in my relationship with Chad. Something big. And I can't figure out what that is."

Violet had no advice for her friend. She'd always felt that if your instincts told you something was wrong—it usually was. So where did that leave Reagan and Chad? "I'll be praying."

"That's all you can do."

Violet hung up and went back to her list, but Reagan's words kept playing in her head. *That's all you can do.* How many times did Violet have to learn that lesson? She'd often been guilty of trying to fix things herself. She'd make lists and anticipate problems and worry about her decisions. Prayer was her last resort. Her fallback plan. What she did when she couldn't do anything else.

She couldn't help but wonder how things might be different if prayer came first. Before she stepped in to offer advice or to try to solve things. Maybe she'd gotten it backward all her life.

Lord, from now on, I'll go to You first. And not just when there's a crisis or a problem.

Dear Mama,

You're not going to believe it. Nana is letting me go to the school dance this weekend. She wasn't super happy about it, but I think Granddaddy talked her into it.

I'm so excited that I finally get to go and do something.

I made a friend at school named Rachel, and we're going to get ready together. I think her mom is going to take us for manicures. I wish you were here to take us instead.

I'm a little bummed that Thomas didn't ask me to go with him, but he told me he thinks school functions are stupid. He says he isn't even going to walk at graduation. I think that's kind of weird, but I didn't tell him that.

I love you,
Shadow

Chapter 18

Violet Matthews: THE TASTE TESTING IS TONIGHT AT
THE SHOP. SHOULD I SAVE YOU A CUPCAKE? AND TELL ME
SOMETHING ABOUT YOURSELF THAT WOULD SURPRISE ME. . . .
(Text message sent September 29, 10:02 a.m.)

Jackson Stratford: I'LL BE THERE WITH BELLS ON. 7ISH?
AND HOW ABOUT THIS: I TRAVEL TO PANAMA EACH
SUMMER WITH A GROUP FROM CHURCH AND VOLUNTEER
AT AN ORPHANAGE. YOU? (Text message sent September
29, 10:22 a.m.)

Violet Matthews: 7 IS FINE AND THAT IS A SURPRISE. I NEVER
WOULD'VE PEGGED YOU FOR A MISSIONARY. HERE'S MINE:
ONCE WHEN I LIVED IN DC, I HAD DINNER AT THE WHITE
HOUSE. (Text message sent September 29, 10:29 a.m.)

Jackson tossed his phone on his coffee table. This arrangement
with Violet was starting to get dicey. More and more, he found

himself looking forward to her texts or to checking off another date from their list. And it had nothing to do with being ready for their date balance to be zero.

And Kathleen had been after him to bring his new girlfriend to Memphis for the weekend, something he wasn't totally sure he could do. He and his sister had always shared everything. Even through some of the darkest days of his life, she'd known what was going on with him.

The idea of parading a fake relationship in front of Kathleen and her family didn't sit well with him. The deal had started out with the best of intentions, but Jackson was starting to wonder if it was worth it.

The doorbell rang and put a welcome end to his worrying. He wasn't expecting company though, especially on a Saturday morning. He peeked out the window.

His mother stood on the porch, a big smile on her face.

He swung open the door. "Hey, Mom. I didn't expect to see you today."

"Sorry for stopping by without notice." She stepped over the threshold and into the living room. "But I was nearby and wanted to speak to you."

"Come on in," he said, motioning toward the couch.

Donna Stratford sat down on the leather couch and crossed her ankles. "I'm just going to cut right to the chase."

"Of course." Mom always had been direct, a quality Jackson had inherited. When Kathleen and Jackson had gotten in trouble as kids, they'd always joked that Dad was the good cop and Mom was the bad cop. They'd been a great team.

"Your sister tells me you aren't happy that I'm seeing Roger." She leveled her blue eyes on him. "If you have a problem with things, now is the time to speak."

Jackson exhaled loudly. He sure didn't want to get into this with his mother. For one thing, he completely realized how childish it seemed for him to be upset that Mom was moving on. "I'm just worried, that's all." He shrugged. "What do we really know about this guy anyway? Nothing."

Mom smiled. "Actually I know quite a bit about him. Your dad and I were friends with Roger and his wife, Melinda."

It was even worse than he thought. "Don't tell me he left his wife."

"For me?" Mom laughed and shook her head. "Don't be silly, dear." She frowned. "Actually, Melinda passed away a couple of years ago. Cancer."

Jackson sighed. "I'm sorry for his loss. . .but still."

"What do you want me to do?"

"I don't know. Isn't there a nice book club you can join? Or a ladies bowling team?"

Mom shut her eyes and shook her head. "Jackson, you know I love you. And I'm sorry that my dinners with Roger upset you so much. But he understands how it feels to lose a spouse. He's been a great support for me, and frankly, it's nice to have someone to go out and do things with sometimes." She shrugged. "Plus he makes me laugh. And there was a time I didn't know if I'd ever laugh again."

Now he felt terrible. "I'm not trying to cause problems. I just feel like it's a little soon—that's all."

Mom frowned. "Your dad's been gone for more than a year. And

I spent so much of that time too upset to even get out of bed. But Roger has given me a reason to get up and to leave the house. I think that's what your dad would've wanted."

Jackson bristled. There it was again. That phrase he loathed. "Or telling yourself that's what Dad would've wanted is a way to ease your conscience."

"That was uncalled for. You might be a grown man, but I'm your mother and I deserve your respect." Mom stood. "Your sister is happy for me. I suggest you find a way to be on board with this."

Jackson stood up and rubbed his jaw. "I'm sorry. I don't mean to seem unsupportive. I'm just worried." He shrugged. "I don't like change."

Mom smiled. "I know, dear. It isn't easy for any of us. But really try to keep an open mind where Roger is concerned." She walked to the door and turned to face him. "If things go well, he'll probably be at our family Thanksgiving. And I'll expect you to make him feel welcome."

His earlier doubts about the contract he and Violet had flew out the window. Her being there might be the only thing that would get him through. "I'm probably bringing someone, too." He grinned at Mom's expression. He'd never brought a girl home to meet his family. "So I'll expect you to make her feel welcome, too."

Mom gave him a hug. "Deal." She kissed him on the cheek and hurried toward her car.

Reagan leaned her head against the passenger seat and tilted her face toward the sun. "Thanks for driving," she said as Violet got behind the wheel. "I just felt better leaving the van and car seats behind in case there is an emergency."

"No problem. We'll go to the spa, and then I'll show you the space." Reagan headed toward town. "Was the guest room okay?"

Reagan laughed. "It was more than okay. You're the one I should worry about. Sorry that Izzy insisted on sleeping with you. Did she kick you a lot?"

"Only a few times." Violet grinned. "No more than Arnie usually does."

"Oh, that dog." Reagan shook her head. "He is just the sweetest. Have you noticed how he wants to be wherever the babies are? He slept in the doorway of our room last night."

"I wondered where he went. Sometimes he stays in the living room now because it's too much trouble to get up and move to the bedroom."

"He actually makes me think a dog wouldn't be a bad addition to our family," Reagan said. "But not for a couple of years so Izzy and Ava Grace are old enough to help take care of it."

Violet slowed down as she reached Central Avenue. "I'm considering getting a puppy. I know Arnie won't be around forever. The last time we were at the vet, I found out his kidneys aren't doing too well." She sighed. "I'm thinking maybe a puppy will help lessen the blow when his time comes."

Reagan reached over and patted her arm. Arnie had been part of Violet's life since they were right out of college. "I'm sorry. And I think a puppy would be a great idea, if you're sure you have time for the training that goes along with that. Opening a business is going to keep you pretty busy though."

Violet pulled into an empty space near Bathhouse Row. "I know. I just worry about how empty my house will be without a dog in it."

There were days Reagan fantasized about her house being totally empty and quiet. A whole day of quiet sounded heavenly. But it would get old and lonely soon. "Maybe Arnie will pull through the kidney thing and have a lot more great years."

"That would be nice, but he's fifteen. I'm not living under the delusion that he's going to be here forever." She reached into the backseat and grabbed her bag. "You ready for this? No stress. No worries."

Reagan slung her bag over her shoulder and followed Violet to the crosswalk. "Where are we headed?"

"Quapaw Baths and Spa. I haven't been inside since they renovated, but Grandma said it's nice." The bathhouse was built in the 1920s and derived its name from the tribe of Indians that lived in the area. "Did you know there's a cave in the basement near the spring that gives the spa its water? Legend has it that the cave and spring were discovered by the Quapaw Indians when they inhabited this area."

"Cool." Reagan grinned. Violet's love of the past never ceased to amaze her. For as long as they'd been friends, Violet had been providing her with interesting historical tidbits or encouraging her to hold on to the past.

Twenty minutes later they were in full spa mode, complete with robes and slippers. "This is exactly what I needed," Reagan said. "These last months have been so stressful. Just getting away from the house is kind of nice."

"I'm sorry I haven't come over to keep the kids and let you have some time off."

Reagan shook her head. "Don't be silly. It isn't your place."

"Have you told Chad how you feel? That you need some help?"

She couldn't imagine having that conversation with Chad. "He has to know I'm overwhelmed. Everyone with eyes knows I'm overwhelmed." She flipped through a *People* magazine. "Besides. It makes me feel like a terrible mother. I mean, I should be able to manage four kids with no problem, right?"

Violet raised her hands in surrender. "You're asking the wrong person. I don't think I could do it, especially once the twins came along. I'd definitely need some help." She closed the magazine she'd been reading and tossed it on the chair next to her. "And I really think you need to figure out a solution."

"This woman at my gym thinks I should plan a romantic date night with Chad. She says we need some time alone together in a major way."

"I might not be married, but that sounds right to me. You guys used to have date nights, didn't you?"

Reagan nodded. "It was before the twins came along. My mom was really good about offering to keep Izzy and Ava Grace."

"So find someone else. Figure it out. Because I don't think you can go on like this for much longer. Even if you have to get two sitters—maybe someone from church can watch Izzy and Ava Grace and Chad's mom can watch the twins. But you need some help."

Reagan had been thinking the same thing lately. "Chad's mom called earlier in the week and offered to let the kids stay the night with them. I declined the offer since I hated to impose like that."

"She offered. Do it. Impose." Violet grinned. "You and Chad have some stuff to work out. Who knows? Maybe a romantic date night is just what y'all need."

True. She could make a reservation at one of their favorite places. It would be so nice to take some time to reconnect without worrying about the kids. "As soon as he gets back from Miami. . . I'll run it by him."

Violet grinned. "Perfect."

A woman in a white coat walked into the waiting area. "Ladies, if you'll follow me, I'll take you downstairs to the baths." She led them down a hallway and to a staircase. "Watch your step. Once you're finished with the baths, you'll come back upstairs for the massage and facials. The warm water will loosen your muscles," she explained.

They walked past the public baths where bathing-suit clad people lounged in the steamy water. "Look at that," she whispered to Violet. "I've read about the public baths, but didn't realize it would look like a big hot tub."

Violet giggled. "That's why I booked us each a private bath. It will be like we each have a personal hot tub."

It sounded divine.

Another spa worker in a white coat met them at the doorway to the private baths. She held two cups of ice water. "Here you go." She handed one to each of them and motioned for them to follow her into the room.

"Your water is running now," she said, consulting her clip board. "Reagan?"

Reagan stepped forward. "That's me."

"Right this way." She led Reagan into a tiny room with an antique-looking tub in the corner. "I'll start your bubbles," she said. She bent down and flipped a switch, and the water started bubbling. "Is this your first time in the Spa City?"

Reagan shook her head. "I've been here before, but never to the thermal baths."

"Well you're in for a treat. The thermal waters have been used therapeutically for thousands of years. The water is high in silica, calcium, magnesium, free carbon dioxide, bicarbonate, and sulfate." She smiled. "Try to say that fast."

Reagan laughed. "I'm sure I'll enjoy the experience."

"The timer will start when I close the door. You'll hear me knock when it's time to get out." She motioned toward a tray next to the tub. "There's an extra ice water for you to drink. It's recommended that you hydrate your insides as well."

"Okay, thanks."

"There's a bell on the tray—ring it if you need anything and I'll come in." She poured a cup full of salts into the tub. "Green tea to help with relaxation," she explained. "Enjoy." She closed the door behind her.

Reagan sank into the bath. This was heavenly. She could barely remember the last time she was alone without someone banging on the door or having to keep her ears open for the baby monitor. She leaned her head back against the rolled towel and closed her eyes. There was even a bell to ring in case she needed something. Not that she'd ring it, but the thought made her smile.

Tomorrow she'd corral her children back into the van and they'd head back to their home and their full week. Monday, she'd drop Izzy off at school and take Ava Grace to gymnastics and call the pediatrician to schedule Scarlett and Simon for their yearly check up. She'd pick Chad up from the airport and send her mother the new pictures she'd just gotten from the photographer.

For now though, all that could wait.

Now she could just be Reagan, woman at the spa with no responsibilities.

Bliss.

Chapter 19

Reagan McClure: Just left the spa. Hope Miami is
nice. Your mom offered to keep the kids next Friday
so we could have a date. Does that work with your
schedule? (Text message sent September 29, 3:02 p.m.)

Chad McClure: Glad you're having fun. Miami is
rainy. Next Friday sounds great. Love you, babe. See
you soon. (Text message sent September 29, 3:15 p.m.)

Violet pulled a pan of cupcakes from the oven. "Here's the first batch from the bakery kitchen."

"The first of many," Reagan said. "And they smell amazing."

"Thanks. While I wait on them to cool, let me show you what I have in mind for the rest of the shop." Violet motioned for Reagan to follow her to the counter that held the cash register.

"Can I just say that I think this is a terrific setup? You have so much space behind the counter, and having a station to ice cupcakes and an oven and everything right there. . .I think people will love it," Reagan said.

Violet nodded. "I was afraid it would be weird at first because customers will literally be able to see the whole process. But I think it will go really well. In the afternoons, Shadow will work the register while I do any baking or icing. But mostly I'm going to try and get several batches baked each morning before I open."

"What time?"

Violet sighed. "I'm thinking we won't open until ten. And then I'll probably stay open until seven. It might all depend on the season."

"Good plan," Reagan agreed.

"I'll be closed on Sunday and Monday." She glanced over at Reagan. "Do you think that's a bad business decision?" Being closed on Sunday was very important to Violet. She didn't like the idea of having to miss church for work, and she didn't want to have employees that had to make that kind of sacrifice either. The sales she might make just weren't worth it.

Reagan shook her head. "It sounds like a smart idea to me. I totally get where you're coming from. I'm sure there are others who might disagree, but I think it is probably the best choice for you. Besides, I'll bet Saturday will be one of your busy days and you'll be glad you have Sunday and Monday to recover."

Violet nodded. "That's what I'm guessing. I visited one of my favorite cupcake shops in Little Rock a couple of weeks ago and asked them some questions. Their hours are nine until six, which I guess could be a possibility for me in the winter. And they told me Saturday is so busy sometimes they actually sell out." Violet couldn't imagine her cupcakes selling out, but it was a nice dream.

"Have you settled on a name yet?"

Violet groaned and shook her head. She'd been brainstorming names for two weeks and was finding it one of the toughest decisions of her life. "I need something simple. Something that looks good on the sign out front. Something that's fun." She shook her head. "I'm having a terrible time deciding."

"What are your top choices?"

"Icing on the Cake." Violet raised her eyebrows in question.

Reagan shook her head. "Too cutsey. What else?"

"Hot Springs Cupcakes."

"Too boring. Next?" Reagan grinned.

"Cupcakes by Violet."

Reagan made a face. "Too cliché."

"Central Avenue Cupcakes."

Reagan's eyes lit up. "Definitely that one. Central Avenue Cupcakes. That's perfect! It tells the location—and everyone who visits Hot Springs visits Central Avenue. It's simple and catchy." She nodded. "And I think we can definitely create a great logo."

"I hope so." Violet ran her hand along the counter. "Central Avenue Cupcakes. I like it. Thanks for helping me figure it out." She'd been leaning toward that one all week but kept second-guessing herself. It was nice to have her pick reinforced by Reagan.

"You're welcome. Remember that I do have a little bit of experience with that kind of thing," Reagan said.

Violet motioned for Reagan to follow her around the counter and into the large open space right inside the entry door. "I'll leave space for a line to form here." She pointed. "And then I'll get four or five tables to fill the rest of the space. How do you think that will look?"

"Amazing. What kind of tables?"

"Probably mix and match. I found a couple of options at a thrift store last week. I'm going to go back tomorrow and see if they still have them." She knew some people would think it was weird to have tables and chairs that didn't exactly match one another. But she'd been to shops with décor like that and thought the effect was quaint.

"What color?"

Violet grinned. "You know me and my funky style. I'm going to get Shadow to help me paint them. We'll probably do the tables white and then paint the chairs in a variety of fun colors. I may even see about putting some kind of different design on each table." Shadow had mentioned being a good artist, and next week Violet would put that to the test.

"That will look amazing next to the yellow wall." Reagan looked around. "This place will definitely be 'you', if you know what I mean."

Violet laughed. "I do. I'm planning to bring my record player up here and put it in the corner." She pointed to a little nook. "And I have my great-grandmother's quilt squares I'm thinking of framing and putting on the wall." The quilt squares would give it a personal touch, plus knowing she had a family heirloom in her store would make her happy.

Reagan clapped her hands. "This is really going to be an awesome place. I'm so happy for you."

"Thanks. I'm still a little shell-shocked that I'm actually doing it. And I'm so scared of the place tanking." Her mother's words about her impending financial ruin rang in her head every night when she went to bed.

"You didn't buy the building, right?"

Violet nodded. There'd been no way she would've bought the place without a trial run as a renter. What if the business failed and she was stuck with payments on a building? "Just renting for now."

"So if something crazy happens and the place isn't all it's cracked up to be, you'll sell your equipment and move on. But I'm putting my money on you and the shop being a smashing success." Reagan leaned against the counter. "I'm the last person who should be saying this because I'm so guilty of it, but stop worrying. Pray about it and do your best on the shop, but don't worry so much."

Violet smiled. She thought about Jackson and his little pep talk the other day. So many people believed in her. So why did she have such a hard time believing in herself?

Jackson paused on the sidewalk outside of the bake shop. He should've asked more questions about who would be in attendance tonight. The only thing he knew for sure was that Violet had texted to make sure it would count toward their date number.

"Jackson?" a voice called from behind him.

He turned around to see a blond woman striding toward him. "Reagan. Long time no see."

"It's been a long time," Reagan agreed. "I came to see Violet graduate from college—you know, after she had to attend the summer semester. Seems like you graduated that day, too."

He might be making some progress in getting back in Violet's good graces, but clearly Reagan would take more time. "I did. You look well."

She raised an eyebrow. "We went to the spa today. It's been a nice day." She gestured toward the bake shop. "Have you seen the place yet?"

"I helped paint the inside."

The surprise on her face was unmistakable. "I see. I didn't realize you and Violet were such friends."

Jackson winced. So Violet wasn't telling her closest friend about their "relationship" yet? That seemed strange. And kind of hurtful. "We see each other now and then."

Reagan nodded. "She mentioned a while back that you'd let her stay at your lake house, but I didn't know that meant the two of you were actually friends."

"Well we are. She's a great girl."

Reagan leveled her blue eyes on his. "She is. And your antics in college drove her crazy. To tell you the truth, I'm surprised she gives you the time of day."

Had he really been that bad? Sure, he'd messed up their presentation. And caused her boyfriend to dump her. "I don't remember it being that bad."

"Jackson, you told all the guys in your dorm that she put the moves on you. And you printed up a T-shirt with a very unflattering picture of her on it. Do you remember that?"

He'd forgotten. At the time he'd thought it was one of his best, most memorable pranks. "I wore it under my team jersey and told her if she didn't come to all of my intramural basketball games I'd take my jersey off so everyone would see the picture."

Reagan nodded. "And I'm pretty sure you're the one who managed to put her name and phone number with a 'call me, I'm desperate' message on the big screen in the auditorium that showed up during chapel announcements."

Their school had a daily chapel service, which meant Violet had been effectively humiliated in front of the entire student body. He'd forgotten about that one as well. "I guess I gave her a pretty hard time. Honestly, I'd sort of blocked that stuff out of my mind."

"Well I can guarantee you she hasn't. Violet has always felt like an outcast. She's lived her life marching to the beat of her own drum. Because of that, she's never had the best self-confidence. And the one thing that she's always hated is to be the center of attention."

Jackson could admit that he'd been horrible to her. He'd been horrible to a lot of people. But Reagan would never understand his frame of mind at the time, and she obviously didn't think people could change. "I'm trying to make up for all of that now."

They stared at each other for a long moment.

"Just don't hurt her again," Reagan said finally.

Jackson nodded. "Of course." He opened the bake shop door and held it open for Reagan. If she had that much animosity toward him, it was no wonder Violet was counting down the days until their deal was over. Those pranks hadn't seemed so major to him at the time, but looking back now, maybe he had more to make up for than he'd first thought.

"Thanks," Reagan said softly.

He followed her inside the shop and was greeted by the

wonderful aroma of freshly baked cupcakes. He spotted Violet arranging cakes on a platter. "Those look wonderful and smell even better."

She looked up and grinned. "Thanks. Today has been amazing. We got a ton of work done on the marketing stuff." She threw her hand up like a spokesmodel. "Welcome to Central Avenue Cupcakes."

"Nice name. I like it a lot."

She beamed. "Reagan helped me decide which one would be best. And I think she has some really cool ideas for the logo. Hopefully by this time next week, the signage will be ordered for the front of the store and I'll have business cards and flyers." She pointed to the arrangement of cupcakes. "Reagan took a ton of pictures today that I think are going to look awesome on a website. There's just so much to think about."

"Just take a breath. You don't have to have absolutely everything done for the opening. Think of it as a soft opening—just for locals. Then you have the rest of the fall and winter to really beef up your marketing in time for the spring and summer tourist season."

Violet nodded. "You're probably right. I just keep thinking of things I need to do. It's easy to get overwhelmed."

"In my experience, the thing you should concentrate on first is making the best cupcakes possible. Get the inside of the store finished. Then after you've opened and people have sampled the cupcakes and soaked up the atmosphere here, they'll tell their friends. I predict you'll do a lot of word-of-mouth business."

She frowned. "I really hope so."

"Do I still detect some worry?" he asked.

Violet shrugged. "Maybe a little. There's definitely a fear of the unknown."

"But that's what makes it exciting, right? The fact that life is full of surprises."

"Listen to you being all philosophical. What's gotten into you?"

He chuckled. "I've always been philosophical. Maybe you never noticed it till now."

"Whatever. Sometimes I think you're just trying to butter me up."

"Nah, just trying to be the best fake boyfriend I can be," he whispered in her ear. It was the closest he'd ever been to her, and he could smell the sweet scent of her shampoo.

She laughed. "I guess." She motioned to where Reagan stood, talking to an older lady. "That's Mrs. Kemp. She owns the shop next door. And did you get to speak to Reagan?"

"She's not exactly a fan of mine."

Violet shrugged. "Sorry. She has a really good memory, so it's kind of hard for her to accept you and me as anything other than enemies." She grinned mischievously. "I mean, we've always been really good at being enemies. So I can see how she'd be confused."

"I guess. Maybe you should put in a good word for me though." He grinned.

"Maybe I will." Violet returned his grin. "Maybe I will."

Dear Mama,

Thomas broke up with me. It's all Rachel's stupid fault. She put a picture on Facebook of the two of us getting ready for the dance. Thomas told me he couldn't possibly go out with someone who was such a conformist.

I don't think me wanting to go to a school function with my friends makes me a conformist, do you? Either way, I'm not speaking to Rachel right now. I told her not to post it because I didn't want him to see.

She said it was silly of me to be that way and that Thomas is the one who is stupid. Actually she called him pretentious.

Oh well. Next week is the week I start working normal hours at the bake shop. It has a name now—Central Avenue Cupcakes. I think that's a pretty good name. Violet told me at church yesterday that my job this week is going to be helping her paint the tables and chairs! I told her I was fine doing whatever, but to tell you the truth, I'm pretty excited about painting.

I kind of like hanging out with her, too. She's not like Stephanie. She doesn't try to force me to be her buddy or whatever. She just treats me like a normal person.

I miss you,
Shadow

Chapter 20

Violet Matthews: THANKS FOR YOUR HELP! THE LOGO IS AWESOME. ARE YOU OKAY? (Text message sent October 3, 10:22 a.m.)

Reagan McClure: I'M SO GLAD YOU LIKE IT! I'M AMAZINGLY PRODUCTIVE DURING NAP TIME AS LONG AS I IGNORE MY DIRTY LAUNDRY AND DISHES. CHAD'S MOM IS COMING TO GET THE KIDS FRIDAY MORNING. WE'LL SEE HOW THIS GOES. . . . (Text message sent October 3, 10:30 a.m.)

Violet unloaded the last of the chairs from Grandpa's truck. It was a good thing he still had the old thing, otherwise she'd have made fifteen trips from the thrift store.

She dusted off her jeans and looked around her garage. She and Shadow had a lot of painting ahead of them.

"Is that the last one?" Shadow asked.

Violet nodded. "Yes. Now the real work begins." She pointed to a table and four chairs in the corner. "Those are ready to paint.

They've been sanded and primed. Do you want to give it a try while I start sanding the rest?"

Shadow beamed. "Yes, yes, yes."

Violet grinned. "It's nice to see you so enthusiastic about the project." She was a little surprised at the teenager's attitude. When Mrs. Kemp had first mentioned her hiring Shadow, she'd been a little hesitant. The first couple of times she'd been around Shadow, the teenager had been so sullen and sarcastic. It seemed to be lessening now. "And that's a cute outfit. Are those . . .cowboy boots?"

Shadow held out a foot encased in a red cowboy boot. "They are. Aren't they darling?"

Between the boots, dark jeans, and flannel shirt, Shadow looked like she'd just stepped out of an ad for a dude ranch. "The braid is cute, too. You look like you belong on the show *Hee Haw*."

Shadow wrinkled her nose. "What's that? I've never heard of it."

Violet groaned. She hadn't felt too old until she started spending regular time with a sixteen-year-old. "It's a TV show that was based in Nashville. I used to watch it with my grandparents."

"Oh." Shadow knelt down to look at the variety of paints. "These colors are awesome. Are we really painting the chairs different colors?"

Violet nodded. "We are. I have spray paint for the chairs."

Shadow made a face. "Are you sure that will work?"

"I saw it on HGTV. It worked for them, it'll work for us." At least she hoped so. "Before you get started, do you want to change clothes? I have some old T-shirts and sweatpants. I'd hate for you to get your clothes messed up."

Shadow shrugged. "I guess so."

Violet led her into the house. "Hang on a second and I'll go grab some clothes for you."

"Cute dog." Shadow sat down next to Arnie on the couch.

"Thanks. He's fifteen and almost totally deaf."

"Wow. He's almost as old as I am."

Violet nodded. That really put Arnie's age into perspective. "I've had him for a long time. But he's not doing too well right now."

Shadow leaned her face close to Arnie and talked to him softly. "Sweet, sweet dog. I have a dog in Texas, and I miss him very much." The sadness in her voice was evident.

Violet hurried to grab the clothes then went back to the living room. "These should do fine." She tossed them to Shadow. "You won't have to worry about getting them messed up. If they get paint on them, it might improve their looks." She grinned and pointed to a door in the hallway. "There's the bathroom."

Shadow gave Arnie one last pat and went to change clothes.

Violet thought about how judgmental she'd been when she first saw Shadow in her Goth attire. She'd never imagined all the trials the girl had faced. Her mother's death, her dad remarrying and having another child, leaving her pet behind to come live with her grandparents. . .it was no wonder she seemed so lost.

Lord, give me the wisdom to know how to help Shadow. Open her heart to letting me be her friend and mentor, and help me to guide her down a path that will lead her closer to You.

Jackson slid into the booth at Chili's and grinned. "Sorry I'm late. Traffic was terrible."

Jeff shrugged. "Don't worry about it." He motioned toward the appetizer platter. "More for us."

"Oh, you two. Stop with the small talk. Tell us about the girl." Lauren banged her hand on the table like she was calling a meeting to order. "I'd kind of hoped she'd be with you tonight."

Jackson smiled. "Patience doesn't mean anything to you, does it?"

Lauren scowled.

"Okay, okay. I didn't ask her to meet us because she's really busy right now getting ready for the grand opening of her bakery."

"Fine. Just as long as she is in fact a real person and we will get to meet her soon." Lauren popped the rest of her mozzarella stick into her mouth.

For a moment Jackson wished he could come clean to them about the arrangement he and Violet had. He'd love to hear their advice. Ever since his run-in with Reagan last weekend, he'd felt remorseful for the way he'd treated Violet all those years ago. "You will definitely get to meet her, and I promise she is one-hundred-percent real." Their relationship, on the other hand, was not.

"Fair enough."

Once they'd placed their orders, Jeff nudged Lauren. "Can we tell him now? Please?"

"Tell me what?"

Lauren smiled broadly. "We're pregnant. You're going to be a faux uncle again."

"Congratulations! That's very exciting news. I didn't realize y'all were going for number three."

Jeff beamed. "With Bennett in school now and Levi starting

next year, we figured it was the right time."

"I'm hoping for a girl to even out some of the testosterone in my household." Lauren grinned. "Maybe a little less rough and tumble would be nice."

"Levi has his arm in a cast right now because Bennett convinced him to try jumping from the top bunk." Jeff shook his head. "It's always something."

"We're on a first-name basis with the nurse at the walk-in clinic." Lauren laughed.

Jackson was happy for his friends. Lauren and Jeff were great parents. They seemed to have found just the right balance between too worried and too laid back.

"So. . .not to pry, but do you think this girl could be 'the one'?" Lauren made quote marks in the air with her fingers. "Or is she just a way to pass the time?"

Jackson took a sip of sweet tea. "Violet has a lot of wonderful qualities. She's smart and funny and very pretty." He grinned. "And she's a good person. She lives her life striving to do God's will." He shrugged. "But I don't really know where things will go with us." Actually, he was pretty certain they'd lead to a breakup the third week of January, but he didn't dare mention it.

"Sounds like a keeper to me," Lauren said. "And it's about time. You haven't had the easiest road."

Jeff sent his wife a dirty look.

"What?" she asked. "He hasn't. We all know how tough things have been at times."

Jackson shrugged. "I don't like to dwell on the past. You know that. By the grace of God, I got through the bad stuff and I'm here now. But everyone has had difficulties. Not just me." He'd always tried to downplay the bad parts of his life, preferring to look at the bright side.

"How's your mom?" Jeff asked, going for a swift subject change.

"Dating." Jackson couldn't help but roll his eyes. "Can you believe that? It's something you don't think you'll ever have to deal with. One of your parents having a love life."

"Yeah, Kathleen mentioned it," Lauren said. "She's good with it though. Says she's glad your mom has someone to talk to and go out and do things with." She grinned. "And for the record, I think it's great, too. I mean, if something ever happened to me, I'd want Jeff to move on." She gave Jeff a wink. "After a very lengthy grieving period, of course."

Jeff laughed. "I'll keep that in mind."

Were they right? Was Mom dating again just the natural order of things? "I've met the guy once at church, but it was only briefly. I don't usually attend where Mom does, so I haven't really been around him. But she says he'll be at our family Thanksgiving."

"Will your girlfriend be there, too?" Lauren asked.

He nodded. "She will."

Lauren shot him a cat-that-ate-the-canary grin. "I'm liking this more and more. I cannot wait to meet her and see how cute you guys are together."

"I think I may have the perfect time for us to hang out." Jeff scrolled through his phone. "The Razorbacks are playing at War Memorial in a couple of weeks. Does your girlfriend like football?" The University of Arkansas football team played most of their games at the Fayetteville campus, but one or two games each year were played at Little Rock's stadium.

Jackson had no idea if she liked it, but she'd signed a contract agreeing to attend a game. "We've actually talked about going to that game."

"Let me see what I can do. I think I can get us four tickets together. We can tailgate before the game and get to know her."

Jackson nodded. "Sounds like a plan. I'll talk to her later and make sure her schedule is clear." So far they hadn't tried to convince anyone of the nature of their relationship. He hadn't stayed at the taste testing long the other night, and from what he could tell, Reagan thought they were just friends with potential. But if they went to a Razorback game with Jeff and Lauren, their every move would be under constant scrutiny.

They'd have to come off as a convincing couple. Jackson knew he was on board—he looked forward to it. He was just afraid Violet would balk at the idea. Especially if he held her hand or hugged her. So far when he'd gotten close to her, she'd tensed up.

Was that because he repulsed her? Or was she becoming aware that he was attracted to her?

Only time would tell, but Jackson knew one thing—he was looking forward to playing the role of her dutiful boyfriend in public.

Just how much he looked forward to it surprised him.

Dear Mama,

I met the cutest boy the other day at the feed store. What a strange place to meet a boy! I went with Granddaddy to get some weed killer for his garden and there, standing next to a display of fake turkeys, was the cutest boy I've ever seen.

His name is Dale, and he had on a cowboy hat and everything. He rides horses in competitions. He asked me to go watch him ride a bull sometime, and he got my phone number.

Granddaddy embarrassed me though because he came over to meet him and asked a million questions.

Anyway, he texted me today, so I think he really likes me.

Oh—Violet and I got the tables and chairs painted for the bake shop. They are so pretty. We painted the chairs all different colors—yellow, pink, blue, orange—you name it! And then we did the tables white, but Violet let me do some free-hand painting on the top. I mostly did little swirly designs and stuff to match the chair colors. It looks so neat.

Violet thinks I should take an art class, but I don't know.

Love you,
Shadow

Chapter 21

Jackson Stratford: Two questions: Do you have plans tomorrow night and what's your favorite color? (Text message sent October 5, 9:09 a.m.)

Violet Matthews: Working at the shop I guess. Why? And purple is my favorite color. Did you really have to ask? How about you? (Text message sent October 5, 9:15 a.m.)

Jackson Stratford: How about dinner at 7? And yeah, I guess that one should've been obvious. Mine's green, although violet is a close second. (Text message sent October 5, 9:18 a.m.)

Reagan stood in the driveway and waved good-bye to the kids. There'd been a few tears from Ava Grace, but when Chad's mom had promised that she and their Paw Paw would take everyone for ice cream later, the tears had miraculously disappeared. Ava

Grace was a girl after her mom's own ice-cream-loving heart.

She glanced at her watch. It wasn't quite three yet. She'd be able to take her sweet time showering and getting ready for her date with Chad. In some ways, she was as nervous as a teenager. They'd spent so little time together during the past few months, and when they had, their conversation centered on the kids. What if they didn't have anything to say to each other anymore? What if Chad couldn't help but compare her to Reese?

Reagan pushed the thought from her mind and took the longest, steamiest shower she'd had in a very long time. It was pure joy to get to wash *and* condition her hair and even shave her legs. Motherhood trumped things like personal pampering.

She wrapped herself in the plush robe Violet had given her when Ava Grace was a baby. She'd called it a spa robe. Whatever the name, it was made from the kind of material that seemed to envelop her in a warm, fluffy cocoon.

Reagan took her time drying her hair, making sure all the kinks were straightened out. Her long blond hair was her one throwback to her pre-mommy days. Chad's mom had chided her for not getting it cut short when she had kids, claiming it would be so much easier to care for, but Reagan had resisted.

Chad had told her once that her hair was the first thing he'd noticed about her. So she'd kept it long, even though it meant more trouble.

And as her family grew, it became more of a hassle, yet she still kept it as a reminder to herself that she was still in there somewhere—the girl Chad had fallen in love with.

She painted her fingernails and toenails red and sat down on the bed for a moment. Still plenty of time left.

She couldn't resist leaning back and resting her head on the pillow just for a second. Last night she'd been up almost every hour with someone, and by the morning when it was time to get Izzy to school, she'd been exhausted.

Reagan burrowed into the soft robe and closed her eyes, thinking about the fun she and Chad would have tonight.

Just like old times.

She heard a loud noise and sat upright. The bedroom door was closed. That was weird. "Chad?" she called. "Are you home?"

The door cracked open, and Chad peeked inside. "Hello, Sleeping Beauty. It's about time you joined the land of the living." He grinned.

She stood up. Her brain felt so foggy. No wonder she didn't nap anymore. "Sorry. I'll be ready in just a sec."

Chad laughed. "Ready for what? The kids will be back soon. You were asleep when I got home last night so I cancelled our reservation and closed the bedroom door." He grinned. "I slept in the guest room so I wouldn't wake you."

Reagan sank onto the bed. "Wait. It's tomorrow? Already?" She closed her eyes. "I don't understand how this happened."

"Babe, you're exhausted. There was no way I was going to wake you up. No dinner was that important." He sat down next to her. "You look upset. Are you mad?"

"What? No." She bit her tongue. "Actually yes. I'm mad." She stood up. "I can't believe you didn't wake me up. You know how much trouble I'd gone to. I arranged for your mom to take the kids, I made a reservation." She frowned. "I even made chocolate-dipped strawberries for dessert."

"I know. I had them as a little snack while I watched *SportsCenter* last night."

He thought he was being funny. "It's me, isn't it? You didn't want to have a romantic night with me." She'd planned to fill him in on her gym membership last night. She'd expected that if they actually had some time alone together, he'd finally notice that she'd lost almost ten pounds. But he hadn't. Because he hadn't woken her up.

"Don't be silly. I was looking forward to the night, too. But you looked so cute asleep, I didn't want to wake you up."

She glared. "Don't try to make me feel better by saying I looked cute." She sighed. "You aren't attracted to me anymore." Hot tears sprang into her eyes. "Are you?"

Chad groaned. "Reagan, that's crazy. And you know it."

The doorbell rang.

"That's Mom with the kids." He stood up. "This conversation is not over." He walked out of the bedroom.

As far as she was concerned it was over. Ten years ago, there was no way he would've just let her sleep through what was supposed to be their first romantic night together in months. No kids. Just the two of them.

It was just as she'd suspected. Something was off between them. And she had no idea how to fix it.

Violet glanced around the shop. It was amazing how much she'd gotten done this week. The taste testing had sent her into full-on panic mode, and she'd felt like she was moving in fast forward all week.

Shadow had turned out to be a huge help, painting and then helping to transport the furniture.

Violet sat down in an orange chair and ran her hand across the smooth tabletop. The multicolored swirls added an extra kick. She couldn't help but smile. This place was a dream come true.

A tap at the door startled her. She glanced up to see Jackson on the other side of the glass, a grin on his face.

"I didn't mean to lock it," she said, opening the door.

He chuckled. "With you up here alone, I think I feel better knowing it was locked. Most everything on this street is closed or closing for the night." He walked past the tables. "Someone's been busy. It looks incredible."

"Thanks. I'm really happy with the way it all turned out."

He pulled back a turquoise chair and sat down. "Can I be honest?"

She nodded. "Always."

Jackson grinned. "When you first told me the plan—the yellow walls and the multicolored chairs and mismatched tables—I couldn't imagine how that would possibly look okay." He glanced around. "But you had a real vision. It looks perfect for a cupcake shop. People are going to love it."

She sat down across from him. "I hope so."

"Still a doubter, huh?" He shook his head. "What am I going to do with you?"

Violet shrugged. "Give me a guarantee."

"There are no guarantees in life. You know that. Put your trust in the Lord. Do your best." He smiled. "And pray a lot. I guess that's my best advice." His blue eyes were the same color as his sweater.

"Pretty good advice I guess." She pushed a strand of hair from her face. "Did anyone ever tell you that your eyes are nearly the same color as denim? Kind of a gray blue?"

He laughed. "Can't say that they have." He raised his eyebrows up and down. "But thanks for noticing."

She blushed. Great. Now he thought she was checking him out. "Just an observation." She stood up. "What are you in the mood for tonight?" As soon as she asked the question, she wished she could take it back. The gleeful expression on his face told her he was about to make an off-color joke.

"Well. . ." He trailed off and chuckled at her dirty look. "What?" He held up his hands in surrender. "I was just going to say pizza. I'm in the mood for pizza."

"Right." Their stupid contract with that ridiculous first kiss flashed through her mind. She knew he might spring it on her any time. Every time she thought about it, she grew uneasy. She liked surprises, but not that one. Not from him.

"Or something else if you don't want pizza." He shrugged. "I'm flexible."

"Actually, pizza is good with me. Would it be weird to just go back to my house and have it delivered? Arnie isn't doing all that great, and I've been gone a long time today." Her voice caught at the mention of Arnie, and she hoped he hadn't noticed. His stance on inside dogs still angered her.

"That sounds like fun. I'll follow you there."

She grabbed her bag and turned off the lights. Just a few more weeks and the shop would be bustling.

Hopefully.

Jackson stood on Violet's front porch and waited for her to get out of the car. It sure was dark out here. She'd been excited to find a place outside of town, but he wasn't sure if it was such a good idea. Her nearest neighbors were pretty far down the road, and there wasn't much of a light out front.

"You look lost in thought," she said as she walked toward him.

He frowned. "I was just thinking about how dark it is out here."

"Funny how that happens at nighttime," she said with a smirk.

Jackson groaned. "I'm serious. Why don't you let me put one of those motion sensor lights out here? You're awfully far from the road, and you don't even have neighbors nearby."

"Are you worrying about me?"

He shrugged. "I guess."

"I'm flattered. But I'm fine." She grinned and stuck her key in the lock. "Really. I haven't been scared once since I moved in."

He followed her into the living room, and she flipped on the light.

"Arnie boy, do you want to go outside?" she asked, bending down and shaking the dog lightly.

Arnie slowly opened his eyes then jumped up, startled at the sight of Jackson. He barked a few times in Jackson's direction.

Violet put her hand on the dog's head. "It's okay," she said. "Come on." She steered him toward the back door.

"Everything okay?" Jackson asked once she came back into the room.

She shrugged. "He's not doing that well. I need to take him to the vet to get his kidney function checked again, but I'm afraid of what I'll find out." She frowned. "I'm giving him a special kind of food and also cooking for him some."

"You cook for him? Like on the stove?"

Violet glared. "Yes, I do. I know you can't possibly understand the attachment I have to him, but rest assured that it's a big one. He's been with me for a lot of years. When people have let me down, Arnie has been by my side. Happy to see me when I come home—whether after a day at work or a trip that lasted a week. It's hard to find unconditional love anymore."

That was true, he'd give her that much. But still. . .the dog hair and dirt and messy yard seemed like a real pain. "I'm sorry. I didn't mean anything by that. My sister is the same way about their Lab. Her husband jokes sometimes that Max is the real love of her life."

Violet's mouth quirked into a smile.

Finally. "Speaking of my sister. . ." He trailed off. He'd been putting this off because he wasn't sure what her reaction would be. "She's invited us to come to her house in Memphis next weekend. I know you're busy with the shop, but if we don't go before you open, it will be almost impossible for you to find a free weekend."

"Memphis for the weekend?" She sat down on the couch. "I don't know."

Was she torn about going somewhere with him, or was it just because she was so close to the opening? Jackson wasn't sure he wanted to know the answer. "I can tell her no if you can't make it."

"Yes. I'll go." She gave him a tiny grin. "It was part of the contract after all. I know we're going to have to be around our friends and families soon, and this thing between us needs to look believable."

Jackson let out a breath he hadn't realized he was holding. "So you'll go?"

She nodded. "Count me in. I'm sure it will be a blast. I love Memphis. Grandpa can come over and let Arnie out."

"We'll leave next Saturday morning and be back Sunday afternoon." Jackson couldn't remember the last time he'd taken a woman on a road trip. And he'd never taken anyone to his sister's house.

"I'd better order the pizza." Violet stood up and grabbed her phone. "Pepperoni okay with you?"

He nodded and watched her dial the number. He knew without a doubt that Kathleen and Violet would get along wonderfully. They could probably be pretty good friends.

A sinking feeling washed over him. He couldn't risk Kathleen letting the truth about his past slip to Violet.

And that meant one thing.

He'd have to tell her himself.

Chapter 22

Violet Matthews: THE SIGN FOR THE FRONT OF THE STORE ARRIVED TODAY! I HAVE THE MOST AWESOME DESIGNER EVER! ACTUALLY, I'VE ALREADY HAD SOMEONE ASK FOR YOUR CONTACT INFORMATION. ARE YOU UP FOR ANY FREELANCE WORK? (Text message sent October 9, 1:23 p.m.)

Reagan McClure: ARE YOU SERIOUS? I'VE NEVER THOUGHT ABOUT IT, BUT I LOVED CREATING YOUR STUFF SO MUCH. HADN'T REALIZED HOW MUCH I'D MISSED IT. SO SURE! FEEL FREE TO PASS MY INFO ALONG! (Text message sent October 9, 1:35 p.m.)

Violet hung the last of the framed quilt squares in the bakery's dining area. Perfect.

"What do you think?" she asked Grandma. The older woman had stopped by the shop on her way to the grocery store.

Grandma looked at her with watery eyes. "My mother would be so proud that she's part of your store." She smiled and wiped her eyes. "I'm just glad I saved them." She held up a bag. "And even happier about this." She handed the bag to Violet.

"What's this? Grandma, you didn't have to get me anything."

Grandma shrugged. "It isn't anything I paid for."

"Grandma, are you stealing again?" Violet teased.

The older woman burst out laughing. "I guess that did sound pretty bad, huh? It's just something that I think you can use."

Violet reached into the bag and pulled out a purple and yellow apron. It was a little faded, but that added to its character. "I love it."

"It was mine. A gift from your grandpa in the early fifties." She smiled. "I always thought I'd pass it on to whichever of my granddaughters married first, but I believe you will cherish it a lot more than Amber." She smiled. "I'll buy her a brand-new apron, and she'll be thrilled."

Violet slipped it over her head and quickly tied the ribbon in the back. "What do you think?" She twirled around the shop.

"Perfection." Grandma smiled.

Violet walked over to the counter and checked her list. Things were surprisingly on target. "I'm set to open the week of Halloween," she said. "What did you think of the sign?"

"I think you're going to be very busy. It looks wonderful."

Violet handed her the mock-up of the flyer and business cards. "Here are the other things Reagan worked on. They're at the printer now."

"She's very talented. These look great." Grandma tapped the paper. "And these cupcakes look delicious even in the photo." She handed them back to Violet. "Is there anything I can do to help?"

Violet shrugged. "Just spread the word. I'll give you the grand opening flyer and some business cards, and you can help me distribute them." She sighed. "And there's the possibility I might need a little help behind the counter. I'm not at all sure what to expect." She grinned. "But I'll be looking to hire someone before it gets out of hand, so don't think I'll be calling on you all the time."

Grandma chuckled. "I'll be glad to help out however I can, even if it's just going to the grocery store for you or running other errands. But I think working behind the counter sounds fun."

"I was hoping you'd say that." Violet grinned. "And I think Shadow will be a great help."

Grandma nodded. "Betty's just thrilled that she seems to be blossoming a little bit. She's made a couple of good girlfriends at school who are in the youth group with her at church."

"She's becoming a little more talkative here, too. I think she likes the creative side of working here. Her painting is beautiful, and she told me yesterday she'd like for me to teach her how to ice the cupcakes." Violet had been thrilled that Shadow might want to learn some of the baking. When she'd hired her, she'd expected that the teenager would only be interested in packaging preorders and working the cash register.

"That's wonderful." Grandma bit her lip. "Can I ask you something?"

Violet stopped checking things off her list and nodded. "Of course."

"Now I don't mean to pry, but Betty says she met your young man the other night. And your grandpa tells me you've asked him to care for your dog this weekend." She patted Violet's arm. "Are you going somewhere with him?"

Violet felt the heat rise up her face. "We're going to Memphis to visit his sister."

"Meeting the family. . .that sounds serious."

She didn't want to mislead her grandmother. "It's complicated. Jackson and I—we haven't always gotten along. Sometimes we still don't." She shrugged. "We knew each other in college."

"Betty was quite taken with him. Said he was very polite and charming." Grandma raised an eyebrow, an ability Violet had never quite mastered. "And I just wondered if you thought it was going anywhere."

The last guy she'd dated who was polite and charming had lied to her, cheated on her, and turned out to be a world-class jerk. She could see why Grandma might worry. "I think that for now we're just learning to be friends." It was way too complicated to try to explain. And even if she admitted the agreement she and Jackson had made, she knew her grandma would probably think it was a terrible idea.

"Being friends is nice." Grandma smiled. "You know, your grandpa and I weren't exactly friends from the beginning. He thought I was way too headstrong, and I thought he was too uptight." She chuckled. "But we worked that out and figured out our differences only made our relationship more interesting." She gave Violet a hug. "I pray that you'll find the same thing someday."

"Thanks." Violet watched her grandmother go. It was hard to wrap her mind around people thinking she and Jackson might actually be a real couple. But she'd better get used to it because in two days they'd be in full-on couple mode.

Reagan collapsed on the gym floor. "Is it my imagination, or is today's workout harder than last week's?" she asked Maggie.

"This instructor is used to teaching the advanced class."

"*Now* you tell me." Reagan grinned. "I was beginning to think I'd gone backward on my fitness goals."

Maggie shook her head. "I'd say you're just right." She nodded her head toward Reagan. "You look great. How do you feel?"

Reagan sighed. "I feel better about everything except for Chad. He let me sleep through our date night last week."

"Maybe you needed the rest."

"I'm sure I did, but it still stings that he'd do that. I mean, we haven't had time alone in eons." She'd refused to discuss it anymore with Chad, but he'd claimed he was only trying to do what was best for her. "And I can't shake the feeling that he's hiding something."

Maggie narrowed her eyes. "Have you told him about the gym yet?"

"No. But only because I want him to *notice* that there's something different about me. He lives with me. He sleeps in the same bed as me. You'd think he'd catch on that I've lost nearly ten pounds."

"Oh, he probably notices. He might not know what's different, but I'm sure he knows something is." Maggie chuckled. "But why don't you just schedule another date night? Now that you know you can let someone else watch the kids for a while, maybe you should take advantage of that."

"Maybe you're right."

Maggie nodded. "I am. Trust me." She grinned. "I was right

about Zumba, wasn't I?"

"I guess. Although if I shimmy much more today, I might have to be carted out of here on a stretcher."

"Don't sell yourself short. Here *or* at home." Maggie took a sip of water. "By the way, the family I work for is moving at the end of December. You know anyone who might need a nanny?"

Reagan laughed. "I wish. But I'm pretty sure Chad would never go for that. His mother has told me a million times how the best decision she ever made was leaving her job so she could stay home. He's always wanted me to stay home with our kids."

"But don't you think that's something the two of you should agree on? I'm not even saying you shouldn't stay home. I'm saying that maybe you need some help. Even another mom you can trade some time with."

"Well, I do have some exciting news that might mean I need a little bit of time without the kids." She filled Maggie in on the design work she'd done for Violet. "And I got an e-mail this morning from a business just down the road from Violet's shop that sells soaps and lotions. They're interested in having me design a new logo for them and possibly renovate their website."

"And is that something you're passionate about?"

She nodded. "I'd really like to accept the job, but I'm not sure how I'd swing it. I did Violet's project because she's my best friend, but I had to let a lot of stuff slide at home. I'm still catching up on laundry."

Maggie laughed. "It's a black hole, isn't it?"

The instructor called everyone back from the break.

"Just think about it, okay? I think it's time you and your

husband had an honest conversation about things."

Reagan pondered the advice. Maybe Maggie was right. But what if it drove an even bigger wedge between her and Chad? She wasn't sure the distance between them could get any farther. Because if it did, they'd be dangerously close to being two strangers who happened to share a house and a last name.

Dear Mama,

I am so excited about this weekend! Rachel and I are going to watch Dale in some kind of bull-riding competition. I think it will be so cool to see him ride.

I'm working on my schedule for next semester, and I'm considering taking an art class for one of my electives. Violet and I had a talk the other day about my classes, and she told me all about how she became a lawyer for all the wrong reasons and how excited she was to finally be going after her dreams. She thinks I should try different things to see what kind of stuff I'm good at and enjoy. It makes sense, I guess, but I don't know how I'll feel about getting a grade for my artwork.

You know that's always been something I just did for fun. What if I'm not really talented?

I guess there's only one way to find out, but it's kind of scary.

ILY,

Shadow

Chapter 23

Jackson Stratford: WE'LL BE THERE AROUND NOON
TOMORROW. WHAT'S THE PLAN? (Text message sent
October 12, 8:22 a.m.)

Kathleen Morgan: YAY! WE'RE SO EXCITED. THE KIDS HAVE
MADE WELCOME DRAWINGS FOR VIOLET. LUNCH WILL
BE READY WHEN YOU GET HERE. LOOKING FORWARD TO
GETTING TO KNOW VIOLET! (Text message sent October
12, 8:34 a.m.)

Jackson stood outside Violet's house, wondering if this was a huge mistake. Showing up unannounced wasn't usually his style, but he really needed to see her. He knocked on the door.

She opened the door, the surprise evident on her face. "Jackson! What's wrong?"

"I know we aren't leaving until tomorrow, but, uh, I kind of needed to talk to you." He shifted uncomfortably.

"Of course." She opened the door wider. "Come on in." She

smiled. "And excuse the mess. I'm trying to go through my giant collection of paper."

"Paper?"

Violet laughed. "I can't seem to throw it away. I'm seriously drowning in stacks of paper." She gave him a sheepish look. "Something I'm sure you can't understand."

"I don't hold your paper hoarding against you in any way," he said with a laugh. "At least you know you have a problem." He flipped through a stack of magazines.

"So what's up?" she asked.

He sighed. He'd known when she accepted his invitation to Memphis that he'd have to come clean about his entire past, but it might be harder than he'd expected. "Let's sit." He motioned toward the couch.

Once they were settled, he took a deep breath. "Violet, I'm really sorry for the way I treated you when we were in college. I'd sort of forgotten most of it until I ran into Reagan the other day. She was more than happy to refresh my memory."

Violet shook her head. "You don't have to apologize. That was a long time ago."

"I do." He frowned. "You need to know how genuinely sorry I am."

She furrowed her brow. "I appreciate you telling me."

"There's more." He cleared his throat. "I think there was a rumor in college that I'd taken a gap year or something and gone to Europe." He shook his head. "That wasn't the truth."

Violet widened her eyes. "Yeah, I'm pretty sure I heard something like that."

"I actually started college at the U of A with some of my friends. Summer after my freshman year, I lived there in an apartment with some other guys." He chewed on the inside of his lip. "We were dumb guys, you know? It was the first taste of freedom for many of us, and we did some really stupid stuff." He sighed. "The stupidest by far was one night toward the end of the summer when I got in the car with one of my buddies. He'd been drinking." He swallowed. "We both had."

She shook her head. "What happened?" she whispered.

"There were several of us in the car. We were so stupid." He'd never had to tell anyone the story before. It was much harder than he'd expected. "Richie lost control going around a curve. I was thrown from the car. The last thing I remember is hearing the girl I'd been seeing—her name was Jenna—scream." He took a deep breath. "Jenna didn't make it. I barely did."

"I'm so sorry." Violet reached for his hand and squeezed it.

"I had a lot of injuries. I went through multiple surgeries and a lot of rehab. It was terrible." He sighed. "Not only that, but I felt immense guilt over Jenna's death. I hadn't dated much before college, so she was my first real relationship. And it was my fault that we were in that car. I knew better. I'd been brought up better."

"You were young."

He shook his head. "That's not really an excuse." He cleared his throat. "Anyway, it took me a long time to recover. And there was a lot of pain—so much that I was on a lot of pain medication." He shrugged. "My parents were so upset with me over my behavior at the U of A that they insisted the only school where they'd pay tuition was Harding. They wanted me surrounded by Christians in the hopes that it would help turn me back to the straight and narrow."

"And did it?"

He shrugged. "It was definitely better for me to be in that environment after everything I'd been through. But in some ways, it caused me even more problems. I felt like I wasn't good enough to be there."

"I'm sorry you felt that way."

"It just felt like everyone I met had these perfect lives. They did and said the right things. And then there was me, with this big, awful secret. Even worse, I had a very hard time getting off the pain pills. Probably a lot of the time you had interaction with me, I was refusing to face the fact that I might be addicted. That made me feel even worse about myself."

"It sounds like you had a really rough time. I had no idea."

"I was miserable, and I tried to make everyone around me miserable. I came to that campus acting like I was some kind of hotshot. I picked on anyone who might be an easy target just to make myself feel better."

"Including me."

He squeezed her hand. "I'm really sorry. You have to understand that I'm a different person now. I've worked really hard to put all of that behind me."

Violet regarded him for a long moment, and Jackson couldn't help but wonder if she was going to dissolve their contract and send him on his way.

Violet's mind reeled. Jackson's story was not at all what she'd expected when he'd shown up on her doorstep. She'd thought he might want to prep her for the visit to his sister's house. But she'd never expected anything like this. "I can't imagine what you've gone through."

He sighed. "I don't want pity or anything. I just need you to understand that the guy you met fifteen years ago was carrying a lot of burdens. I was in pain—both physical and emotional—and nothing helped. I think it was during that time that I lashed out at those people I saw as having it all together. People like you."

"You thought I had it all together?"

He gave her a tentative smile. "Yeah. You were the kind of person who just floated through life. You never seemed to care much about fitting in with a certain crowd. You just did your own thing."

"I dealt with stuff of my own. Nothing like you did, but still. My life was far from perfect."

"I know that now. It's something I guess you learn with age. We all have our own issues, our own insecurities."

She nodded. "So how did you get your life back together?"

"After graduation, I went to grad school. I worked hard to get off the pain meds completely. It was hard. Very hard. But I had a good support group at the church I attended. I think I told you that grad school was when I feel like I really formed my own relationship with the Lord and developed my own faith. That had a huge part in my recovery and eventually helped me to become a better man. It's hard knowing I hurt people."

"It's weird how you never know the things a person might be dealing with just by looking at them, isn't it?" She glanced at him. "When I met Shadow and she was all decked out in black clothes and had fake tattoos and piercings, I jumped to a conclusion about her. And back in college when I met you, I thought you were a pretentious frat boy who made fun of everyone and everything." She shrugged. "I was wrong in both cases. Shadow has dealt with tremendous loss for a child so young. And you must have felt such remorse over the accident and the fallout that it's no wonder you lashed out."

Jackson nodded. "I think for me, one of the worst things was the division it caused within my family. My parents fought a lot during those years, and I know a big reason was because of the stress I put on the family. It can't be easy to see your child make terrible decisions and almost get himself killed. And my parents knew about my problem with pain meds, but they were helpless to stop it." He shook his head. "I finally realized that the pain I was trying to end wasn't really from my physical injuries—but it took a long time to figure that out." He gave her a sheepish look. "Now that you know the truth, do you think I'm too messed up to deal with?"

She smiled. "Not at all. I know it wasn't easy for you to tell me all of that. But look at you now. You have your life together, you're successful in your career, and you're about to receive an award from your alma mater." She bumped against him with her shoulder. "And you have the best fake girlfriend in the history of fake girlfriends."

Jackson chuckled. "That I do."

Violet could tell he was glad to have gotten it off his chest. And she was glad for him. Sometimes it seemed like harboring secrets wound up causing more hurt than just letting them out in the open.

She wondered what that meant for their arrangement. Would the secret they shared come back to haunt them? She certainly hoped not.

Chapter 24

Reagan McClure: GUESS WHAT? I AGREED TO DO THE FREELANCE JOB. WHAT DO YOU THINK OF REAGAN MCCLURE DESIGNS? (Text message sent October 13, 8:14 a.m.)

Violet Matthews: THAT'S AWESOME! WHAT DOES CHAD THINK? WE'RE ON OUR WAY TO MEMPHIS TO VISIT JACKSON'S SISTER. . . . (Text message sent October 13, 8:22 a.m.)

Reagan walked into Ava Grace's room to see what the commotion was about. "What's going on in here?" she asked. Blankets were spread all over the floor, most of them with dolls or stuffed animals on them. Two of the blankets were empty.

Ava Grace cast a woeful gaze at her mother. "They're in time-out." She pointed to a stuffed bear and a doll missing an arm.

"You're putting your babies in time-out?" She couldn't hide her smile. Time-out was a concept Ava Grace had picked up at Sunday school. "Were they bad?"

The little girl nodded. "They didn't share." She put the back of her hand to her forehead. "It was terrible."

Reagan burst out laughing. "Oh, drama."

"I'm not drama. I'm Ava Grace." She lifted her chin defiantly.

"That you are," Reagan said. Her kids were so funny. She knew every mom in the world must think they had the funniest kids, but she was pretty sure hers really were.

"Mama, I can't find my gymnastics bag," Izzy yelled.

Reagan hurried to help hunt the lost bag. Chad had promised to take Izzy to gymnastics today, which would help out a lot. Once Ava Grace and the twins were down for their naps, she could get some housework done and maybe play around with a few ideas for her freelance job.

"When was the last time you saw your bag?" she asked Izzy. In the span of a couple of hours, she'd managed to tear her room apart. "And what happened to your room? It was clean this morning."

Izzy shrugged her shoulders. "I'm trying to find my bag."

"Is your version of trying to find your bag tossing everything off the shelves and onto the floor?"

"Pretty much." Izzy grinned, showing the gap where her two front teeth were missing. Soon she'd have her permanent teeth. She was sure growing up fast.

"Want me to put your hair up for class?"

Izzy thought for a moment. "Can you do a bun? Like a ballerina?"

"I can try." She grabbed a brush from the bathroom. "Come here."

Izzy stood in front of her and watched in the mirror.

Reagan brushed her long, straw-colored hair. "You've got some tangles today. Did you sleep standing on your head?"

Izzy giggled.

Reagan quickly wound her daughter's hair into a bun. "There you go. You look like a princess." She hugged her. "Now let's go see if your bag is in the laundry room. I think I remember seeing it there."

They walked past Ava Grace's room where she'd put two more dolls in time-out and was fussing at them for arguing with each other.

Just a typical morning at the McClure house.

"We're going to be late," Chad said as Reagan and Izzy walked into the kitchen.

"There's a missing bag. You'll have to hold on one second," Reagan said. She scanned the laundry room that also served as the entry room from the garage—and thus the catchall room. Shoes, bags, blankets, toys. You never knew what you might find in there. "Here it is." Reagan handed Izzy the bag and kissed her on the forehead. "Have fun."

Chad walked past her and grinned. "We'll be back soon." He gave her a quick peck on the cheek and ushered Izzy out the door.

Once she had put Ava Grace, Scarlett, and Simon down for naps, she sat down at the computer. Reagan McClure Designs. It had a nice ring to it. She should talk to Chad tonight.

Unless she waited until she had a couple of clients. If her freelancing didn't pan out, there was no need to have started an unnecessary argument.

Yes, that was a much better plan. She'd do a couple more jobs, and then if she had success, she'd tell him her plans.

Even though she hated keeping things from her husband, she was pretty sure there was something he was keeping from her. He'd never been good at keeping things from her, and the past few weeks he'd been very closemouthed about meetings and had been constantly glued to his iPhone. She wasn't sure what was going on, but she feared the worst.

Jackson took Violet's hand and helped her out of the car. "Ready?" he asked.

"Ready as I'll ever be. You?" She'd had fun on the trip to Memphis. Now that Jackson had gotten the news about his accident and bad behavior off his chest, it seemed he'd loosened up some. They'd discussed everything from their favorite movie moments to the next presidential election.

Violet had never been so open with a guy before. She knew part of that was because their relationship wasn't what they claimed it to be. So she felt like she could be herself. She could say anything.

"Uncle Jack!" A brown-haired girl who looked to be about five raced toward them.

Jackson picked her up and tossed her in the air. "Hello, sweet Olivia. When did you get so grown up?" He put her down, and she gave him a gap-toothed grin.

"I'm not grown up, silly. I'm in kindergarten." She looked at Violet. "Tyler and I have presents for you," she said shyly.

Violet knelt down. "I'm Violet. Thank you for letting me stay in your house tonight."

"Oh, you'll have to thank my mommy for that." She grinned again. "I'm not allowed to have sleepovers yet."

Violet laughed.

Olivia took Jackson's hand and then held her other hand up to Violet. "Can you swing me?"

They walked the rest of the way to the house swinging Olivia between them. She giggled each time they lifted her in the air.

"She's great," Violet murmured to Jackson as they reached the porch.

"There you are." A petite woman with the same steely blue eyes as Jackson opened the door. "Olivia has been sitting out here waiting." She grinned at her daughter. "She was supposed to come tell us when you got here, but I'll bet she was too excited." She held out a hand to Violet. "I'm Kathleen Morgan."

Violet introduced herself and followed her into the house. Meeting the family was a new experience for her. Zach's family had lived out of state, and she'd never met them. "Thanks for having me."

"Are you kidding?" Kathleen grinned and gave Jackson a side hug. "We're thrilled that Jackson has found someone he wanted to introduce to us." She nudged him with her elbow. "But Mom is jealous that we're meeting Violet first and she lives right there in town."

Jackson chuckled. "Thanksgiving will be here before you know it."

He'd filled Violet in on his mom's dating life. She'd tried to be supportive of his feelings, but had finally pointed out that he might be overreacting a bit. "I'm looking forward to meeting her though," Violet said.

Kathleen led them into the kitchen. "The guys are gone to get Tyler a new pair of soccer cleats, but it could take a little while to find just the right pair. Let's go ahead and eat while it's hot."

An hour later after the dishes were cleared, Jackson went to the backyard with Olivia so he could see her new swing set.

"Would you like a cup of coffee?" Kathleen asked.

Violet smiled. "That would be wonderful."

"That's why I love my Keurig. I can have fresh coffee at the touch of a button." Kathleen handed Violet a steaming cup. "There's creamer in the fridge and here's sugar and Splenda, whichever you prefer."

Violet poured cream and sugar into her cup and stirred. "Thanks again for the hospitality."

"I'm just glad to finally meet you." Kathleen motioned for Violet to follow her to the kitchen table. "Jackson says you guys knew each other in college."

Violet nodded. "Not well." She smiled. "And we didn't get along."

"No one got along with Jackson back then." She met Violet's eyes. "He's changed a lot."

"Seems that way." Violet took a sip of coffee and stared out the bay window at Jackson pushing Olivia in the swing.

"He speaks very highly of you. He's really excited about your bake shop."

Violet grinned. "The grand opening is just a little over two weeks away." Butterflies swarmed her stomach. Soon it would be time to sink or swim as an entrepreneur.

"Jackson seems to think it will be a raging success. And being able to spot good business opportunities is kind of his specialty."

"True. That does make me feel better."

"I'm glad you're here, Violet." Kathleen grinned. "I hope we see a lot more of you."

Violet's heart sank. This was part of the deal she hadn't bargained for. She actually *liked* Jackson's family. It made her sad to think that in a matter of months, they'd learn there'd been a breakup and never hear from her again.

Maybe she should just enjoy one day at a time and not worry that she was becoming attached to Jackson and his life.

"Told you they were going to love you," Jackson said once they were alone in the car. "Kathleen pulled me aside earlier and told me I'd found a winner."

Violet laughed. "Did you tell her I'm really just a loser masquerading as a winner?"

"Don't talk that way about my fake girlfriend." He glanced over at her. "Seriously though, they all adore you."

"They're pretty great, too. Olivia and Tyler drew me the sweetest pictures."

Jackson frowned. "Yeah, I didn't get any pictures. I don't know about all of that."

She laughed. "It's just because I'm a novelty. Where exactly are we headed? I haven't spent a ton of time in Memphis."

"We don't have a ton of time. Kathleen said the birthday party she was taking Olivia and Tyler to would last about an hour and a half. So I thought we'd go downtown. We'll eat some barbecue and then walk around a little bit. Maybe we'll hear the blues." He grinned. "Then we're supposed to meet them for cupcakes. Kathleen gave me directions to a place called Muddy's Bake Shop. She says it's one of their favorite places in town and maybe you'll get some ideas for your own shop."

Violet smiled. "That sounds wonderful. I'm definitely open to ideas."

Jackson flipped on his blinker. "Kathleen felt terrible that they had something planned." He grinned. "I told her not to worry about it and that I'd be glad to entertain you by myself for a little while."

"You certainly are entertaining." Violet laughed as he almost turned down a one-way street. "Do you know where you're going?"

"I'm not that familiar with downtown, but I know where the parking garages are. I come with my friend Jeff to see the Memphis Grizzlies play a few times each season."

"Fun." She gave him a sideways glance as he maneuvered into the nearest parking garage. "Is Jeff the one we're supposed to go to the Razorback game with?"

Jackson pulled into a spot and turned off the engine. "Yes. His wife, Lauren, and I have actually been friends since kindergarten." He grinned. "Jeff started attending our school in sixth grade. I think you'll love them. They have two adorable boys and another baby on the way."

"I'm looking forward to the game," she said as they walked toward the busy downtown area. "It will probably be my last weekend free for a very long time."

"That's right." Jackson looked over at her and smiled. "The opening is creeping up on you."

Violet nodded. "I can't believe it's October already. It seems like just yesterday that summer was starting." She shook her head. "It's like I blink and a whole month passes."

"Do you think that gets worse as you get older? When I was a kid, time seemed to drag on. But now it goes so fast it makes my head spin."

She smiled. "I think it must feel that way for everyone. Remember how when you were in school, classes felt like they lasted forever? My workday always seems to fly past." She laughed. "Unless it's the Friday before a holiday or something."

"I thought we'd go to the Rendezvous if that's okay. They're famous for ribs, but the barbecue sandwiches are good, too." He took her hand. "It almost feels like you're on some kind of movie set getting to the place though. It's kind of hidden down an alley." He liked the way her hand felt in his.

"That sounds great. I love barbecue."

They walked hand in hand down Union Avenue.

"I think this is the right street," he said.

They found themselves on a narrow, deserted street.

"I smell the barbecue. We must be headed in the right direction," Violet said.

Thirty minutes later they were seated and had ordered.

"You don't talk about your work much," Violet said. "Do you enjoy it?"

Jackson smiled. "I guess I'm weird about that kind of thing. When my dad passed away last year, I promised myself that I'd never get so bogged down with work that I wouldn't see what was really around me. You know?" He took a sip of sweet tea.

"I do, actually. I've known people who are so focused on work it's like they're not really present. Their body is there—at the dinner table, sitting in the bleachers, visiting with a friend—but their mind is elsewhere."

"I don't ever want to be that person. I want to be present in my own life and not just at work." Jackson sighed. "It's tough to find a balance, especially if you enjoy what you do. I think you just have to put priorities on your personal relationships over your career."

"Easier said than done. I have a friend that's sort of struggling with that right now. You know Reagan."

Jackson nodded. "Doesn't she stay home with her kids?"

"Yeah, but she's miserable. She loves her kids. She'd do anything for them. But I think she really needs to do something outside of the house occasionally." Violet filled him in on Reagan's freelancing opportunity. "I get the idea that she's worried her husband might think it means she's putting more emphasis on herself and her career than she is their kids. It's a tough spot to be in."

"Maybe they can work out some kind of compromise that will make them both happy."

Violet smiled. "I sure hope so." She folded her straw wrapper into a tiny piece. "What about you? What would you do if you could do anything?"

"I love what I do. Working to bring new industry into a town that desperately needs it is very rewarding. But if I were ever going to explore other options, I'd probably look at Heifer International. They have positions in Little Rock, and I think it's the kind of place

I'd enjoy being a part of." Heifer International's mission was to end hunger and poverty by providing livestock to people in need and encouraging them to then pass along the offspring of their livestock to other people in their community who were in need. Jackson appreciated the "pay it forward" approach.

"That would be fulfilling." Violet grinned. "And I bet you'd get to travel to some pretty far-off places to see the programs in action."

He shrugged. "For now I'm happy doing what I do. But if I ever change careers, I'll probably go the nonprofit route. If not Heifer, then another one I believe in and that will help me to feel like I'm making an impact."

The waitress placed their food on the table. "Let me know if you need anything else, you hear?"

Jackson offered a quick prayer before they dug into their food.

This was turning out to be the perfect weekend.

Chapter 25

Violet Matthews: The weekend was fun. Thanks for taking me! And now: if you could have a special talent, what would you want it to be? (Text message sent October 16, 4:23 p.m.)

Jackson Stratford: Thanks for going! Have fun working at the shop this weekend. I'll probably stop by at some point. And I can't wait until next weekend for the game! Oh, as for my talent—I wish I could sing! You? (Text message sent October 16, 4:29 p.m.)

Violet Matthews: I wish I were good at speaking in public—it terrifies me! Plenty to do at the shop—stop by and I'll put you to work! And I'm looking forward to the game, too! (Text message sent October 16, 4:35 p.m.)

Violet pulled a test batch of cupcakes from the oven. Her Memphis trip had inspired her to try her hand at an Elvis-themed cupcake.

"Banana cupcake with peanut butter icing?" Shadow read the recipe over her shoulder. "That sounds kind of gross to me."

Violet grinned. "Don't knock it until you've tried it. If it was good enough for the King, it might be good enough for you."

"The King?"

"Yeah. You know. The one and only Elvis Presley." Violet curled her lip as much as she could. "Thank you, thank you very much."

Shadow shook her head. "What's so great about Elvis?"

Violet stuck out her tongue. "You'd better be kidding." She dusted her hands off on her apron and went over to the record player. "Just you wait." She slipped her favorite Elvis album out of the sleeve and put it on the turntable. The familiar crackle of the needle on the record filled the shop, followed by Elvis's smooth voice. " 'Jailhouse Rock' is one of my favorites."

"It's not bad," Shadow said once it was over. "But I still don't know about peanut butter and banana cupcakes."

Violet laughed. "I won't have them on the menu every week. But I want to have some variety. So if you ever think of another flavor that might be fun, let me know and we'll give it a try."

Shadow nodded. "Sure." She hobbled across to the counter to get the icing Violet had just made and put into the tube.

"Are you okay? You're walking funny."

"I'm going out with a new boy who rides horses," she explained. "So I took a riding lesson yesterday after school." She grinned. "My whole body hurts."

"So is it serious with this cowboy?" Violet asked.

Shadow shrugged. "I think he's getting ready to tell me he doesn't want to see me anymore." She dramatically threw herself into a chair. "I don't understand why I meet a boy and think he likes me, but then in a couple of weeks, he dumps me."

"Do you think it's possible that you're picking the wrong boys?" Violet asked gently.

Shadow shook her head. "No. I'm picking the right ones. It's just that they aren't picking me back."

Violet hid a smile. She might be far removed from her teenage years, but it was nice to know dating was just as full of angst as ever. "Hang in there. I'm sure a special one will come along soon who'll choose you over all the rest." She grinned. "As long as you choose him right back."

Shadow brightened. "I hope so."

Violet didn't say so, but she hoped the same thing for herself.

Reagan bent down to touch her toes before class started. She wanted to limber up because the advanced teacher was leading the class again today.

"You're here early," Maggie said as she took her place next to Reagan. "What gives?"

Reagan grinned. "I'm trying to get up an hour earlier in the mornings to get stuff done around the house." She shrugged. "The up side is that everyone in my house was ready on time as a result."

"So the best way for the whole family to get somewhere on

time is for Mom to lose another hour of sleep?" Maggie asked.

Reagan nodded. "Doesn't seem fair, does it?"

"Many things in life don't."

"I think this is going to be my last month here," Reagan said. "Things are just too hectic for me to try and fit the gym in."

Maggie narrowed her eyes. "Does this mean you're accepting freelance work?"

"Yes. I finished another job earlier in the week. And I've had a couple more inquiries just based on word-of-mouth advertising."

"What about your weight-loss goal?"

Reagan sighed. "That's partly why I'm making myself get up an extra hour early. I'm going to start training for a 5K or maybe a half marathon. Plus having to load three kids up twice a week and bring them here and then unload and then go pick up Izzy from school was getting to be too much. I'm literally taking kids in and out of my van nearly nonstop."

"So this way you'll still be working out, but won't have that extra burden."

Reagan nodded. "Exactly. And early in the mornings, Chad will be in the house with the kids, so he can take care of them if they happen to wake up. Which probably won't happen unless someone's sick, in which case I probably won't feel like running anyway."

Maggie frowned. "I'm going to miss you. Zumba won't be the same without watching you try not to trip over your own feet." She laughed.

"We weren't all blessed with the shimmying flair that you were."

Maggie wiggled her hips. "It's all about the hip action."

Reagan laughed. "I guess so." She did another stretch. "Did you find another family looking for a nanny?"

Maggie shook her head. "I think my full-time nannying days might be over. My husband is home more now that he's retired, so it's probably for the best. I'm trying to find something a couple of days a week."

An idea formed in Reagan's head. "You might be the answer to a prayer. If my freelancing business actually takes off, I'd like to look into having someone come to the house for a few hours a couple of days a week so I can get some work done."

"What does Chad think about it?"

Reagan wrinkled her nose. "He doesn't know yet because it might not even pan out. So why argue over something that might not happen?"

"I'd be glad to come over to your house to watch the kids." Maggie smiled. "But I don't like the idea of caring for kids unless both parents are onboard. In fact, before I ever agree to a permanent arrangement, I prefer to meet with both parents just to get a feel for the family."

"I'll keep that in mind. And obviously if this is something that would actually be a permanent arrangement, I would bring Chad into the decision-making process."

Maggie nodded. "Good. After class I'll give you my references in case you ever decide you want to have me come watch them. I'm certified in CPR for children and infants and also have taken a course in wound care."

It sounded perfect to Reagan. Maybe Chad would agree to a part-time nanny just for a few hours a week so Reagan could get some things done.

The loud music filled the room for the warm-up.

Reagan let herself forget all the outside stresses and focus on only one thing—trying to stay on her feet.

Violet stood on the porch at Jackson's the following Saturday and waited for him to answer the door. Since the Razorback game was in Little Rock, it made sense for her to meet him at his house. Which was fine with her—she'd always thought you could learn a lot about someone by their home.

She glanced around the brown brick exterior. Just as she'd expected, everything was clean and well-maintained. Either he spent a lot of time doing housework or he hired it done.

The door swung open, and Jackson stood on the other side, decked out in a long-sleeved Arkansas Razorback T-shirt and faded blue jeans. He wore a baseball cap with a razorback emblazoned on it. "Come on in," he said.

She stepped into the living room and looked around. Gleaming hardwood floors, wall-to-ceiling mahogany bookcases, and a matching leather couch and love seat screamed that it was a man's house. "Very masculine."

"I should hope so." He winked. "I decorated it myself."

She perused his bookshelves. Impressive. Classics, the typicals— Grisham, Koontz, and Dekker, and a variety of nonfiction ranging from Dave Ramsey to Stephen Covey. "So I gather you like to read?"

"Guilty." He smiled. "You have your vintage typewriter and records, I have my books. That's the one thing I can't throw out."

Based on the fact that the rest of his house looked as spotless as a magazine ad, she believed it. "Do I get a grand tour?" she asked.

"Absolutely." He pointed to the crown molding. "I installed that myself. And I know you're turning your nose up at my brown walls, but I like them."

She laughed. "I'd feel like I was living inside a cardboard box, but to each his own." She followed him into the kitchen. "Now this I like. Yellow walls, stainless-steel appliances." She smiled. "It gets my stamp of approval."

"That means more than if it came from *Good Housekeeping*." He grinned. "Down this hallway is the master bedroom, guest bedroom, and office."

She peeked in each room. Each was tastefully decorated in muted tones and expensive furnishings. "It's really pretty. Definitely more modern than my place." She preferred to pick up pieces with a history, and her favorite thing was to find a piece of furniture meant for one thing and repurpose it for another. She'd found the most gorgeous dresser a few months ago, and after some sanding, paint, and new hardware, it made the neatest sideboard in the dining room.

Jackson led her back to the kitchen. "Those french doors lead to a deck and a fenced-in yard."

"Without a dog to enjoy it." She shook her head. "Such a shame."

He grinned. "Arnie is welcome to visit the yard anytime, as long as he doesn't dig or go to the bathroom."

She laughed. "Okay, I'll let you be the one to inform him of that." She ran a hand along the granite countertops. "It's really pretty. I'm impressed."

"Thanks. I know it isn't all warm and cozy and cottage-like the way your place is, but it suits me."

"Yes, I suppose it does." She smiled.

"How's the shop? The opening is just days away."

She sighed. "Don't remind me." She'd spent the last week and a half perfecting recipes and training Shadow on the cash register. "Thanks for your help last week though. You really play the role of a disgruntled customer well."

He chuckled. "I just wanted to make sure Shadow was prepared to deal with the public."

"Well it was great training. She really took to you."

Jackson shrugged. "What can I say? I have a way with the ladies."

Violet laughed. "And you're so modest."

"Are you ready? We should get going. Traffic will be terrible. Jeff and Lauren went early to get a good tailgate spot, so at least we don't have to worry about that."

She followed him out the door and to the vehicle. She'd been at ease meeting his sister, but she was a bit more nervous about meeting his best friends. "Sounds perfect."

They headed toward the stadium in bumper-to-bumper traffic.

"Do you go to many games?" she asked.

Jackson nodded. "I used to have season tickets, but now I just go to a handful of games each year. Jeff and I usually road trip to one away game. My dad and I used to always try and make it to one game in Fayetteville and one in Little Rock each year." He took the exit for the stadium, and they waited in a long line of traffic. "Jeff texted earlier to tell me where they're set up. They're bringing the food." He grinned. "Lauren said that if I'd bring you, they'd do the cooking. I'm pretty sure she doubts your existence."

Violet laughed. "So does that mean you haven't introduced them to many girls?"

Jackson made a face. "Can I confess something to you? Because Lauren will probably tell you if I don't."

"Spill it."

"I've introduced them to a couple of girls over the years, but none of them have really been my type. They're sort of what prompted our arrangement in the first place. I've had a habit of dating what Lauren calls 'bubble heads,' and I promised her I'd bring someone suitable to the awards banquet." He sighed. "The last time I introduced them to a girl, it turned out Lauren used to babysit her. She was only ten years younger than us, but still. Lauren said she was really tired of me bringing girls on double dates who have no recollection of the eighties other than from VH1."

Violet chuckled. "Sounds like Lauren and I will get along just fine."

"Yes, I suspect you will." He pulled into a parking space on the golf course next to the stadium. "Here we go."

She waited for him to open the passenger door and took his hand when he offered it. "This will be fun."

He squeezed her hand as they walked toward the tailgate area. "It sure will."

Chapter 26

Jackson Stratford: ARE YOU READY? THREE DAYS UNTIL THE GRAND OPENING! YOU WERE A HUGE HIT WITH LAUREN AND JEFF YESTERDAY. THEY'RE READY TO GET TOGETHER AGAIN. (Text message sent October 28, 2:33 p.m.)

Violet Matthews: GETTING THERE. IT'S HARD TO BELIEVE THAT IN JUST A FEW DAYS THERE WILL BE REAL CUSTOMERS! (I HOPE!) AND I REALLY LIKED JEFF AND LAUREN, TOO! (Text message sent October 28, 2:39 p.m.)

Violet put the finishing touches on the menu board. It looked great. Shadow had put her artistic skills to use to paint a beautiful border of multicolored gerbera daisies, and they'd painted the inside with chalkboard paint so the menu could be changed weekly.

"How does this look?" she asked Shadow.

Shadow beamed. "Awesome. I can't believe my artwork is on the main menu. People are going to see *my* drawings. That's so weird."

"You're very talented," Violet said. "Have you given any more thought to art classes?"

Shadow nodded. "I'm using one of my electives. It still makes me nervous to think about being graded. And then there are things like competitions and stuff."

"It takes a lot of courage to let the real you come out, doesn't it?" Violet asked. "I think of all the years I spent trying to be someone else. Someone whose dreams were a little less scary and a little more safe." She shrugged. "But scariest of all is waking up one day and realizing you've kept your true personality, your true dreams, bottled up inside."

Shadow sighed. "I guess."

"Maybe you should talk to my friend Reagan. She majored in graphic design in college, but minored in art. She's the one who designed the logo for Central Avenue Cupcakes. She also took the photographs and designed the layout for the website and business cards."

"It's really pretty," Shadow said, holding up one of the grand opening flyers. "Does she like to paint, too?"

Violet nodded. "She used to. I think her eye for art helped make her successful at designing logos and things. You have that same eye for colors and designs. I never would've thought to put some of the colors together on the tabletops, but you did and they look so pretty."

"Thank you. My mom used to paint. Sometimes she'd have me sit for portraits and stuff." She smiled at the memory. "Of course, she wasn't so happy when I got into her paints and painted a picture on the wall in the family room." She giggled. "It was just a tiny picture, and I even signed my name. Mama got on me about it, but she left it on the wall. When Daddy got home from work, she told him we'd acquired a new piece of art for the family room." Shadow sighed. "Stephanie painted over it when she had the colors redone."

"All the painting over in the world can't take the memory away, right?" Violet didn't know what to say. Such a tragic life.

Shadow's mouth quirked into a tiny smile. "I guess it would've been kind of embarrassing to have that on the wall forever. And Daddy made sure to take a picture of it."

"That's neat."

"I'm supposed to fly to Dallas for Thanksgiving. I wish Nana could go with me."

Violet straightened one of the quilt squares on the wall. "It will be nice to see your dad though, right? And I'll bet your dog has missed you a ton."

Shadow's face brightened. "That's true."

Violet wondered how her own Thanksgiving would go. She and her mother had argued about it already. Landry's parents were coming to Thanksgiving this year, and Mom thought she should make an effort to be there. When she'd explained that she already had plans, Mom hadn't exactly been thrilled. *"If you're spending Thanksgiving with this guy and his family, I think it's time to introduce us."* But Violet was determined not to let Jackson get any more involved in her life than he already was.

Otherwise their inevitable fake breakup might feel more like a real one.

Dear Mama,

Well, me and Dale broke up. Sometimes I wonder what's

wrong with me. I meet a cute boy and have a good time talking to him or texting him, but after two or three weeks, it fizzles out.

Violet taught me how to make icing this week and how to ice the cupcakes so they'll look pretty. She mostly does all of that, but I will help out sometimes. I got my food handler's certification this week—I had to take a little class and a test online and then I got to print a card with my certification number and name on it.

I'm flying to Dallas for Thanksgiving. Daddy and Nana talked about it and decided that I could miss a couple of days of school so I could spend the entire week there. I think Nana is kind of sad that I won't be here with them. I hope I get along okay with Daddy and Stephanie while I'm there.

Nana has finally started letting me drive her car sometimes, but she reminds me of every single driving rule before she hands me the keys. Granddaddy says it's no reflection of my driving skills—that she's just nervous about me being behind the wheel because of your accident. After he told me that, I stopped being so annoyed with her.

Ily,
Shadow

Jackson pushed the paperwork across the table to the project manager of Edison Appliances. "I'm pleased the last property you looked at was to your liking and specifications. And I think you'll find the workforce in Lonoke County and the surrounding area is ready to meet the needs of your company." He smiled. This might be his biggest coup yet. "If you'll just sign next to each *X*, we're all set."

Mr. Anderson scribbled his signature on the papers and passed them back. "It's been a pleasure working with you, Jackson. We look forward to opening our doors in Arkansas and are thankful for all you've done to make that possible."

Jackson shook hands with the group from Edison and showed them to the lobby. He couldn't believe it. Just when he'd been sure they were going to set up their distribution center in Mississippi, they'd changed their minds. He'd like to think he'd had something to do with that. "Any calls?" he asked Sheila.

She smiled. "Only one from a Rocky Balboa. He says you have his number."

"I sure do. Thanks, Sheila." He hurried into his office and closed the door. "Okay, Mr. Balboa. What's going on?" he asked once he'd dialed Jeff's number.

Jeff laughed. "I just wanted to tell you that RSVPs have started trickling in for homecoming."

"Already? But the brochures only went out last week."

"What can I say, man. It's the hottest ticket in town."

Jackson groaned. "Whatever."

"Actually, I was just going to let you know that your mom sent her RSVP in already. She's bringing Roger."

Jackson had figured as much. "Thanks for the heads-up."

"And I'm guessing we can just put you down with Violet as your guest?"

"That's right." The fact that Mom was taking Roger as her date didn't bother him as much since he'd have Violet with him. She had a way of calming him down and putting him at ease. It was the craziest thing.

"Don't mess it up, man. I think she's the best thing that's ever happened to you."

Jackson had already had the same thought. "Why do you say that?"

"Lauren and I were talking about it after the game. You guys just fit together. I think you bring her stability, and she loosens you up. And you're obviously so happy. I'm really proud of you, man. I know a committed relationship has never been your thing—I don't guess I've ever known you to give your heart away. But I think this is a really good thing you've got going."

Jackson nodded. "It sure is."

Chapter 27

Jackson Stratford: Happy Grand Opening! It's going to be incredible. I'll be there as soon as I get off work. (Text message sent October 31, 7:30 a.m.)

Violet Matthews: Thanks! I hope I'm still in one piece by the time you get here. (Text message sent October 31, 7:39 a.m.)

Jackson Stratford: You will be. Just save me a cupcake! (Text message sent October 31, 7:42 a.m.)

Violet tied on the apron her grandmother had given her. "Well, what do you think?"

Grandma smiled. "Perfection." She sniffed the air. "And so is that smell."

Violet grinned and motioned toward the nearly full glass case. "This is the last batch for a while. We'll just play it by ear and see which flavors go faster before I bake anything else."

"Good plan. Thanks for letting me be your assistant today."

Violet laughed. "Thank *you*. You being here until Shadow gets in from school is amazing. I think most days I'll manage on my own—at least until the summer season. But since I don't really know what to expect, I feel much better with you being here."

"So tell me the plan."

Violet filled her in on the pricing and the cash register. "It's very simple to operate."

"Famous last words," Grandma said with a laugh.

"These little bags are for to-go cupcakes. If they get three or less, they get a bag." Violet pointed to a stack of small white bags. "Three cupcakes fit perfectly in those. Then fold the top of the bag down and put one of these stickers with the logo on it to seal."

"They look so cute."

"If they get four, five, or six cupcakes, put them in one of these white boxes." Violet pointed to a stack. "Shadow put them together already. All you have to do is put the cupcakes inside and tape it closed. The logo sticker is already on the top of the box."

"What if they want more than six?" Grandma asked.

Violet pointed to a sign. "For orders needing more than half a dozen, they'll have to place the order and come back later. I don't have the space or the manpower right now to risk someone coming in and buying out the case." She shrugged. "But if it's preordered, I can bake ahead and be ready."

"You're a smart girl. I never would've thought of that."

Jackson had helped her come up with the idea last week when she'd been worrying about all the things that could go wrong. "I had some help coming up with it." She smiled at the thought of him. He'd be here tonight and hopefully things would be calm enough for her to at least get to talk to him.

The bell over the door chimed, and a woman with a little girl in tow walked in the door.

"Welcome to Central Avenue Cupcakes," Violet said. Her first customers. Would it be weird to ask to take their picture? She could hardly wait to see what flavor cupcakes they chose.

"Do you have a restroom?" the woman asked. She pointed toward the little girl. "It's an emergency," she whispered.

Violet tried to keep her smile from slipping. They only wanted the restroom. "Go straight back and to the left."

"Let's go potty and then come back for a cupcake," the woman said.

The little girl skipped to the bathroom.

Violet let out a sigh of relief. "Oh thank goodness. I was so worried they didn't come in for cupcakes at all."

Grandma laughed. "We might want to put a 'No public restroom' sign out front, just to be on the safe side."

"Good thinking. I'll have Shadow make one when she gets here."

Violet turned her attention to the next customer. It would be hard to get into the swing of things and figure out the best way to do everything, but standing next to Grandma, serving cupcakes while an Elvis record played in the background, was by far the happiest day she'd ever had at work.

Jackson parallel parked in front of Aunt Teak's. The grand opening last week had gone so well that he'd barely gotten a minute with

Violet all night. He couldn't wait to see how the first full week had gone.

He opened the door and walked inside.

"Welcome to Central Avenue Cupcakes," Violet said with a grin.

"A Beatles song playing on the record player, the sweet smell of cupcakes, and the prettiest girl I know behind the counter. Is this heaven?"

She laughed. "Very funny."

"How has today been?"

She pointed toward the nearly empty case. "Does that answer your question? Shadow and I have been running around like crazy."

Shadow peeked her head out of the storeroom door. "Did you call me?" She noticed Jackson. "Hi, Jackson. How's it going?"

He nodded. "Pretty good. You?"

She wrinkled her nose. "I fly to Dallas in two weeks. I'm spending the entire week of Thanksgiving at my dad's."

"Chin up. Someday he might not be around, so use your time wisely." He and Shadow had talked some about what it was like to lose a parent. He felt for her. "Ask if you can have a daddy-daughter date one night to catch up."

She smiled. "I will. Thanks." She looked at Violet. "I'm through in the storeroom. I think everything is set for next week."

"Thanks, Shadow. Do we need to give you a ride home?"

She shook her head. "Nana left her car for me and got a ride home with Granddaddy." She smiled. "Have a good rest of the weekend."

"You, too. I'll probably see you at church tomorrow, unless I make it to the early service. Otherwise I'll see you Tuesday after school." Violet finished wiping down the counter.

"Bye," Shadow called as she hoisted her bag over her shoulder and walked out the door.

"Anything I can to do help?" Jackson asked once Shadow was gone.

She shook her head. "I think we're all done here." She grinned. "I survived the first full week."

"I'm proud." He smiled. "And I have something special planned now."

She widened her eyes. "What's that?"

"Dinner at the Arlington Hotel. I know how you love historic places. I think they've already put their Christmas lights up." The Arlington was the most historic hotel in Hot Springs.

She clutched her purse. "That sounds like so much fun."

Jackson ushered her out the door and waited until she locked it. "You okay with walking?"

"It's a perfect night for a walk."

They crossed Central Avenue and paused in front of Fordyce Bathhouse.

"It's so pretty," Violet said. "I toured it a few weeks ago just for fun. It's like stepping back in time."

"Is it a museum now?" he asked.

She nodded. "Yes. It's run by the National Park Service." She pointed down the row of ornate bathhouses. "Reagan and I went to the Quapaw Baths to the spa a few weeks ago. It was very nice. The Buckstaff is next door, and it's supposed to be good, too. I'll have to give it a try next."

"Is that the one with the blue awnings?" he asked.

Violet nodded. "Yep." She tugged on his hand. "Have you ever walked along the Grand Promenade?"

"I don't think so."

"Do we have time? We can get to the Arlington Hotel from there."

"Sure."

They walked on the sidewalk that ran between two of the bathhouses.

"You can hear the water," he said. "That's so cool."

She laughed. "Actually it's hot. It's one of the open springs. During the day you can see the steam coming off the water." They climbed a set of stairs that led to a brick paved path. "This is the Grand Promenade. Back in the heyday of the baths, people would walk along this path between baths."

"Interesting."

They walked along in silence for a moment.

"See that spot?" she asked, pointing to an overlook. "I like to stand there and look out over Central Avenue."

"Do you come here often?" he asked.

She shrugged. "I bring Arnie here for walks sometimes. It's a nice area, and there are a ton of trails. Technically this is part of Hot Springs National Park." She pulled him over to the overlook. "Isn't it amazing?" she asked.

He stared at her. "It sure is."

Violet turned toward him. "It's crazy that I never gave much thought to living here before, considering how much I like the past.

The mobster history here fascinates me. I mean, Al Capone himself had a suite at the Arlington. I met a friend of my grandpa's who was one of Capone's drivers back in the day. I can just imagine all the mobsters in their suits and the women in their colorful dresses with their jewels." She grinned.

Jackson smiled down at her. "The mobster history in Hot Springs is very cool. But I'm more partial to the baseball history."

She furrowed her brow. "I don't guess I'm very familiar with that."

"Spring training originated here. Babe Ruth was a frequent visitor, using the bathhouses or visiting Oaklawn when he wasn't playing ball." Oaklawn, Hot Springs's horse-racing track, opened in the early 1900s and was home to the Arkansas Derby.

"I guess I learn something new every day," she said.

He slipped an arm around her waist. "I guess so."

Violet was suddenly all too aware of how close he was. "Are you ready to go to the Arlington? There's a staircase we can take that leads down to the lawn in front of the hotel."

"Almost." His voice was husky. He turned her toward him. "Violet, I've really enjoyed these past weeks. I never thought we had so much in common or would actually have such a good time together."

"Me neither," she murmured.

Jackson pulled her closer and tipped her chin. "I've waited a long time to do this." He bent down and pressed his lips to hers.

She kissed him tentatively at first. It seemed so strange to kiss him, even though she'd known it was coming. The kiss deepened, and Violet wrapped her arms around his neck. It might have been fake, but it sure didn't feel fake.

When he finally pulled away, he was breathless.

Violet balanced herself on the brick overlook. "Guess we've got that first kiss out of the way."

He grinned. "Guess so." He took her hand and led her to the staircase.

Violet's heart still pounded from the kiss. "One down, two to go, right?"

"Right."

Somehow that didn't make her feel better. What was wrong with her? This wasn't a relationship. Just a good first-kiss story in case they ever needed it.

Chapter 28

Jackson Stratford: I TOLD MOM YOU WERE PLANNING ON
BRINGING DESSERT FOR THURSDAY. SHE SAYS YOU DON'T
HAVE TO DO THAT, BUT I TOLD HER YOU INSISTED. HA-HA.
REALLY I JUST WANT ALL THE CUPCAKES I CAN EAT! (Text
message sent November 19, 7:39 a.m.)

Violet Matthews: I'M GLAD YOU LIKE THEM THAT MUCH.
DOES THIS MEAN YOU'LL STILL BE COMING BY MY STORE
TO GET YOUR CUPCAKE FIX EVEN AFTER JANUARY? (Text
message sent November 19, 7:46 a.m.)

Jackson Stratford: COUNT ON IT. (Text message sent
November 19, 7:52 a.m.)

Jackson pulled into the driveway of his childhood home and
parked next to his sister's van. He took a deep breath.
"You okay?" Violet asked.
He shook his head. "I kind of dread this."

"Because of your mom's friend?"

"I'd probably dread it anyway, just because being here without my dad is still so hard."

Violet reached over and took his hand. "You want your mom to be happy. Right?"

"Of course. I just wish moving on wasn't the only path to happiness." He frowned. "But I know how childish that sounds."

"Your sister told me there's been a marked difference in your mom since she started seeing Roger. She said it's helped her get back to her old self."

Jackson frowned. "And I'm sure she told you it's what my dad would want. Right?"

"She may have mentioned something like that, yes."

"That's the thing. People keep saying that. They keep claiming to know what my dad would say or do or want. But how do they know?"

Violet smiled. "I didn't even know your dad and I'm pretty sure I can answer that question. Your dad sounds like the kind of man who would've wanted his family to be happy. So I'd say that's how they know. He'd want whatever it is that would give his family the most happiness."

Jackson sighed. "I guess you're right."

"Trust me." She smiled. "I know how hard holidays must be for you. But remember they're hard for the whole family. And probably even Roger. I'm sure holidays only bring home the fact that he lost his wife."

"I guess you're right."

She held up the canister of cupcakes. "Now, are you ready to go inside? They're probably wondering why we're sitting out here for so long."

Jackson laughed. "They probably think we're out here kissing and getting that all out of our systems before we go inside."

A pink blush spread across her face.

"Are you thinking about our first kiss?" he asked, grinning.

She scowled. "No."

"Good. Me neither." It wasn't quite the truth. It was all he'd been thinking about since it had happened. But there was no reason to tell her that now. "Let's do this."

Dear Mama,

Well, Thanksgiving wasn't as bad as I expected it to be. Maybe being apart has been good for us. Daddy and I went out to dinner one night, and I told him all about my life in Hot Springs. He is really happy that I haven't been in any trouble at my new school. (Remember the great graffiti incident of last year?) And he's also pretty pumped about my GPA. I'm doing really well in my classes.

Stephanie is okay. She isn't as cool as Violet though. But I guess I can put up with her.

Daddy and I talked about college. He didn't seem too surprised when I told him I was looking at schools in Arkansas. Rachel is going to Harding. I think I'll go look at the campus this summer. Violet told me since that's where she graduated from, she'd be happy to take me on a tour of campus.

It isn't set in stone yet or anything, but it's a possibility. Daddy seemed pretty okay with it. I think he misses me, but really wants me to be happy—even if it means I'm not in Texas.

Love,
Shadow

Reagan sketched out the design she was considering for an author's website. She'd been hard pressed to find time to work on it between the madness of Thanksgiving and now trying to get Christmas shopping done. It was hard to believe it was already December.

She held the paper up and gave it the once over. Perfect. The woman wanted something professional, yet fun and inviting, and Reagan was pretty sure she'd be pleased with this.

The office door burst open, and her pencil went flying.

"Why is there a strange woman downstairs playing with our children? And what is this for?" Chad put a large FedEx package on her desk. "What is Reagan McClure Designs?"

Her heart sank. She'd planned to tell Chad everything this weekend. "The woman downstairs is Maggie Denton. She's a nanny."

"Where did you meet her?"

He would have to ask that. "Actually, I met her at the gym."

"The gym? Since when do you go to the gym?" Chad looked at her like she'd grown horns.

Reagan pulled the office door closed. No sense in alarming the kids by their raised voices. "I don't anymore. I did for a couple of months though."

"You never told me. How could you not tell me something like that? Who kept the kids while you were there?"

She bristled. "Actually, the reason I chose the gym I did was because they have a wonderful daycare facility on site. Everyone is very professional, and I signed the kids in and out, so they were never in any kind of danger." She sat down at her desk. "Maggie and I took a class together and got to be friends. The family she works for as a nanny is moving at the end of the month, and I asked her to watch the kids for a couple of hours today while I got a few things done."

Chad frowned. "Don't you think you should've run that by me first?"

"I never would've left them *alone* with someone without talking to you about it. But I'm right upstairs. Ava Grace has been up here a couple of times to show me the crafts she's been working on. It's a really nice setup." She took a breath to calm herself down. "And I checked Maggie's references. They're impeccable."

"What are you working on? What is Reagan McClure Designs?" Chad asked angrily.

"Just calm down. I was planning to tell you this weekend. I wanted to wait and see if it was even a possibility before I broached the subject."

"What?"

"I designed the logo and did some website stuff for Violet's bake shop, Central Avenue Cupcakes. A few people asked her for the designer, and she gave them my information." She shrugged. "I took a couple of jobs just to see if I was interested and see if I was going to even be successful at picking up freelance work." She grinned. "I'm confident that there's enough work out there for me to work as much as I want."

"So you want to go back to work? Like full-time?" He drew his brows together.

She shook her head. "No. But I'd like to consider working a couple of days or even just a couple of afternoons a week." She held her breath.

Chad frowned. "Why didn't you tell me this sooner?"

"I knew you might not be happy, so I wanted to be absolutely sure before we discussed it."

"I'm less happy that you hid it. What were you thinking?"

Reagan sighed. "I was thinking it might be a big, fat failure. And if it was, I didn't want to have bothered you with it."

"Since when is talking to me—your husband—about something that's obviously important to you the same thing as bothering me?" Chad stood up and paced the room. "And the gym thing? What's the deal?"

Reagan's anger flared. "In case you didn't know it, I wasn't exactly happy with myself a few months ago. I had to do something to get out of the funk I was in. And it was hard. My body has been through a lot over the last year. My first two pregnancies were easy. The last one was not. And then I found that the weight wasn't coming off as fast as it had the first two times." She shrugged. "So I decided to go to the gym. Honestly it was as much mental as it was physical. It really helped clear my head to know that a couple of times a week I was going to just be myself. No one would be crying for me or clinging for me or needing something from me. Sometimes that can be exhausting."

Chad sat back down. "I'm sorry you feel that way."

"You don't notice me anymore." She gestured toward herself. "I've lost more than ten pounds. You haven't even said anything."

Chad frowned. "Are you having an affair?"

"You have got to be kidding me. You are the one who travels with young, attractive women. Yet you have the audacity to ask if *I'm* having an affair?" It was completely laughable.

"Sorry. It's just the secrets and the gym and the freelancing." He shrugged. "I feel like you've been pulling away from me."

"I don't even remember the last conversation we had that wasn't about the kids. Do you? So do you blame me for pulling away?"

"Date night soon? Just us? No kid talk?" he asked.

She nodded. "And I won't take on any more freelance work until we discuss it."

He leaned forward and kissed her on the cheek. "I miss us. A lot."

Reagan did, too. Now if they could just figure out how to get back to being the couple they used to be.

Chapter 29

Violet Matthews: WISH ME LUCK! JACKSON AND I ARE
HEADED TO THE BIG WEDDING WEEKEND. (Text message
sent December 13, 4:45 p.m.)

Reagan McClure: I HOPE EVERYTHING GOES WELL. SEND
ME A PICTURE OF THE WEDDING. HOPE Y'ALL HAVE FUN.
HAVE YOU DECIDED WHAT THIS "THING" WITH JACKSON IS
YET?? (Text message sent December 13, 4:52 p.m.)

Violet leaned her head against the seat of the Range Rover. "It's
hard to believe it's already here."

"Yep." Jackson looked over at her and grinned. "You ready?"

"Ready for it all to be over."

He sighed. "Do you mean us or the wedding?"

"The wedding first." She grinned. "We still have a few more
weeks before we're over."

Jackson pulled into the hotel parking lot. "So what's going on
tonight?"

"It's kind of weird. If you ask me, it's just my sister looking for an excuse to be the center of attention for as long as possible." She sighed. "Tonight there is a dinner that is just for our family and a few close friends. Tomorrow there are activities planned during the day and then the rehearsal and rehearsal dinner. Then Saturday is the wedding."

"Three days of wedding fun."

"Exactly." She took a breath. "Are you ready to put on your boyfriend hat?"

He smiled. "Always."

Violet waited for him to open the passenger door for her. She hated to admit it, but having him for a boyfriend, fake or not, was kind of nice. He'd turned out to be one of the biggest and best surprises of her life. "Thanks," she said as he offered her a hand.

"You look amazing tonight, by the way."

"Thanks. You're not so bad yourself." He wore a charcoal suit with a french blue shirt. A blue-and-gray striped tie completed the look. Very classic."

Jackson reached over and took her hand. "Let's do this."

"Violet," said Aunt Darlene when she met them at the hotel lobby door. "Who is this handsome man?"

"This is Jackson Stratford," she said.

Jackson shook Aunt Darlene's hand. "Nice to meet you."

"Your mother told me you had a new boyfriend. I hope this one's a keeper." Aunt Darlene patted her on the back.

Violet leaned close to Jackson once Aunt Darlene had moved on to another guest. "It's not too late to run to a galaxy far, far away."

"Is that a *Star Wars* reference?" he whispered.

She cocked her head. "Maybe."

Jackson leaned down and planted a quick kiss on her mouth.

She laughed as he pulled away. "Check." She made a check-mark motion in the air with her finger. "Two down."

"Stop it." He grinned. "Can't you just humor me and act like you enjoyed that?"

The truth of the matter was that she didn't have to pretend. At least he'd made this one quick. She pushed the thought of their first kiss out of her mind. This was just pretend. "Of course. The next time I promise not to count down." Because that would be at the end of their little ruse and they both knew it. By the time their third kiss happened, they'd be about to part ways.

"Did I just see a little PDA over here?" Amber walked over with her entourage in tow. "Because I'm pretty sure the spinster sister isn't allowed to have more fun than the bride."

Violet tensed. "Hi, Amber. Everything looks just beautiful."

"Thanks." She eyed Jackson. "Aren't you going to introduce me to your man? I've been hearing tales of him, but haven't actually seen him with my own eyes." She grinned at Jackson. "I was beginning to think you were just a figment of Vi's imagination."

He grinned and pulled Violet closer to him. "Not at all. I'm completely real." He held out a hand. "I'm Jackson."

She looked at him with narrowed eyes. "You look really familiar."

"He has one of those faces," Violet said.

Jackson chuckled. "Thanks a lot, babe." His term of endearment might be fake, but Violet liked the way it sounded.

Amber waved at someone across the room. "I want you to meet my maid of honor."

A blond girl bounded over to where they stood. "Amber, it looks so pretty in here." Her eyes widened at the sight of Jackson. "You're the last person I expected to see here. I didn't think weddings were your thing."

Violet felt Jackson tense next to her. "Hi, Whitney. It's been awhile," he said finally.

She stuck out her lower lip. "You just, like, stopped calling."

No way. This could not be happening. Jackson used to date Amber's best friend.

Jackson gripped Violet's hand tighter. "Sorry about that. I just realized we were looking for different things."

"Clearly he was looking for someone older and more mature," Amber observed. "Or maybe just older." She laughed at her own joke. "How did y'all meet, anyway?" she asked Violet.

"We were actually in college together," Jackson explained. "So we've known each other for quite a long time."

Violet forced a smile. "We'd better go say hi to Mom and Dad." She tugged on Jackson's hand and led him away from Amber and her angry bridesmaid.

"I'm so sorry about that," Jackson whispered in her ear once they'd walked away. "I only went out with her a couple of times, and it was last summer. She was way too young for me, and we had absolutely zero in common. I'm sorry if that was awkward for you."

Violet enjoyed the way his breath felt against her ear. It sent shivers down her back. "It's okay. It isn't like we were in our fake relationship back then." She smiled.

He rolled his eyes. "True. But aren't you a little bit jealous?" he whispered.

"Hardly." She grinned when he made a face. "How do you think this is going? Do you think they were suspicious?"

He pulled her to him and gave her a big hug. "Not at all. In fact, anyone looking at us right now thinks I can't keep my hands off you," he whispered.

She grinned. "Got to keep it believable, right?"

"Right," he whispered again, sending another wave of shivers down her spine.

Jackson had to admit, he was having fun. Much of the time, he and Violet kept their relationship very businesslike. But when they were with family and friends and were supposed to be a real couple, he was free to treat her like a girlfriend.

And he liked it.

A few weeks ago when he'd kissed her for the first time, he'd been hit with the realization that his feelings for her went deeper than just someone he had a business arrangement with. And Thanksgiving with his family had shown him how it could feel to have a partner and a friend. He'd leaned on her as he'd dealt with another holiday without his dad and the pain of watching his mom move on.

But tonight was the first time he truly felt like they were a real couple. That spark between them was unmistakable. It wasn't the kind of thing that could be faked.

And he was pretty sure she felt it, too. In the beginning, she'd tensed when he'd come near her. But tonight she leaned into him. She'd been the one to take his hand, and earlier when he'd whispered in her ear, he'd seen chill bumps on her arms. And he was hoping those were a good sign.

"So you're sure you're going to be okay staying here tonight?" he asked.

She sighed. "There was no getting around it. Mom wanted me here in case I'm needed. Of course, after dinner the bachelorette party is happening."

"Bachelorette party, huh? You aren't planning to cut loose are you?"

She laughed. "I'm not going. For one thing, I wasn't invited. For another, that's not really my thing."

He was a little relieved. He didn't like the idea of Violet going out with those girls and being hit on by a bunch of guys. Plus he knew how miserable she'd be. That definitely didn't sound like Violet's idea of fun. "Well if I need to come rescue you tomorrow on my lunch break, just text me." He grinned. "Have you heard from anyone at the shop? How are they managing tonight without you?"

"Shadow sent me a text earlier. It's been a slow night. She and Mrs. Kemp are doing fine." Violet grinned. "I'm a little nervous about being gone for two more days, but I think things will be okay. Sometimes I can't believe I get paid to do what I do."

"And you were scared you'd fail." Central Avenue Cupcakes had far exceeded her expectations so far, and it looked like business would only pick up as more people heard about the cupcakes and the atmosphere.

She shrugged. "I still am sometimes. But it lessens every day."

"I hope I've helped instill some confidence in you. Always know that no matter what, I believe in you."

She blushed. "Are you saying that as my fake boyfriend or as yourself?" she asked softly.

"Myself." He brushed his lips against her forehead. "And don't forget it."

"Dinner is served," a waiter announced to the small crowd mingling in the lobby.

Jackson took Violet's hand and led her into the ballroom. He glanced over his shoulder. It had been a shock running into Whitney. But hopefully she'd behave herself and leave them alone.

Because the last thing Violet needed was any kind of scene this weekend. And Jackson was going to do all he could to ensure that things went smoothly.

Dear Mama,

The closer we get to Christmas, the more I miss you. Violet's boyfriend, Jackson, told me not too long ago that holidays were hard for him, too. His daddy had a heart attack and died last year.

But he told me it made him feel better to think about his daddy in heaven. That God had been the one to decide it was time for his daddy to go home, and even though it was hard for him to understand, he had to trust that was the best plan.

I'm trying really hard to believe that, but sometimes it

isn't easy. I wish God had decided that I needed you more than He did. But I guess it doesn't work like that.

Maybe someday I'll understand. But for now, I guess I just have to accept it, even if I don't completely understand.

Today for the first time, I looked in the mirror and saw you. That was kind of cool. Nana says that you'll always be with me. Maybe that's what she meant—that I have a piece of you in me.

I hope I make you proud.

Love,
Shadow

Chapter 30

Shadow Simmons: EVERYTHING IS ALL CLOSED UP FOR THE NIGHT. NO PROBLEMS. NANA SAYS NOT TO WORRY. WHENEVER WE RUN OUT OF CUPCAKES, WE'LL JUST PUT THE SIGN IN THE WINDOW EXPLAINING THAT WE'RE SOLD OUT AND WILL REOPEN ON TUESDAY. (Text message sent December 13, 10:43 p.m.)

Violet Matthews: THANK YOU SO MUCH FOR YOUR HARD WORK AND YOUR HELP! A CHRISTMAS BONUS IS DEFINITELY COMING YOUR WAY. TEXT ME IF YOU NEED ME. (Text message sent December 13, 10:45 p.m.)

Jackson walked out of the hotel hand in hand with Violet. Despite the tension between Violet and her sister, they'd had a nice evening. "So what time do I need to be back tomorrow?" he asked.

"The rehearsal is at six and is scheduled for half an hour. I'm not planning on going to that. The dinner is right afterward. So maybe get here around six fifteen or so? Just call me and I'll come down and meet you so we can go to the dinner together."

He pulled her close. "Day one of the wedding extravaganza is over, and you're still in once piece."

She smiled. "Barely. And if you weren't here, I definitely wouldn't be okay."

"Good to know." His heart pounded. He wanted to kiss her again, a real kiss. Off the contract. But he had no idea how she'd feel about that. "I'd better get home. Work tomorrow."

Violet nodded. "Good night," she said softly.

He held her for a long moment, relishing the way she fit against him. "See you tomorrow."

She nodded. "Of course." Her phone buzzed, and she pulled it out of her purse. The screen lit up the darkness around them. "It's Reagan." She looked up at him with a worried expression. "It's not like her to call so late. I'd better take it."

He nodded. "See you tomorrow."

She waved and held the phone up to her ear.

Jackson watched her walk up the path to the hotel. He'd fallen hard for her, and he was pretty sure she had no idea. And he was even less sure about the way she felt about him. He'd caught glimpses of what he thought was genuine interest, but at the same time. . .he couldn't be sure until they talked about it.

He climbed in the Range Rover and looked down. Violet had left her overnight bag in the floorboard. She'd need that stuff tonight. He hoisted the bag over his shoulder and hurried toward the hotel.

He heard her before he saw her. She must still be on the phone with Reagan.

"I'm so sorry," she said. "I think you should really talk to Chad though. You might be surprised by things."

Jackson hated to eavesdrop, but he also didn't want to interrupt. Maybe he should just leave the bag at the hotel desk.

"Okay, stop right there," Violet said. "If I'm not allowed to judge your relationship, you're not allowed to judge mine."

Jackson froze. She was talking about him. About them.

"We're just friends, nothing more."

He nearly dropped the bag. He knew that was the party line she was giving Reagan. She'd claimed she couldn't pretend to Reagan that they were really in a relationship, so she was just telling her they were friends who enjoyed hanging out. Still though, it hurt a little to hear her say they were nothing but friends.

"I'm *not* falling for him. Stop saying that. Do you really think I've forgotten the past so easily? And it isn't like he has a successful relationship track record. I mean, he's a mess and you don't know the half of it. I'd end up getting hurt, and I've been hurt plenty of times before. So don't worry."

Jackson's heart fell. Violet knew everything about him. Everything about his past. He'd opened up to her in a way he never had with anyone else.

And he wasn't good enough. It didn't matter that he'd changed. That he'd overcome the problems he'd faced in the past and was trying hard to live the kind of life that would make his loved ones proud. But clearly Violet wasn't proud to be with him.

At least he knew.

Now he wouldn't make a fool of himself by declaring his feelings. He'd even thought about telling her he was in love with her. That he'd never felt this way about anyone. But hearing what she really thought of him had set him straight.

He took the side entrance to the hotel and left her bag at the desk. "Please leave a message for Violet Matthews and have her pick this up."

The clerk nodded. "Yes, sir."

"There you are," a familiar voice said. "I was looking for you."

He turned to see Whitney walking toward him. "I thought y'all were headed to a bachelorette party."

She laughed. "We are. But I thought you might want to hang out first."

Jackson glanced at the main entrance. Violet would probably be coming through the door any minute. And he had no desire to see her right now. "What did you have in mind?" he asked Whitney.

She smiled. "There's a little restaurant across the street that's still open. Want to grab a bite to eat and catch up?"

He looked again at the entrance. Violet must still be outside, bashing him. By now she was probably telling Reagan the real reason they spent time together and what a mistake their arrangement had been. She should really consider theater, though, because she'd had him fooled. "I could go for some food."

"Excellent."

He followed Whitney out the side door and ignored the sick feeling in the pit of his stomach. Violet had made it crystal clear to Reagan there was nothing between them. Which meant everything had been fake. And even worse, all the bad things he'd ever thought about himself were the reasons she'd given for not wanting to be with him. That made it even worse—hearing those same insecurities echoed from the person he cared so much about. "What have you been up to lately?" He turned his attention to Whitney and tried to push Violet from his mind.

"You aren't going to let this go, are you?" Violet asked, clutching the phone to her ear.

Reagan laughed. "Not when you're clearly delusional. I know you well. Very well. And you don't fall for just anyone. I'm just saying. . .maybe there's more to Jackson than I thought."

Violet had tried denying Reagan's accusations, but she wasn't getting anywhere. "Fine. Yes, the past couple of months have been pretty amazing. And tonight I don't know what I would've done without him."

"So you admit it."

Violet groaned. "Yes. I admit it. I have feelings for him. Real feelings. But I'm still a little apprehensive."

"That's to be expected. Not only have you had your heart broken, but Jackson has hurt you before."

"He's not the same guy he used to be. Not at all." The Jackson she knew now was kind and sweet. He would never hurt her on purpose. "Besides, the more I've learned about him and his life, the more understanding I am about the stuff he did when we were in college. He really is remorseful."

"I know. Both times I've seen him at the bakeshop, I've felt like he's trying hard to redeem himself where you're concerned."

Violet smiled. "Now I just have to decide how to handle the

situation. Do I wait and see if he tells me he has feelings for me? Or do I just tell him? And what if I'm way off base and he only sees me as a friend?"

"If he does, don't you think you should find out soon before your feelings grow any deeper?" Reagan asked.

"You're probably right. Maybe I'll get up the courage soon. Or maybe I'll just wait and see what happens."

"I hope everything goes okay. Keep me posted."

Violet nodded. "I will." She clicked off the phone and headed back into the hotel. She glanced at her phone. Jackson had had time to get home by now. The past few weeks they'd started texting right before bed. It was weird that he hadn't sent one.

She scrolled through her messages and chose his name. Just reading back over their texts from the past months made her smile. She quickly sent an "are you home yet?" message to him and waited for his response.

Thirty minutes later, she climbed into bed. He must've gone straight to sleep when he got home, but she put her phone on the nightstand next to her bed just in case.

Because now that she'd realized her true feelings, she didn't want to miss a moment with him.

Chapter 31

Whitney Anderson: LAST NIGHT WAS FUN. MAYBE WE CAN DO IT AGAIN SOMETIME. SEE YOU TONIGHT AT THE REHEARSAL DINNER. (Text message sent December 14, 2:33 p.m.)

Jackson Stratford: I DON'T THINK SO. I WISH YOU THE BEST IN THE FUTURE THOUGH. (Text message sent December 14, 2:39 p.m.)

Jackson had a hard time making it through the workday. Between wondering where he'd gone wrong with Violet and realizing he'd made a huge mistake by going to the restaurant with Whitney, he couldn't concentrate. He knew Whitney was bad news, but last night he'd been so hurt he wasn't thinking clearly. Obviously. Otherwise he wouldn't have done something so rash.

"You okay, Mr. Stratford?" Sheila asked. "You're not coming down with something are you?"

Just a big case of stupidity. "Nothing a weekend won't cure."

He smiled. "In fact, I'm about to head out. You can leave early if you want."

"Thanks," she said. "Have a great weekend."

Jackson was pretty sure the odds of his weekend being great were slim to none. Actually less than none, whatever that would be. He took his suit coat from the hook behind his office door and slipped it on.

Violet had sent him a couple of texts today, but he'd just sent back minimal responses. Nothing like the exchanges they'd had during the past few months.

He still couldn't believe he'd been so stupid as to fall for her. The fake relationship had been his idea. He'd thought it was a no-brainer with no strings.

He certainly hadn't counted on developing real feelings. And he definitely hadn't expected to fall in love with her.

Twenty minutes later, he pulled into the hotel parking lot. He pulled out his phone and sent Violet a quick text letting her know he'd be in the lobby.

He walked into the luxurious building and sat down on a surprisingly uncomfortable seat. Just another example of how looks could be deceiving.

"You ready for round two?" Violet asked.

He looked up to see her standing before him. She'd gone all out tonight. Her green cocktail dress was a throwback to the fifties. "You look like you could be Marilyn Monroe's red-haired sister."

Violet laughed. "I don't know about all of that. I suppose this dress is a bit Marilyn inspired."

Jackson stood. "Let's get this done." He offered his arm, and she clutched it. He couldn't bear to take her hand. Not now. Not knowing how she really felt about him.

"I'm guessing we'll have assigned seats?" he asked as they reached the ballroom. It was best to keep the conversation as impersonal as possible.

Violet nodded. "Oh yes. My sister loves the idea of telling a room full of people what to do." She tugged on his arm. "I think we're going to be seated with my grandparents."

Once they were seated, she glanced over at him. "I guess you had a busy day, huh?"

He shrugged. "About normal."

"I just figured since you didn't text much, it meant you were in meetings and stuff." Violet gave him a worried look.

Jackson would've thought her obvious insecurity would've given him some satisfaction. But it didn't. Instead he just felt sad. "Looks like the rehearsal is over. I see your parents and sister."

"Let's get this party started." She grinned. "I think there's some kind of video first. Another of Amber's ideas." She leaned closer to him. "You know how I hate to be the center of attention? She's the complete opposite. I fully expect for this to be an hour-long slide show full of as many flattering pictures of Amber as possible."

Jackson laughed in spite of himself. "Surely not."

Just as Violet had predicted, the lights flickered in the dining room and a movie flashed on the screen behind where the wedding party sat. "Welcome to the wedding rehearsal dinner of Amber and Landry," Violet's dad said from the podium. "We're thankful you're here to share in this joyous occasion with us. And now, without further ado, is a video presentation." Mr. Matthews sat down at the table he shared with his wife and what Jackson assumed were the groom's parents.

The video flashed a variety of pictures of Amber and Landry at various stages of adolescence. "Look at you," Jackson said to Violet when her face flashed across the screen. "That's some big hair."

"It was a perm. Big mistake." She shrugged. "It was 1989."

He chuckled. Maybe they could pull off the fake relationship after all. At least he knew how she felt about him. He could just suffer through, forget about his attraction to her, and they'd be through with each other in less than a month.

The screen went dark signaling the end of the show, but one final shot popped up on the screen like an afterthought.

"What is that?" Violet hissed, gripping his arm.

The shock at seeing his own picture on the screen rendered him speechless. Whitney had held up her phone at the restaurant and taken a self portrait of them. He hadn't thought another thing about it.

Until now.

"That's what you were wearing last night," Violet said in a low voice. "Did you go out with her after you left the hotel?"

Heads began to turn in their direction.

Jackson met the angry eyes of Violet's grandmother before turning to look at Violet.

"I can explain," he started.

Violet's body trembled. There was no explanation needed. She couldn't even have a fake relationship without being cheated on.

"Hope everyone enjoyed the slide show," Amber said from the podium. "And in case y'all didn't know, that last picture was of my maid of honor and my sister's boyfriend, taken last night." She shook her head. "Poor Violet. She has a knack for picking the wrong guys, doesn't she?" Amber turned toward Violet's table. "Sorry you had to find out like this, Vi, but better now than later, right? Seems that Jackson just couldn't resist going out with Whitney last night to rekindle their old flame."

Violet could only watch in horror the train wreck that was her life.

Amber waved at Landry. "I guess they can't all be keepers like my Landry." She smiled. "But maybe Violet will be able to move on now that she knows the truth."

A murmur spread through the room as more heads turned in Violet's direction. She jumped up. No way was she staying for another second. Without another glance at Jackson, she hurried out of the room.

"Violet, wait!" he called.

She kept going through the lobby and out the door. If she hadn't had on those stupid high heels, she might've run forever. Instead she stopped at a bench outside the building and sat down.

"Please, Violet." Jackson sat down next to her. "I'm so sorry."

"How is it that you've managed to publicly humiliate me again, all these years later? And I'm so dumb, I didn't even see it coming."

"That isn't fair. Your sister orchestrated that. She could've asked me about it in private, and I would've told her she was wrong. But instead she made you a laughingstock."

Violet shook her head. "She wouldn't have had any ammunition if not for you. As far as I'm concerned, this is your fault."

"I overheard you last night on the phone with Reagan."

She drew her brows together. "What? So now you're listening in on my phone calls?"

"I came back to give you your bag. I heard you saying all that stuff about me. About how messed up I am. How the whole thing means nothing." He shrugged. "I guess I figured if you really felt that way about me, you wouldn't mind if I hung out with Whitney."

Violet glared. "You had me fooled. You certainly didn't act like you had any interest in her when we ran into her. But I guess you are a good actor after all, I mean you've convinced most everyone we know that you're crazy about me." She took a breath. "Did you really end things with her over the summer or have you been seeing her all along?"

Jackson groaned. "When would I have had time to see her? I was too busy helping you move and paint and giving you pep talks."

She flinched. "I think you should just leave."

"We need to talk about this."

Violet shook her head. She was suddenly very tired. "No. We don't. There's nothing left to say. You betrayed me. With some girl you used to date who happens to be my sister's best friend. You know my sister and I don't get along. Somewhere in the back of your mind, it had to occur to you that going off with her *maid of honor* might come back to bite you." She buried her head in her hands for a long moment. There was no way she was giving him the satisfaction of seeing her cry.

"Please, Violet. I'm sorry. You have to believe me. Absolutely nothing happened."

She couldn't think of a single thing he could say to make this better. "You need to go. And I need to face my family."

"How will you get home?" he asked.

She'd driven her car to his house yesterday so they could ride to the hotel together. "I'll manage. I managed fine before you came along." Stupid Mimi the matchmaker. If not for her, none of this would've happened. Violet would've probably met some nice guy online and they'd be in the hotel right now enjoying their rubbery chicken.

Jackson walked away without another word.

Violet sat for another moment on the bench. In just a few short minutes, her life had spiraled out of control. There had to be some lesson in it though, right? Some takeaway to make it worth the pain.

Because right now, not only did she have to face a humiliating room full of people, she also felt empty. She'd gotten used to having Jackson by her side. She'd started to have real feelings for him. Feelings she hadn't been sure she'd ever have about anyone.

And just like that—it all blew up.

Chapter 32

Jackson Stratford: I REALLY THINK WE NEED TO TALK ABOUT WHAT HAPPENED. (Text message sent December 15, 9:02 a.m.)

Violet pulled the covers over her head to block out the sunshine. She wanted today to be dark and dreary to match her mood. But no. Of course Amber's wedding day had to be bright and beautiful.

Last night had been the worst ever. Aunt Darlene had given her a ride to her car, and she'd decided to go home. She didn't care if she missed her sister's wedding. Amber had tried to claim that she was only looking out for Violet, that she felt like she needed to be warned that Jackson and Whitney had gone out after dinner. But Violet knew her sister too well.

Whitney had apparently felt bad for her part in things and had apologized to Violet. She'd confided that Amber had sent her to see if Jackson was on the up-and-up.

As far as Violet was concerned, they all deserved each other.

Once again she'd been the one made to look foolish, the one to be pitied.

So today would be business as normal. No wedding for her, sister or not. She'd go in to the bake shop this afternoon and throw herself into baking the best cupcakes she could.

The phone buzzed. She glanced at the caller ID. "Hey, Reagan."

"Do I need to come over? Because I will. I can call someone to keep the kids."

Violet smiled in spite of the situation. "That's okay. I'm fine. Or at least I will be." She let out a huge sigh. "I'm still having a hard time processing everything that happened."

"I don't blame you." Reagan didn't say anything for a long moment. "Have you heard from him?" she asked finally.

"He's texted and called. I haven't responded to either. What could he possibly say to make this better?" Violet had tried to imagine one thing that could change things. But there was nothing.

"Hang in there. It's nearly Christmas. A time for joy, no matter what is going wrong in your personal life."

Or a time for pain. Violet knew how much Jackson was dreading Christmas without his dad. Now it looked like they'd both be alone on Christmas. "Do you want to get together sometime next week?" They didn't exchange big gifts, but usually got each other a little something.

"That sounds good. Let me know when and where. I could stand to do a little kid-free shopping." Reagan chuckled. "Chin up, Violet. God will take care of you."

Violet hung up the phone and finally peeled herself out of bed. It was time to get on with her life. She padded into the living room to let Arnie out.

He lay still on his bed and didn't move when she walked by.

She knelt next to him. "Arnie?" She shook him gently.

Nothing.

She shook him a little harder. "Arnie, please wake up."

He opened his eyes slowly.

"Thank goodness." She put her head close to him.

The dog's breathing was very shallow.

Violet stood up and clapped her hands, hoping he'd get up and follow her outside.

He started to raise his head, but it appeared to be too much effort, so he rested it back on the pillow.

Violet grabbed her phone and dialed the number to the nearest vet. She quickly explained the situation.

"I think you should probably bring him in, ma'am. Because you know he's been in renal failure, it's likely that it's gotten worse. We'll need to check his kidney function."

Violet had no idea how she could possibly get him to the car by herself. He'd be sixty pounds of dead weight. But she'd have to try. And there was no one she could call. Her entire family was at Amber's wedding, and she sure wasn't calling Jackson for help.

Maybe there was one person. She dialed the bake shop.

"Central Avenue Cupcakes, this is Shadow."

"It's Violet. Arnie is really sick. I need some help getting him to the vet. Are you busy today?"

"We're almost sold out. Nana has the sign all ready to go."

"Are there any customers?"

"No. One just left."

"Can you or your nana come help me get Arnie to the vet while the other one closes down?" She heard Shadow explaining the situation to Mrs. Kemp in the background.

"I'll borrow Nana's car and come help you. She'll close up and then go next door to Aunt Teak's. Granddaddy is manning the shop for her today."

"Great. See you in a minute."

Violet threw on some clothes and twisted her hair into a bun. It would have to do. She went back to Arnie. He didn't look good. "Hang in there, boy. Please." Her tears fell on his fur. She knew she should probably keep calm so she wouldn't upset him, but it was not going to be easy. She stroked his neck and rubbed his tummy. "Arnie, you've been the best dog a girl could ever have. Sometimes I've felt like you were my only friend." She wiped her tears, but more fell in their place.

There was a knock at the door. Violet opened it and ushered Shadow inside. "Let's try and slide him on his bed to the door, then we'll lift him into the car."

Shadow nodded.

They worked together to slowly slide him to the door then hoisted him to the car.

"I can drive if you want to sit in the back with him," Shadow offered.

Violet handed her the keys. "Thanks." She cradled Arnie's head in her lap and continued to stroke his fur. *Please Lord, be with Arnie. I know he's lived a long life, but I'm not ready to let him go just yet.*

Jackson sat in his Range Rover outside Jeff and Lauren's house. After the disastrous weekend, he needed to talk his problems over with someone else.

Lauren opened the door, concern written all over her face. "You look terrible."

"I haven't slept in a couple of days. Is Jeff here?"

She jerked her chin toward the kitchen. "Come get a cup of coffee. He's putting the boys in bed, but he'll be down in a minute."

Jackson sat numbly at the kitchen table.

"Here you go." She'd known him long enough to know how he liked his coffee.

He nodded. "Thanks." He wrapped his hands around the warm cup and thought about Violet.

"Hey, man." Jeff walked into the room. "Everything okay?" He glanced at his wife but she shrugged.

"It's over," Jackson said. "Violet and I. We're done."

Lauren furrowed her brow and sat down across from him.

Jeff leaned against a bar stool and crossed his arms. "What happened?"

"It isn't a nice story." Jackson hung his head. What would they think of him once he explained?

Lauren shook her head. "Breakups never are. Now tell us what happened."

Jackson told them everything, from the matchmaker to the contract to the eventual blowup. They both sat still, wearing nearly identical shocked expressions. Lauren spoke first.

"A contract?" She shook her head. "I'm sorry, but I don't get it."

"Violet and I were both looking for something specific—to get everyone off our cases and have a crutch at those events." He shrugged. "It made perfect sense at the time."

"So you're trying to tell me that it was all fake? What we saw at the Razorback game that day was just an act?" Jeff asked.

Jackson nodded. "That's exactly what I'm saying."

"Uh-uh. I don't buy it." Lauren shook her head. "You can't fake chemistry like that, and you two had it. I don't care if you went into it thinking it was a sham—what we saw was real."

"Yeah, well. . .it was real on my part. Not hers." He shook his head. "I heard her plain as day telling her friend that I was a mess that she wasn't going to get involved with. That it was all an act."

"Maybe she was saying that, but there's no way she meant it." Lauren was adamant. "I'm telling you what I saw, and it went both ways. It was *not* an act."

"I can't help what you think you saw." Jackson rubbed the stubble on his jaw. He hadn't shaved in a couple of days, hadn't even gone in to work today.

Jeff paced the length of the dining room. "Do you think there's a chance you misunderstood?"

Jackson laughed. "At this point, it wouldn't even matter. She says I betrayed her by going off with Whitney."

"She's kind of got a point. What were you thinking?" Lauren asked.

"I've never been in love. Until now. I just. . .when I heard her saying those things, it made me feel horrible. And I just wasn't thinking when I went to that restaurant with Whitney. I was just going to go with her to that restaurant because I didn't want to go home right then with my thoughts."

"And what happened?"

"As soon as we got to the restaurant she started asking me questions about my relationship with Violet. How we met, when we met, where our first date was—stuff like that. She kept on and kept on, and finally I just snapped and told her to back off—that being there with her was a mistake." He shook his head. "Then she snapped that picture of us, and the rest is history. Nothing happened at all." He sighed.

"Violet's sister sounds like a pretty terrible human being," Jeff said. "Any chance she's behind it?"

"In hindsight, absolutely. She was positively gleeful standing at that podium outing her sister. But I didn't really know how much animosity she had until I saw that."

"And now Violet feels humiliated," Lauren remarked.

Jackson sighed. "The problem is that it isn't the first time she's been humiliated because of me." He explained their relationship in college. "Y'all know that I went through a rough time back then. I was horrible to a lot of people."

Lauren groaned. "Just when I think it can't get any worse."

"What can I do? How can I fix things?"

"I'm not sure that you can," Jeff said. "Sorry man. That's a tough position to be in."

Jackson couldn't accept that. There had to be something he could do.

He just had to figure out what.

Chapter 33

Shadow Simmons: ARNIE IS REALLY SICK. HE MIGHT
NOT MAKE IT. JUST THOUGHT YOU SHOULD KNOW. (Text
message sent December 19, 2:42 p.m.)

Jackson Stratford: THANKS FOR TELLING ME. HOPE YOU'RE
DOING WELL. (Text message sent December 19, 2:45 p.m.)

Jackson pulled into Violet's driveway. This might not get him
anywhere, but he had to at least give it a shot. He'd waited until
the bakeshop was closed and she had plenty of time to get home
before he showed up.

He hurried up the path and knocked on the door before he lost
his nerve.

The living room curtains parted slightly, and then the porch
light came on.

Jackson held his breath. The porch light was a good sign, right?
It meant she was going to open the door. With each passing second,
his heart pounded faster.

Finally the unmistakable sound of the dead bolt being unlocked reached his ears. He breathed a sigh of relief.

Violet opened the door, her face an unreadable mask. "Yes?"

"Can I come in? Please?"

She pressed her lips together. "Just for a moment. It's been a long day, and I need to get to bed." Her red hair was twisted into a messy bun, and her face was scrubbed free of makeup, clear indications she was in the process of getting ready for bed.

Jackson walked inside and sat down on the couch. His eyes fell on Arnie's empty dog bed. "Is he. . .?"

Violet sighed and sat down in the recliner. "He's hanging in there. The vet thinks he'll make it this time. His kidneys are just failing." She shrugged. "The diet I have him on is helping to prolong things, but the end is inevitable. I'm bringing him home tomorrow." Her eyes were bright with unshed tears.

"I'm sorry." He remembered how he'd poked fun at her cooking special food for the dog. She'd been doing it to keep him healthy, not because she was an overzealous owner. He should've been more sensitive to that. "But I'm glad you'll get to bring him home."

She nodded. "I'm planning to have a special day for him next week. The shop will be closed for the week of Christmas, so we're going to do some of his favorite things. Go for a ride in the car, go for a walk at the park, and then I'll fix him a special meal." She smiled a tiny smile. "Maybe steak and then ice cream. He likes that." A tear dripped down her face. "I think that will be a nice memory to have."

"A special day to celebrate the good years you've had together. I think that's perfect." Jackson smiled. "I might not have an inside dog, but when I was a boy, we had a golden retriever. I loved that dog, and in the summertime he was my constant companion. He died my freshman year of college, and going home after that was never the same."

She nodded. "I'm glad to know you aren't completely heartless."

"Not completely."

Violet stood up. "Would you like something to drink? I think I'd like some hot chocolate."

Jackson followed her into the kitchen. Her formal, polite demeanor was what she'd use if he were a stranger. That stung. But at least she wasn't yelling. "That sounds good." He sat down at the counter and watched as she pulled out a container of cocoa. "You're making the real stuff—not from a mix?"

She looked up and nodded. "Cocoa, milk, and sugar on the stovetop. That's how my grandma always makes it, and it just tastes so much better than water and a mix."

"Old school." He grinned. "That's what I've come to expect from you." He thought he saw a hint of a smile but wasn't sure.

She worked deftly, not bothering to measure. Her practiced ease in the kitchen always amazed him.

"So why are you here?" she asked after minutes of silence. "And who told you about Arnie?" She poured cocoa in two red mugs and handed one to him.

"Shadow sent me a text. I'm glad she did." He took a sip. "This is delicious. Perfect for a December night. I can't believe it's nearly the first day of winter."

Violet nodded. "Why are you here?"

"I'm here to apologize. You have to know that nothing happened with me and Whitney. It was dumb of me to go to that restaurant with her in the first place, but you have to understand that I was really upset. I overheard you talking to Reagan and telling her all that stuff about how you'd never fall for a guy like me."

She watched him for a moment. "You gave my sister the perfect ammunition to humiliate me in front of a crowd. How in the world did warning bells not go off in your head? You saw how ugly Amber was to me about you in the first place."

"She's jealous of you."

Violet snorted. "No. She's not jealous. She's vindictive. Always has been. I love her because she is my sister, but I don't like her. That's water under the bridge though. The issue here is that you and I had a contract. We were supposed to be on each other's team for the duration. And you going off with Whitney like that completely violates it."

The contract? That's what she was mad about? "Wait. You're upset with me for breaking the contract? Not because I was with Whitney?" he asked.

She narrowed her eyes. "You shouldn't have been with anyone. Especially not the same night you debuted as my boyfriend in front of my family. That's just totally inappropriate and inexcusable."

He'd been hoping part of her anger was because he was spending time with someone else. But it looked like that wasn't the case. "I don't think you understand why I went with Whitney."

"Do you want to explain it?"

His heart pounded. He'd never done this before. Thirty-five years and what seemed like a million dates and he'd never given his heart to anyone. Until now. "Violet, I love you."

Her green eyes widened. "What?"

He regained his composure and lifted his chin. "I love you. This thing between us might have started out as fake and all because of a contract, but it isn't fake to me any longer."

She leaned against the counter. "Is this some kind of joke? Are you just trying to make me feel secure so I'll continue our game and go with you to your banquet?"

"This has nothing to do with my speech. Nothing to do with a game. Everything to do with you. I've never met anyone like you. I love the way you walk and the way you talk and the exasperating way you never let me get away with anything." He smiled. "Your hair and your vintage clothes and your obsession with old pennies." He shrugged. "The whole package. I love you."

"Stop saying that," she whispered. "Just stop."

He took a step toward her. "But why? It feels good to finally say it. I've been thinking it for a long time. You must have known after the first kiss. I've never felt anything so powerful." He grinned. "And I'm kind of old, so that should mean something."

She didn't smile at his joke. "If you loved me, you never would've gone off with Whitney. No matter what. Even if you were hurt or mad or whatever. You would've stayed and talked to me. Or something. Not end up out with your ex-girlfriend who happens to be my sister's maid of honor."

He rubbed his jaw. This was not working out the way he'd planned. "Please, Violet. Let's put that behind us and move forward as a real couple. Tear up the contract. Forget the rehearsal dinner."

"No. I can't. I'm sorry." Her voice was so quiet he could barely hear her. "That can't be undone. All those people laughing at me, thinking you're just a big cheater. That feeling of knowing you'd gone and done something behind my back." She shook her head. "I don't think I can trust you."

He'd driven past a yard full of Christmas decorations on the way here, and one of the inflatable ornaments lay in a pitiful puddle, the victim of a hole. That's how he felt. Totally deflated. "What can I do to earn your trust back? How can I get you to believe that I really love you—that I'd do anything for you?"

Violet shook her head. "There's nothing you can do." Her mouth turned down. "I think you should go."

Jackson looked into her eyes for one more moment. This couldn't really be the end, could it? "Please think about what I've said." He turned and walked through the living room and out into the chilly December night.

Somehow, some way, he had to figure out how to make her believe him. Had to get her to trust him.

Unless she really meant all those things she'd said to Reagan. If so, there was nothing he could ever do to fix it.

Reagan turned the van radio up loud. She so rarely got to drive anywhere alone anymore; she'd forgotten what it felt like to listen to real music and not a CD of children's songs.

Her in-laws had offered to come by the house this afternoon and watch the kids while she did some last-minute shopping. She had to admit, Mrs. McClure might be getting a little better now that she'd kept all four kids herself. The overnight trip that was supposed to have been date night for Reagan and Chad had apparently been torturous for Chad's parents.

Mrs. McClure had made the mistake of trying to put Bah in the washing machine before bed, and Ava Grace refused to go to bed without him. Her cries woke the twins, and Izzy used the distraction to get into the cookie jar.

Reagan had put on her best "I'm sorry" face during the story, but inwardly had laughed. After that experience, Mrs. McClure had been much less judgmental of Reagan's parenting and had stopped using their weekly after-church lunch as a time to dispense helpful advice.

She whipped into a space at the mall just as her phone rang. She picked it up and checked the caller ID. It was a forward from the house phone. She'd figured that would be one less thing for Chad's parents to worry about. "Hello?"

"Could I speak to Chad, please? I tried to call his cell but didn't get him, and this was the alternate number he gave." The woman's voice was breathy.

"This is his wife. Who's calling, please?"

There was a long pause on the other end. "This is Holly. And it's about a personal matter."

Reagan snorted. "A *personal* matter? Please. Just tell me what this is in regards to."

"I'm sorry. I'm not at liberty to discuss it. I'll just contact him at a later time."

Reagan stared at the phone after Holly hung up. Unbelievable.

So much for shopping. She backed out of the space and drove straight to Chad's office, not even bothering to make small talk with the receptionist. She flung the door open to his office and walked inside.

Chad looked up in surprise. "Reagan." He rose from his chair. "Is everything okay?"

"No. Everything is most certainly not okay." She pointed at his seat. "Sit down. We need to talk. Who is Holly?"

Chad didn't sit down. Instead he walked toward her and took her by the elbow. "We're not doing this here. Let's go outside." He led her into the hallway. "Reese, I'll be out the rest of the afternoon," he said as they walked past an open door two offices down from his. "Can you take my calls?"

She peered at them and smiled, her glossy hair like a halo around her. "Nice to see you again, Reagan. It was nice to meet you at the office Christmas party last week."
Reagan forced a smile.

"I'll be glad to take your calls." Reese nodded at Chad. "Y'all have a nice afternoon."

Chad kept a grip on Reagan's elbow until they reached the parking lot. "Who has the kids?" he asked.

"Your parents. I was going to do some Christmas shopping. For *your* gift."

He pointed toward the van. "Let's go for a drive. Maybe get a cup of coffee or something."

She let him open the passenger door for her. It was the least he could do.

Once they were on their way, she turned to him. "I forwarded the house phone to my cell. Apparently she tried your cell first but didn't get you, so she called the house."

He slapped himself upside the head. "What a dummy I am."

"You can say that again." She glared at him. He was even smiling. The nerve.

Chad slowed down and turned into the Starbucks entrance then pulled into a space. "I'll go grab coffees. Peppermint mocha, right?"

"Wonders never cease. That's my favorite of their holiday flavors."

He grinned. "I know. I've been married to you for ten years." He winked and hopped out of the car.

For a man who'd clearly been caught up to no good at something, he was certainly jovial. She leaned her head against the seat and closed her eyes. *Lord, please don't let me say anything I'll regret. Guide my steps. And show us the way back to where we need to be.*

The door opened, and Chad held out her coffee. "Here you go."

"Thanks." She took a sip as he climbed back in the driver's side. "Now do you want to tell me who Holly is, or do I need to guess?"

Chad laughed. "Holly is a travel agent. I'm sorry she called you. It was supposed to be a surprise."

Reagan furrowed her brow. "What are you talking about?"

He sighed. "I don't know if you've noticed it, but I've probably been acting strange for the past few months."

"You don't say? I have definitely noticed and have been pretty sure you were hiding something from me."

He frowned. "Kind of like the way you were hiding the gym and the freelancing from me?"

She met his eyes. He was right. "Even?"

"Works for me."

"So why do you need a travel agent? And if you tell me that your work is sending you to Timbuktu for a few weeks, I'm getting out of the van."

Chad chuckled. "That's not it at all. You know how we had our tenth wedding anniversary in the summer? And you were still breast-feeding so we didn't really go anywhere to celebrate because you weren't comfortable leaving the twins yet?"

She nodded. "Yes. I just wouldn't have enjoyed going anywhere at that stage." Plus she'd been fifteen pounds heavier and would've had to wear maternity clothes and endure people asking her when she was due and watching them cringe when she explained that her babies had already been born. Not exactly her idea of fun.

"Well I knew then that I wanted to do something amazing for our next anniversary." He grinned. "So I'm taking you to Italy for two weeks over the summer." He beamed.

"Italy?" Reagan and Violet had spent a semester there in college. "It's always been my dream to go back."

"I know." Chad took her hand. "That's why I'm taking you. I want to do something really special for you. Something that will show you how much you mean to me and how thankful I am that God gave me you."

Tears sprang into her eyes. "And I came at you all accusatory. I'm sorry."

"I admit, it must've seemed suspicious."

"But you hate to fly." Chad loathed planes, and if possible, he drove for work trips.

He nodded. "But I'll make an exception for this. I know we always said that you and Violet would go back to Italy someday, but she's so busy now who knows when she'll have time off. And I know this is something you've wanted to do."

Reagan thought about his words. He wanted to do this for her. Chad would've been happier just going to the lake or something. "Have you already booked it? Like paid the money?"

He shook his head. "That's probably what Holly was calling about. She was putting some packages together. I've been researching for a few months for itineraries and stuff, but finally decided a travel agent was easier."

"What if we do something else? Instead of Italy?" she asked. "Something for both of us?"

He widened his eyes. "What do you have in mind?"

"Hear me out before you say anything, okay?"

He nodded. "Of course."

She took a breath. "I'm really enjoying the freelancing business. More than I expected. Just a few months ago, that wasn't even on my radar, but I was really miserable. I want to be one of those moms who adores staying home five days a week with her kids." She shrugged. "But I'm not. I need to do something that has nothing to do with them and nothing to do with the household and nothing to do with you—even if it's just for a few hours a week. That's one thing the gym membership taught me." She glanced at him. "Do you think that makes me selfish?"

He took her hand. "You are not selfish. I guess that if the tables were turned, I'd probably feel the same way. You're really good at what you do. I don't blame you for wanting to keep at it in some form."

"I'm not saying I want to go back to work. Or even work daily.

I'm just saying that I'd like to pick up freelance jobs here and there. I'll schedule them so I'm not overloaded because I want my main focus to be you guys." She smiled. "I think having something that's my own again will really go a long way in making me happy."

"And I want you to be happy. When you told me you felt like the only role you played anymore was that of a maid/cook/chauffeur/nurse, it made me feel terrible."

"Then let's use some of the money from the trip and put it toward hiring someone to come in two afternoons a week to watch the kids. I'll freelance upstairs in the office or go run my errands without having to load up three kids in the van."

"Do you think your friend Maggie would be interested?"

She nodded. "Unless she's found another family. She's only looking for something part-time, so this could be perfect."

Chad leaned over and planted a kiss on her lips. "I love you. And I do want you to be happy."

"We can go away for our anniversary, maybe for a long weekend, just the two of us."

"The lake?" he asked with a grin.

She nodded. "Sounds heavenly."

"Why didn't you tell me this sooner?" he asked. "If you were unhappy enough to go behind my back, you had to be pretty miserable."

Reagan shook her head. "I felt like a huge failure." Tears filled her eyes. "You have worked hard to give me the opportunity to stay home with our children, and it doesn't make me as happy as I thought it would. I feel like I'm letting you down—letting the kids down—by even needing some time to myself."

Chad reached over and wiped away a tear. "You are an amazing wife and an amazing mother. You are not a failure or a letdown." He rubbed her back. "Needing a few hours a week to yourself doesn't mean you're deserting us."

"Thanks," she whispered. She reached over and gripped his hand. "There's one more thing though."

He furrowed his brow. "What?"

"I think we should go to counseling. There's a guy at church who works with couples." It had been on her mind for a long time.

"Do you think we need it?" he asked.

Reagan reached up and stroked his face. "I think this has been a tough year. You've taken on more stuff at work, and we've added two more people to our family. You and I have to work on communicating. And I have to be less of a control freak about dumb stuff like what brand of detergent or what kind of coffee creamer."

He nodded. "And I guess I need to do a better job of focusing on you at the end of the day instead of the TV or my iPad."

"So you'll go with me? I think it could really help. I have a friend who says it's made a huge difference in her marriage."

He leaned over and kissed her again. "Sign me up."

Chapter 34

Mom: I WANT TO MAKE SURE YOU'RE COMING TO OUR
HOUSE ON CHRISTMAS DAY. IT WILL JUST BE THE THREE
OF US SINCE AMBER IS ON HER HONEYMOON. DADDY
SAYS THIS NEWS WILL MAKE A DIFFERENCE TO YOU. (Text
message sent December 23, 8:22 p.m.)

Violet Matthews: I'LL BE THERE. AND DADDY'S RIGHT.
(Text message sent December 23, 8:29 p.m.)

Jackson knew he was probably the dumbest guy in the universe, trying to win the heart of the woman he loved. He might be even worse than those guys on *The Bachelorette*.

He took the packages from the passenger seat and hurried up the path to Violet's door. He'd debated whether to just leave them and then text her to get them off the porch or give them to her in person.

He'd settled on in person because he wanted to see her face. Each gift had been so carefully selected, he at least wanted the satisfaction of seeing her happiness.

He rapped on the door and waited.

Violet opened the door. Her Christmas apron and the smidge of flour on her cheek told him she was baking.

"Bad time?"

She shook her head. "No, why?"

"Once you told me sometimes you baked when you were upset. I was just hoping you aren't upset about anything." He tried to peer into the house to make sure Arnie was on his bed.

She stepped back. "Come on in. I'm fine."

Jackson walked inside and noticed Arnie standing in the kitchen doorway looking pleased. "So he's better?"

"His kidneys are still failing, but the vet thinks he's got a little time left." She grinned. "And that very satisfied look on his face is because today was Arnie Day. He just finished his steak. I'm actually baking him some homemade doggy treats now."

Jackson laughed. "He does look pretty happy."

"What's in the bag?" she asked, eyeing him suspiciously.

He grinned. "Your Christmas gift."

Violet shook her head. "You didn't need to do that. At all."

"I had to. Most of this I'd gotten before the wedding. So this has kind of been in the works for a long time."

"I don't feel right taking gifts from you, not after everything that has happened."

"You mean like me giving your sister a way to humiliate you in public and then having the audacity to tell you I love you?" He grinned. "I figure I've got two strikes. I deserve one more, right?"

"This doesn't change anything."

"I know. I don't expect it to." He hoped it would, maybe, but he certainly didn't expect it.

She wiped her hands on her apron. "Fine. Sit down."

He sat on the couch and pulled the wrapped gifts from the bag.

Violet's eyes grew wide. "Four presents? You went way overboard."

"Here you go." He handed her the first one. "This one I've been working on for months."

She held it up to her ear and shook gently. "It clinks."

"Could be broken glass." He smiled.

Violet tore the paper away and pulled a red glass jar from the box. "It looks like the Fiestaware I have in my kitchen."

He nodded. "Open the lid."

She gently took off the lid and looked inside. "Pennies?" She pulled out a handful and peered at them. "All from before 1984." She smiled. "I love it."

He'd been collecting pennies from all over the place. "Here's the next one." He handed her a square, flat package.

She tore off the wrapping paper. "No way!" She held up the Bon Jovi record and grinned. "I love it. I don't have this on vinyl, so this will be great to have at the shop."

"And this one's next." He handed her a larger box.

Violet shook her head. "Really, you didn't have to do this." She lifted the package up and down. "This one is kind of heavy." She raised an eyebrow. "I'm intrigued."

He laughed. "Just open it."

Violet took the paper off the box and lifted the lid. She let out a squeal. "I love this." She lifted a yellow mixing bowl from the box.

It had a white flowered pattern in the center of the bowl. "Vintage Pyrex. I love this stuff." She beamed.

"I thought it would look good at the shop." He'd seen a picture in a magazine of some actress's vintage Pyrex bowl collection and had immediately thought of Violet. "Plus, it combines two of your favorite things—vintage and baking."

She smiled. "I love it."

He carefully pulled the final gift from the bag. "This one is the recent addition. I hope you like it." He handed it to her. He'd had to pick it up on his way here.

She eyed him suspiciously. "This one is bigger than the rest."

"That settles it, Sherlock. If we ever have to solve a mystery, I want you on my team."

Violet burst out laughing. "Let's just consider that my Captain Obvious moment of the day."

"Open it." He hoped the fact that she was laughing and joking with him was a good sign. Could she be coming around?

She carefully tore the paper off the large rectangular package. "Oh! It's just beautiful. I can't believe you had this done." She tore off the rest of the paper and held up a painting of Arnie. "It looks just like him. It's amazing."

"I hired Shadow to paint it," he explained, pointing to the signature in the corner.

Violet looked at him with tears in her eyes. "This is the most amazing thing anyone has ever done for me. I love it so much." She held it out and looked at it. "She captured him perfectly."

Jackson leaned closer to her to look at the painting over her shoulder. "I wanted you to have a portrait of him that was more unique than just a photograph."

"Thank you so much." Violet smiled. "I mean that. I know you and I aren't exactly in a good place, but this means a lot. No one has ever put so much thought into gifts for me before." She gestured to the stack of packages. "And I love every one of them."

He smiled. "I'm so glad." He stood. Maybe the best thing to do was leave while he was ahead. "I should go and let you get back to your baking." He crossed the room to the door.

"Thanks," she said.

He turned to face her. "Merry Christmas, Violet. I hope you get everything you want." Jackson walked out the door and down the driveway to his Range Rover. He climbed inside and started the engine.

Violet stood at the door, watching him leave. She waved.

He slowly backed out of the driveway. He'd tried telling her how he felt. Hopefully the gifts would be a way to show her.

He'd tried his best. If she still didn't return his feelings, there was nothing more he could do. So he turned the car toward the highway and headed back to Little Rock.

"Merry Christmas, darling." Mom opened the door, and Violet walked inside, her arms full of gifts.

"You, too, Mom." She put the stack of gifts beneath the tree in the living room. "The tree looks awesome." The tall fir tree had white lights and uniform red and gold decorations. It was a far cry from Violet's own smaller tree with its multicolored lights and ornaments that came in all shapes and sizes.

Mom smiled. "Thanks. I got new ornaments this year at the Junior League's Holiday House. I decided I was ready for a change when it came to my Christmas decorating color palette."

"Well it looks pretty." Violet held up a container of cookies. "I brought some Christmas cookies."

"Put them in the kitchen. Your dad will be thrilled. He loves your baking." Mom straightened a wayward ornament.

Violet walked into the kitchen and set the container on the counter. At least Mom hadn't mentioned the rehearsal dinner fiasco or her absence from Amber's wedding. Yet.

"Please tell me those are homemade goodies from your kitchen," Dad said as he walked into the kitchen.

Violet turned to face him. "They sure are." She opened the lid. "Help yourself."

He reached in and got a cookie shaped like a candy cane and popped it into his mouth. "You've outdone yourself."

She smiled. "Thanks."

His expression grew serious. "Can I have a word with you?"

"Sure."

"Let's go into my study." He winked.

"Certainly, Professor Plum. I'd be glad to." When Violet was eight and her favorite board game had been Clue, she'd started calling her dad's office the study. Dad had thought it was quite funny, and it had been a running joke between the two of them ever since.

Once they were seated—he at his desk and her in one of the leather chairs—he sighed. "I need to confess something to you."

"What's that?"

"I didn't make you a partner in the firm because I knew how unhappy you were."

She raised her eyebrows. "Really?"

"I debated about whether to tell you, but I hate the thought of you thinking for a second that I didn't want you to be partner. I did. But more than that, I wanted you to be happy." He shrugged. "And I thought the best way to ensure that was for you to decide to leave the practice."

"Thanks, Daddy. I appreciate you telling me that."

He smiled. "Also, I'm very sorry for what you went through at your sister's rehearsal dinner. Regardless of what the young man of yours did, Amber had no right to humiliate you that way. I don't know what gets into her sometimes."

"Switched at birth? Dropped on her head? Possessed?" Violet couldn't help but try to joke. Sometimes it was the only way to deal with a bad situation.

Dad pressed his lips together. "Any of those would be better than the truth, which is that she's spoiled and a little bit narcissistic."

"You think?"

He finally smiled. "And maybe a little bit jealous of her older sister. You haven't been the easiest to live up to."

"Whatever. She hasn't been jealous of me a day in her life."

Dad leaned back in his chair. "I don't think that's true. You've always been so unique and such a leader. Amber grew up hearing us praise you, and I fear she felt like things were some kind of competition. Looking back, I realize we should've done a better job of making sure you both knew we supported your individual endeavors."

Violet sighed. She still wasn't convinced Amber's problem was as much jealousy as it was that she was just a completely different kind of person than Violet.

"Your sister, for all of her acting out the other night, has a lot of good traits. She assured us the reason that photo was in the slide show the other night was because she wanted to make sure Jackson didn't hurt you the way Zach did."

Violet opened her mouth to dispute that theory, but Dad cut her off.

"I'm not saying she went about it the right way. Obviously letting you know privately would've been better. But your sister seems to thrive on drama." He shrugged. "That doesn't make it right, but it is what it is."

"I'm sure that somewhere deep down in her Grinch-sized heart, she thought she was doing the right thing. But it was pretty heinous."

Dad shook his head. "I'm guessing you and Jackson are no more then? Too bad. I kind of liked him."

"He mentioned that he liked you, too. But yes. It's over." Violet thought about the assortment of Christmas gifts he'd given her. It was hard to let someone go who knew her so well. But it was for the best.

A knock sounded at the door.

"Yes?" Dad called.

"Are you ready to open gifts?" Mom asked, peeking her head inside.

Violet shrugged. "I guess."

"We're only opening one until Amber gets back. Then we'll

have a good, old-fashioned family Christmas."

"Yay." Violet stood up. "I'm sure that will be super fun." She knew she'd get over the rehearsal dinner and Amber's outburst. But it might take a couple of months.

Mom led them to the living room. She pulled out a flat box, wrapped in red and gold paper. "I want Violet to open this first."

"Thanks." She held it up and shook the box. "Sorry. Habit."

Mom laughed. "You've done the same thing all your life. We've come to expect it."

Violet ripped off the shiny paper and pulled out a canvas painting. The background was yellow, and painted in purple, curly script were the words: *I praise you because I am fearfully and wonderfully made. Psalm 139:14.*

"Do you like it?" Mom asked in a worried tone. "I saw it not too long ago, and it just reminded me so much of you."

"I love it. But why did it remind you of me?"

Mom swallowed. "You've always been your own person, Violet. Even when you were a teenager and everyone was trying hard to be cookie cutters of each other—you were your own person. I've always admired you for that."

"You've admired me?" Violet couldn't help but ask the question. Mom was always giving her a hard time about something.

"Of course. Especially this year. I'm sorry for doubting the bakeshop. I just worried that you were making a hasty decision. But as I've watched you throw yourself into the business and seen how it's grown, I know you were right to give it a try. If it had been me, I would've just stayed in a job I hated."

"I've had some tough times and some growing pains, but never second-guessed the decision to leave the firm and give the bake shop a try."

"Well your work is paying off," Dad said. "I have a client from Hot Springs who mentioned your store a couple of weeks ago. He raved about the moist cupcakes and the atmosphere. I think you have a winner."

She smiled. "I owe a lot to you guys for raising me to always be true to myself. Sometimes that's harder than other times. But I think I'm finally able to realize how important that is." Violet couldn't help but think of Reagan and Shadow when she thought about the concept.

And then an idea took hold.

A brilliant idea.

An idea that would, at least for a little while, take Violet's mind off Jackson.

Chapter 35

Violet Matthews: HEY, YOU TWO. SORRY FOR THE GROUP MESSAGE. WHO'S UP FOR A GIRLS' NIGHT AT MY PLACE FRIDAY NIGHT? I WANT THE TWO OF YOU TO GET TO KNOW ONE ANOTHER ANYWAY. (Text message sent December 26, 1:11 p.m.)

Shadow Simmons: I'M THERE. (Text message sent December 26, 1:13 p.m.)

Reagan McClure: SOUNDS GREAT. I MAY NEED TO TAKE A LITTLE NAP WHILE I'M THERE. SUGARY CHRISTMAS CANDY + NEW TOYS = TIRED MOMMY. (Text message sent December 26, 1:46 p.m.)

Violet sat cross-legged on the floor next to her Christmas tree. "I'm so glad y'all could come."

"I'm glad you let me take a thirty-minute nap while you made Chex Mix." Reagan popped a handful of the spicy mix into her mouth.

Shadow grinned. "And I'm glad to be out on a Friday night." She made a face. "It's still two months before I'm allowed to date."

They laughed.

"How's Arnie?" Shadow asked.

Violet reached over and smoothed the dog's fur. "Hanging in there." She smiled.

"I hear you painted an amazing portrait of him," Reagan said. "I haven't seen it yet though."

"It's already hanging in the shop," Violet said. "But I have a picture of it on my phone." She grabbed her phone from the coffee table and scrolled through her pictures. "Here it is."

Reagan peered at the screen. "That's amazing. You are really so talented." She handed the phone back to Violet. "And I'd love to hire you sometime to do a portrait of my kids."

Shadow beamed. "Really?"

Reagan nodded. "Are you kidding? I have trouble every holiday trying to find grandparent gifts. That would be unique and beautiful."

"Cool." Shadow took a sip of her Dr Pepper.

"Okay, girls." Violet stood up and took two identical packages from beneath the tree. "I have something for y'all." She looked at the tags and handed them out. "Don't open yet. I have something I want to say."

Reagan and Shadow exchanged curious glances.

"Just hear me out, okay?"

They nodded.

"I spent a lot of years pretending to be someone I'm not. I worked as a lawyer even though I hated it because it was safe. I let Zach fill my head with how stupid it was to like things with a history. I've really had to work to finally accept who I am and be okay with it." She smiled. "And I think I'm finally in that place." She motioned for them to open their packages.

Shadow pulled hers out first. "Oh, I love that verse."

" 'Fearfully and wonderfully made,' " said Reagan. "That has a nice ring to it, doesn't it?"

Violet nodded. "This is a reminder for both of you. You are both amazing women. Reagan, I don't know how you do it all. You are a wonderful wife and mother, and at the same time you're also an amazing designer. I'm so happy that you and Chad have figured out a way for you to find a balance." She turned to Shadow. "And Shadow, I've watched you blossom during the past months into a confident young woman. You asked me once why every boy who you liked stopped liking you. It's because you tried to change for them. And they don't want that. They want you to be you. There's only one you." She bent down and gave Shadow a hug. "And don't you forget it."

Dear Mama,

I can't believe it. Another Christmas without you has come and gone. I guess you had a good one though— Christmas in heaven must be pretty awesome.

I have so much to tell you. Jackson hired me to paint a portrait of Violet's dog. He paid me! It's my first sale as an artist. And it turned out really well. Violet hung it at the bake shop so she can see it every day. I kind of thought she'd hang it there, so I put some stuff in the background of the painting that she'd like—this apron with purple and yellow flowers on it and her record player with a stack of records. She told me those little details were what would someday make me a very successful artist.

Last night we had a girls' night at Violet's house. Her friend Reagan came, too. She's a graphic designer, and we talked about how fun it would be for me to do an internship with her sometime, and she wants me to paint a portrait of her kids. Anyway, Violet gave us both these neat canvases that had a Bible verse on them. It's that verse about being fearfully and wonderfully made.

I guess that even though I know that's been a memory verse before, I never really thought about what it meant. Violet and I had a long talk later about how every time I meet a new boy, I start to dress and act like him. She told me I'm perfect just the way I am—that I don't need to change to make someone like me. Maybe she's right. When school starts back in January, I'm going to try and just be me. To tell you the truth, I'm kind of tired of pretending I like stuff I don't like. God made me who I am—and that means an artist and a writer and a girl who mostly likes to wear jeans and T-shirts with funny logos on them. So that's who I'm going to be!

I love you,
Shadow

Chapter 36

To: violet@centralavenuecupcakes.com
From: JuliaMatthews@myinternet.com
Date: January 11, 5:01 p.m.
Subject: Open Now! High Importance

Violet, attached are some candid shots from the first night's dinner during Amber's wedding weekend. I think you should take the time to look at them closely. I'm not privy to everything that goes on in your life, but I will say that upon meeting Jackson, my initial thought was that he genuinely cared about you very much. In these photos, I think you'll see the real emotion on his face as he's interacting with you—and the same can be said for the way you're looking at him. I don't know if you've moved on, or if he's moved on—but perhaps you'd be remiss not to at least consider that what the two of you shared was real and worth fighting for. That picture Amber included in the slide show, though unfortunate, didn't necessarily

mean something improper was going on. Just food for
thought.

I love you,

Mom

P.S. I'd like to come spend some time with you and help
out at the bake shop. Even if I just empty the trash, I'd
like to help!

Violet read her mother's e-mail for the second time. She was
taken aback to say the least. Maybe Mom noticed more than
Violet gave her credit for. And the fact that she offered to come
empty the trash at the bakeshop just so she could be involved spoke
volumes. It was her way of giving her stamp of approval and sharing in Violet's happiness.

She hovered the mouse over the attachments. Since the wedding
disaster, she'd tried to push Jackson from her mind, but seeing the
Christmas gifts he'd given her made it seem like a part of him was
there. Sure, she could've hidden them in a cabinet or boxed them
up—but she couldn't stand the thought.

She clicked on the attachment, and a picture popped up on
the screen. It was right after he'd kissed her in the hallway. They
were frozen in time, eyes locked on one another, each wearing the
faintest hint of a smile.

Violet sighed and moved to the next one. Jackson leaned close
and whispered in her ear. She remembered the way his breath had
sent shivers up her spine.

The final picture was after they were seated in the dining

room. Jackson had his arm draped casually around her chair and was looking at her with adoration as she laughed—no doubt at something he'd said.

Violet shut down the computer and put her head in her hands. Jackson had told her he loved her—even though he'd heard her say terrible things about him to Reagan. He'd come back again with gifts he'd been collecting for months—gifts he knew would make her happy because he knew her so well.

She thought about the first kiss they'd shared, the only kiss they'd shared that was for them and not for an audience. She'd almost had to hold on to the wall to keep from falling over—and Jackson had been breathless when he pulled away. Was it possible that it was because what they had was the real thing?

He'd apologized for going off with Whitney. He'd explained it away. And although it had been a bad decision, she could admit it was probably done because he was so hurt by the things he'd heard her say.

He wasn't like Zach. He didn't try to change her. His Christmas gifts told her that he accepted her for the person she was.

Violet's iPhone dinged, dragging her back into the present.

She glanced at the screen, expecting to see a text or a Words with Friends prompt. Instead, it was a calendar reminder. *Don't be late! Tonight's the last night of our masquerade. See you at 7!*

Jackson must've put it on her calendar weeks ago. She'd let him look through her pictures from the Razorback game, and he must've taken it upon himself to set the reminder.

Enough time had passed that he probably had another date for his event. The thought made her sick to her stomach.

She jumped up and hurried to her closet. It might be too late. But if she didn't go—if she didn't see him make his speech—she knew she'd always regret it.

Jackson smiled out at the crowd as Jeff introduced him. He glanced over at the table that had been reserved for him. Mom and Roger, Kathleen and Andy, and Lauren and Jeff had been his guests. As far as he was concerned, only two people were missing: Dad and Violet. He felt pretty sure that Dad was with him tonight, smiling down on him, hopefully proud of his son. Violet stung a little more. He should've been honest with her much sooner about how he felt. Maybe that would've prevented the eventual outcome. She might not have returned his feelings, but at least she wouldn't have been betrayed by her sister.

He stepped up to the podium as the crowd clapped. "Thanks for having me here tonight and especially thanks for this honor," he began. He scanned the crowd, happy to see many familiar faces of people who'd known him since childhood. "This is even more special to me because my dad, whom many of you knew, received this very honor when he was my age." He smiled. "I remember sitting at that table." He pointed to the table where his own family sat. "And watching Dad give his speech." He took a breath. "Many of you who know me know that my dad and I were very close. Losing him last year has been one of the most difficult things I've ever experienced. The thing that brings me comfort is knowing what kind of man he was, what kind of Christian he was—and knowing that he is truly in a better place. It makes me strive to be a better man and hopefully be a good example to others—just as he was for me." He noticed the door in the back of the auditorium open and a lone figure step inside. "During the past months, my priorities have begun to shift in ways I never expected. I've begun to realize and embrace that the best moments of my life won't be spent in a boardroom, but will be spent with the people I love. I'm pretty sure that was something my dad knew as well." He paused. He'd written the next part last night, but wasn't sure if he should say it. His eyes drifted again to the figure in the back, and just for a second, the light caught the gleaming red hair.

Violet.

She'd come.

He took a breath. "Most of you know that my life hasn't always been perfect. I've done and said things I wish I could take back. So many of you have stood by me and encouraged me—even when it wasn't pretty. For that I'm grateful. I truly believe it's by the grace of God that I'm here today, and I'm thankful for the people He's put in my life at just the right moments." He smiled and watched as Violet walked to the front and sat down next to Lauren. "If I can leave you with one final thought, it's this—seize the day. Tell people how you feel about them. Don't leave things left unsaid. If I'd learned those lessons long ago, my life would've gone much more smoothly." He grinned. "Thanks again for this wonderful honor, and I look forward to many more years of celebrating the good works done at Brookwood Christian."

He stepped away from the podium as the crowd clapped. His eyes drifted again to Violet. She must've felt like she had to come tonight to fulfill the contract. For some reason, that made him sad instead of happy. Because the only reason he wanted her here now had nothing to do with a contract.

Jeff took the podium and smiled at the crowd. "Thanks, Jackson, for those nice words. I think we can all learn a lot from this man." He motioned at Jackson again. "And for one more treat, we have a second speaker to tell us a little more about Jackson and why he's so deserving of being named our Alumnus of the Year."

Jackson furrowed his brow. They hadn't told him about this. What if it turned into more of a roast than a toast? He scanned the crowd to see who might be coming to speak and was stunned when Violet stood up from her seat and made her way to the podium. Her mouth twitched into a smile as she passed him.

He couldn't believe it. Violet hated crowds. She hated spotlights. And she was terrified of public speaking.

"Ladies and gentlemen, thanks for giving me a moment of your attention," she said, her voice a little shaky. "This was unplanned, and Jackson had no idea I was going to be here, so I'm sure he's a bit surprised right now."

He nodded his head vigorously, and the crowd laughed.

"I have something to say about him though and decided this might be the best place to do it."

Jackson cringed. After everything that had happened between them, from his behavior in college to the rehearsal dinner debacle, she could very well tell the world that he'd been awful to her.

"Jackson and I haven't always gotten along. We met fifteen years ago, and it seemed that we were always at odds about something. When we reconnected last fall, we did so with a preconceived notion that we'd never actually be friends." She glanced over at him and smiled. "But we were wrong. We slowly built a friendship, and I found myself surprised again and again at Jackson's integrity, humor, and positive attitude. I was in the process of opening my own business, and I can honestly say that I don't know if I could've done it without him. He cheered for me and gave me advice and painted walls—and did everything he could to help me see that the only thing missing in my business plan was confidence in myself."

He couldn't hide his smile. It was a shock to hear her publicly say such nice things about him.

"In closing, I must speak directly to Jackson." She turned toward him. "I'm choosing a public forum because you know how difficult that is for me. We could just walk away from each other after tonight. I know I said some things to you I wish I could take back. So I'm here to make it right. I love you. I've loved you for some time now. I was just too scared to admit it. But I admit it now."

He held his arms wide, and Violet threw herself into them as the crowd cheered. "I love you, too," he whispered.

She pulled back and grinned. "I think there's still one kiss left on that contract, right?"

He kissed her gently on the lips. "Check," he said, laughing.

Violet took his hand and led him to the table where his family waited.

"So now what?" Jackson asked once they were alone in his car.

Violet laughed. "You're sure you aren't mad at me for just

showing up like that?" She'd never done anything so impulsive in her life.

"Not at all. It might be the sweetest thing anyone has ever done for me. I can't imagine how much courage it took for you to step into the spotlight like that, knowing how you fear it."

"I feared losing you more." She looked down at their intertwined hands.

Jackson leaned over and kissed her on the cheek. "You don't have to worry about that anymore. I'm here for good."

She grinned. "Even when things are messy?" That's what she worried about the most. "Because you've been around enough to know that my life isn't perfect. I'll always have a dog tracking mud and grass in my house. I'll probably always have a pile of recipes I've cut out and meant to file and a stack of newspapers I mean to read. I'll lose track of time when I'm baking or at a thrift store, and I'll never want everything in my house to match."

Jackson nodded. "I'll love you even when things are messy. Life's messy. I don't know why I try and pretend it isn't. I've spent enough time with my niece and nephews to know that sometimes the best moments are the ones that include a little dirt or a little Popsicle juice or some mad finger-painting skills."

"I think you should know something."

He furrowed his brow. "Something bad?"

She shook her head. "No. But that night you heard me say that stuff to Reagan about you—I was just in denial. I was totally scared. That night I realized how much you meant to me. I was completely afraid of admitting it to anyone because I was afraid you really were just acting because of the contract."

"If I were that good of an actor, I should be getting my Oscar any day."

"If you'd stuck around a little bit longer, you would've heard me finally confess to Reagan that I had feelings for you."

"So in other words, the next time I should just keep eavesdropping a little longer? I guess I can handle that." He chuckled.

She laughed. "No. There won't be a next time. Because you and I are done with secrets. We kept the contract a secret from our closest friends and family. We kept our feelings about each other a secret, and it was almost too late once we admitted them. I've seen Reagan's marriage almost blow up this year because she and Chad were keeping secrets from one another—under the guise of 'it's in the other person's best interest' even though that wasn't the case." She gripped his hand. "So no secrets."

"Do you want me to write that up in a contract?"

She playfully slapped his arm. "Very funny."

"No secrets," he said. "I like it. We'll share everything. The good, the bad, and the ugly."

Violet smiled. "No holding back."

"No holding back." Jackson winked. "How about we seal this one with a kiss instead of a contract?"

She met his gaze. The love in his blue eyes was evident. "Sounds perfect."

He cupped her face with his hand and gently pressed his lips to hers.

Violet kissed him back and let herself get lost in the moment.

Epilogue

Five months later

T he ceremony is about to start. Are you ready?" Jackson asked. Violet nodded. "I sure am." She grinned. "Have I mentioned how handsome you look? I know it isn't easy to wear a tie in June in Arkansas."

He laughed. "The only thing getting me through is knowing that when we're finished here, we'll spend the rest of the day at the lake house." He took her hand and twirled her around. "You look beautiful, too."

She curtseyed. "This old thing?" She laughed. "The operative word there is *old* because this is vintage 1950s."

Jackson kissed her on the forehead. "It suits you."

"There's Shadow," she said, motioning toward a small group of people standing underneath a willow tree. "She said she has a special date for the wedding."

He grinned. "As do I."

She laughed and grabbed his hand. They walked over to where

Shadow stood, talking to a handsome guy.

"Love that dress," Violet said. She'd helped Shadow pick out the blue maxi dress last week. It was the same shade as her eyes.

Shadow beamed. Her light brown hair had a few golden highlights in front from the time she'd spent at the lake. "Thanks." She linked arms with a tall guy. "And this is Neil." She quickly made the introductions.

"I've heard a lot about you," Violet said. "You met in art class, right?"

Neil laughed. "And she agreed to go out with me despite my lack of talent." He pulled Shadow to him. "She's the artist."

"He's planning to go to film school in the fall," Shadow explained. "He thought taking art would be an easy A for his final semester."

Neil nodded. "And I wouldn't have gotten out with even a B without her help."

Violet grinned at Shadow. "Enjoy the weekend. I'll see you bright and early Tuesday at work."

"Can't wait," Shadow said.

"She's certainly blossomed during the past months," Jackson observed as they walked toward the wooden seats that faced an arch. "Is she staying with the Kemps until she finishes high school?"

Violet nodded. "She'll be a senior in the fall, and I think she and her dad agree that this is the best place for her. Her grades have risen, and she's really a joy to be around." She took a seat on the second row.

"I suspect part of that is because she has you as a role model." He sat down next to her.

She smiled. "I hope so. And she's been good for me, too. Someday if I turn out to be okay at being a mom, I think it might trace back to my relationship with her."

"Looks like they're about to get started." Jackson put an arm around her.

A man in a dark suit stood beneath the flower-trimmed arch. "Welcome to the vow renewal ceremony of Reagan and Chad McClure," he said.

Jackson reached over and took Violet's hand.

Louis Armstrong's version of "What a Wonderful World" began to play as Izzy and Ava Grace walked down the aisle, each holding the hand of a wobbly twin. The three girls were decked out in matching white dresses with yellow bows, and Simon wore a pale yellow seersucker shorts set.

"They're all barefoot," Violet whispered. "Isn't that adorable?"

"Seems appropriate for a lakefront wedding." Jackson grinned. "I've always thought this place would be nice for an event."

Reagan and Chad's mothers helped the kids into their seats, each taking a twin for their lap.

"As Time Goes By" began to play as Reagan and Chad walked down the aisle and took their place at the altar.

Tears filled Violet's eyes as Reagan and Chad made new vows to one another. They promised to put God first. They promised that their marriage had to come before everything else—even their children. They vowed to set aside certain nights for just the two of them and to never keep secrets.

When they kissed, everyone cheered except for Izzy who loudly proclaimed it to be gross.

"That was perfect," Violet whispered after the minister had said a prayer.

Jackson put an arm around her. "Can I steal you away before the reception?"

"Of course."

He led her down a path that led to the water. "I know it's only June, but there's something I want you to consider," he said.

"What's that?"

His blue eyes sparkled. "I have an event in December, and I'd like to go ahead and lock you in now to be my date."

She burst out laughing. "Oh yeah?"

Jackson grinned and pulled a folded paper from his pocket and handed it to her.

"Please tell me this isn't a contract." She unfolded it and froze as she read the words at the top of the paper. "Is this for real?"

He dropped to one knee. "Nothing has ever been more real. Violet, I love you. You are the best thing that has ever happened to me. You're wonderfully unique. You make me strive to be a better man." He pulled a ring box out of his pocket and flipped it open. "Will you marry me, Violet Matthews?"

Violet smiled through her tears. "Yes," she whispered.

Jackson slipped the ring on her finger then pulled her into an embrace.

Violet hadn't expected to find love, especially with Jackson. But now that she had, she couldn't imagine her life without him. *Thank You, Lord, for your perfect timing.*

Annalisa Daughety, a graduate of Freed-Hardeman University, writes contemporary fiction set in historic locations. Annalisa lives in Arkansas with two spoiled dogs and is hard at work on her next book. She loves to connect with her readers through social media sites like Facebook and Twitter. More information about Annalisa can be found at her website, www.annalisadaughety.com.